A Sprinkle of
SORCERY

Also by Michelle Harrison

A Sprinkle of
SORCERY

BY MICHELLE HARRISON

HOUGHTON MIFFLIN HARCOURT

BOSTON   NEW YORK

In loving memory of Fred Clifford
1950–2017

Text copyright © 2020 by Michelle Harrison. First published in the U.K. by
Simon & Schuster in 2020.

hmhbooks.com

The text was set in Berling Lt Std.
Illustrations by Grace Kum
Cover design by Celeste Knudsen
Interior design by Celeste Knudsen

Library of Congress Cataloging-in-Publication Data is available.
ISBN 978-0-358-19333-3

Manufactured in the United States of America
1   21
4500826876

Prologue

THERE WAS ONCE A POWERFUL WITCH who lived on the edge of a marsh. She lived alone except for her familiar: a large, black raven.

Every day, people would come to her, seeking help, and every day, the witch would assist them in return for some small token or favor. Her magic could cure many things: from warts to worries, from broken fingers to broken hearts.

One day, she had a visitor—the lord of the land—who had come in disguise. He was a cruel man who had heard stories of the witch's magic, and he couldn't bear to think that anyone was wealthier or more powerful than him. While he was quickly satisfied that the witch was far from rich, he unexpectedly began to fall in love with her. But the witch did not return his feelings, even when he threw off his disguise and revealed who he truly was.

Unable to forget her, the lord returned to visit her again. He couldn't understand why the witch did not love him back, and he flew into a rage and ordered for her to be blinded. "If you will not look at me and love me, you will not look at anyone," he declared. But the lord's men took pity on the witch and left her with one good eye.

"You can take my eye," she told him, "but I will always see you clearly." And she enchanted an old stone with a hole through the middle to act as a magical eye for the one she had lost.

When the lord returned a third time and the witch's feelings toward him had still not changed, he lost his temper again. This time, he demanded that her voice be taken.

"If you will not say you love me," he said, "then you will not speak at all." And he ordered his men to cut out her tongue and throw it into the marshes. But after the lord left, the witch's raven croaked in a harsh, rasping voice: "You may have taken my tongue, but you will never silence me."

On the lord's final visit, he saw what he had done to the witch, and he could not bear to look at her. "See how ugly and strange she is!" he cried. "See how she speaks through her raven, a messenger of death! Get rid of her!"

Conjuring a marsh mist, the witch escaped in a little wooden boat with only her cauldron, her raven, and her magical hagstone and rowed far out over the marshes and into the sea. There she found a tiny scrap of land, surrounded by water for as far as she could see, and she and the raven made it their home.

For a while, the witch and the raven lived simply and happily, and were bothered by no one. She was older now and had no concern for the petty requests of others.

Then one day, she was spotted by a group of fishermen who had been swept near to her island by a wayward tide. Pitying them, she blew into a large seashell and summoned a wind that set them safely back on the path home. Once there, they shared stories of the strange woman who had helped them so magically. Before long, these stories reached the ears of the wicked lord. He was married now and had forgotten about the witch long ago, but the tale awakened his curiosity and he found he could not sleep easy with the thought that the witch was still alive.

Taking a boat, he rowed out to sea until he found the craggy rock where the witch lived with her raven. At first, he barely recognized her, for she was old and crooked and gray, battered by a thousand sea storms. But when the raven spoke, he knew it was her, and she remembered him, too.

"I have come to beg your forgiveness," he said. "I wronged you and I am sorry."

The witch considered his request. Despite her bubbling resentment toward him, there was still good in her heart, and so she decided to offer him a chance to redeem himself.

Filling her cauldron with seawater, she threw in a feather from the raven and some items that had been washed up on the shore: an old boot, a torn fishing net, a button, a butter knife, and a horseshoe. Into the mixture, she added the hagstone that she used as her magical eye.

When the pot had boiled dry, all the items had been transformed in some way. The raven's feather was now a golden egg. The boot had transformed into a beautiful new pair of shoes, stitched from the finest leather. The horseshoe had become a lucky rabbit's foot, the button a cape of the softest velvet; the butter knife, a jeweled dagger; and the fishing net, a ball of strong yarn. Only the hagstone remained unchanged. The witch plucked it from the cauldron and cast it far off into the sea.

"You have a choice," croaked the raven. "Whatever you decide will lead you to what you deserve. The stone is now an island. If you truly want forgiveness, find the island and bring back the first living thing you encounter there. If you do, you'll be forgiven. Take an object from the cauldron, but be warned: only *one* of these things will be of use to you, for it is enchanted. The others will bring great misfortune."

The lord's eyes shifted craftily. "What else is on the island?"

"At its heart, there are riches that will last forever," the raven replied. "But you need not concern yourself with those. You are already wealthy."

Without hesitation, the lord reached into the cauldron, picking over the strange items before finally deciding on the dagger. He set off, thinking about the mysterious island, but vowed he would do as the witch asked and return with the first living thing he saw. But by the time he neared the island, his mind was full of thoughts about what might lie at its heart.

I am rich, *he thought, but there are men far wealthier, and I would like to be among their number.* And before long, his eyes glinted as brightly as the jewels in his imagination.

"I will grab the first living thing I see," he said to himself, "before going on to find the riches. Then I can give it to the witch on my return and she will never know."

As he moored his boat, he noticed a small, twisted root that grew in the cracked rocks at the island's edge. He plucked it out and pushed it into his pocket, then clambered onto the rocks. At the same time, a clap of thunder rolled across the sky. The lord's foot slipped, becoming wedged into a deep crack that had opened up from nowhere. Try as he might, he could not free himself, even with the dagger, for its blade buckled and bent like a reed in the wind . . .

He was never seen again.

And while this was the end for him, it was also the beginning of a story that would be passed down for generations: the tale of a one-eyed witch who set out to trick the greedy and reward the worthy. Over time, the story changed, as stories often will, but the island remained, along with the witch and the raven and the strange items, which sometimes altered, depending on the retelling. For years on end, the story would die out, but every so often, it resurfaced to reach the ears of the needy, the ambitious, and the greedy. For stories, like magic, can outlive the people who tell them.

And magic, like stories, will always, *always* leave a trace.

Chapter One

The Poacher's Pocket

THE PRISON BELL STARTED CLANGING just after teatime.

It was a low, monotonous *dong . . . dong . . .* like the bell was taking a breath in between short bursts of gossip.

Inside the Poacher's Pocket inn, the gossip began blazing as brightly as the fires.

Betty Widdershins stopped sweeping and glanced up in alarm as murmurs rippled through the pub. Her older sister, Felicity—whom everyone knew as Fliss—looked up from the spilled beer she'd been wiping up on the bar and caught Betty's eye. The bell was a warning: Keep off the streets. Stay inside. *Lock your doors.* Fliss set down her cloth and began serving the regulars who were flocking to top up their drinks. Wagging tongues made customers thirsty.

"Someone's escaped, haven't they?" asked a scowling Charlie, the youngest Widdershins girl. She was sitting at the bar, poking unenthusiastically at a lacy ruffle on the dress she was wearing.

"Yes," Betty replied. She cast her mind back, thinking of other times when the bell had rung. Living so near to the prison just across the marshes was one of the worst things about Crowstone. And while escapes were rare, they still happened and sent the place into turmoil every time.

"It's a right racket!" Charlie complained, sticking her fingers in her ears.

"That it is!" The girls' granny, Bunny Widdershins, banged down a pint of Speckled Pig bad-temperedly, slopping beer over a grizzle-haired customer's hands. "This is the last thing we need today of all days!" She gave the customer a withering look. "And I thought I told you to smarten up, Fingerty? It's bad enough that we're sur-rounded by riffraff on the outside, let alone having our customers looking like scruff-bags, too!"

"I did!" Fingerty protested with an injured look, but even so, he pulled a comb from his top pocket and began tugging it through his straggly hair as Bunny stomped off, probably for a crafty puff of her pipe.

Fliss slid a nip of port next to Fingerty's glass with a small smile. "On the house," she said. "Don't tell Granny." Fingerty smacked his lips, his grumpy expression softening.

Betty leaned the broomstick against the nearest fireplace and looked around, trying to imagine the pub through a stranger's eyes. It was difficult, for the Widdershins not only worked at the Poacher's Pocket, but they lived there, too. Betty was so used to its shabbiness that, half the time, she barely noticed the threadbare carpets and peeling wallpaper. But today the tired interior stuck out like a robin among crows.

She brushed a hand across her damp forehead. It was rather too warm for all the fires to be lit, but Granny had insisted on it to make the place feel cozier. Betty and her sisters had been hard at work all day, topping up firewood, sweeping the floors, and polishing the brassware until it gleamed. Fliss had even baked in order to fill the place with a homey smell. So far so good . . . except for Granny's mood souring the atmosphere.

Betty approached Charlie, who was now hovering by the steamed-up window for the third time in ten minutes.

"Granny shouldn't talk to customers like that," Charlie said. "Or we'll have none left!"

Betty snorted. "You think? The Snooty Fox is nearly two miles away, and their beer's double the price!" She leaned closer to the glass, wiping a clear patch to peer through. "They should've been here by now."

"Wish they'd hurry up so I can take off this rotten dress!" Charlie muttered, fidgeting furiously. "Posh clothes are so ITCHY!"

"At least it makes a change from nits," said Betty.

Charlie grinned, her freckled nose crinkling. For once, she looked presentable, with her brown hair neatly brushed and in two glossy pigtails tied with ribbons. Betty knew it wouldn't last.

"Ain't had nits for ages," Charlie answered proudly, sticking her tongue out through the gap where her front teeth were missing. "Six whole weeks!"

"Goodness!" Betty murmured absent-mindedly, still staring out of the window. Daylight was fading fast over Nestynook Green, but a few bright spring flowers could still be seen nodding in the breeze that ruffled the grass and set the sign fixed to the wall of the Poacher's Pocket creaking. Betty eyed it, the two bold words swinging back and forth like a hand waving to attract attention: **FOR SALE**.

"They'll be here," she said, but with each passing minute, she felt less sure. The sign creaked again, like something chuckling nastily at them. A black crow had perched on top of it, and as it watched Betty with eyes like bright beads, it was joined by a second and then a third. An old crow superstition of Granny's popped into her head:

One for marsh mist,
Two for sorrow,
Three, you'll journey far tomorrow . . .

Betty watched as the third crow took flight, leaving only two. She didn't believe in all that nonsense, so why was she feeling so jittery?

"The pub will be sold by spring, you'll see," Father had told them after he'd fixed the sign up in the first week of the new year. But it wasn't. The weeks had stretched into months, and now it was almost May. Granny hadn't even wanted to put the Poacher's Pocket up for sale at first. It had been Betty's idea, and it had taken a lot of persuasion to make Granny see that it was time to spread their wings and leave Crowstone.

"We could go anywhere!" Betty had coaxed. "Just think! Perhaps open a little tea shop by the sea or even an ice cream parlor . . . something more cheerful for us all."

Naturally, the mention of ice cream had been enough to convince Charlie, and the idea had taken root.

But leaving wasn't as easy as Betty had thought it would be. While the Poacher's Pocket wasn't as shabby as it had once been, it was far from grand. Not a week went by without a tile coming loose or a window shutter being in need of repair. Even now, their father was upstairs mending something.

"It's a fixer-upper," Granny had said brightly to the only two people who had come to look at the place since the **FOR SALE** sign had gone up. "Been in the Widdershins family for years!"

However, the real problem, as they all knew, wasn't the pub. It was the location. Set upon bleak, drizzly marshes and overlooked by a vast prison, Crowstone wasn't a place people came to unless they had to. It was the largest of a cluster of four islands known as the Sorrow Isles. Many of those living on Crowstone had relatives in the prison that they wanted to be near to. And the prison held a lot of inmates from all over the islands.

Dangerous ones, Betty thought with a shudder. Fraudsters, thieves, and even murderers . . . all locked up just a ferry ride away on the island of Repent. Beyond this was the smaller island of Lament, where Crowstone's dead were buried. The final island was called Torment, the only one of the islands Betty and her sisters had never been to, for this was where banished people were sent, and it was out of bounds to everyone else.

Betty glanced at Fingerty, still slumped on his barstool. A muscle in his wrinkled forehead was twitching in time to the clanging bell.

Everyone knew of his past, first as a prison warder, then later as a crook himself. He alone knew more about Torment than anyone else in the Poacher's Pocket because he had once helped to smuggle people who were desperate to escape off the island.

"Of all the rotten timing," Fliss said. "We've made everything so lovely and cheerful, and now that horrible din out there is spoiling it all!"

"It's not spoiling anything," Granny said, emerging from the door that led upstairs. "Telling the truth, that's what it's doing!" She gestured helplessly around, glowering at the lit fires as fiercely as the flames. "Who did we think we were kidding? Trying to make out this place is anything but a drinking hole for the . . . the dregs of society!"

"Granny!" Fliss exclaimed. "That's a dreadful thing to say."

"It's true!" snapped Granny. "We can scrub this place up all we want, but it won't make any difference. I said it all along: you can't make a silk purse out of a pig's ear!"

Charlie looked affronted. "Yuck! Why would anyone want to do that?"

"It doesn't really mean that," Fliss explained. "What Granny's saying is that it's no good trying to pretend this place is something that it's not."

"Does that mean I can take off this dress?" asked Charlie immediately.

"Not yet," said Betty. "They might still come."

"They're already fifteen minutes late," Granny said darkly.

"Maybe . . ." Fliss looked hesitant. "I mean . . . would it be so bad to stay here?"

"*What?*" Charlie looked outraged. "Why would we do that when we could open an ice cream parlor?" Her green eyes grew round and greedy. "Think of the flavors . . . the bumbleberry sauce . . ."

"Not to mention sharing a room with you two is driving me crazy," Betty put in.

"I like sharing a room!" Charlie protested.

"So do I, but we're running out of space," said Betty. "What with all your creatures and Fliss's mountain of love letters."

"Hardly a mountain," Fliss muttered, flushing scarlet. "The point is, this is home."

Betty felt a bubble of frustration rise up. *Trust Fliss to be sentimental!*

"I know." Granny sighed, her voice softening. "But the thought that we *can't* leave . . . well, it makes it feel less like home and more like . . . like a prison."

The girls fell silent, exchanging glances. They knew better than anyone how it felt to be trapped. Until Betty's thirteenth birthday, the Widdershins had lived under a curse preventing them from leaving Crowstone. But together, Betty and her sisters had broken the curse . . . with the help of a little family magic. It was a secret only the three of them shared. And the Widdershins sisters were good at keeping secrets.

"Fliss," Charlie said suddenly, sniffing. "What's that smell?"

"Jumping jackdaws!" Fliss cried, rushing away through the door that led upstairs. A couple of minutes later, she returned with a tray of blackened gingerbread shapes and began offering them around.

"Can't eat that," Fingerty exclaimed, inspecting a singed piece. "I'll break me teeth!"

"It's only burnt at the edges," Fliss said, offended. She pushed her dark bangs out of her eyes, blinking hard.

Betty reached for the least charred piece she could see, trying not to cough as smoke went down her throat. "Mmm," she mumbled unconvincingly.

Before Fliss could retort, Charlie helped herself to two large pieces. "One for me, one for Hoppit."

"Are you on about that rat again?" Granny asked, placing her hands stoutly on her hips. "Oh, Charlie. If you *must* have an imaginary pet, why can't you have a nice one?"

"Rats *are* nice," said Charlie, crunching determinedly. "And don't worry, Granny. He's safe in my pocket."

"Well, make sure he stays there," Granny muttered.

Betty left Charlie and Granny to their imaginary rats. Once out of Fliss's sight, she threw the burnt gingerbread on the nearest fire. Heading to the window again, she stared past a sprig of dried rowan berries and Granny's other lucky charms into the twilight. An evening mist was creeping in from the marshes, and the bad feeling Betty had felt before deepened. She'd always scoffed at Granny's superstitions, but no one would deny that the Widdershins had had more than their fair share of bad luck. Perhaps it was something they couldn't escape easily . . . like Crowstone itself.

Through the wispy gray, a figure came into view. A

warder was prowling the street across the green, knocking on doors. There would be more of them, Betty knew. Searching for whoever had dared to escape. The warders wouldn't stop until the prisoner had been found. Soon they'd cross the green and arrive at the Poacher's Pocket, sniffing around and bringing questions and suspicion.

A movement under the vast oak tree on the green caught Betty's attention. Two figures were standing in the shadows under the branches, staring toward the Poacher's Pocket. It was hard to tell, but they looked like men. Betty's heartbeat quickened. These *had* to be the people they were expecting, the potential buyers . . . brothers, Granny had said. From their movements, Betty could tell they were having a disagreement.

One of them gestured impatiently, taking a step toward the inn. The other shook his head, pointing first at the inn, then at the warder going from door to door. Betty watched, heart sinking, as they turned in the direction of the ferry, their footsteps in time with the clanging prison bell. She could imagine the conversation: *Not worth the bother . . . What kind of place is this? We can find something better . . .*

Her eyes smarting with smoke and disappointment, she stepped back from the window. *Granny was right,*

Chapter Two

The Sign of the Crow

"CHARLIE!" FLISS EXCLAIMED. "*Why* are there crumbs all over my bed?"

"'Cause I couldn't sit on mine." Charlie cuffed butter off her chin and gestured to the bed she shared with Betty. "She's taking up all the room. As *usual*."

Fliss wafted into the bedroom, toweling off her short, dark hair. Steamy, rose-scented air followed her. She brushed the crumbs off her pillow and then stood at the looking glass, combing out her wet hair and sighing happily.

Betty glanced up from the maps she had spread all over the bed. "At least one of us is pleased about Granny's new two-baths-a-week rule," she said.

It was evening now. Darkness pressed in against the drafty windows, and below them murmured voices could be heard as Granny prepared to close up the Poacher's Pocket for the night.

Earlier, when the warders had arrived, rapping their batons and barking their questions, a hush had spread throughout the place, making the bell outside seem even louder. "Two runaways," they'd said, sending whispers scurrying around the pub once more. "One washed up, half-drowned, not expected to survive the night. The other still at large . . ." Then, about an hour after the warders had cleared out, the bell had finally stopped.

Betty had expected to feel relief—they must have found whoever they were looking for—but she was still unable to shake the feeling of unease. She tried to tell herself it was just the menacing presence of the warders. The last time they'd appeared in the Poacher's Pocket like that was a couple of months back, to investigate two warders who'd vanished without a trace—and they'd put everyone on edge then, too.

"Can't wait till we sell this place," Charlie said now, jolting Betty back to the present. She stuffed another piece of toast into her mouth. "Then we can stop all this dressing up and washing. One bath a week is bad enough."

"Soap dodger," Betty muttered, even though she

secretly agreed. Not that she minded baths, but they were just one of several things that made her hair so annoyingly frizzy.

"What you looking at this time?" Charlie asked, perching on the edge of the bed.

"Places," said Betty. For a moment, the nagging worry she had been feeling eased and she felt a sudden rush of excitement, the way she always did when she was studying maps. So many places to explore! There was a whole world waiting for them away from Crowstone. Where would they end up?

"What about this: Great Snodbury? That sounds exciting. There's a forest and a castle ruin—"

Fliss snorted. "You can't tell what a place is like just by the *sound* of it!"

"You can with Crowstone," Betty retorted. "It sounds gloomy and it *is*."

"What about there?" Charlie asked, pointing a sticky finger dangerously close to Betty's precious maps. "That's near a beach. Beg . . . Beg . . ."

"Beggars' Roost," Betty finished. "Sounds about right. Beggars can't be choosers—that's what Granny always says. And that's us." She swiped Charlie's hand away. "Have you been hogging the lavender jam again, you greedy beast?"

"Yep." Charlie hopped off the bed, licking her fingers. She wandered over to the chest of drawers and picked up a set of painted wooden nesting dolls, fiddling with them craftily.

Betty, seeing what Charlie was up to, mouthed *Don't*— but it was too late. In one movement, Charlie had twisted the halves of the outermost doll a full turn counterclockwise, her eyes trained on Fliss in impish expectation.

Fliss, who'd been dabbing homemade scent on her wrists, suddenly shrieked as a three-legged brown rat appeared before her seemingly out of nowhere.

"Charlie!" she exploded. The perfume bottle slipped from her fingers and landed on the floor, leaking its contents. "You and that blasted rat! *Stop doing that!*"

Charlie scooped up the rat, erupting in giggles. "Oh, Hoppit," she whispered gleefully. "We got her good, didn't we?"

Fliss pursed her lips. "Those dolls aren't toys, you know."

"Fliss is right," Betty said, rolling up her maps and putting them away before plucking the nesting dolls from her little sister's hands and giving Charlie's pigtail a gentle tug. "They're not some magic trick you can use whenever you feel like it." Betty stroked the smooth wood fondly.

"They're a secret . . . and they're special. The most valuable thing we possess."

She had received the dolls on her thirteenth birthday, a gift that had been passed down through generations of Widdershins girls. But these were no ordinary dolls.

"I call it a pinch of magic," Granny had said. And Betty had watched, utterly thrilled and disbelieving, as she'd learned of the dolls' strange power. For, by placing something small of her own inside the second largest doll, Betty could make herself vanish. And, by hiding something belonging to someone else in the *third* doll, that person would disappear, too. In both instances, the dolls had to be placed one inside the other, exactly aligned. At the moment the halves of the outermost doll were perfectly matched up, the intended person—or people—would vanish. To reverse the magic and become visible, the top of the outer doll had to be twisted a full turn counterclockwise.

As Betty opened up the dolls, she shook her head. There, in the center of the third doll was a long, thin rat's whisker.

"Only *you* would think to hide a rat with them," Betty said, a smile tugging at her lips as she ruffled Charlie's already-messy hair.

Charlie tapped her little upturned nose and grinned. "Got to keep him hidden from Granny somehow."

"Wish you'd keep him hidden from me, too," Fliss grouched.

"Keep who hidden?" a voice boomed, making all three of them jump.

Instinctively, Betty closed the dolls, lining up the outer halves so Hoppit vanished in Charlie's arms. She whipped the dolls behind her back as their father popped his head around the doorway.

"No one!" the girls chorused.

Barney Widdershins grinned, his cheeks round and ruddy like Granny's and his hair as much of a bird's nest as Charlie's. "For a moment there, I thought Fliss was hiding another boyfriend," he joked.

Fliss blushed and swatted him with her towel.

"Going somewhere?" Betty asked, noticing that Father had his coat on.

He nodded, scratching his bristly chin. "Catching the last ferry to Marshfoot. There's a pub being auctioned in the morning, but I figured I might be able to interest someone there in this place. I should be back by dinnertime tomorrow." He tweaked Charlie's nose. "That's if you haven't eaten it all!"

Their father's easy words smoothed away more of

Betty's niggles. If anyone could sweet-talk a buyer for the Poacher's Pocket, it was Barney Widdershins. He possessed a knack for charming people, something Fliss had inherited (along with a tendency to blab things that were better left unsaid).

After whiskery kisses for them all, he creaked down the stairs. Betty watched from the window as he vanished across Nestynook Green into an ever-thickening fog, carrying their hopes with them.

Sometime later, Betty woke up with a jolt as the windowpane rattled, sending a damp draft scuttling over her pillow. With sleep tugging at her, she burrowed farther down under her covers. Then something made her open her eyes.

The room was quiet. *Too* quiet. Betty turned over and squinted blearily. Charlie was a noisy sleeper, and normally the silence was punctuated by snuffles and snores. But now Betty heard nothing except the sound of her own breathing. She blinked the last of her sleepiness away.

Charlie's side of the bed was a rumple of sheets. And Charlie wasn't in it.

Betty sat up, listening. Could her little sister be raiding the larder as she sometimes did in the night? Charlie had been told enough times not to pilfer, but her bottomless tummy always got the better of her. Last time, she'd eaten her way through half a loaf of bread meant for breakfast. Granny had been *properly* cranky and threatened to make her clean out the creepy cupboard on the landing.

Well, Granny can deal with it in the morning, Betty thought with a yawn. But still, she sat, listening and waiting for some telltale rattle or clink from the kitchen to betray her sister's whereabouts. None came. With growing curiosity, Betty slid out of bed and stuffed her feet into her boots.

On the far side of the room, Fliss slumbered soundlessly. She looked like a pixie, Betty thought, with her short, dark hair sticking up in tufts around her oval face. Even in sleep, her older sister was far too prim to do anything as unattractive as snore.

Pulling a shawl around her shoulders, Betty crept to the door and paused. Rumbling snores came from Granny's room. She glanced in the direction of the kitchen. It was silent and dark.

She stepped out into the hallway and headed for the stairs. The smell of beer and Granny's pipe smoke deepened as she reached the bottom. Slowly, she pushed the door, then froze. Granny's lucky horseshoe above the door frame was upside down. How had *that* happened? Everyone knew how finicky Granny was about it being the right way up, so the luck wouldn't trickle out. Quickly, Betty straightened it and silently scolded herself. Horseshoes, crows . . . she was getting as bad as Granny! And yet . . . that niggling, uneasy feeling was back.

Betty glanced past the empty tables and chairs, the air still faintly warm from the glowing embers in the fireplaces. Still no Charlie.

Her pulse quickened. *Stay calm*, she told herself. *Six-year-old girls don't just vanish.* Especially not ones as rambunctious as Charlie Widdershins.

Could she have had bad dreams and crept into bed with Granny? It was worth checking. Betty turned to go back upstairs and tripped over something warm and hissing at her feet.

"Oi!" Betty hissed back (partly because she was annoyed and partly because this was, in fact, the "something's" name). The cat shot her a filthy look and skulked to the back door. He raked his claws down the wood with a low, demanding *meow*.

"I am *not* your servant!" Betty whispered, but as Oi fixed her with a poisonous, yellow glare, she knew that actually she was. The price for not letting the cat out was both unpleasant and stinky, and it was usually Betty who had to mop it up the next day.

"Darn cat," she grumbled, reaching for the key to the

door. To her surprise, she found it was already unlocked. "Surely not . . ."

A chilly gust of wind whistled around her ankles as Betty pushed the door open. She stepped out into the courtyard, with Oi zipping past her feet. The moon was a hazy smudge in the sky and the air was filled with the salty smell of the marshes. Betty strained to see through the blanket of fog that had enveloped her and which was even thicker than a cloud of Granny's pipe smoke. The cobblestone yard was full of crates of empty glass bottles and stacked beer barrels waiting for return to the brewery.

Betty edged around the crates, peering into the shadowy corners of the yard. A faint whispering noise reached her ears, and for the tiniest moment, local stories flooded back to her. Tales of fishermen and escaped prisoners who'd been lost to the mists and now haunted the local marshes. Then Betty shook herself and remembered she was determined not to believe in that sort of thing.

"Charlie?" she whispered into the darkness. "You out here?"

Silence. Then another faint whisper, followed by shuffling. A small head with two untidy pigtails emerged from behind a beer barrel. Two wild eyes stared back at her.

"Meddling magpies, Charlie!" Betty grumbled, her

racing heart slowing as thoughts of ghosts melted away. "What are you doing out here in the middle of the night?" She shivered into her shawl and hurried over to the farthest corner of the yard, where there was a tiny area of boggy grass and a sparse flower bed.

Charlie, too, had dressed in her outdoor clothes, her dark coat melting into the shadows.

At her feet by the flower bed lay a trowel and a matchbox, with something small and feathered inside. It wasn't moving. Betty's heart sank. No doubt Oi had been up to his usual tricks.

"Charlie!" Betty's pity turned into exasperation. Now she knew why her animal-crazy little sister had sneaked off in the night. She gestured to the flower bed, where rows of twigs stuck out, each one marking a tiny grave. "You *know* Granny said no more burying dead creatures!"

She broke off, noticing that Charlie was barely listening.

"What's the matter with you?" Betty asked. "Why are you being so weird?"

Charlie shifted, pointing with a shaky finger.

Behind her, a small child was wedged into the shadowy space between two crates. Betty stared. She was probably about the same age as Charlie, six or seven perhaps. Her thin, grimy face was streaked with tears, and the look of poverty hung all about her, from the patched, hand-me-down clothing to the hunger in her eyes.

"Who . . . who is that?" Betty breathed.

"Dunno," Charlie whispered. "I just sneaked down here to do the bird funeral, and I found her hiding there."

The child stared back at them, wide-eyed and trembling. Charlie knelt and reached out a small hand.

"Who are you?" she whispered. "It's all right. We won't hurt you."

The little girl shivered but didn't answer. Her untidy hair hung in tendrils, and her clothes clung damply to her skin.

"How did you get in here?" Betty asked, her voice sharper than she meant it to be. The girl shrank back into the shadows, but there was a glow about her, Betty noticed. The glass bottles nearby were glittering in places the moonlight couldn't reach. Did she have a lantern back there?

"Look." Charlie pointed to the gate. It was locked, but there was a gap where a section of wood had rotted away. "She must have squeezed through."

Betty frowned. Something was prickling at the back of her mind like a needle.

"Why you hiding?" Charlie persisted gently, as if to a

frightened animal. And then she snatched back her hand with a gasp as a glowing orb emerged from behind the girl's raggedy dress.

"A wisp!" Betty hissed. She grabbed at Charlie as the orb loomed in front of them. "A will-o'-the-wisp! She's come in off the marshes!"

Charlie scrambled backwards, the trowel clattering at her feet. Her small face was pinched with dread. Quickly, she made the sign of the crow, just like Granny had taught them, to ward off evil.

Betty hesitated, then did the same, even though it went against her practical nature to believe in such super-stitions. *Better safe than sorry*, she thought grimly. Granny had always warned them that the will-o'-the-wisps on the marshes were bad news. The people of Crowstone had grown up with stories of the glowing balls of light leading travelers astray in the fog, never to be seen again. Like Granny, many believed them to be ghostly echoes of lives lost crossing the marshes.

The wisp hovered in front of the girl but didn't come any closer. Its eerie, silvery light cast strange shadows on her thin face, making her appear older suddenly.

"Charlie," Betty whispered. "Go inside. And you." She turned to the girl. "You'd better go back to wherever you came from."

"I can't."

The whispered words were so faint that for a moment Betty wondered if she'd imagined them. But the desperation in the girl's eyes was plain, and there was something else there, too. *Determination.*

"I can't," she repeated, louder this time. "And I *won't.*"

"Betty," said Charlie, her eyes fixed on the girl. "I think she needs our help."

"Charlie Widdershins!" Betty hissed. "I told you to go inside! We don't know anything about her, or what she wants, or why she has that . . . that *thing* with her!"

"It won't hurt you," the girl began, but stopped as scuffling footsteps sounded on the other side of the walled yard. She shrank back again, looking so young and afraid that Betty couldn't help feeling a stirring of sympathy. Charlie was right. The girl was clearly in trouble. But why?

A gruff voice spoke. "I'm telling you, there was a light. A lantern or something."

The gate rattled as someone shook it. Betty froze as a flashlight beam shone through the gap in the rotten wood, sweeping over the glistening, damp cobbles. She grabbed Charlie and ducked behind a large, empty beer barrel just in time. The beam of light flickered over the yard and Betty pressed her finger to her lips, motioning to the girl and Charlie to keep quiet. For once, her little sister did as she was told.

Betty bit back a gasp as something—a fist?—hit the gate, sending splinters of wood flying over the cobbles. One strong kick and the gate would crash down. No wonder Granny had been nagging their father to fix it for weeks.

Betty's heart thumped wildly. What could they want with this scrap of a girl? Could *she* be one of the people who'd escaped? Surely not. The bell had stopped tolling hours ago . . . and as far as anyone knew, the only prisoners on Crowstone were men. Betty prepared herself for the gate to shatter, but a second voice from the other side of it barked a steely command: "No."

Silence, then a muddle of whispers too low for Betty to catch. Two pairs of heavy footsteps thudded away from the gate. She listened, straining her ears for sounds of movement until she could hear nothing more. Shakily, she beckoned to Charlie. After a moment's hesitation, she gestured to the mysterious girl and pointed to the back door, mouthing, *Inside now!*

Chapter Three

The Black Feather

BETTY CLOSED THE BACK DOOR behind them as quietly as she could and grappled with the stiff bolt. It shot into place with a loud snap that made all three of them jump. Betty muttered under her breath, her eyes and ears fixed on the stairs. There was no movement from above.

"In there," Betty whispered with an *oof* as Oi twisted past her ankles again, making her stumble. "Blinkin' cat!"

She ushered Charlie and the girl into the bar area, where they immediately made a beeline for the nearest fireplace. "Keep the lights low," Betty warned. "And don't add any more logs to the fire. Fresh smoke from the chimney at this time of night could look suspicious."

But to whom? she wondered, as she hurriedly checked the windows, making sure all the curtains were drawn to shut out prying eyes. Who was out there, and had they *really* gone? She tested the front doors, ensuring they were locked. Outside, the **FOR SALE** sign creaked in the wind.

Once she was satisfied all was locked and bolted, Betty hurried back to the fire just in time to snatch the poker off Charlie, who had set about stirring the embers into life. The little girl had stretched her hands out toward the last of the glowing coals, trying to soak warmth into her frozen-looking fingers. Her skin was deathly white, and she was shivering.

"Here," said Charlie, producing half a sandwich from her pocket. "I saved this from munch for my rat."

"*Lunch,*" Betty muttered. "Not munch."

"Same thing." Charlie shrugged, holding out the sandwich toward the girl generously. "You look like you need it more."

Betty watched the girl—and the wisp—closely. The girl was stuffing the sandwich into her mouth, not appearing to care that it was curled and dry. Thanks to Granny filling their heads with so much superstitious nonsense over the years, it was hard not to think of tales of malevolent imps and fairies turning up on the doorstep and tricking you into feeding them so you could never get rid of them. In the dead of night in the dimly lit room, the stranger's arrival certainly felt like bad luck. The wisp hovered near the hem of her damp dress. A couple of times it drifted closer to the fire, as if hypnotized by something glowing other than itself, but then it quickly returned to the strange girl's side.

Goose bumps dotted Betty's skin. She'd seen wisps on the marshes before but never this close up. A faint flickering came from within it, like a heartbeat of white, glittering embers. It was eerily beautiful, almost bewitching, and easy to see why people followed them . . . With a stab of fear, she blinked, forcing her eyes away.

"Five minutes," Betty said a little more sharply than was necessary. "By the time you've eaten that up, the coast should be clear for you to go."

The girl made no sign that she had heard and simply stared into the flames with lost, haunted eyes.

A pang of sympathy tugged at Betty's heart. Had it not been for the wisp, she wouldn't have been so suspicious, but the sight of it floating there was deeply unsettling. Granny would be furious, *so furious*, if she knew Betty had invited it in. The thought made the back of her neck itch. Part of her wanted to help the girl; the other part wished they had never set eyes on her. Blast Charlie and her creatures!

"What's your name?" Charlie asked, hunkering down next to the fire. From another pocket, she produced a nibbled piece of burnt gingerbread and offered it to the girl.

She crunched on a mouthful and glanced at the wisp, hesitating. "I . . . Willow. Perhaps you should just call me that." Her voice had dropped to barely above a whisper, so that Betty now struggled to catch it, and she felt it best not to try. The less they knew the better.

"How old are you?" Charlie asked. "I'm six, but I'll be seven next week."

"I'm nine," said Willow. "People say I'm small for my age."

"Like a runt?" Charlie said helpfully.

"No more questions, Charlie," said Betty, uneasy. "You need to get back to bed." *And Willow needs to go before Granny wakes up,* she thought, refusing to ask the girl any questions of her own, even though she had several. It was safer not to know, especially when there were strangers outside looking for her.

Charlie paid no attention, clearly enjoying having a guest close in age. "Want to stroke my rat?" she asked. "He's invisible."

Willow looked up from her gingerbread. "You have an imaginary rat?"

Charlie grinned. "No, invisible, like I said. Here."

"Charlie!" Betty warned, but it was too late. Charlie had delved into her pocket and, after rooting around with a, "Come on, Hoppit!" she withdrew her hand and held it cupped in her lap. Willow stared at it, then at Charlie.

"Go on," said Charlie. "He's right here!"

Willow reached out with a hand even grubbier than Charlie's, clearly expecting a trick of some kind. Then she gave a small cry.

"Oh! There *is* something in your hand! It's all warm and . . . *furry.*"

"Told you," said Charlie proudly. "I have to keep him invisible because Granny would make me get rid of him if she knew."

"But . . . how?" Willow began to ask.

Betty shot Charlie another warning look, but she needn't have worried.

"Nope, I can't tell you that," Charlie said. "It's a secret. Only me and my sisters know." She nodded to the wisp, which was drifting closer to Charlie in little, bobbing movements, as if uncertain. "What about that?"

Willow stared at the wisp thoughtfully. "What have you heard about them?" she asked at last.

"Lots of things," Betty heard herself saying, dimly aware that she was transfixed by the wisp once more. "That they're evil spirits, or imps, or the souls of people who've died on the marshes. Some people even say they're nothing, just marsh gases." She stared at the wisp, which was bobbing even closer—*more bravely?* she thought—to Charlie's outstretched hand. "But looking at that, I can see it's not marsh gas. It's too . . . alive. Too curious."

"Alive?" Willow said hoarsely. "Not exactly, but it was once."

"Who . . . who was it?" Charlie asked.

Willow said nothing. She stretched her hands toward the fire once more, wiggling her fingers. As she did so, her sleeve drew back, revealing a small, dark mark inked on her wrist.

"What's that?" Charlie asked, leaning closer.

But Betty already knew, and the sight of it filled her with as much fear and dread as the wisp.

"A crow feather," Willow said softly.

"So you *are* the one who escaped," Betty said, her heart quickening. "But . . . but not from the prison. From *Torment!* You're one of the banished folk!"

Willow nodded, eyes wide. "Please don't call the warders," she begged. "I'll go soon. I just . . . just needed a place to hide, to think for a few minutes. Once I'm gone, you can pretend I was never here, that you never saw me."

"But it doesn't make sense," Betty said slowly. "Why stop ringing the bell if you hadn't been found?" She thought back to the warders' words. *Two runaways . . . one washed up, half-drowned, not expected to survive the night.*

"Who . . . who were you with?" she asked carefully.

"My mother," Willow croaked. "I'm not sure if the warders even knew it was both of us, that I was with her . . . but then something went wrong . . ." Confusion flashed across her face. "I . . . we got separated and everything happened so quickly after that, and then I . . . I couldn't find her. And then the bell stopped, after what seemed like forever. So I know now that she's . . . that they've . . ."

"They've caught her," Charlie finished, breathing hard.

Betty looked away, troubled. The washed-up body the warders had described had to be Willow's mother, but Willow appeared to have no idea. Somehow Betty couldn't bring herself to admit what she knew.

Willow swallowed noisily, nodding. Her eyes shimmered in the dull light. One hand went to her pocket, patting it as if to reassure herself of something inside.

The wisp hovered around her, making Betty think of Fliss bobbing around Charlie with a handkerchief every time Charlie scraped her knees.

Charlie reached out and gently took Willow's hand, studying the feather inked on her skin. "Did it hurt?"

Willow's lip trembled. "Yes." She had calmed a little now, staring into the fire, but not really seeing it. "Everyone on the island gets marked. I'm one of the lucky ones. Mine's only small—"

Charlie gawped. "You mean some people have to get bigger ones?"

"Yes. I got a feather because the crime wasn't mine," Willow explained.

"Then whose crime was it?" Betty asked, unable to contain her curiosity. Much was said about life on Torment, but very little was known. What they did know was that there were dangerous people there. Ex-convicts, released from the prison, who had nowhere else to go, as well as others who'd been banished from Crowstone. It was a dumping ground for wrongdoers.

Before Willow could answer, they were interrupted by an indignant squeaking from Charlie's hand. The wisp was buzzing around her palm, clearly intrigued by the rat it couldn't see.

"Calm down, Hoppit," Charlie said, tucking her hand

into her pocket. Betty watched the fabric moving as the unseen creature burrowed into Charlie's cozy warmth.

"They sense life," Willow said quietly. "They're drawn to it. That's why, when people see them on the marshes, they come closer. Most of the time they're harmless, but others—"

A loud rap on the door made them jump.

"Open up!" a voice barked. "By the order of Crowstone!"

"Warders!" Betty hissed, horrified. They stared at one another, frozen, not daring to move. Upstairs, bedsprings creaked as someone stirred. Then silence.

"Perhaps if we stay quiet, they'll think we're asleep and go?" Charlie whispered, but she had barely finished the sentence when another loud bang shook the door. The latch lifted and rattled.

"They're not giving up," Betty said, her voice faint.

"They mustn't find me here," said Willow, trembling. "Please! I'll go out the back. I—"

"No." Betty thought quickly, springing into action. "They've seen the broken gate in the yard so they've probably worked out you're here. For all we know, they could have someone waiting out back in case you make a run for it."

"Please don't hand me over to them," Willow begged.

Betty hesitated. Anyone caught sheltering escaped

prisoners was thrown in jail or even banished. She suspected helping people from Torment carried similar pun-
ishments. But if they handed Willow over . . . the penalty
for trying to escape was death.

The pounding at the door made her decision for her.

"OPEN UP!" a voice roared.

"Quickly, this way!" Betty grabbed Charlie's hand and
pushed Willow toward the stairs, her heart thumping as
violently as the door.

"Betty?" Charlie gasped, half stumbling.

"Shh," Betty whispered, urging her sister and Willow
ahead of her. The wisp floated along beside them, darting past ankles as it tried to stay close to the strange girl.
Betty bundled them into the bedroom. On the other side
of the wall, the bed creaked again, and then a heavy tread
stamped across the floor.

"Granny's up," Charlie whispered.

"Into bed now!" Betty instructed. Her eyes darted
to the shelf, quickly searching a row of books, bottles of
Fliss's homemade rosewater perfume, and Charlie's lat-
est ransom note to the tooth fairy. But what she wanted
wasn't there.

"Betty?" a voice whispered into the darkness. "What's
going on? Who's at the door?"

Betty spun around, heart racing. Fliss was sitting up

in bed, her dark hair still poking up in short tufts. She rubbed her eyes, peering at Willow. "Who is that?"

"No time to explain. Warders are here," Betty whispered, her eyes still raking over the room. "Fliss, the nesting dolls! Where are they?"

"The nesting . . . What? Why?"

Sharp cracks rang through the air, wood on wood. Fliss's eyes widened—she was now fully awake—and she stumbled out of bed, shivering.

At the same moment, Granny charged past their room.

"ALL *RIGHT!*" she bellowed. "I'M COMING!"

"Fliss, the dolls, *now!*" Betty hissed. "Charlie, *bed!*"

"I hid them earlier, out of the way of Charlie's mischief," Fliss burbled, digging the dolls out from the bottom drawer of the chest. Then she froze, clutching her hands to her chest. "B-Betty . . . is that a . . . a . . . ?"

"A wisp? Yes." Betty rushed toward her sister, knocking a pile of laundry over. Grabbing the dolls, Betty quickly pulled the outer doll apart, then did the same with the second and third dolls. They were empty, save for Hoppit's whisker inside the third.

"Now listen," Betty said fiercely to the girl, "I'm going to help you stay hidden from the warders, but you can never reveal to anyone what's about to happen. *Anyone!* Got it?"

"But, Betty," said Charlie in a small voice, "you said they were a secret."

"They are." Betty gave Willow another hard look, hoping that her misgivings were hidden. "And they'll *stay* that way."

"What if they don't?" Fliss whispered, her eyes still fixed on the wisp. "Who *is* this girl, and why are you taking such a huge risk?"

"Because *she's* the runaway," Betty said breathlessly. "From Torment. And if she's found here, we're all in big trouble."

Turning toward Willow, she said, "I need something of yours. A bit of hair or some clothing . . . something personal." Her eyes quickly skimmed Willow's dress, realizing it was so threadbare that to try to pull off a button or a loose thread would probably result in the garment falling to bits. Before she had time to think further, Willow stuck a finger up her nose and hooked something out.

"Yuck!" said Charlie.

"Sorry," said Willow. "Good enough?"

"I guess we'll find out," said Betty. She turned Willow toward the mirror above the drawers. "Now watch." She fixed the top half of the third doll in place, then replaced it inside the other two dolls, carefully lining up the tiny, painted key on the two halves of the wooden surface.

Instantly, Willow let out a gasp: she had vanished from sight.

Betty reached for her and took her arm. "You can still be heard and felt." She guided Willow into the corner of the room next to the wardrobe. "Stay here. Keep quiet and don't move."

From downstairs came a heavy dragging sound. Granny was opening the door.

Moments later, the bedroom door creaked open caught on a draft that weaseled its way through the Poacher's Pocket like an unwanted guest. It carried the harsh sound of strangers' voices.

"The warders are here," whispered Betty, faint with dread.

Chapter Four

Deep, Deep Trouble

"**B**ETTY!" FLISS SAID, SOUNDING CHOKED. She pointed a shaky finger. "That . . . the . . . *thing!*"

The wisp! In her panic to hide Willow, Betty had almost forgotten the strange ball of light that was hovering near the corner where the girl was hidden.

"We can't hide it," she realized. It would be like trying to grab on to air. But they couldn't get caught! Images of the prison pushed their way into Betty's mind. The stink, the rats. The swinging noose on the gallows . . . *No!* She forced herself to focus and stared around the room, looking for hiding places—*the wardrobe? Trinket box?*—before dismissing them all. Her eyes settled on an old oil lamp on the shelf and an idea flared. A daring idea, but one that might just work . . .

"Willow," she whispered urgently, pointing to the lamp. "Can you make the wisp go in there?"

"I-I'll try, but . . ."

"Good," said Betty. "Do it—now." She kicked off her boots and dived into bed, motioning for Fliss to do the same. Pulling up the blankets, she felt Charlie shivering next to her and looked across at Fliss. Her older sister was white-faced, eyes fixed on the wisp, the only light in the dim room. Betty turned to watch it, too, catching faint, shaky breaths from Willow in the corner. Then, thankfully, it glided up and settled within the rounded glass, glowing gently, just like a flame.

In the silence of the room, Betty could hear only the quick breathing of herself and her sisters. Then Granny's voice rang out below, shrill and defiant.

"I'm telling you, there's no one here! Just me and my granddaughters asleep upstairs. Now, if you please—"

A steely voice cut across her. "How many granddaughters?"

"Three," Granny answered icily. "Why? We've nothing to hide, I tell you!"

"Then you won't mind us looking."

"Might I have your name?" Granny inquired, the

shrillness gone. Her voice was dangerously low. "So I know who to complain about?"

"Warder Wild" came the sneering response. "This is Warder Goose. And you've nothing to complain about, lady. Let us do our job, then we'll go."

"Since when has your job been to barge into innocent people's homes in the dead of night?" Granny demanded.

"Our job is to keep order," Wild said coldly.

"And keep people safe," another voice put in.

That must be Goose, Betty thought. He sounded less sure of himself than Wild.

"Fine," Granny growled. "But hurry up. I'm too old for this nonsense!"

Under the bedsheets, Betty tensed, though a tiny part of her couldn't help feeling proud of her fearless grandmother. Everyone on Crowstone was terrified of the warders—everyone except Granny, it seemed. But then most people were afraid of Granny, too, when she was in one of her tempers. If anyone could see those two off, it was her.

"Search this place. I want every corner sniffed out, every cupboard and chimney looked in," Wild said. "But first I need everyone downstairs."

"What?" Granny asked. "Why?"

"I'll ask the questions," Wild said curtly. "Everyone in the household here, *now*. Fetch them."

Betty looked at Fliss, afraid. The sisters knew all too well what the warders were capable of. Their own father had been on the wrong side of them once and spent time in Crowstone Prison. And now warders were here, invading their home.

There came the sound of movement at the foot of the stairs, then Granny called up. "Fliss? Betty? Ch—"

"We're coming," Fliss called out shakily. She slid out of bed, feet bare on the floorboards. Charlie followed, slipping her small hand into Fliss's. Betty grabbed her dressing gown and slipped it on, glancing at the dark corner where Willow was hidden and then to the shelf where the lamp was. To her horror, the wisp had begun drifting up, out of the glass neck.

"Stay there!" Betty hissed through gritted teeth. The shimmering orb bobbed back down.

They filed downstairs in silence, entering the bar area. Passing the back door, Betty glanced out into the swirling fog. She could see nothing, but there were the sounds of barrels scraping across cobbles and glass bottles rattling as Goose went about his search. She headed for the fireplace, where Granny and her sisters had gathered under Wild's watchful gaze.

He was a tall, heavy man, the type who made a room feel much smaller. Badger-like, shaggy hair reached his shoulders, and his face was mostly obscured by a thick beard. His narrowed eyes slithered over each of them, and Betty held her breath, waiting for them to linger on Fliss. Her older sister's beauty often attracted attention, even sleep-rumpled as she was now. But Wild's hard gaze settled on Charlie, and it was then Betty realized their mistake.

"You," he said sharply. "Why aren't you in your nightclothes?"

Granny opened her mouth to object, then snapped it closed again as she got a proper look at Charlie. For the first time, Granny looked not just annoyed but unsettled as she realized something wasn't quite right. The mood in the room shifted, tension crackling.

When a warder comes sniffing, Granny always said, *you make sure nothing stinks.*

Well, Wild certainly looked like there was a rat under his nose now—and not just an invisible one.

Betty watched helplessly as Charlie glanced from her to Granny and then to Wild.

"I wet the bed," Charlie lied without an ounce of shame. She shot an accusing look at Wild. "All the loud banging made me scared. So I got changed."

Wild raised an eyebrow. "That quickly?"

Charlie crossed her arms. "Yep."

Wild took a step toward the stairs. Charlie, realizing he was about to call her bluff, darted in front of him.

"Fine! I *didn't* wet the bed."

"You lied." Wild's eyes gleamed, like a shark scenting blood. "Why?"

"Because I—I . . ." Charlie glanced at Granny awkwardly. "I was burying something outside."

"Oh, Charlie!" Granny said with a groan. "Not again!"

Charlie reached into her pocket and produced the small bundle of feathers Betty had seen earlier. Wild's lip curled in disgust.

"Only a fledgling, too," Charlie said mournfully.

"Enough!" Wild snapped. "Why did the three of you remain upstairs until you were called?"

"How do you mean?" Betty asked, although she suddenly had a good idea of what Wild was getting at and was starting to wonder if this was mistake number two.

"I mean if *my* children had been woken up by someone banging at the door in the dead of night, they'd have been out of their beds and wanting to know what was going on." His cold eyes flashed, darting over Betty and her sisters. "But not you three."

Nerves fluttered in Betty's tummy. Wild was right: ordinarily, the girls wouldn't have kept to their beds. Well, perhaps Fliss might, but Betty and Charlie would have been straight downstairs with Granny, trying to find out what was happening.

"What exactly are you getting at, young man?" Granny asked.

Wild slammed a fist down on the bar, startling them all. "We're looking for a child," he hissed. "A girl of nine years, small for her age, brown hair. A child"—he pointed at Charlie—"just like *her*."

"You mean you don't *know* who you're looking for?" Granny asked, incredulous.

"We have a description," Wild answered. "We can't be expected to know every felon on that cursed island."

"You can't be serious!" Fliss blurted out, finding her voice at last. "This is our *sister*! Not some . . . some runaway!"

Granny looked flabbergasted. "You're not suggesting that Charlie . . . ?" She shook herself. "We have birth papers proving exactly who she is!"

"Get them." Wild snapped his fingers. "Now!"

Granny's face began turning an angry shade of red. With a low growl, she went over to the stairs, stamping even harder than usual. Hot on her heels was Goose, who'd now finished searching the yard. Betty's stomach did an unpleasant squiggle as she thought about Willow —and the wisp—hidden in the girls' bedroom. She was beginning to wish very hard that she had never let Willow into the Poacher's Pocket, or laid eyes on her in the first place.

A shout from Goose made her blood curdle. "Up here!"

Betty's chest was tight with fear. *Please, please don't let him have found Willow . . .*

"Move," Wild commanded, eyes flashing triumphantly. "All of you, where I can see you."

One by one, they stumbled up the stairs. Betty forced one foot in front of the other, her heartbeat pounding in her ears. This was it. They were caught. Done for. Fliss took her hand and squeezed it, hard. But when they reached the top, it was the kitchen Goose was in, rifling through the cupboard next to the sink. Betty glanced at Fliss in confusion, then her eyes went to Granny, who'd appeared at the door with an old cookie tin under her arm.

"Meddling magpies! Is this really necessary?" Granny blustered, but a quavering note had crept into her voice.

Betty's heart sank. Why did Granny seem so shifty all of a sudden?

Goose had swept aside tins of boot polish and a couple of cleaning rags, and a familiar smell wafted out of the cupboard.

"Well, well," said Wild, reaching past them. "What have we here?"

Betty stared at the small tin in Wild's hand . . . and the dozens of identical tins piled neatly in the farthest corner of the cupboard. Now she knew what that distinctive smell was.

"Granny!" Fliss gasped. "Where did all this tobacco come from? And why is it here?"

"Er," said Granny, flustered now. "See, well . . . it was going cheap, and—"

"I've reason to believe these are smuggled goods," said Wild.

"*Granny!*" Charlie said reproachfully.

Smuggled? Betty stared at Granny in disbelief. *Surely not!* But the guilty look on Bunny Widdershins's face said it all.

"Are we . . . are we in trouble?" Fliss asked nervously.

Wild didn't answer but continued to search the kitchen. Betty's uneasiness grew. *Contraband!* The penalties for handling smuggled goods in Crowstone were harsh, but perhaps the warders might turn a blind eye if they were more concerned about the missing girl.

A distinct thud sounded from one of the bedrooms. Wild stopped his rummaging, head tilting like a hound.

"Wait here," he ordered, then left the room. A moment later came the familiar creak of Granny's bedroom door, the groan of floorboards being trodden on, walls being rapped for secret hiding places. Betty's knees shook. The girls' room would be next. What if Wild reached into the corner where Willow was? He would feel something there even if he couldn't see her and then the game would be up.

Betty looked at each of her family in turn. Granny's face was pale with shock. Fliss was also looking anxious, nibbling her lower lip. No one spoke, and the only thing Betty could hear above her own rapid breathing was the crackle of paper as Charlie's hand delved into a bag of raisins she was munching from, occasionally sneaking her hand down to her pocket to feed a couple to Hoppit. She appeared surprisingly calm, but Betty knew she was tense from the speed at which she was chewing.

Wild strode back along the landing to the girls' room, sending Betty's pulse racing even faster. She heard the click of the wardrobe door, clothes being swept aside. She thought of Willow, trying not to move or even breathe in case she gave herself away. Could Wild sense that he wasn't alone in the room? Agonizing seconds crawled by in which Betty tried to think of some kind of distraction. Was there a way she could draw him back into the kitchen without rousing his suspicion? And then he cried out as a yowl cut through the air. Claws scratched over wood, and Oi shot past the kitchen door, fur on end.

"Nothing but a mangy cat." Wild reappeared, his lips pressed into a sour line as he nursed a bleeding hand. He hadn't found any trace of Willow, Betty realized, as her knees began to stop wobbling and Charlie's chewing slowed.

"Come on," he spat to Goose, turning to leave. "We've wasted enough time here."

Betty released a shaky, relieved breath, feeling her heart begin to slow.

And then a small, glowing circle of light trailed into the kitchen after Wild like a ball of yarn. All eyes fixed on it in stunned silence. The wisp skittered curiously over the kitchen floor, weaving this way and that, before finally settling next to Charlie.

Betty knew then that they were in deep, deep trouble.

Chapter Five

Arrest!

GRANNY WAS THE FIRST TO REACT. The cookie tin fell from her hand and landed with a resounding clang on the kitchen tiles, startling them all. Wide-eyed, she muttered under her breath and hastily made the sign of the crow. Piles of letters and papers scattered at her feet, but no one attempted to pick them up. Betty, realizing that they needed to act as though this was the first time they'd seen the wisp, caught her sisters' attention, and the three of them made the crow sign, too.

Wild's grip on his baton tightened so much that his knuckles turned white. A peculiar look crossed his face, leaving Betty to wonder whether he was excited or afraid. It was one thing seeing wisps floating around on the marshes, but quite another to find them inside a home. It made everything seem a little less certain. A little less safe.

"A*ha!*" Wild said hoarsely. But he made no move to approach Charlie, or the wisp, which was now buzzing round her pocket . . . the pocket holding an invisible rat. Goose backed away, pressing himself against the kitchen table and uttering silent words that might have been a prayer.

"Charlie?" Granny croaked. "Move away from it!" Bravely, she grabbed a wooden spoon and approached Charlie, trying to wave the wisp away. It flitted out of reach like a marsh midge before returning to pester at Charlie's pocket.

Betty's heart was drumming now; Wild was already suspicious, and the wisp was making them all look guiltier than ever.

"We were right," Wild purred, his eyes gleaming happily—the same way Charlie's did, Betty thought, when she was taken to Hubbards' sweetshop across the green.

"Right about *what* exactly?" Fliss asked. "We've nothing to do with this . . . this thing! Whatever you're thinking, you've got it all wrong!"

Wild's eyes narrowed. "I don't think so. You see, the child we're searching for has . . . a certain way with wisps.

And this is proof that she's the one we're looking for: the runaway from Torment."

"I *ain't* from Torment!" Charlie spluttered.

"Now just you hang on," Granny interjected. "That there is my granddaughter, and I'll prove it!" She bent down, knees clicking, and began to rifle through the papers scattered on the floor. Quickly, Fliss knelt, too, and began to help.

Betty watched, uneasiness squatting in the pit of her stomach. *It'll be all right*, she told herself. *We can prove who Charlie is.*

"Here!" Fliss pounced, brandishing a piece of paper under Wild's nose. "Charlie's birth papers. These prove she was born here. She's never been to Torment!"

"So there!" Charlie crowed. "Hah!"

But Wild's gloating expression remained as he cast his eyes dismissively over the paper. "This proves nothing. It's just words."

"What?" Granny spluttered. "But it's her birth paper! How can it not prove—"

"All it proves is the birth of a child," Wild continued. "Not who that child is. This, on the other hand"—he gestured to the wisp—"speaks volumes. For now, it's all the proof we need."

"For what?" Granny thundered.

"For taking her back to Torment," Wild finished.

Charlie's head snapped up, eyes full of questions —and, if Betty wasn't mistaken, a hint of excitement. "You're taking me to Torment?"

"You can't!" Fliss gasped. "It's full of . . . full of crooks!"

"Yes, well," said Wild. He nodded at the stash of tobacco. "You'd know all about that, wouldn't you? You took the stolen goods in exchange for hiding her, didn't you?"

"No!" Granny said, horrified. "We've nothing to do with missing people from Torment!"

But Wild wasn't the only warder here, and Betty wasn't about to hand Charlie over easily. "Sir," she said to Goose. "Please listen. My sister's not who you're looking for. If you don't believe us, ask anyone in Crowstone! And we have photographs," she said, her voice gathering strength. "I mean, not that many, because we've never had much money, but if we could just show you."

Goose regarded her, his expression a mixture of pity and uncertainty. He ran his tongue over dry lips. "Perhaps we should listen," he offered feebly. "Perhaps it's not her."

Wild shook his head. "If we're wrong, we'll return her. But somehow I don't think we are."

"Wait!" said Fliss. "The black feather! If she was from Torment, she'd be marked." She swooped on Charlie, pushing her sleeve up. "And she isn't!"

Wild's eyes flickered to Charlie's arm, but his expression didn't change. "Proving only that she hasn't been branded yet," he said evenly. "All the more reason to do it as quickly as possible upon her return."

Betty shared a horrified look with Fliss. Their little sister, branded with a black feather? It was too terrible to think of.

She glanced helplessly at Goose, but already she knew he was too weak to sway Wild. *Don't panic*, she told herself. *It's all just a big mix-up, and soon they'll realize that.*

"What about that?" Goose asked, nodding fearfully at the wisp. "What do we . . . *do* with it?"

"Same as always," Wild muttered. "Don't listen, and don't follow. Who knows what dark magic summoned it . . . what curses it might contain? And this household is placed under immediate curfew," he continued. "No one leaves, and no one enters, you hear me? You'll wait for the morning warders to arrive, when you'll all be properly questioned."

He put his hand on Charlie's shoulder. Charlie immediately shrugged it off.

"Ain't going nowhere, mister. You can't arrest me. I'm seven next week!"

"We don't arrest children," Wild said through his teeth. "We take them into custody."

Charlie stopped wriggling and looked suddenly hopeful. "Custardy?"

Wild gave her a look that suggested he already found her very tiresome indeed, but Betty doubted it was enough to put him off. He clamped his hand down on Charlie's shoulder again, more firmly this time. "Move."

"Now look here," Granny said, stamping over to Charlie. "She's not going anywhere, not without one of us."

"That's not permitted," Wild said. "Might I remind you that this household is now under curfew—"

"Curfew my backside!" Granny growled. "You're supposed to be protecting us! I should be questioning *you* as to why there are wisps floating around and getting into innocent people's homes!"

Charlie looked down at Wild's hand, then gave Betty a sideways glance.

Shall I bite him? she mouthed.

"No!" Betty blurted out, to the confusion of everyone else in the room. She coughed and gave Charlie a warning look.

"Well, I'm coming, too," Granny said, grabbing her pipe determinedly. "Any questions you've got for me can be answered on the way!"

"You are most certainly *not* coming," Wild said coldly.

Granny reached for Charlie's hand. "Watch me."

And suddenly things began to get worse very quickly.

Wild knocked Granny's hand away roughly. Her mouth dropped open and she unleashed a terrible word that made Fliss blush and Charlie's eyes pop.

"How *dare* you raise your hand to me?"

Before Betty's horrified eyes, Granny brandished the wooden spoon she was holding and smacked Wild smartly on the nose.

"Right, that's it!" he bellowed in Granny's face. "You're under arrest!"

"No!" Fliss cried. "You can't! Granny, quick, apologize—"

"I will *not*," said Granny, with a strange, little glint in her eye.

She got herself arrested on purpose, Betty realized with a great rush of love. *So she could stay with Charlie!*

Wild, looking oddly triumphant, simply nodded to Goose. "Cuff her. We'll drop her off at Bootleg Beak."

"You mean . . . she's *not* going with Charlie?" Betty

asked with a sinking feeling, as Goose produced a pair of silver cuffs.

He snapped them on. Granny's wrinkled hands clenched into fists, and another stream of cuss words poured out of her.

Wild turned to Fliss. "The duty warder can deal with her in the morning."

He bundled Charlie toward the kitchen door. Goose followed with a guilty look on his face as he nudged Granny forward. Betty's hands twitched at her sides. She wanted nothing more than to grab both of them back and hold on to them tightly, but she didn't dare.

"How can they do this?" Granny raged. "It's practically kidnapping, that's what!"

"Don't worry, Granny," Charlie said, slipping her small hand into Granny's old one as Wild urged them down the stairs. "At least I'll get to see Torment, and I'm really good at being kidnapped!"

"What do you mean?" Granny murmured. "You've never been kidnapped, Charlie. This isn't some silly game!"

Betty and Fliss exchanged a look. They both remembered what Granny and their father did not. Only the three sisters knew of the adventure they had shared, in which Charlie had indeed been kidnapped.

The slam of the front door shook the Poacher's Pocket. Moments later came a familiar clang as Granny's horseshoe fell from above the door frame. Betty listened to it ringing out as it settled, unable to shake off the sense of foreboding that was digging its claws further and further in. All those little warning signs: the crows, the misplaced horseshoe. Could they have meant something after all?

Despite her belief that the warders would realize their mistake and return Charlie, she had a terrible feeling that something about the whole situation was very wrong.

"Poor Charlie," she whispered. "None of this would have happened if I hadn't let Willow in."

"They'll be all right," said Fliss, rubbing Betty's arm comfortingly, but the look in her eyes betrayed her. She was every bit as afraid as Betty was. "Charlie's a tough egg, and they'll have to bring her back when they realize their mistake."

"We need to get Willow out," said Betty, barely listening. She drew her sleeve across her runny nose, trying to stop sniffling. "We've got to get rid of her. Now."

Betty went into the bedroom, leaving Fliss to clatter around in the kitchen. Her breath was ragged in the darkness. From some hidden space, the wisp emerged, glowing softly as it drifted around her ankles. In the last awful moments of the arrests and Charlie being taken, she had almost forgotten about the eerie orb. Had the warders forgotten, too? Or had they simply chosen not to deal with it now they had captured Charlie? The sight of the wisp so close unnerved her all over again and strengthened her resolve. It didn't belong here, and neither did the strange girl it accompanied.

"Willow," Betty said quietly. "Are you there?"

For one heart-stopping moment, there was no reply, and a terrible thought popped into Betty's head: *What if Willow had silently left, unseen, with the Widdershinses' most treasured possession?* Her eyes went to the chest of drawers where she had hastily—and foolishly—left the nesting dolls. She exhaled shakily. They were still there. She snatched them up and slipped them into her pocket, stepping closer to the wardrobe. The wisp was hovering in the corner, suspended in the air like a tiny moon.

"Willow?" Betty said again, reaching into the darkness. Her hand met only air.

"Over here." The voice came from the other side of the room. Betty stared as the rumpled bedsheets moved seemingly by themselves. It was eerie to watch.

"He was tapping the walls," Willow said softly. "I crept past him as he moved. But after he'd gone I was so cold, and I couldn't stop shivering. Couldn't get warm. So I-I . . ."

"It's all right," Betty said gruffly.

The bedclothes stopped moving and there was a beat of silence.

"I'm sorry they took Charlie," Willow whispered. "This is all my fault."

Betty held back a bitter remark, reminding herself that Willow was just a child. And after tonight, possibly a child who no longer had a mother—just like them.

"It's done now, no point blaming yourself. They'll have to bring her back when they realize she's not you." She glanced at the window. Outside was thick with mist, and doubts began creeping into her mind. Willow was barely older than Charlie—could they really turn her out and let her fend for herself? "Look," she began awkwardly, "you don't have to go right away. It's still so foggy out there—"

"No," said Willow. The bedclothes shifted again as she moved off the bed. "The mist is on my side. I should leave now, while they have Charlie. As long as they think she's me . . . well, that's the best chance I have."

Betty nodded, reaching for the dolls. As she pulled the outer doll apart, Willow snapped into view, huddled at the edge of Betty's bed. The wisp zipped over to her and buzzed around her ankles, but Willow looked so lost and forlorn that Betty hesitated. "I could keep you invisible for a little while longer if you like?"

Willow shrugged. "Maybe. Or maybe it'd only cause more problems—"

"*Aaaaaaaaaaaaaaaah!*"

The scream from the kitchen made them both flinch.

"Fliss?" Betty yelled, her voice bubbling in her throat. Legs wobbling with fear, she ran from the room, afraid of what she was about to see.

Fliss stood with her back to the kitchen sink, chest heaving. Her eyes were fixed on the table, and in one hand she held the kettle. In the other, a large, half-empty bottle. "It just . . . *appeared*," she gasped.

"The whiskey?" Betty asked, eyeing the bottle suspiciously.

"No, the rat!" Fliss squeaked.

Betty turned, finally noticing Hoppit on the table, partially submerged in the open bag of raisins Charlie had been pilfering. "Charlie must've left him behind. Oh, hang on, Oi's on the prowl!"

Devilish, yellow eyes had appeared at the edge of the table, along with the tip of a flicking, black tail. Quickly,

Betty scooped up the rat, shuddering at the feeling of his clammy, little paws and worm tail, and stuffed him into her robe pocket.

"Blasted rat." Fliss dumped the kettle and stepped away from the sink. "Blasted cat, too. Shoo!" she said, sweeping Oi off the kitchen chair.

Willow had appeared in the doorway and was hovering uncertainly. Fliss glanced at her nervously, then away, like she simply wanted her to disappear. Taking an empty potato sack from a hook, she knelt by the cupboard and began stuffing the tobacco tins inside it.

"What are you doing?" Betty asked.

"Ditching Granny's stash." Fliss twisted the sack closed. "If duty warders are coming here in the morning, we should get rid of these. No point incriminating ourselves further."

"But the other warders already saw them."

"Their word against ours," Fliss said stubbornly. "Willow can take them and dump them somewhere when she leaves." She looked at Willow pointedly. Betty glanced at the window again. The swirling mist showed no signs of letting up. A knot of fear tightened in her belly. Why would the warders risk crossing the marshes in this mist? The uneasy feeling was back, pecking at her like a hungry crow.

"All right then," Fliss said softly. "I guess it's time for us to say goodbye, Willow. I hope you get to wherever it is you're trying to reach."

Willow looked at her, her large eyes solemn in her thin face. She opened her mouth to speak, but the words were snatched away.

A sharp rapping at the front door made them all freeze in fear.

"Who in crow's name could *that* be?" Fliss said shakily.

Betty grabbed Willow's arm and pushed her back into the bedroom, fumbling with the nesting dolls. As she connected the two halves of the outer doll, Willow vanished once more. "Stay out of the way, like before," Betty told her, returning the nesting dolls to the chest of drawers. "And get that wisp back into the lamp!"

She hurried down the stairs, Fliss on her heels.

"Perhaps the warders decided to release Granny," Fliss said breathlessly, crossing her fingers for luck. "Or Charlie convinced them to bring her back!"

Betty said nothing as she slid the bolts back from the door, but her thoughts were a jumble. Much as she wanted to believe Fliss, the nagging sense of wrongness wouldn't let her, and even as she opened the door, Betty somehow knew already that it wasn't going to be anything good.

Two figures stood on the step, shrouded by mist.

Warders . . . but not the ones who'd been there already. As their faces appeared in the dim light, Betty drew in a sharp breath. She recognized one of them, even if he wouldn't know her.

"Apologies for disturbing you at this hour," he said. "We're looking for a runaway, and it's vital we search all premises."

Fliss stared at him in confusion. "But . . . but you've just searched here."

The warder stared back at her, eyes narrowing. "No, we haven't."

"I mean your colleagues," Fliss said. "Other warders." She turned to Betty. "Goose and . . . ?"

"Wild," Betty answered, staring at a crease that was deepening between the man's eyebrows and not liking it at all.

The second warder glanced at the first one.

"There are no warders named Goose and Wild."

Chapter Six

A Glimpse Through a Hagstone

"THEY WERE JUST HERE MINUTES AGO," said Fliss, her voice rising. "Asking us questions, searching the place . . ."

The first warder spoke again in a clipped voice. "There are only two of us searching this side of Crowstone now. We split up from the other pair an hour ago. Whoever it was that came here, they weren't warders."

Not warders? The news wrapped round Betty's thoughts like marsh mist, drowning her. She felt lost and terrified.

"B-but they were in uniform!" Fliss continued, her bottom lip trembling. "They've taken our little sister!

Our granny, too. It's all a terrible mistake!" She glanced desperately at Betty. "*Tell* them!"

"It . . . it is," Betty croaked. She saw the plea in her sister's eyes and knew Fliss was begging her to give Willow up, but it wasn't as simple as that. Handing Willow over to the warders wouldn't bring Charlie back. All it would do was incriminate the Widdershinses.

"They thought our sister was someone else, the runaway, and . . . and then, when we tried to stop them from leaving with her, they arrested Granny and said they were taking her to Bootleg Beak . . ." She trailed off as shock gave way to an icy dread spreading throughout her body.

Who *were* these people who had taken Granny and Charlie? What did they want with Willow? Whoever they were, they'd beaten the warders to it. A skittering, panicky feeling took hold of Betty. Everything had changed. If they no longer knew who had Charlie, they had no clue where she was really going, either . . . or *why*.

"Why would they confuse the two?" asked the warder more to himself than to the Widdershinses. "Perhaps we'd better take a look around ourselves."

"Hold it right there," Fliss interrupted, barring his way. "If those weren't real warders who were here before, then how do I know you're who you say you are?"

The warder's lip curled. It was a thin lip, one Betty

74

remembered, for she'd seen this warder before. He was a short, reedy-looking man with a limp moustache resembling a starved rat and a personality to match. He flashed his badge: a golden crow's foot that gleamed even in the dim light. Betty knew his name before he even said it.

"Tobias Pike. And this is Eli Minchin."

Minchin gestured to his badge, too.

"That proves nothing," said Fliss. "The others wore badges."

"He *is* a warder," Betty put in. "I . . . I remember seeing him before. At the prison." This wasn't strictly true, but it was easier than trying to explain to Fliss that she'd first encountered Pike on the marshes last year, when the three sisters had set out to break their curse.

They stood aside to let Pike and Minchin pass. Fliss shut the door behind them.

"And you showed them the birth papers for your sister?" Minchin asked, frowning as they approached the bar. He was more softly spoken than Pike, with a kinder face. He took out a notebook and flipped it open, beginning to scribble in it with a pencil.

"Yes." Fliss ran upstairs quickly and returned with the handful of papers from Granny's old cookie tin. "This is Charlie's. They said it didn't prove who she was and took her anyway."

"Back to Torment?" Pike asked.

Betty nodded weakly. "That's what they said, but if they weren't real warders, then . . ." *Then why would they take her to Torment?* she wondered, the fear in her heart echoed in Fliss's eyes. *And what would they do to Charlie once they discovered their mistake?*

Pike turned to Minchin urgently. "We need to get to the harbor and quickly. In this fog, they couldn't have got far. We'll light the beacons, send search parties out."

"And what about the other warders?" Fliss asked. "Can you ask them to help?"

"We need to find them first," said Minchin. "But if the impostors wore warders' uniforms then . . ." He paused, gulping visibly. "It doesn't look good."

"What I don't understand is why they took Granny," said Fliss. Her oval face was deathly white now, and even her lips, normally deep and rosy in color, were sickly pale. "If they were just looking for this girl, why not take only Charlie?"

"They didn't want Granny. They wanted to scare us," Betty realized. "They created a distraction, throwing us off-guard." Wild's over-the-top reaction made sense now. It was clear Granny shouldn't have been arrested, but it had certainly frightened Betty and Fliss into obedience.

Pike gave Betty a long look. "Is there anything else you need to tell us? Anything we should know that could help your sister?"

Betty shook her head, thinking of Willow in the room above, quiet and listening.

"No." Her voice was hollow. *Such a small word for such a big lie.*

"In that case," Pike said, "we'll get searching right away."

"A description? Or photograph?" Minchin put in.

Betty handed him a small picture from the shelf above the till. Charlie's face beamed out from it cheekily. "Here. This was taken early last year. She's missing her two top front teeth now."

"Please," Fliss said in a wobbly voice. "Please find her. Bring her back."

Minchin nodded gravely and tucked the picture into his pocket.

"You're of age?" Pike asked Fliss.

"Y-yes," Fliss stammered. "I'm seventeen next month."

"Good." Pike nodded curtly toward Betty. "Old enough to supervise this one, then."

Had the circumstances been less serious, Betty would have bristled at this. She was thirteen—she didn't need supervision! But now was not the time for eye-rolling or sarcastic remarks. Now was the time to keep her mouth shut and her eyes open.

The warders left, and the girls bolted the door to the Poacher's Pocket for the second time that evening. As the lock slid into place, Fliss rested her forehead against the dark wood and let out a muffled sob. Betty, already half-way to the stairs, turned back, fizzing with impatience and worry. If one of them dissolved into tears now, then there was a good chance the other would, too. And they couldn't afford for that to happen.

"Come on," she urged. "I know you're upset, but neither of us has time to cry. It won't help us . . . or Charlie!" She raced up the stairs two at a time.

"Help Charlie?" Fliss protested, running after her. "How exactly do you think we're going to do that? We're stuck here in the middle of a fog, and—"

"No, Fliss." Betty reached the top of the stairs and went into the bedroom, pulling out warm clothes from the drawers. "We *aren't* stuck here, that's the point. The warders were fake and so is our curfew." She scooped Hoppit out of her robe pocket and thrust him at Fliss. "Here."

"*Eeeeeeeeh!*" Fliss squealed, shuddering as the rat

squirmed in her hand. "Oh, you know I don't like wriggly things! Can't I just put him down?"

"Not unless you want to tell Charlie that her pet got eaten by Oi." *If we even see Charlie again*, said a horrid little voice in Betty's head. She shook her head, trying to quieten it. "Just hold him, for crow's sake!"

Fliss grimaced, holding the rat at arm's length. "What are you doing?"

"What does it look like?" Betty retorted, flinging her nightclothes aside. "I'm going out to look for Charlie." She raked through several pairs of woolen stockings, grabbing the least holey ones and tugging them on. As she sat on the bed, she felt it shift with an invisible weight and sensed Willow next to her, silently listening. The wisp had gone from the lamp, but there was a faint glow coming from under the bed.

"*G-go out?*" Fliss stammered. "But the warders—the real ones—they're already out looking! Shouldn't we trust them to track Charlie down?"

"How can they when they only know half the story?" Betty said fiercely, pulling on her boots. She buttoned up a thick cardigan over her dress, then took Hoppit from Fliss and tucked him in the pocket. "Anyway, you know as well as I do never to trust a warder. Half of them are corrupt, just look at Fingerty and those two who went missing earlier this year. Who knows what they were mixed up in?"

"But not all of them are corrupt," Fliss argued. "And they have power and weapons. Not to mention experience tracking people down."

Betty grimaced. "So do I. I found you and Charlie last year, didn't I?"

"That was different," Fliss muttered.

"The only difference then was that Charlie was taken because she had something valuable," Betty hissed. "This time she's been taken by mistake, and as soon as they realize that, she'll be worthless to them! And then—"

"Then she'll really be in danger," Fliss finished, her breath coming in quick, little gasps. She went to the wardrobe and began dressing quickly, but the fear and hesitation on her face were plain. "Even if we find her, how will we get her back?" she asked. "We can't hope to overpower those impostors. They'll laugh in our faces!"

"No," Betty agreed. "But perhaps we can outwit them, because we have two things on our side. Two things the real warders *don't* have." She took the nesting dolls from the chest of drawers. "First, they won't be laughing in our faces if they can't see us." She snapped the dolls apart and immediately Willow became visible, poised on the side of

Betty's bed as if she were about to flee. "And second we have her, and she has answers—or at least some of them."

"But I thought she was leaving?" Fliss asked. "We can't risk being caught with her!"

"We've hidden her up till now," said Betty, lacing her boots determinedly. "And the way I see it, we don't have a choice. Whatever it is they want her for and whatever she knows, she's the key to finding Charlie." *And getting her back*, she thought, as a darker idea entered her mind. Could they do a deal, exchanging Willow for Charlie? It was a shameful thought but one that Betty couldn't completely dismiss. Charlie's safety came first, whatever the cost.

"What about that?" Fliss asked, nodding at the wisp, which had emerged from under the bed and was circling Willow's feet. "We can hide her, but we can't hide a wisp!"

"You're right." Betty stared at it. "Perhaps we can release it on the marshes or something."

"I can hear you, you know." Willow's voice was soft but fierce. She coaxed the wisp back into the oil lamp. "And you won't be able to get rid of it that easily."

"What *is* it?" Fliss asked. "Why does it follow you?"

Willow remained silent.

"You have to start talking," said Betty urgently. "We need your help to find Charlie, and there's no time to waste. Every minute that passes, she gets farther away. Do you know who these people are and why they've taken her? What is it they want from you?"

Willow swallowed noisily. "I know . . . I know why they've taken her," she said at last. "But if I tell you, you have to help *me*, too."

Betty glanced at Fliss. At that moment, it was clear that both of them would say almost anything—whether they meant it or not—if it would lead them to Charlie. "What is it you want us to do?"

Willow gazed at the wooden dolls in Betty's hand with a mixture of wonder and apprehension. "I have to get somewhere," she said finally. "But I don't think I can make it on my own. It's too far, and I need a boat, and . . ."

"We have a boat," Betty said, trying to keep the impatience from her voice. "Just tell us where you want to go."

"It's probably easier to show you," said Willow, reaching into the folds of her shabby dress. From it, she withdrew a square of waxed paper, yellowed with age. It had been folded several times and was slightly worn at the creases and edges.

Betty took it, her heart beginning to thud fast again, but this time it was with excitement rather than fear. She unfolded the paper carefully, but even as she did so, she knew it was a map. Hand drawn in black ink, with a decorative nautical star in the corner. For a moment, its beauty quite took her breath away as she skimmed over the detail, but then she frowned.

"It's just a map of Crowstone and the surrounding areas," said Fliss, peering over her shoulder. "Don't you have one a bit like that, Betty?"

"Not really," said Betty, puzzling over something. She turned to Willow. "I mean, I've got maps of Crowstone, but they're larger, more detailed. On this, Crowstone and the Sorrow Isles are too small to hold many details. Most of this seems to focus on the water—and there's nothing much there besides that old shipwreck." She paused, scratching her head. "This is a pretty strange map. Where exactly is it you want to get to?"

Willow bit her lip, hesitating. Then she rested a trembling finger on the yellowing paper. "Here."

Betty studied Willow carefully. She was starting to wonder if this strange girl was what Granny would describe as *one feather short of a duster.* "Willow," she said gently. "There's nothing there."

Silently, Willow reached into her pocket and placed something in Betty's hand. A round, gray stone with a hole all the way through the middle.

"A hagstone?" Betty asked. She ran her thumb over the stone's surface. It was scratchy with tiny barnacles.

"Granny has one of these. They're supposed to be lucky and ward off evil."

"And help you see things that aren't usually visible," Fliss added. "Remember, Granny always told us if you looked through one, you'd see pixies and other hidden creatures?"

Betty rolled her eyes. "*Hmph.* All I ever got from looking through one was sand in my eye."

"Not this time," Willow whispered.

Her words sent a shiver over Betty's skin. She lifted the stone to her eye . . . and gasped. For there on the map, where there had been only water, something else appeared.

"I . . . I don't understand," she breathed, taking the stone away, then putting it back to her eye once more. "How is this even possible?"

"What?" Fliss asked, grabbing at the stone. "What *is* it? Let me see!"

Betty handed the stone to Fliss with a shaking hand. She stared at Willow again, brimming with questions and wonder and the slightest niggle of fear. Finally, her voice emerged as a disbelieving croak.

"It's an island."

Chapter Seven

Bootleg Beak

FLISS GASPED AS SHE LOOKED through the hagstone.

"What *is* this map? Is this some sort of trick?"

"No," Willow replied. "It's real, all of it." She gestured to the dolls. "Just because something can't be seen, doesn't mean it's not there."

"I've got almost every kind of map there is on Crowstone and the surrounding areas," Betty said hoarsely. "I've never seen or heard anything about a secret island." She was breathless and slightly dizzy, the same way she had felt when she'd discovered the nesting dolls and seen their magical ability for the first time. And while she had always craved adventure and the chance to explore the unknown, the magic of this map had a swirling undercurrent of danger about it.

"If everyone knew about it, it wouldn't be a secret," Willow replied.

Betty took the stone from Fliss and examined the map more carefully this time. There it was again, inked in just the same as the rest of the map, with coves and cliffs and an area of water at the center of it.

"It looks like there's some kind of lagoon in the middle," she said. "But none of it's labeled." She glanced across at Crowstone and the Sorrow Isles, tinier than they were on the maps she owned but still large enough for some of the areas to be named: the Devil's Teeth, the prison, and the Three Widows, for instance.

"Why would it be labeled if no one knows about it?" said Fliss.

"But someone *does* know about it," Betty answered. "Well enough to draw it on a map at least. Unless . . ." She hesitated, watching Willow. "I mean, how sure are you that this place really exists? How do we know the map's not a fake? Something made by pirates or smugglers to lure people off somewhere? Where exactly did you get it?"

"It was my father's. And it's all I've got." Willow's bottom lip jutted out obstinately, reminding Betty of Charlie.

A lump rose in her throat. *Charlie!*

"We can't stay here if we're to have any chance of finding Charlie," she said, swallowing down the lump with effort. We have to leave now if we're going to catch up. We've taken too long already."

She handed the map back to Willow. "If you want our help, then you have to be honest with us. Who are these people searching for you?"

"Trappers," said Willow. "That's all I know."

"*Trappers?*" Fliss asked fearfully.

Willow nodded. "They take people . . . people like me."

"Why?" asked Betty. "Is this something to do with the wisp?" It was all she could think of that seemed to make Willow different. "They didn't try to capture it, though . . . They just wanted Charlie—well, you, I mean."

"They didn't want the wisp, not this one anyway." Willow chewed her lip. "They only want me because . . . because they know I can catch them."

I can catch them . . .

The words echoed in Betty's head like unwelcome guests. Even when they faded, they left questions, but she forced herself to put them aside—for now. It didn't matter how Willow could do what she did. All that mattered was that Charlie *couldn't*.

"So where would they have taken Charlie? *Think!*"

"I . . . I don't know," Willow whispered.

Betty turned away from her, frustrated. She grabbed a handful of dry clothes from Charlie's drawer and bundled them at Willow. "Change into these," she said, frowning. "Your clothes are still soaked through."

"I'm not cold," Willow said faintly.

"You're freezing," Betty said as Willow's hand brushed hers. "Even your hair is still dripping wet."

From the rolls of maps next to her bed, Betty selected one and pulled it out of the box. "Hold this," she told Fliss, then went into the kitchen.

She paused, her heart racing. She had spent so much of her life in the Poacher's Pocket, dreaming of adventure. Now she was about to embark on a real one, and like the last time, it wasn't unfolding in a way she had imagined at all. From a row of hooks above the sink, she took a set of keys. Then she grabbed a loaf of bread from the pantry and filled two flasks with water. Her eyes rested on the potato sack that Fliss had stuffed the tobacco into earlier. She grabbed it and threw the other things inside—they could get rid of Granny's stash on the way. Returning to the bedroom, she pulled another thick shawl from the wardrobe. In the freezing fog, one of them was bound to need it. "Let's go." She pocketed the nesting dolls after rendering Willow invisible once more. "And you've got some explaining to do."

Willow didn't reply, but the lamp containing the wisp trembled. Betty took it from her, shivering as their hands brushed each other. Willow's fingers felt like slivers of ice.

The fog was still thick outside. They left the Poacher's Pocket in silence, creeping away from Nestynook Green with the damp air chilling their noses. Betty watched and listened for any sign of warders—or the impostors—but the streets were empty, windows dark. People always kept their curtains tightly shut when the prison bell rang. Little would anyone watching know, Betty thought grimly, that the person who'd escaped was this fragile girl beside them—or that the glow from the lamp lighting their way wasn't all it seemed. Daylight was still some hours away, and she found herself longing for it. Everything seemed worse at night—that was what Granny always said. Fears and worries were bigger when there were shadows for them to prowl in.

"Betty?" Fliss whispered. "Where are we going? What's the plan?" She paused. "*Is* there a plan?"

"I'm working on it," Betty muttered, pulling her scarf up over her rapidly frizzing hair. "All I know is that we should get to the harbor. That's where the real warders were eager to search, so it makes sense for us to look, too —there's no other safe way off Crowstone than by boat from there."

"There are plenty of places they could take a boat from that *aren't* safe," Fliss said anxiously. "Like the caves at Smugglers' Point—"

"Too risky," said Betty, hoping she was right. "They're pretending to be warders. Surely leaving from anywhere else would look more suspicious? And perhaps, if Charlie's been clever, she'll have dawdled, the way she usually does, and we might intercept them." She sped up, cursing herself for losing time by poring over the strange map. It had cost them valuable minutes, and already she had the feeling they were too late.

When they reached the harbor, it appeared empty, as Betty had feared. There were no signs or sounds of movement, except for the faint creaking of boats on the gray water. They crept through the mist, footsteps light on the path as they traced it from one end of the harbor to the other. Their own boat, recently painted a merry green, bobbed along in time with its neighbors. It tugged lightly on its mooring rope as though eager to set sail.

Fliss pointed past it. "Look. The warders' boat."

Through the curling fog, Betty had almost missed it: a small boat at the very edge of the harbor. It was plain and black, but for a crow motif made of iron at the bow, and held three rows of seats. Two were for warders, and the middle one, complete with shackles, was for prisoners.

"So where's the other boat?" Betty wondered. "Pike said there was another couple of warders searching the other side of the island." Something crunched under her boot. She reached down, finding crumbs on her fingertips.

"Gingerbread! Charlie must have dropped it—she *was* here."

"Not anymore." Fliss's voice was solemn. Betty followed her gaze to a thick rope dangling from an iron ring next to the warders' boat. It had been tied with a complicated knot that Betty vaguely recalled seeing in one of Father's boating books.

Her stomach twisted. "At least we know for sure now," she said, pointing to the rope. It had been sliced clean through. "Charlie's not on Crowstone anymore. They've taken her in the warders' other boat."

"Bother it!" Fliss's eyes filled with angry tears. "Why us?" She glared at the harbor, her dark brown eyes fierce. "Even the stupid tide had to be in, didn't it! And this hateful fog, too. Why is luck never *ever* on our side?"

Betty touched her sister lightly on the arm. "Don't give up. And don't blame luck for getting us into this. It didn't. Choices did." *My choices*, she added silently.

"And Granny?" Fliss added tearfully, scanning the harbor, even though it was impossible to see far in the smothering mist. "Do you think she's gone, too?"

"No," Betty said, feeling helpless. The burden of what had happened lay in her stomach like a stone. Normally, Fliss was the one who reassured and comforted, but tonight everything had changed. "It's Charlie they're interested in." She gazed back the way they had come, past their boat, to where a rocky path rose up. Following it would take them past the ferry point and then on to Crowstone's headland. "If those trappers were honest about anything, there's only one place she can be."

"Bootleg Beak." Willow's voice sounded next to her, making Betty jump.

"Yes," Betty muttered, trying to ignore a sliver of fear. With Willow unseen and the swirling fog, it was easy for her mind to play tricks. For a moment, Betty had been convinced there had been no misting of Willow's breath as she spoke into the cold air.

"We should check there," said Fliss. "I need to know Granny's all right. If she *is* there, then she must be in that stinking rat hole of a lockup—"

"But, Charlie!" Betty objected. "We don't have time!"

"*Please*, Betty. We've no way to tell which way they've gone—setting off in the fog like this is crazy! We might even see something from the cliff top, a light from a boat, or . . . or Granny might have heard the trappers say something about where they're going. It's worth a try."

"Fine," Betty snapped. "I just hope this isn't a mistake."

They set off more swiftly than before, though the fog continued to hinder them. As the path rose up the cliff, the air grew colder still. In the lamp at Betty's side, the wisp's glow lit the way. Betty tried to be glad of its presence. After all, it was the only light they had, and without it, there were a number of loose stones and roots they might have tripped on. But the unnatural eeriness of it was something she couldn't shake off. There was something so unearthly and unsettling about it, and it felt decidedly out of place among them.

They continued without speaking, saving their energy for the steep incline of the path. Betty was glad of it, for the effort finally warmed her limbs. How used to being cold she was! Finally, they reached the end of the path, muscles burning, and squinted through the mist, trying to decipher which way to go.

The headland at Bootleg Beak was wide and almost empty: an open space with scrubby grass and not much else save for nesting gulls and crows. Years ago, another path had led down from the cliff tops to several caves used by bootleggers and smugglers, but the caves had since been filled in and the path rendered unusable. There was only one reminder of Bootleg Beak's murky past, only one thing there at all: the lockup.

It was a small stone cell with a single wooden door that held a tiny, barred window.

"This place gives me the creeps," Fliss said in a low voice.

Betty nodded, staring at the mossy walls. There had been a game they'd played with other Crowstone children when they were younger, to see who was brave enough—or silly enough—to get as close as they could to the lockup. The rules were simple: everyone had to put something into the pool (or the "bootleg booty" as they called it). This could be a coin, a sweet, or some other small token, such as an unusual pebble or a shell. Then they'd take it in turns to creep closer and closer to the lockup while the others watched. The ultimate aim was to reach up, touch the bars on the door, and shout, *Bootleg Booty!* but more often than not the winner was the person who dared to get the closest, for few had the gumption to actually reach out and touch the bars. Especially after what had happened to Betty . . .

She gulped, remembering how she had been grinning widely as her hand reached out for the door and how she'd drawn breath to shout the words. But, instead of victory, filthy fingers had shot out from between the bars and clamped around her own. Then came a dry, wheezing cackle from the prisoner within, whose face she couldn't see. That had only made it all the more terrifying. Betty had twisted and yelled and yelled . . . but the fingers didn't loosen. It was Fliss who had seized her courage and the bootleg booty, and flung the fistful of sweets and coins through the bars with a roar: "Let go of my sister!"

And it had worked. The dirty hands released her as the prisoner scuffled around on the floor of the lockup to collect the goodies that had been thrown through.

Betty glanced down at her hand, remembering the feeling of those horrible fingers on hers.

"That was the first time I ever saw you scared," Fliss said faintly.

"First time I ever saw you brave," Betty replied with a small smile. They stared at each other for a short moment, not needing to say anything else. They had both seen each other scared—and brave—many more times since that day.

They approached the lockup cautiously, creeping around in silence from the rear. Their footsteps made little sound in the damp, overgrown grass. Willow's seemed to make no noise at all.

When they reached the front, the door was shut, a heavy padlock holding it in place. Surely, then, it couldn't be empty? The barred window was too high to look through without being obvious. Betty held a finger to her lips, straining to hear above the light rushing of the wind. For a moment, there was nothing. Then a slight movement came from within. Her heart seemed to leap from her chest into her throat. Someone *was* in there!

She hit the door with her fist three times, pounding on the wood. "Hello? Who's in there?"

A scuffling movement sounded—someone getting up from the floor. Hands appeared on the bars: strong wrinkly ones that Betty knew, before their owner even spoke.

"Betty, is that you?"

"Granny!" Fliss exclaimed, hugging Betty with relief. "Yes, it's us!"

Betty sagged against the cold stone wall, her knees suddenly weak. "Thank goodness you're here." Swirling mist nipped at her nose. Fliss had been wrong: there was no hope of seeing any lights on the water from the cliff top. They couldn't even see where the land ended. Until the fog cleared, their only chance of picking up Charlie's trail now was Granny.

"Don't thank anything that I'm here," Granny retorted. "Arrested at my age! It'll be the talk of Crowstone."

"It won't," Betty cut in, the truth drying her mouth out. "Because it wasn't a real arrest. Oh, Granny, you were tricked—we all were!"

"*Tricked?*" Granny was incredulous.

"They were just pretending so they could take Charlie," said Fliss.

"*What?*" Granny said, enraged. "Take Charlie where? Who *are* these people? Get me out of here so I can get my hands on them!"

"We don't know yet," said Betty, motioning for Willow to stay quiet. "All we know is we need to go after them—they've taken her on a boat. Maybe they haven't got too far yet in the marsh mist." She glanced around, suddenly realizing something. "Perhaps, for once, it's our friend."

"Betty Widdershins," Granny said in a voice as sharp as needles, "you're not to go chasing after criminals, do you hear? You're to fetch the real warders and get me released, then we'll deal with this together."

"The real warders are already out looking," said Fliss. "They'll have to bring a spare key to get you out. But, Granny?" She swallowed nervously. "We can't just sit around, waiting for someone else to rescue Charlie.

We . . . we've got things the warders haven't. We're going after her."

"Never mind what you've got," Granny replied. "How do you think you're going to catch up with them—you just said they've taken a boat!"

"They have," said Betty. "But so can we."

"What?" Granny spluttered. "You're thirteen! You can't sail a boat!"

"I can," Betty retorted. "I've been on the boat with Father every spare minute. I've watched and I've learned. I *can* do it, and I have to if we're going to get Charlie back."

Granny's hands loosened on the bars. "This is my fault. I should have fought harder. If your father had been there, none of this would have happened. They were never going to listen to a silly old woman."

"Don't ever say that!" Fliss said, shocked. "It wouldn't have made any difference. They fooled us all. And honestly, Granny, you're *twice* as scary as Father! The way you stood up to them—"

"You were wonderful," Betty added fiercely. She reached up and took Granny's hand, squeezing her papery fingers. "And you can't blame us for going after Charlie, because that's exactly what *you'd* do."

Granny squeezed back, sniffing. "That's not the point."

"We have to figure out where they've taken Charlie," said Betty. "Was there anything, *anything* at all those warders said that might give us a clue?"

"No," Granny said dejectedly. "They didn't mention anywhere except Torment. But if they're not really warders, they won't be taking her there."

"So they kept up the lie," Fliss said, her voice cracking with disappointment. "Whoever they are, they're good at what they do."

Granny took a sharp breath. "Wait. There was one thing I thought I heard them say after they locked me in and were starting to walk away."

Betty pounced. "What? Where?"

"Not where," said Granny. "And like I said, they were already leaving . . . it was faint. But I thought I heard the word *swindles*."

"Swindles." Betty frowned. "There's only one Swindles that's ever talked about in Crowstone."

"Rusty Swindles," Fliss breathed. "The notorious smuggler?"

"*Dead* smuggler, you mean," Granny interjected. "Anything linked to him and his crew can only be bad news."

"Why would they be talking about him?" Betty puzzled before a flicker of an idea sparked within. "Unless . . . perhaps it *did* mean something! Or rather, some*where*."

"Betty?" Granny said in a warning tone. "You can't do this — it's crazy! Fliss, talk some sense into her."

"Sorry, Granny," Fliss said, "but Betty's right. We're Charlie's best chance right now."

Granny gave a disbelieving splutter. They all knew that Fliss could usually be relied on to be the sensible one. But there was nothing usual about tonight, and Fliss wanted Charlie back every bit as much as Betty did.

Hearing Granny shiver, Betty suddenly remembered the extra shawl she had brought. She pulled it out from the potato sack and pushed the edge of it through the bars in the door. "Here. Take this to keep warm." She hesitated, then poked through a tin of the tobacco, too.

"Don't suppose you brought any whiskey?" Granny asked hopefully.

"Er . . . no," said Betty, seeing Fliss grimace at the mention of it. "But we'll be back as soon as we can."

"Betty, no . . . wait!" Granny demanded, but Betty had already begun to stride away, back toward the cliff path to the harbor. Fliss followed wordlessly, and with every step, Granny's voice grew fainter — and more desperate.

"Betty Widdershins, if you don't get back here this minute, I'll . . . I'll . . ."

But they never heard Granny's threat, for her words were whipped away as they stepped onto the path. Betty was grateful for the wind whistling in her ears, drowning out all else. A cross Granny was something she was used to, something she could deal with. A frightened, desperate Granny . . . wasn't. It made her angry. No, *furious*. That fury was something she needed, something which chased away the fears and doubts.

"Betty," Fliss said, hurrying to keep up. "Wait!"

Betty kept walking, big strides that sent her blood pumping and added to her anger. Making her brave.

"Betty!" Fliss pleaded again. "Say something. Why do you have that look on your face? What are you thinking?"

"Plenty," Betty answered grimly, trying to put her clamoring thoughts in order. "But I'll tell you something: whoever they are, those people who've taken Charlie? They've messed with the wrong family."

Chapter Eight

Rusty Swindles

WHEN THEY REACHED THE HARBOR, Betty's nose and fingers felt half-frozen. She pushed her hands in her cardigan pockets to warm them and was startled by the feeling of a little, wet nose and tickling whiskers nuzzling her fingertips. She had forgotten about Charlie's rat. She stroked his ears, glad of his furry warmth in her hand.

"Which boat is it?" Willow asked from beside her. Her voice, coming out of emptiness, startled Betty more than it should have. She moved so silently, like snow through air, that it was hard to tell she was there at all.

Betty looked past the rows of boats, some flaking and shabby, others brightly colored and well kept. "There," she said, pointing out a small fishing boat. "The green one."

"*The Traveling Bag*," Willow read from the decorative, painted letters on the side, as they approached. "What's a traveling bag?"

"Something magical that could take you away to anyplace you wanted—or to anyone," Betty said wistfully. She grabbed the mooring rope and began to heave at it, tugging the boat closer to the wall.

"Something magical . . . like the dolls?" Willow asked. "You had something like that once?"

"Once." Betty averted her eyes. How she wished they still had Granny's scruffy, old carpetbag! But it was long gone and no amount of wishing would ever return it. "Not anymore."

"It's still a funny name for a boat."

Betty shrugged. "No funnier than *Knot Working*," she said, wanting to change the subject. She nodded to a ramshackle thing floating next to them. "Or that pink monstrosity over there: *Summer Love*."

"I like that one!" Fliss objected.

Betty snorted, still hauling the rope. "You would."

The boat bobbed closer, half a step from the wall. "Go on, Fliss, you first," Betty instructed.

Fliss stepped onto the boat with a predictable

nauseated gurgle. Betty felt cool air swirl past her as Willow boarded as soundlessly as a cat and then climbed on herself.

Fliss plopped down on the bench, staring determinedly into the distance while taking deep breaths.

"What's the matter with your sister?" Willow asked as Betty unlocked the wheelhouse and dumped the potato sack inside. A faint odor of fish rose up, a smell no amount of paint could disguise.

"She gets seasick, that's what," said Betty. "She can barely look at a boat without turning green."

"But we aren't even moving yet."

"I take it you're at home on the water, then?" Fliss asked snarkily.

"My family are fishing people," said Willow. "I've probably spent more time on water than on land."

"Good," said Betty, feeling a droplet of water land on her hand that she felt sure had dripped off the little girl. "You'd better go into the wheelhouse and keep warm. Fliss, give me a hand with stoking up the engine."

Together, Betty and Fliss heaved coal from the hatch below deck and shook it into the furnace, sneezing as coal dust flew into their faces and blackened their fingers. Though the fog was clearing a little, there were still no signs of life at the harbor. Soon steam began to puff from the funnel. Betty wound in the mooring rope and lit the lamp at the front of the boat, even though it could not help them see far through the mist.

"Fliss," Betty called, heading for the wheelhouse, where she took the wheel. "Coming in?"

Fliss gave a pained nod and followed, taking a spot on a cushion propped on the wooden seat. Its checked cover matched the thin curtains at the windows, which the girls had insisted on making to brighten up the little fishing boat after Father had painted and repaired it.

Once inside, Betty twisted the dolls, allowing Willow to be seen. Though she hadn't voiced it, the knowledge that Willow was there with them, unseen and so very silent, was spooking Betty more than she cared to admit. As the girl came into view, she felt slightly better. There was something about her quietness that made it easy to imagine she could be invisible even without the magical dolls.

Willow squeezed into the narrow space after them and sat opposite Fliss. Slowly, the little boat chugged across the harbor and into the night.

"I wonder if Granny's been found yet," Fliss murmured, more to herself than anyone else.

"Doubt it," said Betty, peering through the mist, her fingers clamped tightly on the wooden wheel. She steered to the left, willing the fog to clear. "She would've come straight down to the harbor after us."

Fliss leaned back, closing her eyes and resting her head. "We'll be in for it when we get back."

"At least you're thinking positively," said Betty.

Fliss opened one eye, raising a perfectly arched eyebrow. "That's positive?"

"You said 'when,'" Betty replied. "That's good enough for me."

"Great," Fliss muttered, closing her eye again, and giving a little *oooh* as the boat rode a small wave.

With her feet, Betty nudged a tin bucket toward Fliss. "Lucky we left when we did," she said, noticing a nearby water marker. "The tide's starting to go out. Much longer and we'd have been stranded."

"Always lucky, that's us," said Fliss, sarcastic for once. "Anyway, you still haven't said where we'll be coming back *from*."

Betty reached into the potato sack and removed the map she'd brought along: a roll of thick parchment with slightly tatty edges. She opened it below the window in front of her, pinning its curling edges down with two stones Father had brought aboard as paperweights. It was similar to Willow's map in that it showed Crowstone and the Sorrow Isles: Torment, Lament, and Repent on a small scale in the lower right corner. Above it was the mainland, starting with Marshfoot and leading to Horseshoe Bay and beyond. But it was the area to the left that was of interest to Betty, in the expanse of water that, on Willow's map, held the location of the mysterious, hidden island.

On this map, the area below the secret island was where Betty's finger trailed, where the first of two unusual landmarks lay. She tapped the parchment, eyeing Willow.

"Know what this is?"

Willow stared at the map. "A shipwreck."

"Not just any shipwreck," said Betty. "The most famous one of all."

Fliss's eyes flew open again. *"The Sorcerer's Compass?"*

"That's the one," said Betty. "Although *infamous* is probably a better word. And do you know who that ship belonged to?"

"Rust . . ." Willow frowned. "Rusty . . . ? The smuggler you mentioned earlier?"

"Right," said Betty. "Rusty Swindles."

"We heard the tale a lot when we were younger," said Fliss. "Sometimes from Father, sometimes from Granny." She paused. "You never heard the story?"

Willow looked uncertain. "My family isn't from Crowstone. We've only lived on Torment for the past year, since my father was put in prison. But there was something about a cursed shipwreck, only people told it differently. I guess that's the thing about small places. The same stories get . . ."

"Retold?" Fliss said gently. "That makes sense. Up until recently, we'd never left Crowstone." She gazed past Betty into the thinning mist. "Our world was very small, but on Torment, yours must have been smaller still."

The words hung in the air, sinking into Betty's damp clothes and weighing them down. She had thought about life on Torment before, of course, and wondered what it must be like, but not in any real depth. She had been too busy plotting her own freedom to give much consideration to the people who had even less than she did.

"The story goes that Rusty Swindles was one of the most notorious smugglers in these parts," Fliss continued. "And his most valuable stolen treasure was rumored to be a magical compass that had once belonged to an old sorcerer—"

"Some say magician," Betty interjected. "And the compass was rumored to lead its owner anywhere they wanted to go—or to anything they wanted to find. After he stole it, Rusty even renamed his ship to celebrate his victory."

"Big mistake," said Fliss, appearing to forget her

queasiness a little as she warmed to her subject. "Our granny always says that renaming a ship leads to terrible luck, as Rusty was about to find out. Shortly after the compass came into his possession, the ship was ambushed by pirates who wanted it for themselves. Although Rusty was killed, his body was never found—and neither were any of his stolen treasures. But they say he went down with the wreck—and the compass with him."

"How did they know he was dead?" Willow asked, her eyes as round as buttons.

"Some of his crew survived to tell the tale," said Betty. "And, as you've heard, the shipwreck's said to be cursed by the ghost of Rusty Swindles. Anyone who tries to move it, or rob it, meets a grisly end."

"So . . . do you think . . . ?" Fliss bit her lip, pondering. "If the trappers mentioned Rusty Swindles, could they be searching for something of his? His treasure? The compass?" Her face crumpled suddenly. "What if Granny misheard? And even if they *did* say Rusty's name, how do we know there's a link at all? Perhaps it was something they said in conversation, or to throw Granny off the scent!"

"No." Betty gripped the wheel tightly, feeling more and more certain that she was on to something. "They didn't *need* to throw Granny off the trail—think about it.

She was already locked up, out of the way! As far as the trappers know, no one's following them." She narrowed her eyes, glancing at the map in front of her. "And if you'd just kidnapped two people, you'd be focusing on your plan, wouldn't you? I know *I* would. Not talking about old smugglers and shipwreck stories for the fun of it."

"So where does Charlie come into it?" Fliss asked. "Or rather Willow? You said they wanted you because you can . . . can catch wisps?"

Willow nodded. "My parents always warned me I'd be in danger if I was found out," she said, her voice barely above a whisper. "We tried so hard to keep it a secret, but someone must have been watching us." Her lip trembled. "And when we escaped, they took their chance . . . to catch *me*."

"But why?" asked Betty. She turned to Willow as a thought flared in her mind. "Back at the Poacher's Pocket, you said that wisp was alive once . . . so it must be true that they're souls, just like Granny always said." A chill colder than the mist wrapped around her heart. She had always preferred to think of the wisps as marsh gases, a practical explanation that suited her. But having had the chance to watch this one closely, she could see it was no such thing.

"Who?" Fliss whispered, ashen-faced. "Who was it? What does it want from you?"

"I think it's someone who can clear my family's name," Willow murmured finally.

"Why do you think that?" asked Betty.

When Willow spoke again, her voice was haunted. "Because it appeared today—the day my mother and I set out for the island I showed you on the map."

"So what's there?" Betty asked. If anything, she found Willow's answer more troubling. "Why is the island hidden? Is it even *safe*?"

"I . . . I don't know." Willow's voice had risen, and the wisp seemed to share her agitation, for it zipped out of the lamp and swiftly circled around Betty's legs.

Betty exhaled sharply, prickling with fear. How had Willow come by the map? And what exactly did she expect to find on the island? "There seems to be a lot you don't know," she muttered. *Or won't say.*

She gazed at the wisp, and for the first time, a pang of sadness touched her. It wasn't just a little light on a marsh. It had been someone once. Living, breathing, with hopes and feelings and memories. Was this all that remained? "If they want *you*, to be able to trap a wisp, and not just *any* wisp . . ."

Fliss gave a little gasp. "Then that must mean they want Charlie to . . . to . . ."

Betty stared at the wisp, dread clutching at her. "To capture the spirit of Rusty Swindles."

Chapter Nine

The Wisp Catcher

"THEY WANT CHARLIE TO RAISE the *dead?*" Fliss squeaked.

"We can't know for sure," said Betty, swallowing hard. "But I think it makes sense. To take the risks they have, it would have to be something *big*. If they want Rusty Swindles, they must be heading for the shipwreck—*The Sorcerer's Compass.*"

They were approaching Repent now, the second largest of the Sorrow Isles, and Crowstone's closest neighbor. But although the population was higher here, there were no families on Repent—only families divided. A huge, ugly stone prison took up the bulk of the land.

Through sheets of drifting mist, Betty caught glimpses

of lit beacons at the edge of the island, serving as warnings of the land mass to passing boats. Beyond them, dim lights flickered from a handful of windows where warders were on their nightly duties. Though they were not visible now, Betty knew that there were hundreds more windows. Each one was barred, keeping in a prisoner. It wasn't long ago that their own father had been locked away there for selling stolen goods after gambling all their money away. Thankfully, those days were past them now — but Betty shuddered, remembering the stink and despair of the place only too well. On the far side of the island, separate from the prison, stood an ancient stone tower reaching into the low cloud.

She caught Fliss's eye, memories passing between them. As well as the prison, Crowstone Tower had been part of the Widdershinses' past and the terrible curse that had hung over their family for generations. Though it no longer posed any threat to them, Betty had no wish to look at it. *Or to return to it ever again.*

She was so caught up in her own thoughts of Repent that it took her a moment to notice that Willow had gone completely rigid and was staring at the prison with haunted eyes. It was a look Betty recognized.

"Willow?" she said softly. "Earlier, you said you and your mother escaped but that you weren't on Torment because of something you'd done." She glanced at the prison, leaving the unspoken question hanging in the air.

Willow nodded, her gaze dropping. "My father," she whispered. "When he was jailed, my mother and I were sent from our home in Merry-on-the-Marsh to Torment." Once again, her eyes took on the look of someone who was much older. "We haven't even been allowed to visit him."

"Oh, Willow." A tiny part of Betty's hardness softened. She knew how it felt: the shame of a father locked away, the ache of missing him, the sting of having visits denied. She reached out and touched Willow's hand. It was still worryingly cold, though Willow seemed numb to it. She wondered what Willow's father had done. It must have been something serious to get his family banished, but before she could ask, Fliss spoke.

"Betty, what if the boat's stopped and searched?" Fliss gazed out of the window fearfully, searching the waters for any sign of warders. "They'll still be looking for Willow."

"We keep her hidden," Betty replied. "You're the eldest, so you'll have to say we've received word our cousin in Marshfoot has fallen ill, and we're going to look after him."

Fliss nodded but didn't look particularly happy about it. "You know I hate lying."

"Well, it's not your lie, is it?" Betty reasoned. "It's mine, and I don't mind lying at all. You'll just be the one actually saying it."

"All right," Fliss said rather ungraciously.

"Speaking of keeping hidden," Betty added, "we'd better put something of ours inside the dolls, just in case we all need to disappear." She pulled the dolls from her pocket and passed them to her sister.

Fliss twisted the dolls apart, then plucked one of her hairs out and placed it into the third nesting doll. Betty added a hair of her own to the second doll, wistfully noticing how dull and frizzy it was compared to her sister's glossy, smooth one. She stacked the dolls inside each other again but kept the outer halves not quite lined up so the girls remained visible—for now.

Fliss shuffled along the seat to get a better look at the map, bumping into the potato sack. "It's about time we dumped this, isn't it?"

"Perhaps we should keep hold of it awhile," said Betty.

"What?" Fliss demanded. "Why? You know what could happen if we're caught with it! The safest thing to do is throw it overboard and be done with it."

"There's a lot of tobacco in there," said Betty. "Might be worth something."

"Worth getting caught?"

"No," Betty replied. "But it's not like we have any money—this is all we have to trade with!"

Fliss sniffed. "You're starting to sound like a crook."

Betty shrugged. "Crooks have got Charlie. If we're going to get her back, we need to think like them."

Fliss pursed her lips, then clutched the edge of the bench as the boat tilted. "So we have to find Rusty Swindles's shipwreck. How far away is it?"

Wordlessly, Willow handed Betty the yellowed, old map and the hagstone. Betty took them, half-afraid that the map was at risk of being damaged, for Willow's wet hair had trailed damp patches all the way down her front. But when she took it, the map was mysteriously dry. Staring through the hagstone again, the peculiar thrill of it made Betty's fingers tingle.

Betty eyed Willow's map, then compared it with her own. Though Willow's was smaller, she could see it was perfectly to scale and drawn with finer detail than her own. Quickly, she calculated the distance and their speed. "A good few hours at least." She sneaked a look at Willow, who was staring into her lap. "Plenty of time for you to tell us what or *who* that wisp is, and why you escaped from Torment. And then there's the question of where you got this map."

Willow drew her feet up onto the seat, her long hair

falling in straggles around her face. Odd, Betty thought, that it was still dripping, even now. The damp mist had a lot to answer for.

"Come on, Willow," Betty urged. "Time to start talking. We can't help you unless we know exactly what it is you're trying to do." She heard the harsh note in her voice, saw Willow flinching and forced herself to speak more kindly. Willow had already been through enough. "Whether any of us like it or not, we're involved now. All of us."

Willow nodded, sniffling. "Like I said, my mother was with me most of the way. She told me, over and over, that if we got separated, I should follow the signs for Nesty-nook Green and then head for your yard."

"Wait, *what*?" Betty demanded, shocked at this revelation. "I thought you just saw the hole in our gate and got in by chance. But you're saying you headed there on purpose? Why?"

"My mother paid people to get us across," Willow admitted. "A cloth trader. It was all arranged by one of the warders—"

"Jumping jackdaws!" Fliss exclaimed. "You trusted a *warder*? Don't you know half of them are crooks?"

Willow's eyes filled with tears, becoming glassy and distant. "We didn't then. I never saw him, only heard him speaking to Mother downstairs late one night. He said . . . he said it was wrong that we were there, and he wanted to help us escape. He knew I could catch wisps, too. He said it was dangerous, that if the wrong people found out, I'd be in trouble. That's why we trusted him—because he knew and didn't tell. After it was all arranged and Mother had paid him, we never saw him again."

"Never saw him again?" Betty repeated, thinking of the two warders who had vanished.

Willow shook her head. "At first Mother was afraid he'd taken our money and tricked us—or perhaps even been found out—but no one came for us and the day for the escape came closer and closer." She wrung her hands. "It was our only chance—we had to take it. Mother and I hid in rolls of fabric being shipped to Crowstone. She thought it was safer to go that way rather than risk traveling straight to the island from Torment. Our plan was to hide out, then stow away on another boat leaving Crowstone."

"So where does the Poacher's Pocket come into it?" Betty asked.

"The barrels in the backyard," said Willow. "Mother told me to wait until the brewery wagon came to collect the empties, then sneak into one once they were on the wagon."

"And then it'd be shipped off across the water," said Betty. "With you hidden inside."

The fog was lifting, dissolving into patchy puffs over the water. They were almost past the prison now, heading in the direction of Marshfoot.

"Why the Poacher's Pocket, though?" Fliss asked. "The Snooty Fox is on the other side of Crowstone. Surely it would've made sense for you to head there if you wanted to stow away in a barrel? It's much closer to Torment."

Willow hugged her knees. "Mother thought our chances were better from the Poacher's Pocket. We heard it was shabby and run-down, and that getting into the yard would be easier—"

"Shabby?" Fliss fumed, clearly insulted. "*Run-down?*"

"Oh, come off it, Fliss," Betty snorted. "The place is falling to bits! No point getting hoity-toity."

Fliss pursed her lips, looking remarkably like Charlie in a sulk. "And after everything Father's done to smarten the place up, too," she muttered, shooting Willow an injured look.

"That wasn't all we heard," Willow added in a small voice.

"What else, then?" Fliss demanded. "That our granny's a drunk? Or our home-cooked food is lousy?"

"Only when you're cooking," Betty said under her breath.

Fliss glared. "I heard that."

Betty raised an eyebrow. Fliss rarely lost her temper, but seasickness and loyalty were proving an interesting combination.

"*N-no*," Willow stammered. "Nothing like that. Mother heard that the people who lived there were good people. Kind. That . . . that they wouldn't turn us over to the warders if they found us."

"Oh," said Fliss, softening immediately. She shivered, leaning over the bucket. "Better that we're known for being kind than for being wealthy, I suppose."

Betty wriggled her toes in her hand-me-down boots. "There's never been any danger of *that*."

An ugly thought occurred to her, but she kept it to herself. It was all very well being known as kind, but that kindness had led to Charlie being snatched. Kindness had made them *vulnerable*. She shifted uncomfortably at the wheel. Handing Willow over wouldn't have been easy or felt good—but it would have meant that the Widder-shinses would all be sound asleep in their beds. Instead, they'd been scattered to the winds. She pushed the horrid little thought away, clasping the wheel more tightly.

"I don't understand how that would've helped you get to this . . . this invisible island, though. The brewery ship certainly wouldn't be stopping off there, or anywhere close."

"It wouldn't," said Willow. "It would only have gotten me safely away from Crowstone. From there, I needed to get to the Winking Witch. The brewery ship passes close by, close enough to swim to."

"The Winking Witch?" Betty asked, feeling a shiver of fear and excitement trickle down her spine. She examined Willow's map again, peering closer at the two unusual landmarks. At first she'd been too caught up with the mysterious island to take much notice of anything else. There was *The Sorcerer's Compass*, inked as a tiny wreck. Situated between the shipwreck and the secret island was a tiny, craggy isle that showed the silhouette of a standing figure in a distinctive pointed hat. On its shoulder was a large, black bird and beside it a cauldron. Betty had seen the landmark before on her own maps but never detailed so exquisitely as it was here. Ordinary maps offered something far less fantastical: a pile of rocks that vaguely resembled a face with a hooked nose and something that could've been a witch's hat. But on Willow's map . . . there was something odd about the figure, Betty saw now. A fleck of white stood out within the face, like a tiny, white eye.

"Look through the hagstone," Willow told her.

Betty lifted the stone and, for a moment, saw nothing. Then the figure fluttered, as though caught in an invisible breeze. And, unmistakably, there was another movement.

"It winked!" Betty exclaimed, thrusting the map and hagstone at Fliss in shock. "It *winked* at me!"

"Jumping jackdaws—it really *is* winking!" Fliss passed the stone and map back to Betty, fingers shaking.

"I think the Winking Witch is connected to the island somehow," said Willow. "That's why I have to go there."

A frown crinkled Fliss's forehead. "Wait—wasn't there a story Father used to tell us? About a one-eyed witch on the marshes, and an island . . ."

"That's right!" Betty exclaimed. "Something about her granting requests or wishes." Memories of her childhood flooded back, of Betty and Fliss cuddling up to Father as Charlie babbled in her cot, chewing her own feet.

Charlie.

Betty's eyes prickled. *Don't cry*, she willed herself. *This is not the time to cry.*

"That old book—I remember it now. Full of stories, legends of Crowstone."

"Yes," said Fliss, nodding vigorously. "*The Crowstone Chronicles*!"

Betty closed her eyes. She could almost smell the yellowed, musty pages. And in her head, she heard Father's voice, and the story he had told so many times.

She took a breath, opened her eyes, and began.

"There was once a poor man who had three sons . . ."

THE CROWSTONE CHRONICLES

The Crone, the Raven, and the Labyrinth: Part I

There was once a poor man who had three sons. They lived on an island surrounded by marshes, where the only path to anywhere was by water.

As is often the way with siblings, the three brothers were very different. The eldest, named Fortune, was goodhearted but conceited. As the firstborn, he had been given the best of what the family had and was blessed with charm and good looks. The second son, Luck, was brave but foolish, and resented living in Fortune's hand-me-downs. The youngest brother, Hope, was the kindest and wisest of the three but was overlooked.

The family scraped by, just surviving on their father's work as a shoemaker. Where his craftsmanship had once been fine, age made his hands unsteady and his eyesight poor. Customers failed to return. After a particularly harsh winter, the old man was unable to work at all. Fearing for the family's survival, the three sons began to plot how they could save themselves from ruin.

"I will go out and find work," Fortune declared. But he had few skills and only ever managed to bring home copper Rooks and Feathers, which were not enough to feed them all. Then, one day, he came home with something else: a mysterious tale that he had overheard.

The story told of a strange island that hid a vast labyrinth at the center of which were riches beyond compare. But the labyrinth was riddled with puzzles and traps, and the way to it could only be learned from a one-eyed crone who lived on the marshes with her raven.

Self-assured as always, Fortune boasted that *he* would be the one to reach the heart of the labyrinth. Only half believing the story but desperate enough to try anything, their father agreed. So off Fortune went in their small boat, following the directions he had been given across the marshes to find the crone.

Now, there was a reason the crone had chosen to live alone, and it was because she didn't like people very much. She disliked their constant requests for help and the way they turned up unannounced. Most of all, she resented the way they looked at her, because she was different. It so happened that she was also a witch.

When she saw Fortune approach, hollering for her attention, she stirred up the sea into a dreadful storm. Fortune, however, as strong as he was conceited, managed to steer the boat safely to the rocky crag where the crone lived. There, he found that a large, black raven on her shoulder spoke for her in clipped phrases.

Silently, the crone pushed a stone into Fortune's hand. At the center was a hole, crusted with tiny gemstones.

"Look through, look through," the raven instructed.

Fortune lifted the stone to his eye and cried out in wonder. A mass of land that hadn't been there before had appeared on the horizon. Immediately, he knew this must be the location of the hidden labyrinth.

The crone held a cauldron in her hand, which she offered to him now.

"Take one, choose one," said the raven, blinking a yellow eye at Fortune.

In this cauldron, there were all sorts of curious

things: a pair of fine leather shoes that were exactly his size, a plush velvet cape, a jeweled dagger, a lucky rabbit's foot, a ball of yarn, and a golden egg. By now, Fortune had guessed that one of these items would help him, and his mind was ticking. If he failed, he reasoned, wouldn't it be wise to choose something of value? That way he wouldn't return home empty-handed.

"I already have good shoes," he reasoned, "and the dagger and cape will not compare to the riches that await. The rabbit's foot I will not choose because my luck should not be at the expense of another living creature's. The yarn is worthless." In the end, he chose the large golden egg.

Because she was so ugly, Fortune failed to see the witch's scowl of annoyance. He had spent a long time dithering, and the cauldron was heavy. Her old arms ached. However, Fortune, so busy congratulating himself on his cleverness, forgot to thank her as he clambered back into his boat, once again stirring her temper. She conjured a wind that blew his boat off course and set him back another day.

So on Fortune went, using the stone to guide the way. When he arrived at the island, exhausted, he circled it, finding no path, only craggy, white cliffs. Odd branches jutted out where roots had grown in cracks over the years. It was now he realized the crone's storm had resulted in him losing the rope to moor the boat. With nothing to tether it, he had no choice but to leave it drifting.

Wearily, he climbed the cliffs. But the footholds were few, and several times he lost his grip and slid, sending up clouds of dust that got into his throat. Miraculously, the golden egg survived the climb, but already Fortune was doubting his choice. The egg was heavy and cumbersome, and he had a long way to go. It was nightfall when the path came to an end and he found a small area of land before a cave, and he could have cried with joy when he discovered an old stone well tucked away within the greenery.

His joy didn't last. Peering into the well, he saw a bucket floating far below with no means to reach it. The only way to satisfy his thirst was to pull out handfuls of the wet moss that grew inside the lip of the well and squeeze the moisture into his mouth. By then, he was ravenous, too, and had begun to dream about what size yolk might lie inside the egg.

"Only a fool would starve to keep an egg that could feed him," he said to himself. "What use is a golden egg to a dead man?" And he cracked it open.

Alas, a black raven erupted from the egg to cackle at him. Lunging at it in temper, Fortune missed and fell headlong into the well. The bird —for it had been the witch's all along—heckled, "Too bad, too bad!" and flew back to the crone.

And Fortune's little boat drifted farther from the rocks and floated away.

Chapter Ten

A Silvery Veil

BETTY BROKE OFF FROM THE STORY as Fliss pushed past her to the door. A moment later, she could be heard heaving over the side of the boat before returning, pasty-faced, to the wheelhouse. Meanwhile, Betty had been puzzling over the story and unpicking it like knots in a thread. She had always thought the story of the three brothers was merely that—a cautionary tale to be read to children at night. But if there was truth in the legend of the one-eyed witch, then maybe there was some truth in the existence of the island, too. The question was, what was Willow hoping to find there?

Riches beyond compare . . .

She heard Father's voice clear in her mind. Had

Willow and her mother really risked so much and come all this way because they had been motivated by greed? The thought of it filled Betty with anger and disgust.

"What exactly are you hoping to find on the hidden island, Willow?" she asked, her voice icy. "Did you and your mother really risk everything, and did Charlie get kidnapped, all because you thought there was a chance you could get rich?"

"What? *No!*" Willow protested, her face crumpling. Tears spilled down her pale cheeks and dripped off her chin. "I'd never even heard of the riches on the island —it's nothing like that!"

Betty ground her teeth in exasperation. Even if Willow had never heard the story, her mother might have and been foolish—or greedy—enough to think that riches would solve their problems. Perhaps they hoped to buy Willow's father out of jail.

"Betty." Fliss gave her a warning look and shook her head slightly. Betty decided to keep quiet for now. Perhaps Willow might respond more readily to Fliss, who had a way of charming people into doing what she wanted, rather than blundering in like Betty.

"If it's not riches you're after, then why are you so eager to get there?" Fliss continued. "You must know what happens to people who're caught trying to escape! To put yourself through what you have tonight, you must be—"

"Stupid," Betty growled.

"I was going to say desperate," Fliss added. "And we know how that feels, don't we, Betty?"

"Never mind us," Betty snapped, too annoyed to be reasonable. "I want to know about *her*. Because so far, her story is full of holes, and I'm not just talking about the hagstone!"

"We *are* desperate," said Willow miserably. "We knew how dangerous it was to escape, but we had to—for my father. To prove he's innocent."

"Innocent of what?" Betty asked, the coldness seeping from her voice. Could it be true? Could Willow and her mother really have risked their own lives for her father? She glanced back at the prison vanishing behind them into darkness. She and Fliss both remembered how awful it was to have someone they loved locked inside its walls.

"Murder," whispered Willow.

The word rang in Betty's ears. For Willow and her mother to have been on Torment, Betty had known it must be for something serious—but she hadn't been imagining this. She and Fliss each took a sharp breath as things became worryingly clear. Prison sentences in Crowstone were always harsh, but for taking a life, there was only ever one outcome. The worst outcome.

"He's going to be executed, isn't he?" said Fliss shakily.

A small sob escaped Willow's lips and she nodded.

"When?" Betty asked, her voice a dry croak now. She recalled the prison gallows once more with dread. The wooden scaffold, the gloomy prison courtyard. At one time, Granny said, they used to carry out the hangings at the crossroads, for everyone to see. Nowadays they still happened, only inside the prison walls.

"In three days," said Willow, biting her lip. "We tried so *hard* to make them listen, but no one would. And time just kept on running out." She wiped her runny nose. "That's why we had to get away, to try to prove once and for all he didn't do it. And now Mother's been caught, it's down to me. I'm . . . I'm all he has left. I'm his only chance." She buried her face in her hands and wept silently.

Not knowing what else to do, Betty reached out and gently laid her hand on Willow's back. Despite the dry clothes of Charlie's she'd changed into, there was a damp, clammy feel to them. As if the marsh had got its hooks into her and wouldn't let go.

"So then why were you and your mother on Torment?"

Fliss asked, confused. "I thought it was just for people who'd been banished or released from prison and not allowed to return to their previous home?"

"As punishment," said Willow. She rubbed a sleeve over her wet face and sighed. "Before all his happened, we lived on the mainland, in Merry-on-the-Marsh. My father was a fisherman, a good one. But he was also a wisp catcher like me." Her face crumpled. "It was part of the reason his catches were the biggest and the best."

"I don't understand," said Betty. "How could being a wisp catcher help him to fish well?"

Willow shook her head. "It didn't exactly. Father says wisps hold on because of unfinished business. Sometimes it's a feeling: anger or sadness. Sometimes they're vengeful; sometimes they want justice. But they always want to be heard. And that's why they can be dangerous to people who don't know how to listen, who aren't prepared. It's easy to follow them, to forget yourself. That's why folk fear them.

"But Father didn't. He wasn't afraid," Willow explained. "He'd go where others wouldn't. Places full of wisps that most fishing folk would stay away from out of fear. But he . . . *respected* them. And he taught me to once it was clear I had the gift, too." She smiled faintly. "He said I was a born wisp catcher."

"What do wisp catchers do, though?" asked Fliss.

"We lull them."

"Lull?" asked Betty.

"It's a way of calming them, so they lose their power over people," said Willow. "At least for a little while. Father showed me how to do it safely, but he said we must always keep it a secret. That there were people who would try to use what we did for . . . for bad things."

Betty felt a sudden familiar chill. Granny had said something very similar on the night she had given Betty the nesting dolls. About how dangerous they could be in the wrong hands . . .

"One day he went out fishing with his best friend, Saul," Willow continued, frowning. "Mother hadn't wanted them to go. She was worried because I'd seen them arguing about something. I was too far away to hear what they said, but I could see Saul showing Father something—a scrap of paper. Father was shaking his head, and Saul was getting angry. Then finally Father nodded. So they left . . . but something happened, and Saul never came back. Father returned with a bump on his head and couldn't remember how he got it, but there was . . ." She faltered, brushing tears away from her eyes.

Fliss managed to look up, though by now she was

decidedly green again. "There was . . . ?" she coaxed gently.

Willow sniffed. "Blood inside the boat. But Father had no injuries—well, no cuts. Apart from the bump on his head, there were no marks on him. So the blood had to have been Saul's, but they never found him." She gazed at Fliss, then Betty, her eyes troubled and glistening with tears. "After Father was arrested, I searched his boat. There's a tiny secret space where we hid money and food when we were out fishing, in case the boat was ever robbed. That's where I found the map and the hagstone. I couldn't think why the stone would be there, but I remembered stories of how hagstones are meant to be magical, so I looked through it. I was holding the map at the time and caught sight of the island appearing on it by chance. I knew then it must be a clue . . . to whatever had happened to Saul. The way he'd vanished . . . and finding the map with an invisible island, I felt sure the two things *had* to be connected."

"Why didn't you show the warders?" Betty asked. "Surely you'd want to give them any proof of where Saul could be?"

"Mother wouldn't take it to the warders. She was too afraid. They hadn't listened to Father, she said, so why would they take any notice of us? They could accuse us of being the ones to make the map, and then . . ."

"And then you'd be thrown into Crowstone Tower," Betty finished. "Like anyone suspected of sorcery."

Willow nodded, sniffling. "Father's in prison for killing Saul, but he didn't do it! I *know* he didn't . . . but he says he can't remember anything."

"So they sent you to Torment," said Betty, "because they think, by punishing you and your mother, it'll make your father admit to what he did to Saul . . . and where his body is."

Willow nodded tearfully. "And that's why I believe him. Because he would never, ever let us stay on that horrible island!" She slumped farther back on the seat, looking every bit as hopeless as she sounded.

"You said your father has been in prison for almost a year now," Betty said, her voice softer. How terrible to be punished for someone else's deeds if you were innocent!

"Yes," Willow answered. "That's how long we've been on Torment."

"How wicked!" Fliss exclaimed.

"And the wisp?" Betty asked. "Where does that fit into all this? And who exactly is it?" Even though it had been perfectly well behaved since they'd boarded the boat, she couldn't help shuddering a little at the sight of the orb still glowing at Willow's side. At some point while Willow had been telling her story, it had drawn closer, as though it were listening.

"It appeared this evening, after Mother and I became separated," Willow said, her voice trembling. "Something about it . . . seems familiar. Like . . . like it knows me. I think . . . it could be Saul? And he's trying to show me something."

A sick, guilty feeling rose up inside Betty. There was another more likely possibility that the wisp could, in fact, be Willow's mother. The warders had said whoever was half-drowned wasn't expected to survive the night . . . and if Willow sensed there was something familiar about the wisp, then it didn't look good. *But how can I possibly tell her?* Betty thought. *After all she's been through, how can I tell her that her mother didn't make it?*

"But then that means Saul really *is* dead," she muttered.

"It doesn't mean my father killed him," Willow replied with the same determined look Betty had seen earlier.

"No, but it doesn't help you, either."

"It does if he can show me what happened," Willow insisted. "That's why I need to get to the island, to prove Father didn't kill anyone! The island is the key in all this —I can just feel it!"

"It could just as easily be trying to establish his guilt," Fliss said. "You may not like what you find."

Willow glared at them stubbornly, her face streaked with tears. "Maybe not, but if my father's going to die, I have a right to know either way. I *need* to know."

"And if he's guilty?" Betty asked. "What then?"

"Then at least we'll have proof, and the warders won't have any reason to keep us on Torment," said Willow. "They'll have to let us leave. They *have* to."

There it is again, Betty thought. That desperation, the clinging to the smallest of hopes when it was all a person had to keep them going. Rather like she felt now about finding Charlie.

"Earlier, you said that the wisps exist because of unfinished business," said Fliss, her dark eyes troubled. "But what happens to a wisp if whatever they stayed for isn't resolved?"

"They become more dangerous," Willow said quietly. "Their . . . their . . ." She paused, struggling for the right words. "Whatever it is that once made them who they were, that fades. And all that's left is a memory, a feeling, a secret—whatever they were holding on for. And it just drifts, a little light flickering on the marshes. That's what Father used to say—a light that was once a soul, waiting to be heard."

"How sad," Fliss murmured, and promptly retched into the bucket. "Sorry," she mumbled, white-faced. "I'd better go out on deck for some air. It's just too . . . *urgh* . . . fishy in here." She wobbled to her feet and left the wheelhouse, cold air swirling in before she closed the door again.

Moments later, she was back, looking even more ashen and breathing shakily.

"What's up?" Betty asked. "You look even sicker than you did a minute ago."

"I—uh . . ." Fliss quavered, her eyes wide and glassy. She pointed at the windows. "Outside," she managed. "Look outside!"

Alarmed, Betty turned to stare through the glass. She froze as she realized what Fliss had seen.

Wisps, dozens of them, emerging from the marsh mist and shrouding the boat like a glowing, silvery veil. Betty watched, an icy chill rippling down her spine as the wisps bobbed against the windows from all sides.

They were surrounded.

Chapter Eleven

"Don't Listen to the Whispers..."

"I'VE NEVER SEEN THAT MANY BEFORE," Betty whispered. The sight of the glowing orbs clamoring around the boat was deeply unsettling. She could feel the hairs on the back of her neck sticking up rather like Oi's did when anyone tried to stroke him. "It's like . . . like an army of them!"

Willow stood up and peered through the glass. Betty could tell she was trying to seem brave, but there was a telltale trembling of her knees through her dress. She looked scared and younger than ever.

"They must sense the one in the boat," she said. "And us."

Fliss swallowed. "Betty, can we speed the boat up? Go through them, or outsail them?"

"We can't shake them off, not by outsailing them," said Willow.

"Then how do we get rid of them?" Fliss asked, her voice rising. "What do they *want?*"

"To be heard," said Willow. "And seen."

"So how do we get out of this?" Betty was frantic. More and more were swarming the boat—it was getting harder to see past them.

The wheelhouse was filling with an eerie, gray light, making specters of them all. At the edges of the door, thin slices of light glowed and trails of mist leaked under as if reaching for them.

And then came a low whispering sound. Betty whipped away from the window to face Willow and Fliss.

"What?" said Betty, nerves rattling. "Did someone say something?"

"No," Fliss said. "I thought it was you?"

The whispering came again, so softly that Betty could hardly recognize it as being words. She could see now that neither Fliss nor Willow was moving her lips.

"Then who *is* that?" she said faintly. "Who's whispering?"

"*Them,*" said Willow.

There were so many now that all Betty could see was the strange, white light engulfing the boat.

"What do we do?" Fliss croaked.

"We lull them," said Willow. "But the more there are, the harder it is. Even for someone who knows how to do it. They can be wild, unpredictable." Her eyes were wide and frightened. "I've never lulled this many before."

"How do you do it?" Betty asked, her eyes still fixed on the glowing window as her heart raced.

"By singing them a song," said Willow.

"Singing?" Betty's hopes lifted. "Well then, teach Fliss and me! If we all sing it, then maybe we can get rid of them even faster. Fliss's singing usually gets rid of anything."

"This is no time for jokes, Betty," Fliss said tightly.

"I wasn't joking," Betty said in earnest. "Your singing really is dreadful, but that might be a good thing for once!"

"It won't make them go away," Willow said. "It puts them in a daze, so we can move past them, but it's not something I can teach you . . . not in time anyway." She glanced around the wheelhouse. "And we'll need other things . . . nets, jars. Do you have any?"

"Nets and jars?" Betty asked, bewildered. Another

whisper sounded, this time closer, and she swatted at it, unnerved. She ducked down, rooting under the seats. "There are a couple of small nets from when we took Charlie crabbing and one or two jars she used for tadpoles. What do you need them for?"

"You'll see," said Willow. "But we have to hurry." She took a couple of deep breaths, as if readying herself, then reached past Fliss for the door. "After I go out, I need you to wait for my signal. Then bring out the nets and jars quickly. I'll tell you what to do next and, whatever you do, don't listen. You *mustn't* listen to the whispers."

"What would happen if we did?" Fliss asked, in a choked voice.

"That's how people get lost," said Willow. "First by following the light. Then by listening to them, being drawn away."

"And you're going out there *alone*?" Fliss huddled into herself, clearly horrified at the thought of it.

"I have to," said Willow. "If I don't, we won't get away. And more will come."

She seized the door handle and slipped out of the wheelhouse into the swarming glow of wisps. Betty caught one last glimpse of her face, pinched with fear, before she vanished. Betty and Fliss drew closer together, trying to make out the small girl through the silvery light. Everything that happened now, to them and Charlie, hinged on what Willow was about to do.

"Listen," Betty murmured, pressing her ear to the door. "Do you hear that?"

"*W-what?*" Fliss clutched at Betty's hand. Her palm was clammier than Betty had ever felt it before. "Willow said not to listen to the whispers!"

"Not that." Betty leaned closer to the door, a draft tickling her ear. "It's Willow."

It was faint at first, a strangely deep crooning sound that could almost have been coming from an animal. Slowly, it rose and fell like the waves of the sea, and as Betty strained even harder to hear over the whispers, she understood now why Willow couldn't have taught them the song.

"It's in the old tongue," she realized. "Old Crow, the language they used to speak here hundreds of years ago." Granny had tried to teach them some of the few words she knew, but Betty had never managed to grasp them. Above Willow's song, the susurrus of whispers continued, like leaves in a rough wind. Willow went on singing, her voice growing in strength.

"Look!" Fliss pointed, uncurling her fingers from Betty's. "It's working."

Betty's eyes darted to the window, which was rapidly

darkening once more. Fliss was right: the wisps were gliding away, one by one, taking their whispers with them.

"Where's Willow?" Betty asked, craning her neck. "I
don't see her—she must be in the stern of the boat."

"Stern?"

"The back!" Betty said, exasperated.

"What shall we do?" asked Fliss.

"She said to wait for her signal," said Betty. "Once we
get it, we need to stick our fingers in our ears and grab
those nets and jars."

"How can we grab them if our fingers are in our ears?"
Fliss shot back.

"You know what I mean," Betty snapped, unable to
help it as the tension set in deeper.

She eyed the wisp inside the wheelhouse with them,
glowing softly in the lamp once more. At Willow's song,
its light seemed to have been dampened a little, and it
had stilled, as though listening.

They stood, shivering with cold and anticipation.
Betty's hand rested on the latch. Outside, Willow's voice
began to fade. Perhaps her song was drawing to an end
and they would soon be free of the wisps. Betty squeezed
her eyes shut, listening and hoping.

"Betty?" Fliss said urgently. "Does it seem . . . brighter
in here to you again?"

Betty's eyes snapped open. She blinked at the windows, where wisps had begun clamoring once more. Out on deck, nothing could be heard except swirling wind and lapping water.

Betty stiffened. "Something's wrong. Willow's not singing."

"Maybe she's finished," said Fliss uneasily. "But then, why are the wisps back at the window?"

"Exactly," said Betty. She drew in a deep breath. "We have to go out there."

"B-but the signal . . ."

"What if she can't?" Betty said urgently. "She needs our help. I know it."

Fliss hesitated. "I'm scared," she admitted. "I'm not brave like you."

"Yes, you are," said Betty. "I'm scared, too. But we're still going to help Willow, and *that's* what bravery is."

Fliss nodded, looking slightly less terrified. "She who tries triumphs," she murmured. "That's what you always say, isn't it?"

"Mmm," said Betty, because she couldn't think of anything else and she didn't want Fliss to see that her teeth were chattering. She flung a net over her shoulder and tucked a jar under her arm. Then, sticking her fingers in her ears, she indicated for Fliss to do the same before she swung open the door. Once she was sure her sister had covered her ears, Betty screwed up her courage and stepped outside.

They were met by a wall of wisps rising up like the mist itself. Immediately, Fliss shrank back, but Betty gritted her teeth and nudged her onward with her elbow. "Come on! We have to get past them."

The wisps enveloped them, and there was something almost . . . oozing about the movement. Slow, like tentacles or jellyfish. Up close, they were so bright that Betty's eyes were dazzled. And the whispers, louder now, mingled into one another in a low, eerie blanket of words.

"*Come with me . . . need to show you . . . Something you should seeeeee . . . help us, please . . .*"

Betty jammed her fingers in her ears, her courage leaping overboard. Desperately, she searched the deck for Willow, but all she could see were wisps. A terrified gurgle forced its way up her throat. Had Willow fallen overboard? She pushed through the wisps, using her elbows to nudge them aside, although the moment one was elbowed out of the way, another simply replaced it.

"Willow?" Betty's voice emerged dry and raspy. "Where are you?" Around her, the wisps thickened, like curious cats watching a mouse hole. She swatted them away again, momentarily creating a path for herself and

Fliss. But already she was struggling with her sense of direction, disorientated by the floating orbs. She could no longer be sure of where the wheelhouse was, let alone where Willow might be.

Her foot struck something on the deck. Something solid but unmoving. Betty squinted through the wisps, but already, she knew.

A small leather boot, not much bigger than Charlie's. Betty gasped and dropped to her knees. "Willow!" Forgetting the girl's earlier warning, she took her fingers out of her ears and shook the unmoving figure. Instantly, the whispers filled her head, crashing against her own thoughts and making it difficult to focus.

"Set me free . . . just listen, listen . . ."

"Shhhh," Betty moaned, grasping Willow's boot. She followed her leg until she found Willow's face, cupping it in her hand. Her skin was deathly cold, her eyes glassy and staring.

"Is she . . . ?" Fliss's terrified voice cut through the whispering, warm and alive.

"No." Betty's heart leaped. There was a faint movement on Willow's lips. She leaned closer, trying to catch the words. Strangely, she couldn't feel the girl's breath. "She's saying something . . . No, wait. She's still trying to sing!"

She wrapped her arms around Willow, her head thick with the whispering now, thoughts muzzy.

"Betty!" Fliss was yelling now. "Don't *listen!*"

But it was impossible. For out of the whispers, some voices rose above others. Pleading to be heard, demanding to be obeyed. Betty grappled to keep her own thoughts, battling the sensation of slipping away on the night air.

Words crammed into her head: phrases from past lives, songs, promises, threats, secrets. Dimly, she wondered how bright she would glow, how loud her voice would be . . . and what it would say to passing travelers as lost in the mist as she was. The voices drifted over her until she felt her grip on Willow loosening, and she began to float, slowly, away with them.

Chapter Twelve

Seaweed

"**B**ETTY!"

"*Yargh!*" Betty spluttered as cold salt water hit her face. She spat it out, shivering as a thread of it dripped down her collar. "For crow's sake, Fliss!" she yelled, sitting bolt upright. "What are you trying to do, drown me?" She rolled onto her knees, coughing. The deck was damp and gritty beneath her hands. For a moment, she struggled to remember what she was doing out here in the dead of night. Then, from the edges of her vision, the blanket of wisps oozed closer, the whispering taking hold in Betty's mind again.

"I'm *trying* to save your life." Fliss's voice cut through

the whispers in a sterner tone than Betty had ever heard from her.

Betty turned to face her sister. If circumstances had been different, she would have wanted to laugh. Now that she got a proper look at Fliss, she saw her sister looked rather absurd. Her short, normally neat hair was sticking out at all angles from where the sea wind had blown it, and she was brandishing a fishing net fiercely, along with a jar dripping with seawater.

Betty peered closer. "Is that . . . *seaweed* in your ears?"

"Yes." Fliss spoke through gritted teeth. "It was all I could find to dull the noise." Before Betty could protest, Fliss's fingers were deftly poking in Betty's ears, too.

"Oooh." She shivered as the cold, slimy seaweed was stuffed in place. "That feels," she said miserably, "absolutely revolting."

"I know," said Fliss, sounding muffled. "It stinks, too. Now come on." She yanked Betty to her feet and handed her a large glass jar. "Willow needs us!"

Fliss elbowed the wisps out of the way to clear space around them. Willow lay slumped on the deck, unmoving. The whispers were more indistinct now and easier to ignore. Fliss's idea seemed to be working.

"Willow." Fliss shook the girl, gently at first. Her head

lolled to one side, her eyes staring and glassy. "Willow!" Fliss shook harder now, a frantic note entering her voice. "Come on, stay with us! *Sing!* We're right here with you, Willow. Please don't give up. We need you. *Charlie* needs you!"

Fliss turned to Betty, her face a mask of shock and sorrow. "We're too late. We should never have let her come out here alone."

"No," said Betty. "NO!" She thought back, trying to recall Willow's strange, crooning melody. While she knew none of the words, a small part of it looped in her mind, and it was this bit she hummed.

Hesitantly, Fliss joined in, echoing the tune in her warbling, slightly off-key way, tacking on another little section that she, too, had remembered, jogging Betty's memory. And then Fliss must have remembered something else: a single word of Old Crow: *domus*. This she sang, and so Betty sang it, too, and they continued to hum, repeating the only word they knew in what they hoped was the right place.

The boat rocked softly on the water, but Willow remained motionless.

We've lost her, Betty thought, numb with shock. *She's gone, and Fliss and I will be next.* At the thought of this, the whispers edged closer, somehow louder in her head.

She shot a defeated look at Fliss, reaching out and squeezing her sister's hand hard. Fliss squeezed back, humming louder and more tunelessly than ever.

And then Betty saw it: the faintest shift of movement from Willow.

"Fliss, I think it's working!"

They hummed even louder, in time now, if not in tune, singing the one word they knew. And gradually, in shaky breaths, Willow stirred and joined them, correcting the tune and filling in the parts they had missed. Her words were so faint at first that she, too, sounded as though she were humming. Gradually, her voice grew stronger, overtaking theirs as she poured out the strange, old words. She lifted her hands to her ears, blocking out the whispers that were becoming fainter as the song swelled in the air.

Everything stilled—the air, the water, the boat. It was as though the night were holding its breath. The wisps hung motionless around them, like a scene in a snow globe.

Willow stopped singing and sat up. "It's time."

"Time for what?" Betty croaked. She clambered to her feet, and Fliss followed.

"To collect them." Willow took the net from Fliss and gently swept it from side to side. And, instead of darting away like wily fish, the wisps remained unmoving and were collected in the net easily, as if they were nothing more than dandelion clocks, scooped up into the net together in one glowing ball of light, merging together as one. If Betty hadn't come quite so close to being lost, she might almost have found it beautiful to watch.

"And now?" Fliss whispered.

"We move them, gently," Willow said. She ducked through the mass of wisps still surrounding them and shook the net gently over the back of *The Traveling Bag.* "My father always said that, however much we fear them, we must respect them, too."

Hesitantly, Betty set to work with the second net, casting it about as Willow had done, keeping it firmly at arm's length while she collected the wisps before depositing them over the back of the boat. As the net filled, it remained oddly weightless, as if Betty were collecting nothing more than clouds.

She caught sight of Fliss shaking out a jar and wondered if she felt as jittery as Betty did. Her sister's face was gray, but there was a steely look in her eye. Betty had always been the strong one, the one with the quick answers and ideas. It was easy to underestimate Fliss, with her gentle nature and frequent blushes. But when their mother had died, it had been Fliss who took to mothering Betty and

Charlie, nurturing where Granny was brash and fierce. There were different ways, Betty realized, to be strong.

She worked faster, concentrating on the front of the boat. Soon the way ahead was dark and clear.

"We should get going and quickly," Willow said, in a low voice. She'd paused from her work, slightly breathless. "Lulling them only lasts a few minutes, but it should be long enough for us to escape."

Glad to have something more practical to do, Betty stoked the boiler. Slowly, the boat began to pick up speed. She went into the wheelhouse and began to steer. Having cleared the last of the wisps, Fliss and Willow joined her, and Fliss pulled down blankets from an overhead cubby.

Betty's racing heart began to slow, her mind clearing now that the wisps were no longer muddying her thoughts. Here, she felt safer, more in control. Here, it was easier to focus on what she needed to do and why they were out on the boat in the first place. She had to think of one thing and one thing only, which was to rescue Charlie. Her fingers tightened on the wheel, as if by steering the boat she could steer her own mind, too.

Betty glanced at the little clock. It was approaching two o'clock in the morning, yet sleep couldn't have felt further away. She realized, with a stab of worry, that all the while they'd been under attack from the wisps the boat had been adrift. Had luck been with them, taking them in the right direction? Or was it too much to hope that the Widdershinses' ill-fated pattern would change? She glanced at the distinctive shipwreck on Willow's map and consulted her compass, scouring the horizon desperately for recognizable landmarks. The prison, at least, was nowhere to be seen.

"Well," said Fliss, peering out from a nest of blankets, "that wasn't something I thought I'd end up doing tonight."

"No," Betty agreed. "Or ever."

"If Granny could see us now . . ." Fliss's voice was soft, thoughtful. "If she knew what we'd just done . . ."

"She'd be proud." Betty stared through the window, searching the empty waters. "Probably still furious that we dared to take off like that, but yes, proud. Whether she liked it or not. And Father. He'd be impressed."

"Charlie would be, too." Fliss's voice was softer still.

Betty didn't answer. Her throat was aching again with the longing to cry. Charlie *would* be proud. Cross, too, that she'd missed out. *And,* thought Betty, as she caught sight of her reflection in the glass, *Charlie would no doubt be wondering why her two sisters had seaweed dangling out of their ears.*

Chapter Thirteen

The Sorcerer's Compass

THE MARSH MIST HAD CLEARED, leaving a sky so black and clear it was hard to believe the fog had been there at all. After Willow had woken from a fitful sleep, they had shared the bread Betty had brought, but they were still ravenous. A loaf didn't go far between three. Or four, if you included Hoppit.

Betty's tummy grumbled loudly, and she remembered again how there was something about sea air that could make a person so hungry it could send them half-crazy. She knew this was true because she was even reaching the point where the thought of Fliss's burnt porridge made her mouth water.

"Charlie always says being hungry is worse when you

don't know what your next meal will be, or when," Fliss said anxiously. "Poor Charlie. I hope wherever she is that they're at least feeding her properly."

Or at all, Betty thought, but decided not to voice that aloud. "Well," she said, in an effort to sound cheery, "if they're not, she'll probably eat *them*."

A pale moon and glittering stars stretched before them. Once or twice, Betty saw distant shadows that could have been land, but they were too far away to tell. Fliss's eyelids were becoming heavier with sleep, and Betty was reluctant to admit she didn't know exactly where they were since they'd drifted. She was also unwilling to stop the boat and wait until they were sure of their bearings, for the thought of Charlie getting farther away from them was plucking at her like a harp string.

"We could catch fish," Fliss murmured sleepily, as a gurgle sounded from her belly. "We have nets after all. And the little stove to cook on."

"Suppose so," Betty replied. "Although I don't want to gut them, do you?"

Fliss grimaced.

"Thought not." Betty sighed. "Father thinks there're a few types of seaweed that are edible, and some of them don't even taste *that* bad."

"No thank you," said Fliss, her lip curling in disgust.

"You never know whose ears it might have been stuffed into."

Sunrise came, bringing a pale pink sky. Betty looked out over the water. It was as flat as a looking glass, the view clear for miles around. She'd stayed at the wheel while Fliss and Willow dozed and fidgeted, but now that dawn was here, her eyes were gritty and tired. Thanks to the seawater Fliss had thrown, her hair was in a bigger frizz than ever, and her face felt dry and crusty. She licked her lips, tasting salt and feeling a flash of concern. They didn't have much fresh water, either, and there was no way of knowing when they'd next find some.

A sleepy-eyed Fliss stirred and joined Betty at the wheel. Fliss yawned, squinting through the window. A frown creased the creamy skin on her forehead. "Where are we?"

"I've only just started to figure that out," said Betty. "We drifted a little off course last night, but not as badly as I'd feared." She consulted her map, comparing it to the magical one of Willow's. "There's the mainland. We're up past Widow's Point, and the shipwreck should be in this direction. If we keep going, we'll make it by late morning and hopefully intercept Charlie."

"What if they made it before us?" Fliss asked, looking

more awake and worried now. "If they find she can't do what they want, if they think she's useless to them . . ."

"Charlie's smart," said Betty, needing to reassure herself as much as Fliss. "She was onto them, I know it. If she was clever enough to leave a trail of gingerbread, then she'll have thought of ways to stall them. Heck, she's probably pushed them overboard and is rowing back to us already!"

Fliss gave a watery smile.

"We just need to keep going northwest," Betty said determinedly, "and we'll find her."

To think anything different was unbearable.

"And you need to rest," Fliss said gently. "Let me take over."

"You've never sailed a boat," Betty protested. "You think starboard is a darts game!"

Fliss snorted. "How hard can it be? Northwest, right?"

Torn between doubt and exhaustion, Betty allowed Fliss to nudge her out of the way. She sank into the blanket her sister had just shrugged off. It still held Fliss's warmth and a faint trace of rosewater perfume, as well as a whiff of vomit. Nevertheless, she pulled it around her, only now realizing just how tired she was. Across from her, Willow slumbered on.

"Northwest, remember," Betty reminded her sister, sleep tugging at her.

"I remember," said Fliss, more patiently than Betty deserved. "I'm more capable than you think, you know."

"Mmm," Betty murmured. "If it hadn't been for you . . . when those wisps came . . . I was under their spell. How did you resist them?"

"It was luck, really," said Fliss. Her slim, elegant hands looked strange on the wheel of the boat. "That word I remembered . . . *domus*. It's one Granny taught me. It means 'home,' so that's what I thought of. The Poacher's Pocket and everyone there."

"Well, thank goodness you did," Betty said. "I only remember her trying to teach me the words for 'whiskey' and 'tidy up.' If we'd been counting on me, we'd have been lost."

"Don't be silly, Betty." Fliss looked at her fiercely. "It's partly because of you that I knew I could do it. What you said about being brave is true. And I never knew I could be until *you* showed me."

"Really?" Betty mumbled gratefully.

"Really," Fliss repeated. "Well, that and I was also trying very, *very* hard not to be sick everywhere. Turns out it's quite a useful distraction."

Betty didn't feel as though she slept, but she must have, for when Fliss's alarmed gasp roused her from sleep, the sun was high in the sky through patchy cloud. At some point during Betty's snooze, Hoppit had sneaked out from her pocket and was now squeaking indignantly at the wisp in Willow's lap.

Betty sat up on the bench, flinging the blanket aside. "What is it?" she demanded, catching sight of the sick bucket next to Fliss at the wheel and her sister's greenish face.

"We need to slow the boat," Fliss said quietly.

Betty stared across the water, dread creeping over her. The waves were choppier now and the clouds above were casting shadows across the water. Within them, she saw several things at once: rows of jagged rocks; strange, little, floating wicker baskets; and, not too far beyond, a mass of jutting, black wood breaking the water's surface.

"That's it, Fliss," Betty whispered, transfixed by the sight ahead. "That's Rusty Swindles's ship — *The Sorcerer's Compass*!" She picked up Willow's map and pushed her way out of the wheelhouse, the air surprisingly warmer outside now. She shut the dampers, steering the boat away from the rocks as it slowed, and leaned over the bow. A moment later, Fliss joined her, staring out toward the wreckage. Willow lingered a little way behind them, paler than ever in the daylight. Lulling the wisps seemed to have leached her strength even further, for she had hardly said a word since.

"It's so vast," Fliss exclaimed, a tremor of wonder, or perhaps fear, in her voice. "How can it be poking out of the water like that?"

"Father said it rests on a raised part of the seabed," said Betty, unable to take her eyes off the ship. "There are layers and layers of rocks underneath, which is what wrecked it in the first place. And not just any rocks." She opened Willow's map, holding it carefully, half-afraid the precious item might be taken by a gust of wind, and homed in on their position. "Those are the Siren's Claws. And this area"—she pointed to a particularly sharp sliver of rock—"is known as the Siren's Nest because of all the shipwrecks."

"Lots of shipwrecks," Willow murmured faintly, closing her eyes. "Many souls. They can't be seen so easily in the daylight, but they're here. I feel them . . . waiting . . . *angry*."

Chilled, Betty surveyed the jagged rocks glinting like shards of black ice in the sun. It was only the second time she'd ever encountered ones as deadly as these. Off the coast of Lament last year, she had grappled with a smaller formation of rocks known as the Devil's Teeth. Unlike those, which were mostly hidden beneath the water, the Siren's Claws pierced the surface like a cat mid-pounce. They made the Devil's Teeth look like kittens' teeth in comparison.

"And those floating baskets?" Fliss asked, her eyes widening. "Are they . . . are they what I think they are?"

"Memorials," Betty guessed, watching as one of them drifted nearer. It was similar to a small birdcage, with a wicker frame woven from reeds. Inside, she caught glimpses of paper, presumably inscribed with loving words or prayers. It had been waxed to prevent water damage and rolled into a scroll that was fastened with a ribbon of deep red. Tucked into the ribbon was a single black feather.

"Someone loved and missed," said Fliss sadly. "And another over there, look."

The second memorial was smaller than the first and had been made in such a way that the top of it was open, almost like a little chimney. Despite this, some of the wicker was singed, for inside was the nub of a candle long burnt out. Through the water, Betty glimpsed a length of thin rope plunging into the depths, no doubt weighted by a heavy stone to keep it in place. She wondered whom it had been left to remember and whether the poor soul was one of the wisps they had encountered in the misty darkness. Betty didn't want to think about how many lives had been lost in this spot.

They set off again, taking care to avoid the deadly Siren's Claws and the memorials floating ghostlike on the water. Betty couldn't help wondering what lay beneath them, far below on the seabed. How many timber wrecks? How many ghost ships and spilled cargos could there be? Once or twice, they felt and heard the light scrape on wood as some unseen rock grazed the hull of the boat. But they held their breath and carried on, unscathed, with the jutting shipwreck looming ever closer.

Dark clouds were gathering above now, and as the little boat moved into the shade of the wreck, the sudden change in temperature sent shivers across Betty's skin. They all stared up at the wreckage in silent awe.

The front section of the ship was the only part that was visible. The bow reared up from the water like a stallion, tilting to the left and partially exposing the keel. At the front, a beautiful carved figurehead of a mermaid was intact. Though time and water had eroded some of the paint, she was still beautiful, with a sea-green tail, bronzed skin, and shimmering, golden hair.

"I can't believe the ship's still here," Fliss said, looking around in awe. "And the . . . the what's it called . . . the lookout thing on the stick there."

"You mean the *crow's-nest* on the *mast*," Betty corrected, rolling her eyes. How Fliss could live on the coast and know so little about boats was beyond her. "Well, the *fore*mast, actually. The main mast is farther back . . . It must be underwater."

She peered at the water lapping at the sides of the wreck, trying to see into its murky depths. She thought she spotted a porthole below the waves, but the water was difficult to see into, especially with the blackness of the wood fringed with seaweed darkening it further. Whatever else was below the water remained a mystery.

What is down there? she wondered. What secrets or treasure could the massive wreck still hold, if any? Had it been swallowed up by the seabed? Or was everything still inside, as it was the day it sank? Could any loot have been stolen by wreckers? Even as she thought about it, Betty remembered what her father had told her on so many occasions over the years when the girls had been snugly tucked up at bedtime.

"They say *The Sorcerer's Compass* is a cursed ship. Can't be moved or stolen from, though many have tried."

"Who's tried?" Betty had asked, eager as always for the gory details. Next to her, Fliss was half-asleep and Charlie was on her back in her cot, noisily sucking her fist.

"Oh, lots of people," Father replied. "But it's said that Rusty Swindles was a master of booby traps. When he knew the ship was going down and there was no escape, he rigged the entire vessel so none of his loot could be taken, and Rusty and his crew would get to keep their treasure forever. And as the years passed, the legend spread and so did the fear. Stories of a curse began to circulate. But there are always those whose greed will get the better of them."

"And what happened to them?" Betty had asked, exhilarated by the thought of it.

"All sorts of horrible things," Father said, eyes glinting ghoulishly. "Fingers chopped off by falling swords, ghostly visions of dead sailors, treasure plain vanishing or changing into a scourge of rats. But mainly fingers got chopped off . . ."

And every time Father finished the story he would lower his voice to a rumbling, piratey growl, and say the words Betty longed to hear:

> Rusty Swindles, buried deep
> Stolen treasure in his keep.
> Be ye greedy, be ye brave,
> Only fools disturb his grave.

Betty thought back now to Father's bloodthirsty stories of Rusty Swindles and his infamous ship. She had always taken them the same way as any story her father told her: with a pinch of salt. Barney Widdershins was well-known for exaggerating, after all. But as she gazed up at the forbidding shipwreck, it wasn't hard to believe it was cursed.

"So now what?" Fliss asked, interrupting Betty's memories. Her voice was high-pitched, panicked. "There's no sign of Charlie or the people who took her. What if we missed them?"

"We can't have," said Betty, but worry started to gnaw at her. The wisp attack had cost them precious time, but there were two things Betty clung to simply because she had to. "They may have left before us, but they're in rowboats. Ours is bigger, faster. And what Granny told us is our only clue." A clue, she feared, that may not have been enough to go on after all.

A movement by the crow's-nest caught Betty's attention. The "nest" itself was an old barrel, sitting at the top of the mast, and due to the angle of the ship, it jutted sideways over the water. Tufts of straw or something poked out of the cracks, and in a couple of places, weeds had begun to grow. Without warning, a huge gull burst from the barrel and took to the skies, making them all shriek.

"Jumping jackdaws!" said Fliss, clutching her chest and almost knocking Betty overboard. The gull teetered wonkily in the air, as startled as they were, then flapped away.

"Let's look around the other side," said Betty finally. "Perhaps there is a sign someone's been here recently."

But when they arrived, no portholes or areas of deck were visible there, either. Though they had to be above water, the tilting of the ship meant that they were out of view from the girls' position on the smaller boat. There was, however, a crude wooden sign nailed to the hull.

Shakily, Fliss read it out loud:

ENTER NOT IF YE WOULD PLUNDER,
THIEVES WILL ALL BE TORN ASUNDER!

"What does 'asunder' mean?" asked Willow.

"Apart," Fliss said with a gulp. "Thieves will all be torn . . . apart. Well, you said you were hoping for a sign. Looks like we got one!"

"It's probably just there to scare people," Betty muttered. "It could've been written by anyone! It doesn't mean it's true."

"You know what Granny always says," Fliss said

darkly. "There's no smoke without fire. Why would someone write this if there was no truth in it?"

"Perhaps 'someone' has a terrible sense of humor," Betty said. She stared at the sign, which seemed more sinister the longer she looked at it. "Or perhaps . . . perhaps there really are things inside that are of great value."

Images of precious gemstones and golden goblets filled her mind. Chests of priceless coins and antiques . . . One item alone might be enough to feed a family for years. She felt a strange tingle of anticipation. "Perhaps there really *is* something here worth stealing."

"Betty Widdershins," Fliss said disapprovingly. "Our family has never been rich and probably never will be. That doesn't make it all right to take what isn't ours."

"I don't mean for us, but once those warders arrive, we'll need something to trade for Charlie. They're after Rusty's treasure—but what if we got to it first?"

"*Us?*" Fliss spluttered. "Take the treasure? I'd like to keep all my fingers, thank you very much!"

"We wouldn't be the ones keeping it," Betty said. "Perhaps we could even leave something in its place, so we don't make Rusty's spirit angry."

"And what exactly do you think we have that Rusty Swindles would be interested in?" Fliss shot back. "*Hmm?*

Because the only thing I can think of is the nesting dolls, and I sure as eggs don't think we should give those up."

"No," Betty agreed. "Neither do I. But what about Granny's swag? I mean, pirates like tobacco, don't they? And all the better if it's stolen. What do you say, Rusty?" she murmured. "Deal?"

There was a beat of silence in which Betty imagined that the old ship would creak in reply. Nothing came— only the soft lapping of waves against wood. She turned to Fliss, who was looking less certain with every minute.

"So who's going in first, then? You or me?"

Chapter Fourteen

Salt Water and Spit!

AFTER SOME DELIBERATION, they returned to the other side of *The Sorcerer's Compass*, where the side of the wreck was fully submerged.

"There's something down there," said Fliss, wide-eyed. "See that glow, through the porthole? What if it's a wisp—or worse . . . a whole crew of them?"

Betty stared down into the water. There was an eerie, bluish glow filtering through it. "It could be plankton," she said, trying to put Fliss at ease.

"Or Rusty Swindles," Fliss retorted, clearly unnerved.

"Maybe. We'll have to see if it's wearing an eyepatch," Betty joked, then stopped smirking as Fliss gave her a stony look. "Whatever it is, we have to look. If there's anything inside that can help us bargain for Charlie, we need it. It's not like we have any other options."

The mention of Charlie made Fliss purse her lips determinedly. "I'll go," she said. "I'm the oldest."

"But I'm the strongest swimmer," Betty argued. "*I'll* go."

In truth, all three Widdershins girls were fine swimmers, even Charlie with her frenetic doggy-paddle. But Betty could see Fliss wasn't convinced by her idea, and the thought of losing a nail was usually enough to make her sweat, let alone the thought of losing a finger.

"What about me?" Willow asked in a small voice. "It's all because of me that this is happening. I should be the one to go."

Fliss shook her head at once. "No way. We wouldn't let Charlie dive down into something this dangerous, so you're not going, either."

"She's right," Betty added. Besides, she didn't think Willow looked up to it—at all. In the bleak light of day, she looked more washed out than ever. Almost . . . *faded*, Betty thought, and she seemed to be swaying on her feet. The strain of lulling so many wisps must have weakened her.

"Oh, this is such bad luck," said Fliss, starting to pace back and forth. "You do realize that, don't you? How unlucky it is to rob a grave? That's what we're about to do, you know!"

"Oh, for crow's sake," Betty muttered. "You're as superstitious as Granny!"

"Not just Granny," Fliss shot back. "It's something all sailors say."

"We're not sailors," Betty pointed out. "We're three people on a rescue mission—"

"Yes, and we need all the luck we can get!"

Betty ignored her. Talking about it wasn't going to help—she needed to act. Scooping Hoppit out of her pocket, she passed him to Fliss wordlessly. For once, Fliss didn't even complain.

"Betty," she began, but Betty cut her off.

"I'll be careful." She whipped off her cardigan and dress and removed her boots and stockings, then perched on the edge of the boat. Slowly, she lowered her feet in, preparing herself for the drop in temperature. She took a deep breath, held her nose, and plunged into the water.

The shock of it! Like ice water numbing her fingers and toes and seeping into her ears. *Ooooh!* She allowed herself a moment to adjust to the cold, focusing on not releasing her precious breath. Then she opened her eyes, lowered her head, and began to swim.

The salt water stung her eyes, but she kept them

open, trying not to stir up any silt. Thankfully, the water was clearer than she had imagined it would be, and she was able to make out the porthole a short way off to the right. Reaching for it, she felt the edge with careful fingers. Whatever glass had once been there was now gone, leaving only a few soft, rotting splinters. Squinting inside, she felt a surge of adrenaline. There *was* a glow, stronger now. And past that, a brighter flash of broken light from above—another porthole? Betty's fingers gripped the flaking wooden frame.

She squeezed her head and shoulders inside. Immediately, her heart beat faster. Despite the glow ahead, it was much darker in here and even colder, for this was a place the sun hadn't seen for decades. Already her lungs were feeling the tremendous pressure of holding her breath in, and combined with the energy it took to keep moving, Betty already knew her time was running out. She headed for the glow, reaching out in the murky underwater light.

Something smooth and slimy brushed underneath her, making her recoil. She whirled in the darkness, catching sight of something long and tentacled slithering out of the rounded porthole. *An octopus.* She shuddered, turning back to the faint glow. Now she was closer, she saw, to her relief, that it wasn't a wisp after all. Her fingers found the cold, smooth surface of glass. It was a mirror, not much bigger than Betty's hand, the kind that fixed to the wall and tilted. Something about it struck her as odd.

But Betty had no time to ponder it further. She needed air. She turned and headed back to the porthole, chest burning with every kick. She squeezed through, collecting a splinter in her thumb, and kicked for the surface. She came up with stinging eyes, sucking in huge lungfuls of cold, salty air. Clinging to the side of *The Traveling Bag*, she barely regained her breath before spluttering out a jumble of words.

"It's not a wisp down there; it's a mirror. Don't you think that's strange?"

"Everything about this place is strange," Fliss replied, though she sounded heartily relieved that Betty had resurfaced safely.

Betty stared up at the mast hanging over the water, getting her breath back. Every so often, a light creaking noise came from the wreck, like it was fidgeting in its resting place. "Right. I'm going back in for another look. Now I've a better idea of the space, it should be easier. And there's another porthole—above water. Maybe I can swim up and take another breath from there."

"Betty, please don't take any risks," Fliss begged. "Charlie's been kidnapped, Granny's in the lockup . . . the last thing we need is for something to happen to you."

"I can do it," Betty promised, gazing up at her sister's worried face. Unexpectedly, the sun broke through the cloud above and warmed her shoulders. She readied herself, then took a deep breath and slid under the water once more. This time she was faster, navigating her way into the darkened space beyond the porthole more easily. Again, the drop in temperature was tangible, and the sensation of swimming alone in the darkness took hold of her senses. It was lighter this time, thanks to the sun's rays filtering into the water and turning everything around her a murky green.

It was then that Betty had an idea. She swam to the mirror, pulling it away from the side of the ship to angle it closer to the light streaming in from the porthole. The niggle she had felt earlier deepened, the feeling that, in this ancient wreck, a mirror seemed out of place. The silvery frame was smooth under her fingers, the glass unblemished. Surely something old would have tarnished after all this time underwater? And what was a mirror doing in a pirate ship, anyway?

It was new, she realized with an unsettling jolt as she tilted the glass. The mirror connected with the sun from above, sending a thin beam of light into the wreckage below.

The murkiness of the green water lightened enough

for Betty's straining eyes to make out several details. The salt water made her sore eyes smart, but she could see a few bits of furniture on their sides, slicked with swaying seaweed and half rotted away. An iron safe covered in barnacles, door open. And then a heavy-looking chest laced with chains and locks.

A pounding began in Betty's head, the only thing she could hear in the watery silence. The chest looked old . . . but it certainly hadn't lain there undisturbed. It had been put there recently.

The urge to breathe was building, the porthole temptingly close. But Betty had to know. To her horror, something came loose from the chains piled on the chest: a pale, skeletal hand that slid toward her. A stream of bubbles left her mouth, and she darted back in fear before realizing that it was, simply, just bones. But whose? Someone like her, who'd been snooping where they shouldn't? Betty swam back toward the chest, heart pounding. There must be something in there. Kicking closer to the chest, she wriggled her fingers under the lid and heaved. The locked chains held it tight, but the lid lifted the tiniest crack. It was enough for a glimpse within: silver stacked upon gold, glittering and priceless.

She let the lid fall, reeling back. *This isn't just a shipwreck*, Betty realized, fear mounting. The warning outside . . . it wasn't only to deter would-be pillaging of Rusty Swindles's loot. No, *The Sorcerer's Compass* was more than that. It was a lair, a den for thieves who were using the wreck to hide their plundered goods—and Betty had blundered right into it.

I've got to get out of here, she thought. *Before whoever this all belongs to—or whoever stole it—comes back and finds us.* Were these the same people who had taken Charlie? She whipped away, catching her elbow on a padlock. Bony fingers scraped her back, tangling in her tank top, trapping her. Panicking, she tugged at her shirt, black dots swimming at the edge of her vision, terror and the need to breathe combined. She wrenched herself away, kicking the chest, and felt the tear of fabric as she got free.

Desperate for air now, she realized that the nearest porthole was the one on the opposite side from which she had entered. It lay above her at an angle, a bright disc of light above the water. To her right, the rest of the ship's interior was inky black, and the tilt of the entire wreckage angling down was making her feel off balance. She tried to block it out, focusing on the circle of light, letting it guide her like a beacon.

The mirror made sense now, Betty thought grimly. Whoever was stashing stuff here must be using it the same way she had, to direct light from above into the water below. She came up for air just a short way below the porthole itself. She stayed there, breathing deeply, steadying herself. From the other side of the wreck, she caught drifts of words from Fliss, still going on about bad luck and jittery about how long Betty was taking. The water lapped in Betty's ears and her drenched hair lay heavy down her back. Reaching up, she pulled herself smoothly out of the water, resting her elbows on either side of the porthole.

Betty opened her mouth to call out and reassure her sister, but the words stuck in her throat when she saw what else she had missed—what they had all missed—from below.

A damp, white shirt and a pair of trousers were laid out not far from the porthole. They were crinkled from being wrung out and lightly steaming in the sun. Her stomach lurched horribly. Who could they belong to?

As if in answer, the mast gave a light creak. Betty's gaze swung upward, to the crow's-nest hanging over the water.

Surely not . . .

Anxiously, she edged out of the water, squeezing droplets from her hair and underclothes as quietly as she could, thankful that the lapping of water against the wreck was masking the sounds of her movements. Above, the gull was back, circling and squawking, but this time Betty was glad of its cries. She stared hard at the crow's-nest, her eyes seeking out the gaps in the wooden barrel.

There it was. A slight movement from inside. Bigger than a nesting bird. And as Betty's gaze suddenly rested on a larger gap near the base, she saw something that was unmistakably a toe.

There *was* someone in there!

Betty shrank back, afraid. All this time, the girls had been busy focusing on what they might find within the wreck. But someone had been here all along, watching them. Seeing everything they had done and no doubt hearing all they had said.

She moved slowly to the porthole. Perhaps she could slip back through to the other side, quietly warn Fliss and Willow, and then they could leave before anything happened.

But Charlie . . .

If they left now, they could miss their chance, and it would mess everything up even more. Betty felt a sudden flash of anger and resentment at whoever it was hiding up there. Hadn't they been through enough for one night? Granny arrested, Charlie gone. And now this spying sneak could be about to scupper the only plan they had.

Well, there are three of us. And only one of them.

The thought popped into Betty's head, hot and angry, like a bun straight from the oven. Before she knew what she was doing, she was creeping toward the mast. The black wood was thick and sturdy, with plenty of footholds leading up to the crow's-nest. Betty began climbing, her bare feet soundless as she advanced. She could see Fliss and Willow now. Both were leaning over the water, too absorbed in searching for her to think of looking up.

The crow's-nest was just an arm's length away now, but Betty's weight was bending the mast, bringing it closer to the water the closer she got to the top. She brought herself up another rung, just a pounce away. Surely, any moment now, the person inside would feel the mast dipping.

She held her breath, waiting. Who *was* it in there?

A hand crept over the rim of the barrel, then was joined by another. They were large, grubby hands with short fingernails caked with dirt. Golden hairs sprouted from the knuckles, or at least the knuckles that weren't grazed or scabbed over. Betty stared at them, a little bit of her courage fading. She'd seen enough fistfights in the Poacher's Pocket to know what trouble looked like. And it looked like that.

A moment later, a head emerged from the barrel. A boy with tousled, dark-blond hair that was threaded with gold peeked out. Betty stayed as still as a cat as he leaned farther out and looked down at Fliss and Willow. He hadn't noticed Betty yet, but she could see his profile. He had a thin, straight nose and amber, almost honey-colored eyes. His chest and shoulders were bare and bronzed, but Betty could see the rippling of goose pimples every time the breeze lifted. He was bigger than her, but not that much older—fourteen perhaps—and somehow this restored her courage a bit. She also had the element of surprise on her side . . .

Betty did the only thing she could. She leaped, reaching out for the boy's arm and grabbing it with a yell as she plummeted down, taking him with her. Plunging into the water, his arm slipped out of her grasp and he wriggled away, his foot catching her in the chest as he kicked out and away from her.

Betty rose to the surface, spluttering.

"Betty!" Fliss shrieked. "Who *is* that?" She reached out, grabbing Betty's hand, and began hauling her back onto the deck of *The Traveling Bag*. Betty flopped over the side, gasping. Water rolled off her and she could feel herself shaking, breath coming faster than ever. She scanned the water, its surface churned and rippling.

"Where is he?" she cried. "Where's he gone?"

"Maybe he drowned?" Willow said in a small voice as she peered over the side.

The boy came up a little way in front of them, coughing water. His face was a furious red, but whether it was from anger or lack of breath, Betty couldn't tell. When he went under a second time, it was clear.

"He's in trouble," Fliss said. "Betty, throw him the life buoy!"

"There *isn't* a life buoy!" Betty yelled. A sudden dread gripped her. What if the boy *was* in trouble, and she had caused it? She had meant to take him by surprise, but she hadn't wanted to really hurt him.

"Then a rope!" Fliss searched the deck, flinging things aside. "We can't just let him drown."

"There's no rope, either," said Betty, silently cursing Father for leaving the boat so ill-prepared. She grabbed the only thing she could think of: the larger net they'd used on the wisps. Leaning over the side, she threw it at the boy. "Grab on! I'll pull you in."

The boy managed to glare at her in refusal before sinking again. He reemerged, making a horrible gargling sound, and relented, grabbing hold of the net. Warily, Betty pulled him in until he was bobbing right below them.

Up close, and now that the grime had been washed off him, his skin was an even deeper shade of burnt gold and there was a thin sprinkle of hairs starting to sprout from his chest. He wore a thin brown leather strap around his neck, and dangling from it was a creamy, pointed seashell. What in crow's name was he doing out here all alone?

"Take my hand," she said, sounding as stern as she could manage. "You'll be all right. You've just swallowed some water."

He grabbed Betty's hand, and she prepared to pull him in . . . then gasped in shock as he yanked her arm with surprising strength. Too late, she saw the arrogant twist of his mouth and the determination in his startling, golden eyes. Her balance gone, she tumbled overboard and hit the water headfirst.

Salt water stung her eyes, flooded her mouth, which had opened in shock. She'd forgotten how much it hurt when water went properly up your nose. Her throat burned with pain and humiliation. Of *course* he could swim — he'd *tricked* her! Of all the sneaky, rotten things to do . . .

She burst to the surface in time to see the boy ably hauling himself up with lean arms to scale the side of the boat. Beyond him, Willow and Fliss stood frozen, and in an instant, Betty knew that he meant to knock all three of them overboard and take their boat for himself.

"NO!" she bellowed, then coughed again, bringing up seawater. She began kicking for the boat, but the shock had left her weak and already the boy was advancing on Fliss. She stared back at him like a terrified deer.

Betty reached the side of the boat, scrabbling for a hold. She swung one arm over, then the other. Already she knew she wouldn't make it in time. There was a strange pause as the boy's eyes lingered on Fliss's face a moment too long. But to her astonishment, the frightened look vanished from Fliss's face and she ducked out of the boy's path and rolled away from him. In one swift move, she had seized the smaller fishing net, whipped around, and jammed it over the boy's head.

He let out a roar of surprise as Fliss gave the net a mighty shove, forcing him over the side of the boat for the second time. She pulled back the net, then swooped to help Betty clamber back on the boat.

Fliss examined the net. "Say, these could really come in handy at closing time back at the Poacher's Pocket."

Betty grinned despite herself.

They eyed the boy warily as he floundered, thrashing and swearing. He spat through his teeth and stared sullenly up at them, treading water.

"Who are you?" Betty demanded. "And why were you spying on us?"

"It's my job." He spat again, sending an arc of water Betty's way.

She took a couple of steps back and glared at him, folding her arms. "That was a dirty trick you pulled just now."

He shrugged, narrowing his eyes at Fliss. "No dirtier than hers."

"Who *are* you?" Betty repeated, only half expecting a reply.

"Spit," he said.

"I am *not* spitting," said Fliss immediately. "It's a rotten, filthy habit."

"No, *Spit*," he said again. "That's my name." He turned his head and spat again, away from them this time.

"Spit?" Betty said incredulously. "That can't be your real name! Who names someone Spit? It's a nickname."

"Ain't a nickname." He looked annoyed now. "It's the only name that was ever given to me, all right?"

"So what are you doing here?" Betty asked. "Apart from being a rubbish lookout?"

Spit bristled. "Who says I'm a rubbish lookout?"

"You left your shirt drying up by the porthole," said Betty. "That's what gave you away."

Spit shrugged. "Lots of people come out here, looking for things. Trying to take what doesn't belong to them. Most of them heed the sign."

Without warning, he deftly hauled himself up again

189

and swung onto the boat before any of them could object. Betty took a step back. Spit was stronger, taller. And she could see from the look in his eyes that she wouldn't be able to take him by surprise again. He was ready for her now.

The hairs on Betty's arms rose like hackles. "What's that supposed to mean?"

"I mean that people who try to pillage from this wreck don't get away with it," Spit replied. "See, this is *ours*."

"Whose?" Willow asked timidly.

"My crew's," Spit said with a hint of pride. "The Rusty Scuttlers."

"So that's your treasure down there?" Betty blurted out.

Fliss and Willow both gasped. "There's *treasure* down there?"

Spit sighed and shook his dripping head. He took a step toward her, and Betty instinctively took one back, realizing her mistake. Why, oh why had she mentioned the treasure?

"I mean, you must have something down there, right?" she waffled, trying to backtrack. "Not that I saw anything —it was so dark . . ." She trailed off, alarmed by the solemn look on Spit's face.

"I was hoping you wouldn't have seen nothing," he

said gravely. "The Rusty Scuttlers . . . they don't like people talking about them or knowing things."

"I didn't *see* anything!" Betty protested, but it sounded like a lie even to her. "I don't *know* anything!"

"Yes, you do." Spit sighed again. "And I'm afraid that . . . complicates matters."

Fliss stepped forward, placing her hands on Willow's shoulders. "There's no need for any unpleasantness," she said softly. "We're not here to cause trouble—we've enough of that already. So you just forget you ever saw us, and we'll be out of your way."

Betty saw Spit hesitate as he looked into Fliss's soft brown eyes. He lowered his gaze. "I'm sorry," he said at last. "But you know too much. I can't let you go."

Chapter Fifteen

Pirates!

FLISS BLINKED A FEW TIMES, her long eyelashes fluttering against her cheek. Spit, however, seemed determined not to look at her.

"Now, listen here," said Betty, impatient. If Fliss's charm failed to work, then the only other option was to be blunt. "There are more of us than you. If we want to leave, you can't stop us. It'd be madness to try."

Spit fidgeted and spat twice in a row. Fliss grimaced.

"I might not be able to stop you," he said gruffly. He pointed past *The Sorcerer's Compass* to the open water, where a craggy row of rocks stood in the distance. "But *they* will. And, trust me, there's more of *them* than you. Many more."

Betty stared at the rocks, holding her breath. She could see nothing, only shimmering water under the sun.

"Is this some kind of bluff? There's no one there!"

"There will be," Spit said almost apologetically.

And then Betty saw it: the long prow of a ship nosing out from behind the rocks. A large ship, she realized, which must have been hidden from view on the other side.

"People don't realize how high those rocks are from here," said Spit softly. "The distance, it makes it deceiving."

Betty swallowed nervously. Next to her, she saw Fliss's shoulders stiffen as she saw it, too. They watched as the boat advanced relentlessly.

"How did they know?" she asked, choked. "You signaled somehow, didn't you?"

"He can't have!" Fliss protested. "Surely we'd have noticed—"

"I signal them when it's safe," Spit said. "Every hour on the hour." He nodded to the wrecked ship's crumpled sail, floating in the water next to them. "One of those ropes is rigged all the way to the crow's-nest. A quick pull and the sail goes up high. That's how they know all's safe over here. When it doesn't go up, they know something's amiss."

"What . . . what will happen to us?" Willow asked,

staring at the oncoming boat in fright. She was horribly white now, almost translucent. Betty felt a sudden urge to protect her.

"Hard to say," Spit replied. "The last person they found here was made to walk the plank."

"*The plank?*" said Betty. "Now, hang on." The chill she felt was deepening into alarm. "If you were listening to us all the while you were up there, you'll know we never intended to *take* anything. We were never after your treasure. There's only one thing we came here for."

Spit scratched the back of his head, then inspected his fingernails. "They might go easy on you three, seeing as you're young. But it really depends on what kind of mood they're in."

"Mood?" Betty repeated, her temper rising up to drown her fear. "*Mood?* Don't talk to me about moods! I'm in a terrible one. Our sister's been kidnapped and we're about to be taken prisoner by a bunch of . . . of *pirates!*"

Betty stepped forward and poked Spit hard in the chest. "We're going to leave now," she said sharply. Her eyes bored into Spit's. "And you tell them, when they get here, that we were just sightseers, here to look at the wreck and nothing more. Say you fell asleep and that's why you didn't raise the sail."

"I can't tell them that!" he blustered. Two spots of color appeared high on his cheeks and were deepening every time he looked in the direction of the approaching ship. It was well past the rocks now, sails rippling in a lively wind. "I'm here as lookout, one of the lowest jobs there is! If I say I fell asleep, I'm as good as useless to them."

"Then say we stopped to ask directions . . . that our anchor got caught in the sail so you couldn't lift it," said Fliss beseechingly. "Please don't hand us over."

Spit stared into her eyes. A sheen of sweat was now visible on his forehead and upper lip. "Look, if it was up to me, I'd let you go, but they make the decisions, not me." His voice was flat. "As soon as that sail didn't go up, they'd have been watching. You leave here, and they'll come straight for you."

"But we haven't *done* anything," Willow objected.

Spit projected another arc of saliva over the boat's side. Betty began to suspect that this habit was something that increased when he got nervous.

"I know that," he said. "You just have to convince *them*."

"Why should we?" Betty said angrily. "Your crew doesn't have a claim over this wreck any more than we do!"

"This is the sea," Spit muttered. "Only one rule counts: the strongest always win."

"Oh, really?" said Betty. "Well, the rules might be about to change." She glanced at Fliss, trying to convey her unspoken thoughts. Fliss gave a slight, almost imperceptible nod.

"Because you see, Spit, there's something rather unusual about us," Betty continued. "We have a way of disappearing without a trace. So I'd suggest you get your story straight before they arrive and you're left with a lot of awkward questions to answer."

"Huh?" Spit's eyes shifted from Betty to Fliss, then back again. "Disappearing? What're you talking about?"

"Vanishing." Betty snapped her fingers. "*Poof!* Gone. It's all very peculiar."

"But how . . . ?" he began, then shook himself. "It's not possible. No one can disappear." He glanced anxiously at the approaching boat. "Listen, you might think you're being clever, with some kind of hidden stowaway or secret panel, but trust me, if they find you, if they learn you've tricked them, they'll kill us all."

Fear twisted Betty's gut. "They won't," she said at last. "As long as you keep your mouth shut, we'll all be safe."

"And your boat?" Spit asked, still frowning incredulously. "Will that disappear, too?"

"No," Betty replied. "Just us. So let them think they've got the boat. They won't have it for long."

She clenched her jaw, her mind working furiously as a plan began to weave itself. A daring, harebrained plan that depended on them all to pull it off. She cast a desperate look at the advancing pirate ship, then at Fliss. They were running out of time. "Just answer one thing truthfully: before we came here this morning, was there anyone else? Two men in warders' uniforms and a little girl?"

"Warders?" Spit said, looking shocked. "What kind of trouble are you in?"

"They're not real warders," Fliss put in. "They're impostors, and they kidnapped our sister. Please answer the question."

He shook his head. "No," he said at last. "You're the only people to come here since sundown yesterday."

"You swear?" Betty asked with a hard look at him.

Spit spat on his fingers and saluted. "On my word. Not seen another soul."

Betty's breath caught in her throat. She couldn't tell if she felt dismayed or relieved. Perhaps it was both: relief that they had not missed Charlie, dismay that there had been no sighting of her since she'd left the Poacher's Pocket. Emotions curdled wretchedly in Betty's stomach, mixing with seawater.

"And you?" he asked, still looking doubtful. "Are *you* telling the truth? I've heard some stories and seen some strange things out here, but none so strange as what you're claiming you can do."

"I'll prove it," she said. "Give me something of yours, quickly. That shell around your neck."

Spit passed it to her warily. "I'll need that back."

"I'm not stealing it."

"Betty," Fliss said with a warning look.

"It's all right," Betty murmured. She had no intention of revealing the dolls to Spit and giving away their secrets. *Let him wonder,* she thought. A little mystery here could go a long way. Hastily, she grabbed her clothes and swept toward the wheelhouse.

"Where are you going?" said Spit. "Stay where I can see you!"

"I'm getting dressed," Betty said, hoping she sounded convincingly haughty.

Spit averted his eyes. "Be quick."

Inside the wheelhouse, Betty checked the wisp. It was still in place, flickering in the old oil lamp. Panic rose up in her mind. Her plan wasn't even fully formed yet and already there were holes in it when it came to the wisp, something that couldn't be hidden. She draped the lamp with a scrap of cloth and pulled on her clothes. There was no time to worry about that part.

Carefully, she placed the tiny shell of Spit's into the third doll next to Fliss's hair and Willow's nose pickings, then checked her own hair was safe in the second doll before pressing both the inner dolls' halves in place. She slotted the halves of the outer doll together but not quite aligned. Concealing them in her pocket, she kept her hand on them, feeling the engraved key under her thumb. Then she stepped out onto the deck.

With a jolt, Betty saw that the Rusty Scuttlers had gained on them considerably. The boat was so close now that she could see tiny figures on the deck—lots of them—and she knew she had to hurry. If they could see the pirates, then the pirates would be able to see them, too.

"Look at your reflection," she told Spit. "Look into the water."

"Is this another trick?" he asked, evidently suspicious. "You push me in again and I'll—"

"Just do it," she snapped. "Or look into the window. It doesn't matter, either way. Just find your reflection."

Spit folded his arms and stared at the window, a muscle twitching in his jaw. "Go on then."

Betty took a breath and pretended to chant under her breath, moving her lips soundlessly.

Beneath her clothes, her finger and thumb were twisting the top half of the outer nesting doll, bringing the two parts of the key together. She continued the silent chant, watching all their faces reflected back at them. The moment the two halves aligned, their reflections vanished, leaving only the sky and sea shimmering back at them in the glass.

"*W-what?*" Spit stumbled back, staring at the glass, then at Betty in confusion. He turned to Fliss, Willow, then to the glass again. "It d-doesn't make sense . . . I can still see you, but we're not here!"

"We've all vanished," said Betty. "We can see each other, but no one else can."

Spit approached the glass, cupping his hands to it. "This is some kind of . . ."

"It's not a trick," Betty said. "It's real. Check the water if you don't believe me."

He shot her a wary look, then stumbled to the side of the boat to look for his reflection, his expression becoming increasingly shocked.

"We're gone, all of us," said Betty. She cast a desperate look at the pirate ship. Jumping jackdaws, just how big was this Rusty Scuttlers crew? New figures seemed to be appearing every moment, sending ripples of fear down into her stomach. They were running out of time, and she needed to think fast.

"All right, listen," she said urgently. "Spit, I'm going to make you visible again. So here's what you're going to say. Tell them that one of us went down to the wreck and got into trouble. The others went searching, but none of us have come back up."

"Oh, Betty!" Fliss said, horrified. She hastily made the sign of the crow. "We can't say that! It's tempting fate."

"We can if it'll save our lives," Betty said grimly. "And that's the only thing that's going to work without anyone getting hurt." She looked Spit straight in the eye. "Including you."

Spit gulped. "But what if they discover you? Or realize I'm lying? It won't end well for any of us. You don't know them like I do." A tremor entered his voice. "I've seen it before. A traitor is the worst thing a pirate can be. I can't . . . I can't do this." He stuck his chin out, trying to look defiant, but Betty could see it was an act.

"You have to," said Betty, using the moment she had while Spit was looking out to sea to remove his shell from the dolls and place it in her pocket. Quickly, she snapped them back together to render herself, Fliss, and Willow unseen once more. It provided a small measure of comfort to know that now, at least, the pirates could not see them. "Because if you don't, I'll make you disappear. *Permanently.*"

He turned, alarmed to notice his reflection visible again in the glass while the rest of them had vanished. "You what?"

"I'll make you invisible for good. And I don't suppose that'd go down too well with your pirate pals."

"Oh, I don't know," said Spit, his eyes darting everywhere, clearly unsettled now he couldn't see any of them. "My crew might think it's pretty useful to have an invisible member. Wouldn't have to worry about squeezing into that stinking crow's-nest for a start."

Betty hesitated, taken aback. Instead, it was Fliss who spoke up.

"Some of them might like it for a while," she said. "But pirates are a superstitious lot, aren't they? They wouldn't be happy about having someone cursed aboard. You'd be cast out. Just another lonely voice lost on the sea, not much more than a wisp, really."

"Nah," Spit said, folding his arms, though doubt began to flicker on his face. "Still can't do it. I pledged to be a Rusty Scuttler. And I owe *them* my loyalty, not you." He lowered his voice, speaking under his breath. "Whatever they've done. And whatever trouble you're in."

"That's a shame." Fliss clicked her tongue. "Especially for someone so . . . so *handsome* not to be seen."

Spit's chest puffed out like a pigeon's. "H-handsome?" A bead of sweat ran down the side of Spit's face. He brushed it away, glancing at the Rusty Scuttlers' boat. "All right then!" he growled. "I'll do what you want. But if you're found out, I'm taking no blame for it! I'll say you fooled me as well."

"Fine," Betty growled back, thankful for her sister's charm.

"Betty," Fliss breathed, rigid with fright as the Rusty Scuttlers drew ever closer. "They're nearly here. What'll we do about our boat? Even if we stay on it, invisible, the pirates will steal it! We'll lose our chance to find Charlie!"

"We won't lose it," Betty said in a low voice. Her mouth was dry with salt and fear, and she could hardly believe what she was about to say. "Because we're going to split up."

"Are you out of your *mind*?" Fliss hissed. "We've already lost Charlie! I'm not losing you, too! No way. I absolutely refuse!"

"Fliss, we have to," Betty insisted. "It's the only way. You and Willow stay invisible on the boat and find a hiding place. First chance you get, when the Rusty Scuttlers lower their guard, you cut loose and come back for me."

"And where will *you* be, Betty?" Fliss demanded. "You can't possibly think this will work!"

"We don't have a choice," said Betty. "If Charlie comes" —she corrected herself—"*when* Charlie comes, one of us has to be here. We can't miss our chance. I'm staying with Spit on *The Sorcerer's Compass.*"

"This might be the worst plan you've had yet, Betty Widdershins," Fliss muttered, trembling now.

"Well, it's the only one we've got," said Betty. "If we're going to find Charlie, then we have to do it."

"But—"

"No buts," Betty whispered fiercely. "There's no time. They're here."

Chapter Sixteen

Dead or Alive

THE SHIP CUT THROUGH the water and surged toward them, details growing clearer with every billow of its deep red sails.

Red, thought Betty grimly. *The color of danger. The color of blood.*

On the largest red sail, there was an emblem of a huge crow's skeleton, a key wedged into the dead bird's beak. *We'll find your treasure,* the key seemed to threaten. *And your secrets. We can unlock anything and take it for ourselves.*

Once again, Granny's warning floated back to Betty, as clear in her mind as it had been the day it was spoken, when Granny had given Betty the magical nesting dolls for the first time.

"You must never use these objects without care, especially in a place like Crowstone. Most people here are connected to the prisoners in that prison. Dangerous people who'd go to any lengths to get their hands on these things."

They'd learned the hard way that Granny's fear was justified when Charlie had been kidnapped so her magic might be used for a prisoner to escape. Back then, the thought of the inmates in Crowstone Prison had been threatening, but as Betty was starting to realize, there were things—and people—even scarier out in the world. The prisoners at least were behind bars. But out here on the open sea, there was no one to keep the Rusty Scuttlers in check. They made their own rules and answered to no one.

"Quickly, hide," Betty instructed Fliss and Willow, terror clutching at her. "Our boat will be swarming with pirates any minute! Remember you can still be heard—and felt. If they find you, they'll kill you!"

For an awful moment, it seemed Fliss was too frozen with fear to act. Desperate, Betty shoved her. *"Move!"* Finally, Fliss jerked into life, urging Willow underneath one of the benches before tucking her own slim frame under the other.

Betty crept past Spit, feeling him stiffen as her clothes brushed against him. She slid her legs into the water, taking care not to make a ripple that would give her away. Immediately, her skirt and stockings became waterlogged, pulling at her heavily. She took a breath and lowered herself down into the water. Above her, she heard Spit pacing the deck of *The Traveling Bag* nervously as his crew got near, and he spat three times into the water, *phlat phlat phlat*, one after the other.

She began to swim to the other side of the ship, behind the vast bulk vanishing into the water. Approaching the Rusty Scuttlers' warning sign, she hooked her fingers into a strip of torn rigging and began to climb up onto the side of the wreck. If she could get high enough, she'd be able to see across the other side to where Fliss and Willow were. Somehow, even though she knew the pirates wouldn't see them, she needed to reassure herself of this. By now, she could hear the rumble of voices from the other side of *The Sorcerer's Compass*.

What she hadn't thought of was the rush of water draining from her drenched clothes back into the sea. To Betty it sounded horribly loud, loud enough to give her away. She froze, waiting as the water slowed to a trickle. Carefully, she pulled her skirt up and began squeezing out the rest of the water. It ran down the sloping wooden sides of the wreck, thankfully without a sound.

She crawled up farther. The ebony wood was hot and dry in the sun, warming her chilled body. She passed Spit's shirt, which had stopped steaming now, and paused at the edge where the mast and the crow's-nest were visible. The pirates' ship was close now, virtually alongside *The Traveling Bag*, though it kept a safe distance from the rocks that had brought disaster to *The Sorcerer's Compass*. Like the wrecked ship, the Rusty Scuttlers' ship was huge, dwarfing the Widdershinses' little boat in comparison.

Betty's heart skittered as she took in the figures on deck, swarming below the red sails. There had to be twenty or so of them—and there would be more below decks. Already she saw a rowboat being lowered into the water with three people aboard. The two who were rowing were young men, with strong but lean limbs. The third passenger was a woman who stood at the bow, looking through a spyglass. Straightaway, every nerve of Betty's jangled.

She wore a tan leather waistcoat that was the same color as her skin. Her black hair had been cut very short, but lengths of ribbon and rags had been tied into the roots and flowed behind her like a rainbow. A curved sword was sheathed at her waist, and a dagger was strapped to one of her boots, which were laced to her thigh. Jewels dripped from her wrists and throat. And Betty knew you'd have to be brave, stupid, or invincible to flaunt such riches.

One thing was certain: she didn't look stupid. This woman was not someone to be taken lightly. This was someone used to giving orders—and being obeyed. Strangest of all was the cat standing on her shoulder, looking perfectly at ease. It was white, except for its two front paws, which were as black as ink, and a black slash across its eyes like a robber's mask. It stiffened as the rowboat glided through the water, its eyes fixed on the shipwreck. For a heart-stopping moment, it seemed to stare right at Betty, but then it blinked lazily and looked into the water, as if searching for fish.

Before Spit even opened his mouth, Betty knew how he would address this woman. He drew himself up straight, saluting obediently.

"Cap'n."

"Spit." Though she spoke quietly, her deep, velvety voice carried easily across the stretch of water. Here was someone used to being listened to. She nodded at *The Traveling Bag*, her full lips curving into a smile. "What have we here?"

Spit hoicked into the water, still standing to attention. "A prize bit of booty. Occupants went down to check out the wreck and must've met with trouble—ain't come back up yet." He slapped his hand on the side of the jewel-green boat. The boat Betty's father had painted in secret as a surprise for them all last year.

She felt herself bristling with indignation—but, more than that, hoping with all her might that Spit would stick to the story they'd agreed on. If he gave them up to this woman, they were as good as dead.

"Mmm." The captain cast her eyes over the little boat dismissively, as if it were nothing more than a paper toy. "Might be all right as a decoy. Looks sturdy enough, but it's of no real worth." She reached up to tickle the cat's chin.

To Betty's dismay, the captain stepped neatly aboard *The Traveling Bag* as sure-footed as the cat on her shoulder. Betty held her breath as the captain walked past Fliss, who was cowering under a bench, and paused by Willow's hiding place under another to stare into the water. The dagger in her boot was directly level with Willow's nose.

"Which part did they go into?" Her voice was still quiet but emotionless. Businesslike.

"The deep part, Cap'n," Spit answered dutifully. "Rusty's domain."

"Any sign of the bodies?"

Spit shook his head, and Betty felt weak with relief that he hadn't given them away. It seemed the captain believed him—for now.

"Everything else untouched?" she asked, tapping her spyglass. Spit nodded.

"Well, there we have it," she said. "This is what happens when greed gets the better of people." She gave Spit a scathing look. "What else did you see from up there?"

Spit fidgeted. "Not a lot," he answered. "There were three of them. Big burly looters."

"You'd better not be lying." The pirate woman's clear green eyes were as flinty as her voice.

"No," Spit spluttered. "Course not, Cap'n."

She regarded him for a long moment.

"*Ronia.*"

Betty had been focusing on the smaller boat, but now she looked up. The voice had come from the pirate ship. Flanked by pirates on either side, a stout man sat in a wheeled chair. With a shock, Betty realized that he had no legs. He had only one eye, and even from Betty's vantage point, she could make out a thick scar that ran from his hairline to his chin.

His arms were as meaty as hams, but with not a trace of fat. He had a small knife in one hand, which he was using to pick the nails of the other. The sun flashed on its blade dangerously.

The pirate woman — Ronia — looked up, too. "Father?"

"Search the rest of the boat and the wreck. If there are bodies, I want 'em found. Dead or alive." He grinned widely, displaying a dazzling set of white teeth. He lifted his beefy arm, pointing with the knife at a thin length of wood jutting out from the front of the pirate ship like a needle. "I'm sure they'd make a lovely addition to the gang."

Laughter rippled through the rest of the crew.

Betty blinked in horror . . . and almost fell from where she was perched. For there, hanging from the spike, was a jumbled collection of bones. An arm, two legs and a skull, dangling like baubles on a gruesome yule tree.

"Buckles! Bilge!" Ronia commanded, calling up to her crew on the ship. "You two search the wreck underwater. Check the booty."

Two mean-faced pirates, one with huge gold hoops through his ears and the other with a ring through his nose, glanced at each other before diving reluctantly into the water. Betty tensed. She crouched down, hoping they wouldn't climb onto the wreck itself, for there were few places to go. Moments later, she heard an eruption of water from the second porthole as one of the pirates came up for breath.

"Clear!" he called, then vanished back inside the wreck. Betty waited for the other one to emerge, half expecting him to leap onto the raised part of the ruined ship at any moment and trip over her . . . but when he came up, it was in the exact spot he'd first entered the water.

"No sign of Rusty's domain being disturbed," Nosering confirmed, hoisting himself onto a rope ladder on the side of the pirate ship. He was clutching at something strung around his neck in such a worried way that Betty guessed it was a lucky charm, worn for protection.

"There was this, though." The other pirate had resurfaced, holding a dripping scrap of fabric that Betty recognized immediately as from her top. "Caught in Old Squid's clutches, rest his seaworthy soul."

"He always did have sticky fingers," Ronia remarked.

Squid? Betty thought. *Those bony fingers had belonged to one of the Rusty Scuttlers' crew?*

The rest of the pirates bowed their heads, and those wearing hats removed them as they murmured: "Rest his seaworthy soul."

The pirate hauled himself onto the rope ladder and

threw the wet rag from Betty's tank top to the pirate captain. She held it up.

"Looks like one of them ran into problems down there," Ronia said, smirking.

Betty went very still, imagining how worried her sister would be at this. Had Fliss noticed her shirt had already been torn from her first dive to the wreck? Probably not. Everything had happened so fast, but Fliss was sure to be panicking now, wondering if Betty *had* made it safely out of the water this time.

Betty's thoughts were snatched away as Ronia addressed the two pirates who'd brought her over in the rowboat.

"Take me around to the other side."

A breath caught in Betty's throat. Ronia was coming!

"Nothing there, Cap'n!" said Spit a little too quickly. "Been all over the upper wreck meself."

Ronia silenced him with a steely look. "I like to be sure." She jumped nimbly into the rowboat.

Betty felt sick with fear as the oars lifted, then began slicing the water. The smaller boat turned and vanished from sight. She flattened herself against the warm, black wood, trying to work out what to do. *Just stay calm,* she told herself. *Breathe. She can't see you.* She kept very still, listening for the *shush-shush-shush* of the oars as they drew nearer.

And then stopped.

Hardly daring to breathe, Betty turned to face the water. She could just see the top of Ronia's head, a scarlet ribbon flying in the breeze.

Why wasn't she moving?

"There's something up there." The pirate captain's voice cut through the air. "Something's come out of the water."

Betty looked down, trembling. She'd wrung out her clothes and hair as best she could, but they were still soaked. And as she'd been cowering and watching, she hadn't realized that all the while water was running off her to collect in the wooden grooves of the ship and run down its sloping sides.

Her eyes followed the watery trail. Invisible or not, this was enough to lead the pirates straight to her.

Fear took hold of her. Of all the idiotic ways to get caught!

No! she thought. It wasn't over yet. They hadn't caught her, and no matter how much they were outnumbered, she, Betty, was *invisible*. They might have bones dangling from their masts and more daggers than Fliss had had kisses, but they didn't have a pinch of magic like the Widdershinses did. And they didn't have a motto, which made her feel a smidge braver.

She who tries triumphs, Betty thought, just as Ronia raised her voice for the first time.

"Rusty Scuttlers: ruin and rule!" she yelled.

Oh. So they did *have a motto, after all*.

Betty froze, eyes darting around for somewhere to hide. Could she make it to the crow's-nest without detection? Her heart was pounding, and she could hardly think straight. She wished now that, when Ronia had decided to bring the rowboat around, Betty had taken the chance to get back into the water and swim away from the wreck. At least then she could have trodden water and observed at a safe distance until the pirates were gone. But it was too late now. If Betty entered the water, they'd see the ripples. They'd know something was there.

But wait . . .

Fliss's words came back to her. *Pirates are a superstitious bunch . . .*

Perhaps them seeing *something*, something they couldn't explain, would be enough to rattle them. Even in broad daylight, there was something deeply creepy about *The Sorcerer's Compass*. A little haunting would feel entirely believable . . . and not only that, but it would give her a way to signal to Fliss that she was still alive.

A loud *thunk* caught Betty unaware. She lost her grip and slid on the wet wood a little way from where she'd been sitting. Below her, the deck creaked and Betty knew instantly that Ronia had leaped onto the tilted side of the ship. She spied Spit's shirt, now almost dry, and an idea came to her. With only seconds to spare, she grabbed it and pulled it on, then silently stood up, balancing on the uneven deck.

Water dripped from her hair, running down her body. From her position, she couldn't see any reflection of herself. Would Spit's shirt vanish along with the rest of Betty and everything she was wearing? Or would it stay visible, as it belonged to someone else? She was about to find out.

But it was not Ronia who found her first. Instead, the white cat that had been perched on the pirate captain's shoulders appeared on the angled hull of the ship. It prowled toward Betty, slow and sure-footed. Then it stopped dead—staring right at her—and hissed.

"Bandit?" Ronia stepped into view, balancing as easily as her cat. "Whoa!" She reeled back, almost losing her footing, and stared in Betty's direction.

It had worked. Spit's shirt must be visible, for Ronia's

eyes were wide with shock. Quicker than Betty expected, she whipped out the cutlass from its scabbard and held it before her. Betty stood motionless, unsure what to do next. She was not as steady on her feet as the pirate captain, and if she stumbled it would ruin the ghostly illusion. So she waited, dripping water that soaked slowly into Spit's shirt.

The pirate captain regained her composure. She crossed herself in some sort of protective gesture and, to Betty's relief, began to back away.

"There's something up here!" she yelled. "Rusty's been disturbed!"

She's going to leave, Betty thought, amazed.

But Bandit was not so easily put off. The white cat continued to hiss in Betty's direction and began to stalk closer. The hiss became a low, rumbling growl.

It knows, Betty thought. *Just like Oi knows with Hoppit. It can't see, but it can sense me and smell me.*

Ronia turned, calling to the pirates in the rowboat below. As she edged out of sight, the cat pounced. It leaped straight at Betty, ears flat, teeth bared. Landing on her shoulder, it sank its claws deep into her flesh. Betty couldn't help it—she screamed, a bone-chilling sound that echoed over the water. And the louder she screamed, the more the cat clung to her.

She heard shouts from the rowboat and a scrambling noise—Ronia was coming back. Betty flailed about, trying to shake the cat off. Any moment now, Ronia would see the cat clinging to something—something unseen—and then the game would be up.

A thought came to her. *Cats don't like water* . . .

She reached for her wet hair and squeezed it. A trickle of seawater hit the cat, and with a yowl, it sprang away from her. Encouraged, Betty shook herself like a dog, sending a cold shower of droplets all over the animal. Fur on end, it skulked away just as Ronia returned.

She scooped Bandit up. "There, there," she crooned. "Mummy's here . . ."

Her face fell as she looked in Betty's direction. Betty looked down at herself, and bit back a horrified gasp. Spit's white shirt was spotted with blood.

"Retreat!" Ronia shouted hoarsely. She flung something in Betty's direction, muttering, "Rest your seaworthy soul!" before turning and leaping from the wreck into the waiting rowboat.

The object hit Betty in the chest, then landed in a wooden groove at her feet. With Ronia gone, she knelt to retrieve it.

It was a silver coin flashing brightly in the sun. One side showed a horseshoe, the other a clover. Despite its shimmer, the weight and beauty of it suggested it was old and valuable.

Father had told her something once about coins buying safe passage for the dead to the afterlife. So Ronia *had* been fooled—and if she had been alarmed, then Betty felt sure she could strike fear into the rest of her crew, too. She slid the coin into her pocket and headed to the side of the wreck overlooking *The Traveling Bag* and the Rusty Scuttlers' ship. Ronia drew up alongside it with a fearful glance back at the ruined ship.

A cry went up. One by one, the pirates turned to stare at Betty (or rather Spit's dripping shirt) hovering over *The Sorcerer's Compass*. Some backed away, crossing themselves and murmuring in terror. Meanwhile, more pirates were swarming aboard *The Traveling Bag* and set about searching it. There were heavy clangs as the anchor was raised, creaks as the deck buckled under the weight of muscle and gold. Spit gazed up at his blood-spattered shirt, his face a mask of shock. But it was Fliss Betty sought. Her sister's white, pinched face peered out from her hiding place, crumpling in relief. She knew now that Betty was alive.

Betty wished she could call to her—one last message of strength or at least a goodbye—but of course she couldn't. All she could do was lift her arms, as though reaching for her sister. Fliss's eyes filled with tears.

To the pirates, however, the sight must have looked like a threat, and they scrambled to get away. Betty watched helplessly as the anchor was pulled up and Ronia's ship began to move off, followed by *The Traveling Bag*.

Even though she had known Fliss would be taken, Betty couldn't stop the ache in her throat or the burning sensation at the back of her eyes. What did it matter now if she cried? There was no one to see her. She lowered her outstretched arms and let the tears roll down her cheeks.

Why, *why* did everything have to go so wrong for them all the time? All she'd tried to do was help someone in trouble. Instead, she'd made everything ten times worse. She'd failed Willow, whose father's life was ticking away, and both her sisters were now gone. Her plan was flimsy and dangerously full of holes. This wasn't one of Father's bedtime stories. Fliss and Willow were with real, murderous pirates. The kind who kept human bones as trophies.

Betty's hand felt for the nesting dolls in her pocket. They were all she had now, a sprinkle of sorcery that was her only hope. She'd even lost the magical map, she realized with another wrench. It was in the wheelhouse . . . *with the wisp*. What would happen when Ronia discovered them?

A loud splash jerked her from her misery. Someone had gone overboard from the Widdershinses' boat. Betty leaned forward, feeling panicked, to scan the rippling waves and Spit emerged, looking furious.

"What did you do that for?" he yelled at a weasel-faced pirate leering over the back of *The Traveling Bag*. "You pushed me in!"

The pirate smirked. "Someone's gotta stay with the booty."

Spit shook his fist. "I've been here all night!"

The pirate laughed, tossing a small package into the water. It landed a short way from Spit and immediately began to sink. Growling, Spit dived down after it and managed to catch it, by which time the boat had moved some distance away. All he could do was watch, clutching the parcel and shouting obscenities, as his comrades sailed off without him.

He swam back to the shipwreck, spitting and swearing as he hauled himself out of the water and began climbing up to where Betty sat trembling a short distance from the crow's-nest. He scowled in her direction and spat overboard.

"Look at the state of my shirt," he said. "Ruined! Bad luck, that's what you are." He huffed resentfully. "I was supposed to change shifts now. Get back on the ship while some other underling took over as lookout. But because they all got the heebie-jeebies when they saw you, they ran away." He sniffed, glaring at the crow's-nest. "I hate being up there. Hate it! No wonder it's used as a punishment. The seasickness hits something awful."

Betty was suddenly glad she wasn't alone, though she could never admit this to Spit.

"Well, you're here now, and so am I." Her voice was steady, not betraying the tears drying on her cheeks. "I guess we're stuck with each other."

He folded his arms, a muscle twitching in his jaw. "I guess we are," he said evenly. "But don't mistake me for a friend. The only reason I didn't turn you in to Ronia is because you threatened me. I won't forget that. And I want you gone by sunrise, whether your sister makes it back here or not."

Betty gulped, hoping he hadn't heard. Tears prickled her eyelids once more, and she allowed herself to cry silently as Spit angrily shook out his wet hair. Across the water, unseen on *The Traveling Bag*, Fliss and Willow sailed farther away with every heartbeat. And all the while Betty could practically hear Granny's voice in her head saying: *Betty Widdershins! What have you got yourself into this time?*

Chapter Seventeen

Through the Spyglass

BETTY DIDN'T KNOW HOW LONG she watched for, but she waited until the little green boat was the size of her thumbnail before it followed Ronia's ship behind the row of rocks from which it had first emerged. *Would it stay there?* she wondered. *Or would Fliss and Willow be caught up in Ronia's plundering plans?*

Betty sank down onto the wreck, hugging her knees to her chest. Everything ached: her legs from standing so stiffly for so long, her arms from the swim, her empty stomach and her pounding head. Her heart.

She was sore, too. Crisscrossed with cat scratches. Wincing, she peeled off the bloodstained shirt.

Spit snatched it, his scowl deepening. "What am I

supposed to do with this?" He wrung it out, his lip curling in distaste.

"You might as well wear it," said Betty, her voice flat. "There's no one out here but me to see you, anyway. It'll keep you warm at least . . ." She trailed off weakly. "When it's dry."

"Right." He narrowed his eyes. "I think I've forgotten what dry feels like." He spread the shirt out once more in the sun, eyeing it thoughtfully. "I suppose I could string it up next to the sign. A bit of blood works wonders at keeping people away."

"Mmm," Betty agreed, remembering Ronia's reaction to the bloodied shirt. She prodded her scratches gingerly. "I thought our cat at home was a beast until I met Bandit."

Spit ignored her, clearly in no mood for small talk. He sat a little way apart, swinging his legs over the side to dangle toward the water. He took the package he'd been thrown and began to unwrap it, discarding a layer of waxed paper. Inside lay a golden cob of bread, two apples, and a wedge of cheese. Betty's tummy gurgled loudly, but she looked away. She wasn't expecting Spit's charity and she wasn't about to ask for it. Even so, the crisp crunch as he bit into an apple was torture.

"You know," he began, "it'd probably help us both out if I could *see* you."

Betty turned back to him. To her surprise, he was offering the second apple in his outstretched hand, albeit not quite to her.

"Oh," she muttered, wishing the dolls worked differently. If she tampered with the outer nesting doll containing the smaller ones, she would render not only herself visible, but Willow and Fliss, too. "I can't let you. I mean, not without giving the others away, too." Besides, for all she knew, Spit might be about to trick her. Would he punish her, push her overboard for her part in his being left here? The apple gleamed rosily in the sun. She reached out and took it warily, then sank her teeth into it.

"That really is creepy," Spit muttered, shuddering. "I don't like it. I don't like it at all."

"You don't have to like it," said Betty, between crunches. She wiped juice from her chin. "Why'd you give this to me, anyway? You just said we weren't friends."

"We aren't." He frowned, pulling a knife from his back pocket.

Betty stiffened at the sight of it. For a moment, she forgot to chew, but then Spit cut off a piece of cheese and held it out. She took it, wolfing some down immediately.

"I want you gone," he continued. "Out of my hair. If you keel over or, worse, die on me, you'll be an even bigger pest than you already have been." He lowered his voice, muttering, "Besides, if Fliss comes back, I don't want her thinking I let you starve. So you see my reasons for looking out for you are entirely selfish."

"I should've guessed." Betty rolled her eyes, munching the rest of the apple before beginning on what was left of the cheese. She saved a tiny bit for Hoppit—assuming she would see him again. Spit tore her off some bread and she scarfed that, too.

"Drink?" he said curtly.

"Is there one?'" Betty asked longingly. The mere mention of something that wasn't salt water made her parched throat feel even drier.

Spit leaned back and dug his elbow into one of the wooden boards on the ship's side. It flipped like a seesaw to reveal a hidey-hole underneath. He reached in and withdrew a jewel-encrusted bottle. "Here."

Betty took it in awe, transfixed by the gleaming red stones. It looked very old and was probably worth more than the Poacher's Pocket. "Jumping jackdaws," she whispered. "Are those *real* firestones?" The image of the silver and gold below them in the wreck danced before her eyes once more. If Spit treated something this valuable so casually, then just how much treasure did the Rusty Scuttlers have?

Spit nodded. "Yeah. So don't drop it."

Betty uncorked the bottle and sniffed dubiously before taking a swig. Inside was cool, fresh spring water. She handed the bottle back, wiping her mouth.

"So when can I expect you to be gone?" Spit asked, using the knife to dig bits of cheese out of his teeth.

A piece of apple stuck in Betty's throat. "Soon. My other sister . . . she's being brought here," she managed, swallowing forcibly. But *was* she? Betty fought down a wave of panic. Surely Charlie should have been here by now. What if Granny was mistaken or some horrible accident had happened? What if . . . what if the wisps Betty, Fliss, and Willow had encountered had gotten ahold of Charlie, too?

Stop! she thought furiously. Thinking like that wouldn't help. But every hour that passed made it harder to believe that Charlie was heading here. An unpleasant little part of her wanted to blame Willow for all that had gone wrong. Yet, at the same time, Betty knew it wasn't the little girl's fault. It might have been bad luck that brought her to their door, but Betty had been the one to invite her in.

A horrid sense of shame came over her. It wasn't fair! She hadn't even been looking for trouble this time. All she'd been trying to do was the right thing, and she'd messed it up and gotten it so badly wrong.

Spit sighed, sounding slightly less cross. "Even if she does turn up here, how do you plan on getting away? I hate to break it to you, but your boat will be heavily guarded. Even if Fliss manages to steal it back, Ronia will come after it. She's not one to give up easily."

"Neither am I," said Betty. Her attempt to sound fierce was annoyingly feeble.

He hesitated. "You don't understand. Ronia wasn't born a pirate, any more than her father was. He was a wine merchant, sailing from place to place with Ronia and her mother. One night, their ship was taken by pirates. Ronia's mother was killed outright. Her father tried to fight back, but there were too many of them. He was overpowered, and well . . . you've seen what happened to him."

Betty listened in shock, thinking of the pirate's stumps. She had never imagined they were the result of something so grisly. A boating accident, perhaps—or even a brush with sharks—but not this.

"Ronia was just a child when it happened," Spit went on. "She was so young the pirates never considered her a threat. They decided to keep her as a kitchen skivvy. But gradually Ronia convinced them she had skills—skills they needed. And so they began to trust her. But what she was really doing was *learning*. Biding her time, plotting her revenge. As Ronia grew, so did the size of the crew. She made allies of the new members, ones taken against their will as she had been. Gradually winning them over, earning their trust. Making them her own. And when there were enough on her side, she took the ship for herself."

"How?" Betty whispered, horrified at this already-grisly tale but unable to stop listening.

"With poison," Spit said. "And anyone who survived it found themselves on the pointy end of her cutlass." His eyes were troubled. "So now you know what you're dealing with. She's clever and cunning, and most dangerous of all, she's *patient*." He shook his head. "You made a big mistake when you came snooping around here. We can't have people trespassing or stealing from the wreck. Whenever that happens, Ronia has to set an example. That's if Rusty doesn't get there first."

"What do you mean?" Betty asked. Could Father's stories of grisly curses be true?

"See that bit?" Spit pointed to the far end of the ship below the waves. "That's dangerous territory. That's Rusty Swindles's part of the wreck, and we leave that for him out of respect. Whatever's there is his. Even the Rusty Scuttlers don't attempt to disturb it. Anyone who does . . ." He lifted a finger and mimed slicing across his neck.

"We weren't stealing, though," Betty said through

gritted teeth. "We aren't interested in Rusty Swindles's treasure—or yours. All we came for was my sister!"

"You said she was kidnapped," said Spit. "What happened?"

Betty pursed her lips. "What do you care? Like you said, we aren't here to be friends."

"Nope," Spit agreed, stretching his lanky legs out next to Betty's. "But it gets pretty dull up here with only the gulls for company. A bit of conversation will help pass the time."

"All right," Betty muttered. She straightened her damp clothes and leaned back onto her elbows, her mind working furiously to spin a tale close enough to the truth but which wouldn't give Willow's ability away. Willow's own father had warned her that she'd be in danger if the wrong people learned of it—and Betty could safely assume that pirates were *definitely* the wrong people.

"They're not actually warders who have Charlie. We don't know who they are—all we know is that they took her by mistake. It was Willow they were after. They want something from this wreck, and they think Willow can help them get it."

"What is it they're looking for?" asked Spit, and Betty could hear another question in his voice: *Why would they need a child to help them?*

She squirmed, glad Spit wasn't able to see her. For a pirate, he had awfully honest eyes that were difficult to lie to, and she was sure he knew she was holding something back. "They mentioned Rusty Swindles," she said finally. "So they must be looking for his treasure—or maybe even the actual sorcerer's compass. We thought if we found it first, we could use it to bargain for Charlie."

"Instead of just handing Willow over to them?"

Betty scowled. "Exactly."

Spit nodded slowly. "So how did they end up with your sister instead of Willow?"

"It was a mix-up," Betty said. "And it's sort of all my fault." She screwed her eyes up tightly, thinking back over the previous night. Before she could help it, the story came spilling out: about the prison bell tolling for the Torment escapee, Charlie's discovery of Willow in the yard and Betty's decision to hide her, and the supposed warders taking Charlie. The only things she kept back were the wisp and Willow's mysterious map. The map that was probably now in the hands of the pirates. The thought of it made Betty feel sick.

"Whoa!" said Spit when she'd reached the end of her tale. He raked a hand through his blond hair and blew out a long breath. "You girls really *have* had rotten luck."

"Yeah," Betty agreed. "Bad luck seems to be our family inheritance."

Spit stared out into the distance. The wind had risen, and white crests were appearing on the waves. "Everyone's dealt bad luck at some point." A shadow crossed his face. "It's how you cope with it that counts." He paused thoughtfully.

"Sounds like you've had your share," Betty said. She felt foolish now, for blurting out her story to a stranger—and a pirate at that. It had felt strangely good to unburden herself, but she wanted to change the subject now and shift attention away from her and her family. "How did you end up being part of Ronia's crew?"

The expression on Spit's face closed down immediately. He frowned and spat overboard. "It doesn't matter."

Betty regarded him, curiosity roused. She'd lived in a pub for long enough to sniff out a good story. "You might as well tell me what happened. Like you said, we're both stuck here for now."

"Fine." He scowled. "They found me, all right?"

"*Found* you? Where?"

"Adrift," he said, his amber eyes clouded with pain. He flicked the blade of his knife in and out. "A boat had gone down in a storm. Ronia and her father came across it and were searching the debris scattered over the water. There wasn't much of value, mainly clothes, some furniture. They thought it must be a migrant ship, people looking for better lives. Lots of belongings, but no survivors." He sniffed, looking down at his hands. "Until they found me.

"I was in a floating barrel, half-drowned. A miracle I'd survived, really. They said I'd swallowed so much seawater that I was spitting and spitting to get the taste out of my mouth." He spat again, spurred by the memory. "And it kind of became a habit."

"Oh," said Betty, feeling a pang of sadness. All this time she'd thought this strange pirate boy had just been uncouth, but the tragic story behind his habit softened her. "And . . . your parents?"

"Never found them," he said, lowering his eyes. "If they were even the ones I was traveling with. Guess I'll never know who they were or who I really am." He shrugged. "I'm just Spit, a Rusty Scuttler. They took me in, so that makes me one of them."

"When . . . when did this happen?" Betty asked, shocked.

"Twelve years ago," Spit replied. "They think I was about three, but there's no way of knowing how old I am for sure." He rubbed his nose and took a mouthful of water from the bottle. "I don't even know when my birth-day is. Whenever it's mentioned, Ronia always says it's the day they found me. The day I became Spit." His face darkened. "That's how it all happened, according to her."

Something in his voice made Betty's scalp prickle. "Have others said differently, then?" she asked.

He hesitated. "There was another version. That the Rusty Scuttlers didn't just come across the ship I was on." His voice was quiet. "They attacked it. Slaughtered every-one aboard, except for me. Because . . ."

"Because you were too young to be a threat," Betty finished, horrified, not least because of the similarity to Ronia's tale. "But surely, if the same thing had happened to Ronia, why would she do that to another child?"

"Exactly," said Spit. He forced a hollow laugh. "Any-way, I only heard that story once. It came out during a row, when they'd all been on the rum and gambling. Ronia said it was a pack of lies. She made sure it was never repeated."

Betty's knees trembled. She crossed her legs, trying to stop them shaking.

"But . . . but what if it wasn't a lie?" she asked. "What if Ronia *didn't* really save you? Would you still be loyal to her?"

Spit stayed silent for a long time, his face unreadable.

"It was a lie," he said at last. "I have to believe she saved me, because if I don't, there's nowhere else for me. If I'm not a Rusty Scuttler, then who am I?"

They sat in silence, watching the waves rolling and the gulls swooping for fish. How full of chance the sea was, Betty thought, mulling over Spit's sad story. Sometimes beautiful, sometimes cruel.

A short while later, Spit reached into the hidey-hole again and checked the time on a pocket watch. Then he hopped along the mast to haul the ragged sail out of the water, signaling to the Rusty Scuttlers that all was apparently well.

When he returned, almost tripping over Betty, his mood had shifted like the tide. The sadness had gone, replaced by defiance. It was as if, Betty thought, when Spit had raised the sail, his defenses had gone back up again, too.

"They won't get the sorcerer's compass, you know," he muttered, sitting beside her once more. "These people who have your sister. No one's ever got their hands on it—or any of Rusty's loot. Strange things happen when anyone dares to go in that part of the wreck. *Bad* things. People have lost their minds in there or come out with every hair on their heads turned white. That's if they come out at all. Even the Rusty Scuttlers know better than to try."

"So it exists then?" Betty asked. "The sorcerer's compass?" Despite everything, the part of her that reveled in adventure longed for it to be true.

"It must," said Spit. "Why else would Rusty stay to guard it all this time? Then again, who can say for sure? No one's ever seen it. Maybe it's just another story passed down through generations. A warning to show what happens to people who take what they don't deserve."

"Just another story," Betty echoed, falling silent as she was reminded again of the one about the mysterious island and the three brothers. How did it fit with what had happened to Willow's father and Saul?

"Spit?" she ventured. "Have you ever heard the legend about the one-eyed witch and the hidden island of treasures?"

"Of course." Spit snorted. "Wouldn't be much of a pirate if I hadn't, would I?"

"Suppose not," said Betty. "Reckon it's true?" She glanced at Spit, half expecting him to dismiss it immediately.

"Now, there's the question," he murmured, his thick eyebrows furrowing as he gazed into the distance. "If I answered that now, watching the gulls pecking over there and the sun sparkling on the waves, I'd bet all of Rusty's treasure that it wasn't true. But if you asked me at night when I'm out here alone, and the wreck's creaking, and the moon's casting strange shadows . . . and there are will-o'-the-wisps drifting over the water . . ." He paused, looking thoughtful. "*Then* I'd probably say anything is possible."

The Crowstone Chronicles

The Crone, the Raven, and the Labyrinth: Part II

Fortune's father and his two younger brothers asked far and wide for news of him but received no word. Many believed he had looted the labyrinth's riches and kept them for himself. Others said he had fallen afoul of pirates or tricksters, or gambled it all away. His brothers, Luck and Hope, vowed to go after him, but their father forbade it.

Heartbroken, the family resigned themselves to never seeing him again. Until, one year to the day after Fortune had left, his little boat returned. Empty—except for a large, black feather. Again, Luck and Hope begged their father to let them search for their lost brother, but the old man still refused.

However, Luck was not to be deterred. He stole away in the night to search for the lost Fortune, taking the little boat over the marshes to find the crone. Arriving at the rocky crag, he spotted the raven perched on the witch's shoulder and flew into a rage.

"Where's my brother?" he demanded, throwing down the black feather. "What have you done with him?"

But the only response he received was the gnarly hand of the crone, offering him a hagstone.

"Look through, look through," croaked the raven.

Snatching it from her, Luck gazed into the middle and spotted the island at once. He gasped, then greedily eyed the cauldron.

The raven spoke again: "Take one, choose one."

The crone watched as the foolish youth picked through the cauldron. Like Fortune, he discarded the dagger and the cape, believing there would be bigger riches in store. He dismissed the rabbit's foot, declaring, "I have no need for luck, because *I* am Luck!" The egg he picked up, enchanted by its golden sheen, but decided it would be too difficult to carry. The yarn he gave barely a thought to, for by then he had spotted the shoes.

What a fine pair! And exactly his size. Luck looked down at his own shoes, which had been worn by Fortune first, like everything he owned

—laces frayed, toes scuffed. How he had longed for his very own pair of shoes all these years. "Besides," he reasoned, "this will be a long journey, and my old shoes are not up to it." So he cast them into the sea and set sail without a word of thanks to the crone.

Enraged, the crone winked at the sky and summoned a lightning bolt which struck Luck's boat so it sprang a leak. He quickly realized he had nothing to bail out the water with except his wonderful new shoes. He almost wept as he pulled them off and used them to scoop the water back into the sea. How he wished he had kept the old ones! But it was too late. He had no choice but to carry on, managing to plug the leak with a torn-off strip of his tunic.

Luck made his way to the island, arriving at the same rocky spot Fortune had stopped at a year before. Here he cursed himself again because he had forgotten to check that the boat was properly equipped and the mooring rope Fortune had lost had not been replaced.

Sadly, Luck glanced down at his shoes. Their sheen had gone, replaced instead by crusty trails of sea salt. He pulled out the laces and used them to tether the boat. Then he began to climb. By the time he reached the rocky ledge where the cave mouth was, his shoes were dusty and scuffed, no better than his old ones. When he reached the well, he knew he had made the wrong choice.

Luck peered into the well, just as Fortune had, noticing the bucket in the water below. Finding a copper Rook in his pocket, he threw it in to make a wish, for he had started to wonder if perhaps he was not quite as lucky as he'd first thought. But instead of a splash, a large, silver fish raised its head out of the water.

"Who is throwing coins on my head?"

At once, Luck recognized his lost brother's voice, and the two wept with joy. And then they wept some more because they realized Luck had no way to rescue his brother.

"Go home," Fortune said, "and return with help."

But Luck wasn't about to give up just yet. He had always been in Fortune's shadow, always second best, and this was his chance to prove himself. A chance for glory! Not only would he save his brother, but Luck was determined that *he* would be the one to make it to the riches at the heart of the island.

"I'll search the island," he promised. "If I cannot find a rope, then surely there'll be some strong vines that I can weave into a net to catch you."

Fortune was not at all happy about this, but Luck didn't stay to listen to his protests. He approached the darkened caves, knowing that this was the start of the labyrinth and that he must make it to the center. At the mouth of the cave was a burnt-out lantern, but Luck noticed a cluster of bog beetles glowing brightly nearby. He swept them into the lantern delightedly, for now he had something to light the way.

"What a stroke of luck," he exclaimed.

"Not for us," the bog beetles chirruped sadly. "Please set us free!"

Luck did not hear them, for their voices were tiny. He entered the caves, braver now that the bog beetles were glowing. Ignoring the pinch of his shoes, he journeyed into the twisting tunnels, sure he would soon be out the other side. But before long, the bog beetles' glow began to fade, for they were afraid—and nothing can shine when it is full of fear. Luck became cross and rattled the lantern, shouting, "Glow, beetles, glow!"

Instead they went out, one by one, and Luck was left to roam in darkness. His courage was in tatters, and his feet were now horribly blistered, for the wet shoes had shrunk and were so tight he could not pull them off. He wandered this way and that, tricked by breezes and tiny chinks of sunlight here and there, which never quite led to a way out. And although he called and called for help, no one came. Yet still he cried out, because the loneliness was crippling and even the echo of his own voice was better than no sound at all.

Hocus-Pocus

"**W**AKE UP!"

A voice, low and urgent, hissed in Betty's ear. She shot up with a gasp.

Where am I?

For a moment, she was disorientated as she took in the wrecked ship, the vast expanse of water, and the amber-eyed boy poking her awake. The daylight was fading and a cool breeze ruffled her hair.

Then it all came rushing back: *Willow. Charlie and Fliss gone. Spit with his sad and unsettling past.*

Betty wiped away a string of saliva that had trailed from her chin to her ear.

"What is it?" she asked, her voice gruff with sleep.

Spit offered her a spyglass and pointed. "Over there."

Betty peered into the glass. At first she saw only miles and miles of water, flat and golden in the fading light. Then, as sleep left her eyes, she spotted it. Her fingers tightened around the spyglass. "A boat," she said, the last traces of sleep leaving her. "And it's heading straight for us."

The boat was small and unlit. Against the sun, two figures were silhouetted. One was rowing, the other seated. From this distance, it was impossible to tell who they were or make out any distinct features, but already Betty's heart was sinking.

Two people. No sign of a third.

It can't be them, she thought. *The ones who have Charlie. Unless . . .*

Unless something had happened. Like Charlie escaping . . . or worse. Betty's mind reeled, tormenting itself.

What if she'd fallen overboard, and they'd lost her in the fog?

What if they'd finally believed she really wasn't Willow and had got rid of her?

"You think those are the ones who have your sister?" Spit asked.

"I can't tell yet." Betty's hand shook as she passed the spyglass back. "They're too far off. Either way, she's not with them now."

Her voice hitched and she fought to regain control of it. She was afraid now, truly afraid of what might have become of Charlie. But over the fear and guilt for her part in things, anger began to simmer like a cauldron of witch's brew. Everything that had happened since yesterday had started because of these two and their greed . . . *Well, they will pay*, thought Betty. And one way or another, she would find out where her sister was.

Spit frowned, squinting through the spyglass. "You sure about that?"

Something in his voice made Betty snatch the spyglass back. She gasped. The boat was closer now, and while the figures were still fuzzy, there were now most definitely three of them—and one was a child.

Betty almost slid down the side of the wreck in shock, and the spyglass slipped from her fingers.

"Hey!" Spit grunted, diving for it just before it fell into the water. "Careful with that!"

Betty scrambled back up, her mind whirring, worrying that she might have been mistaken. "What if it's not her?" she babbled. "I need to know it's Charlie. Let me see again!" She ignored Spit's protests and grabbed the glass again.

It was definitely a child. As the boat drew ever closer, Betty was able to make out two familiar, untidy pigtails.

A surge of love and relief threatened to overwhelm her, making her giddy. It took all her willpower to contain it and focus on what she needed to do.

"Charlie!" she whispered, clenching her fists. "Don't worry, Charlie. I'm coming for you." She thrust the spyglass back at Spit. "How much can they see from where they are?" she demanded. "Could they have spotted you?"

"Doubt it. The sun's behind them, but it's darker here." Spit flipped the loose board and stowed the spyglass in the dark space beneath it, checking the pocket watch as he did so. A sudden realization hit Betty.

"Jumping jackdaws! How long do we have?"

Spit looked blank.

"Before you're supposed to lift the sail to signal all's well to the Rusty Scuttlers?" Betty prompted, panic rising. Already she knew Spit wouldn't be signaling—his job was as lookout, after all. But when he didn't . . . it would bring the Rusty Scuttlers right back to the wreck. "If that boat sees pirates charging in, they'll be gone—and so will Charlie!"

"But if I signal to keep them away, the boat will see the flag," Spit argued. "They'll know someone's here. They could take off anyway! If the Rusty Scuttlers find out I didn't signal when I needed to, it'll be my head on the chopping block!"

He was right, Betty realized. Either way, the fake warders would soon realize they were not alone at the shipwreck. A strangled half sob escaped her lips. This was Charlie's *life* in the balance, and Betty's only chance of getting her back.

"Listen," Spit said, "I reckon you can still rescue your sister. It's almost dark, and they're going to be focused on the wreck. If they're stupid enough to go messing about in Rusty's domain, then they won't even see the Scuttlers until it's too late. You can do your hocus-pocus and make Charlie disappear with you. You never know, a band of pirates might even help as a distraction."

Hocus-pocus . . . make her disappear.

Yes, Betty realized, her heart lifting. Provided she didn't twist the outer doll, she could keep herself, Willow, and Fliss unseen and open the dolls to add an item of Charlie's to the third. First, though, she had to reach Charlie. Breathless, Betty gazed out over the water, and her tummy flipped. The boat was approaching quickly now, and she could only guess that the sight of *The Sorcerer's Compass* had spurred the warders on.

The daylight was fading fast, and as dusk fell over the watery wreck so did an eerie stillness. It was easy to imagine things lurking unseen below the surface, waiting.

"I need your help," she said to Spit. "The only way I

can make this work is if I get Charlie alone, but they're going to be watching her like hawks. I need you to hide in the crow's-nest and draw their attention away from her, just for a few seconds."

Spit looked fed up. "Reckon I've already helped you enough, don't you?"

"No," Betty retorted fiercely. "Not if you want me gone."

"Fine," he muttered. "But how will I know when? I can't even see you!"

"I'll knock three times on the deck," said Betty. "That way you'll know when I'm ready. Now quickly—get up there before they see you."

She crouched at the base of the mast as Spit climbed up it. *This was it*. She could hear the oars of the boat now, swishing through the water, and low voices. Then she settled into position, heart drumming ever faster . . . and waited.

The soft lapping of the oars came closer.

Betty's eyes strained to see anything in the gloom. She wished she could use the spyglass but couldn't risk any objects being seen to seemingly float in midair. She smiled grimly. At least not yet.

At last they were near enough for Betty to make out

the features of the two men who had appeared at the Poacher's Pocket the previous night. Her hands curled into fists. Part of her had never wanted to see either of their lying faces again. The other part of her felt a rush of pure relief. Their one slip-up had been enough to track them.

They came closer still, scoping the wreck at the side where the Rusty Scuttlers' warning sign was displayed. If Betty jumped, she'd be almost on top of them.

"Stop." The one who'd called himself Wild raised a hand and lifted his oar from the water to survey the wreck. His cold eyes showed no sign of fear, only antici-pation—and greed. He shifted slightly for a better look, and behind him, Betty glimpsed a small figure sitting in the bottom of the boat under the watchful eye of Goose. Her heart twisted.

Charlie. Tangle-haired and pale-faced, with a scowl fierce enough to sour milk. It was all Betty could do not to leap into the water right away.

"There it is," Wild commented, his eyes raking over the ruined ship. "Time to say goodbye to your loot, Rusty." He raised his voice and it echoed over the wreck. "Do you hear me, you old sea dog?"

Betty saw Spit slowly lean out of the crow's-nest, his

eyes narrowing. His words drifted back to her, stirring up dread: *Strange things . . . bad things . . . people have lost their minds in there. That's if they come out at all . . .*

"I hate this place," said Goose, clutching his oar as though it were a spear. His skin looked clammy and flushed.

"You won't say that when we get our hands on that compass," Wild retorted. "And whatever else is down there." He threw his oar at Goose, his eyes fixed on the wreck. "If that old devil Rusty really is down there, we need to capture him and keep him out of the way."

His words sent a creeping fear over Betty. She'd seen what wisps could do with her own eyes. If Rusty Swindles's soul were summoned, how could any of them hope to control it, when Charlie wasn't even who they thought she was? With Willow gone, there was no one to lull Rusty. They were all in danger of succumbing to any wisps that these fools were about to disturb.

"You can stop glaring at me like that," Wild remarked to Charlie in a voice like chipped ice. "Do as you're told and we'll let you go."

Charlie continued to glower, frowning so hard that her eyebrows were almost resting on her cheeks. "I told you before," she said grumpily. "I ain't no wisp catcher.

And when my sisters come to find me, you're going to be in SO much trouble."

Wild leaned over until his nose was almost touching hers. "Your sisters aren't coming. Your *granny*"—he mimicked cruelly—"isn't coming. No one knows you're here."

"My s-sisters will come." Charlie's bottom lip stuck out in defiance, but even from where Betty was, she could see that it was trembling, too. "You don't know them. You don't know any of us."

I'm here, Charlie! Betty wanted to shout. Her little sister's fierce, unwavering loyalty was warmer than a hug.

"We know enough," Wild said mockingly. "Now stop prattling and sing."

Charlie stared silently at the water, her shoulders slumping in defeat.

"Sing!" Wild growled, his temper fraying—along with Betty's. How *dare* he treat Charlie this way?

"Perhaps shouting isn't going to, uh, help," Goose suggested timidly. "She's just a child."

Wild rounded on his companion, eyes blazing. "A pain in the rear, that's what she is! This was meant to have been over with last night, but it's been one setback after another." He loomed over Charlie, spittle flying out of his mouth in temper. "First, you start leaving a trail, meaning we had to abandon our route and double back. Second, you jump overboard, moments after convincing us you couldn't swim. In the middle of the worst pea-souper we've had for weeks." His voice dripped with contempt. "I almost drowned bringing you back to the boat, you little beast."

"Shame," Charlie muttered.

"And third"—Wild's eyes were bulging now—"you haven't. Stopped. *Eating!*"

"I'm tired," said Charlie. "And I've been freezing my cockles off in a boat all night. Being tired makes me hungry!" She glared at him again and stuck the end of her pigtail in her mouth.

"*Sing,*" Wild growled.

"All right." Charlie cleared her throat and sat up straight. "You asked for it, mister."

Wild nodded at Goose. "Get the jar ready."

Charlie began to sing.

Ohhhhh . . . There was an old man from
 Skinny Woods,
With Crowstone's hairiest knees.
When cut it grew back
So he put it in plaits,
But he couldn't keep still for the fleas!

There was a stunned silence. Then Wild hissed through his teeth. "You think you're funny?"

Charlie hung her head. "If you think that was bad, you should hear my sister's singing."

"I'm talking about the *song!*" Wild raged. "You could sound like a strangled cat for all I care—it's the words that matter! That's what lulls them!"

"There are no wisps to sing *to*, though," Goose objected. He had been keeping watch over the water, his eyes skittering about nervously.

Wild turned on him. "I can see that. I thought maybe they could be lulled *before* I dive down and disturb them, but this brat isn't cooperating."

From the belly of the boat, he took a copper diving mask. "Well, you'll wish you had. And then you'll sing, believe me."

"I want to go *h-home*," said Charlie, all traces of mischief gone. She started to cry. "I don't *know* the song you mean!"

Betty leaned closer, heartsick at her sister's tears. She had to get to Charlie—but how?

"Perhaps . . ." Goose said shakily, wiping sweat from his upper lip. "Perhaps she's telling the truth?"

"I am," Charlie sobbed. "I'm just Charlie Widdershins!"

"If that's true," Wild said quietly, "then you're no good to us."

Charlie looked up through her tears. "So . . . I can go home?"

"I'm afraid not." Wild nodded curtly at Goose. "Get rid of her. And make it look like an accident."

Chapter Nineteen

A Scattering of Pearls

GET RID? AN ACCIDENT? The implication echoed in Betty's head, turning her blood to ice. Surely Wild was bluffing, trying to bully Charlie into doing what he wanted?

"Now hang on," Goose said shakily. "You said no one would get hurt!"

Wild stood over him, eyes flashing. "You want to take her back? Go ahead! I'm sure the Crowstone authorities will be waiting to give you a warm welcome."

Goose hesitated, running a tongue over his lips. "What if we just leave her? She'll be picked up by a passing boat and—"

"All right!" Charlie shouted. "I . . . I'll do it. But it . . .

it can't be done unless the wisps are here." Her eyes darted over the wreck, and she hugged her arms around herself, shivering uncontrollably.

She was stalling, Betty knew. Doing the only thing she could think of, and who could blame her? Charlie knew as well as Betty that Wild had no intention of letting her go home, whether she helped them or not.

This was what would have become of Willow. Betty knew that now. They might have kept her alive longer to make more use of her, but as soon as that usefulness ran out, she'd have been discarded. The difference was that Willow had no one to look out for her. But Charlie *did*.

Wild smiled. "Good. I knew we'd get there in the end."

"H-how do we get the wisps to come to us?" Goose stuttered. "You said we'd deal with them before looting the wreck?"

"We will," Wild answered. "But clearly they need some riling up. We have to draw them out—and Rusty's the most dangerous one of them all."

"But what if they attack while you're down there?" Goose said.

"I'll be out in seconds." Wild's mouth twisted in an arrogant sneer. "I've studied the blueprints of this ship for months—I'd know every inch of the wreck blindfolded. And once I draw them out, she can deal with them while we clean the place out."

Betty watched, hardly able to breathe as Wild tugged on the diving mask and stepped off the little boat. *He's going to do it*, she thought. *He's actually going to enter the cursed part of the wreck, where even the Rusty Scuttlers don't dare to go*. Did he really think that one little girl who could catch wisps was enough? That *he* would be the one to get the better of Rusty Swindles and his cursed wreck when no one else had succeeded?

Fingernails scrabbled over wood, and a grunt followed. The wood below her creaked, just as it had when Ronia had stepped on to the wreck. Now Wild was following in her footsteps. Slowly, Betty backed away, as far over to the edge of the bow as she could.

His arm swung into view, narrowly missing her ankle. She bit back a gasp as he pulled himself up, his breath noisy inside the heavy mask. She watched as he located the porthole that was above the water and slithered down into it. A faint scrape sounded as the copper mask clipped the wood, and then she heard him entering the dark water inside the ship with a faint splash.

Goose began to pace the little boat, breathing hard.

"You'd better do what you said, kid," he muttered, swiping a hand over his face. "Once those wisps are up, there's no getting away from them."

Charlie sat, shivering, saying nothing.

Betty edged forward to peer into the porthole. She caught the faint glisten of the water a short way below it, but nothing else. The round circle gaped like a mouth, giving the eerie impression that Wild had been swallowed whole.

She had to act. With Wild out of the way, this was the best chance she had. Once the wisps were riled up, the danger would escalate—and fast. Between them, perhaps Betty and Spit could overpower Goose—at least long enough to get Charlie away. Betty stared up at the crow's-nest, seeking out Spit. He was peeping out at Charlie and Goose, but as Betty watched, he cast a questioning glance in her direction, clearly waiting for her signal.

Betty rapped three times on the wood, the sound echoing over the water. She saw Charlie stiffen, and Goose stopped pacing immediately.

A noise cut through the night. A long, thin wail, like someone in distress. Betty whipped around and saw Spit's hand cupped to his mouth as he continued to make the disturbing sound. It was a desperate, eerie noise, which would chill anyone's blood, and she could see Goose trembling as he searched for the source of the noise. *Weakening.*

"That's it!" he cried, lunging for an oar. "I'm getting out of this cursed place!"

Betty prepared to jump, but Charlie was faster.

She leaped to her feet, seizing the other oar, and swung it, catching Goose on the cheek. He staggered in shock and teetered, about to regain his balance. But Charlie moved in a blur, jabbing the oar into Goose's chest with all her might. It caught him off-guard, and he toppled into the water with a stunned gurgle.

Charlie grabbed the other oar and quickly sat back down on the bench in the boat. Her face was screwed up in determination as she tried to drag the oars through the water—but they were clearly too heavy for her, and Goose was already recovering himself and lunging for the boat.

"Charlie!" Betty leaped off the side of *The Sorcerer's Compass*. As she plummeted down, she saw both Charlie and Goose whip around at the sound of her voice. It didn't matter now about staying quiet—all that mattered was getting to Charlie before Wild disturbed the soul of Rusty Swindles. She hit the water, shocked by its icy darkness . . . but as she swiveled below the surface, Betty could see that the darkness was lightening. A row of windows stretching down into the seabed had begun to glow. Terror clawed at her: the wisps were coming.

She heard Spit plunging into the water next to her and they broke the surface at the same moment. Goose reared back, his eyes trained on Spit, quickly realizing he was a living, breathing person and not one of the cursed things of the wreck.

"Who are you?" he demanded.

Spit didn't answer. He glanced in Betty's direction, where the water was churned up by her movements. Charlie hadn't spotted it, for she, too, was staring at Spit —perhaps wondering if he had been the one to shout her name. At once, she was on her feet, brandishing an oar.

"Who are you?" she yelled. "Stay away!"

"Charlie!" shouted Betty, swimming for the little boat. "It's me—let me up!"

Charlie turned, her face a mask of astonishment. "*Betty?*" she whispered in disbelief. "Is that really you?"

Betty grabbed the edge of the boat, pulling herself up and rolling, drenched, inside. She landed heavily in a sopping mass of clothes, hearing a *thunk* as the dolls in her pocket hit the deck. Charlie, unable to see her, stared at the water pooling in the bottom of the boat as Betty dragged herself to her feet. She launched herself at Charlie, hugging her fiercely. Charlie returned it, and even though Betty was soaked to the skin it was the warmest hug ever. She had her little sister back.

"It *is* you!" Charlie sobbed. "But how did you—?"

A shout from the water brought Betty to her feet. Goose was tussling with Spit, pulling him back from the boat.

Betty broke away from her sister, leaning over the side of the boat. "Hey!" she yelled, sweeping her hand downward to dash water in Goose's eyes. The two figures leaped apart, with Goose spluttering from a face full of water. For the first time, he and Spit saw the glow beneath the waves spreading and rising.

Spit's eyes widened. "Need to get out of the water!" he gasped.

Quickly, Betty leaned over and grabbed his arm. "*Come on!*" She pulled him into the boat and handed him an oar.

"Who's doing that?" Goose howled, his eyes wild as he searched the boat for the unseen assassin. Then, panicking at the sight of the glowing water, he flung his arm out to the boat.

Spit knocked his hand away, shaking water from his hair. "Row," he told Betty grimly. "We have to move."

"Where to?" Betty asked, staring at the glowing water in horror.

"Away from the wreck." Spit hauled at his oar breathlessly. "It's not safe. They're coming."

"Betty, what's coming? And who *is* that?" Charlie began, as Betty and Spit began to row.

"No time to explain," Betty gasped. Her foot scuffed something in the bottom of the boat, sending it rolling away. "All you need to know is that he's with us."

Light flickered in the blackness. A faint silvery glow was leaking out of the wreck . . . and the porthole that Wild had entered. Betty watched, wrenching her oar, heart hammering. How long had Wild been in there now? Was he still alive? Or had the wisps claimed him already?

Just then a figure burst out and scrambled over the side of the wreck, and then Wild tore off his diving mask. Confusion and terror crossed his face as his eyes swept over the hijacked boat and took in Goose treading water.

He froze on the edge of the wreck, his eyes resting on Charlie. "SING!" he bellowed.

But Charlie didn't even appear to have noticed him. "Betty!" Her little voice rose, and she reached blindly for Betty. "*Look!*"

A cluster of wisps emerged from the glowing water without so much as a ripple. The wisps hovered before them, large and fierce and ethereal. Somehow Betty sensed these were different from the playful thing that accompanied Willow. There was a definite sense of malevolence oozing from them. The wisps drifted closer, as though investigating them.

Betty gulped, keeping as still as she could. Both she and Spit had stopped rowing, frozen with fear. She could now hear the faint whispering in her head, like before when she and Fliss and Willow had been surrounded. Only now the chanting voices seemed less desperate, more menacing. And this time there was no Willow to ward them off. Betty's lips opened, trying to summon the song, but her mind had gone blank. There was no escaping it this time. The whispers grew louder.

"*Not yours . . . not yours . . . not yours . . .*"

They hung there a moment longer, then drifted back over the water, circling a whimpering Goose menacingly.

"Swim!" Wild yelled to him. The glow behind him had risen, casting ghostlike shadows on his face. "The boat, get to the boat!"

Betty stared down through the water. The inside of *The Sorcerer's Compass* was glowing even more brightly now. The glow spread around the wreck, glimmering and glittering. More wisps rose up through the water into the air, surrounding Goose, penning him in. He had nowhere to go.

Several wisps trailed up the side of the wreck to where

Wild was clinging on. Something dangled from his fist: a string of pearls that gleamed like teeth.

"*Not yours . . . not yours . . .*" the whispers sounded again.

"You want this?" Wild babbled, thrusting the pearls clumsily at the swarm of wisps. "Have them! Keep it all." The necklace broke apart in his fingers, and he scrambled back, horrified as the pearls each took on a luminescent glow, rising up and growing into wisps which swarmed around Wild like flies on a carcass. And then another solitary wisp approached him, glowing fiercely. Betty could almost feel the waves of anger coming off it, so blindingly and terrifyingly did it burn—like a white-hot poker tip. She knew, with absolute certainty, that *this* was Rusty Swindles. Wild lifted his hand to shield his eyes, cowering beneath it. His face was a mask of terror.

Betty watched, transfixed and horrified by the pale orbs. Fragments of whispers drifted across to the boat over the water. And a darker voice, that somehow cut across all the other whispers: "*You'll pay . . . you'll pay . . .*"

The sound was rising like a tide, the glow like an icy sunrise.

"Cover your ears, Charlie," Betty warned, but Spit shook his head slowly, squinting in the dazzling light.

"It's not here for us."

"What will happen to those two?" Charlie asked, gazing at her captors and wringing her hands in her lap. Within the glow of the wisps, the impostor warders could barely be seen now, each of them just a smeary shadow against the light.

"Nothing good," Spit replied gravely. "Now let's move."

Betty's fingers tightened on the oar. She rowed harder, eager to escape as quickly as possible. The flickering wisps merged and swarmed around the two figures. The glow seemed to brighten, lighting up the whole of the wreck under the blackened sky. And then there was a flash so blinding that Betty had to look away.

The whispers were suddenly shut off, as if a door had been closed. When Betty looked back, the glow had gone and all she could see were a few flecks of pale light like a scattering of pearls in the night sky. They could no longer see *The Sorcerer's Compass*, but Betty knew it was still there somewhere.

Waiting in the darkness.

Chapter Twenty

A Bargain

CHARLIE SQUEEZED CLOSER AND FLUNG her arms around Betty's waist, crushing the breath out of her.

"*Oof!*" said Betty, gasping for air. She lowered her oar and rubbed Charlie's back as her little sister sobbed into her lap. "It's all right now," she soothed. "I'm here."

"When he said 'get rid of her' . . . I thought . . . I thought . . ." Charlie sniffed, her voice muffled. "If you hadn't been there, they'd have . . ."

"Well, I was," said Betty, lightheaded with relief. "And you weren't making it easy for them. That was a pretty impressive whack you gave Goose."

"I did whack him, didn't I?" Charlie sat up, a little

brighter. There was an object in her sister's lap, Betty realized, glimpsing curved wood, and she remembered now how something had rolled by her feet. *The dolls.* They must have fallen from her pocket when she'd climbed into the boat. Charlie had picked them up.

Charlie eyed Spit suspiciously. "Who *is* this? Where's Fliss? How did you find me? Where are we going?"

"Whoa, Charlie," Betty said gently. "One thing at a time!"

"I'm Spit," he said, turning to spit over the side of the boat but stopping himself just in time.

"He's . . . sort of a pirate," Betty added. "That shipwreck, *The Sorcerer's Compass*, it's where his crew keeps some of their loot."

"Will you *stop* blabbing our secrets?" Spit exclaimed. "It's our best hiding place!"

"Jumping jackdaws," Charlie breathed. "A real live pirate!" She leaned over and poked Spit's legs. "Either of these wooden?"

"Nope," said Spit. "Sorry."

"No eyepatch?" she asked, disappointed. "Parrot?"

Spit shook his head, bemused.

Charlie looked unimpressed. *"Where's Fliss?"*

Betty hesitated, glancing at Spit. "She . . . well. She got a bit kidnapped, by Spit's crew. So did Willow."

"*Kidnapped?*" Charlie looked at Spit, confused. "I thought you said he was with us?"

"He is," said Betty. "But it's . . . complicated." She regarded the pirate boy curiously. Spit had only gone along with her plan because she had threatened to make him vanish. They weren't friends—he'd said so himself. But he'd done more than provide a distraction; he'd helped them back there.

Spit pursed his lips, saying nothing.

"Poor Willow and Fliss!" Charlie breathed. "You mean . . . the three of you came all the way out here for me?"

"Of *course* we did," said Betty.

"What do the pirates want with them?" Charlie asked.

"Well, the pirates took *The Traveling Bag*," Betty explained. "Only they didn't realize that Fliss and Willow were on it, invisible. I'd made us all disappear."

She trailed off, a horrible realization seeping into her as she saw Charlie's expression change, becoming stricken. Betty's eyes went to the dolls in her lap, then to Spit, then back to Charlie. A wave of panic washed over her. Both of them were staring directly into her eyes. She wasn't hidden at all.

"Oh no," she croaked, grabbing the dolls from Charlie's

lap. In the darkness, she hadn't seen, or thought to check. "No, no, *no!*"

"Betty?" Charlie whispered. "I . . . I'm really sorry. I didn't know . . ."

Betty gasped, lifting the dolls to the light. It didn't matter now if Spit saw them. Everything had already gone wrong. She corrected herself. Even *more* wrong.

The two halves of the key on the outer doll were no longer aligned.

"You twisted them, didn't you?" Betty asked. An image of Charlie wringing her hands in her lap flashed before Betty's eyes. Only, she hadn't been wringing her hands after all.

One turn, counterclockwise . . .

"I d-didn't know pirates had Fliss and Willow," Charlie stuttered, her eyes huge and panicking. "I was just scared, and I wanted to see you so badly, I—"

Betty's voice shook. "How long ago was it? A minute? A few?" Her mind buzzed like a beehive. She gripped the dolls, about to twist the outer halves back in place, but something stopped her. "It can't have been long," she whispered, mostly to herself. "But what if . . . what if that was enough time for Willow and Fliss to be found?"

"There would've been crew on your boat, guarding

it," Spit said gravely. "The boat's small. They could well have been captured already."

"I'm sorry," Charlie repeated, beginning to cry again. "It's my fault if they're catched!"

"No." Betty squeezed her sister's hand, even though it wouldn't make either of them feel any better—or help Fliss and Willow. After everything Charlie had been through of *course* she would have wanted to see Betty and reassure herself. "You weren't to know."

The dolls rattled in Betty's hand as it shook with fear and shock. *Why* had she allowed Fliss and Willow to leave *The Sorcerer's Compass* at all? Even if they'd been stranded here without a boat, it would have been better than being split up—and two of them in the clutches of pirates. If she made Willow and Fliss vanish again now, what would happen?

Pirates are a superstitious lot . . .

Could it work to their advantage? she wondered desperately. *Could Fliss and Willow stage a little haunting?* Or were they under lock and key already? If so, they wouldn't be able to slip away, unseen or not. There was just no way of knowing.

"We have to get to them," said Betty. "Right now." She grabbed Spit's arm and shook it. "You have to help me."

He stared back at her almost pityingly. "What do you

expect will happen? That we'll turn up and Ronia will just . . . *hand* them over?" He waved at the shipwreck. "There's more chance of Rusty handing you his treasure!"

"There has to be something we can do," Betty insisted. "You *know* them—you know how they work! There must be a way we can trick them—"

"Whoa!" Spit shook her off, his cheeks flaming. "Do you know what you're saying? No one gets away with tricking Ronia, you hear me? No one! Least of all not one of her own crew. If Ronia finds out I helped you, it'll be my bones up on that mast next."

Betty forced down a sob. Without Spit, any plan for tackling Ronia and her crew was doomed. If only she could persuade him. Not for the first time, she wished she had even a scrap of Fliss's charm.

"Oh, forget it," she snapped. "We have to go, with or without you. We can't just sit here doing nothing—we don't have time! Willow's father doesn't have time!"

"Go where?" Charlie asked, wiping her eyes. "To the pirate ship?"

"Exactly. Go where?" Spit repeated. "Even if you row all night, you won't make it in time."

His words sent alarm spiraling in Betty's head. "What do you mean?"

"They'll be off plundering at dawn," he exclaimed.

"And if they've found Willow and Fliss, they'll be going, too."

"No," said Betty, horror-struck at the thought. Though she had considered the possibility of the girls being caught up in the pirates' skullduggery, she hadn't thought it would happen so soon. If the Rusty Scuttlers took off into the unknown with Fliss and Willow, there was no telling what fate might befall them. Or how Betty would ever catch them. "We *have* to get to them. I'm not losing any more sisters."

She pointed a finger at the rocks. "We're leaving now. So if you're not going to help us, you'd better get off this boat and swim back to your crow's-nest."

"I can't go back there yet!" Spit spluttered. "Those wisps might have vanished, but they'll still be riled up under there. I've never seen them that angry before." He cast a fearful look at *The Sorcerer's Compass*. "No one holds a grudge like Rusty, you know. Except perhaps Ronia."

"Are you *scared*?" asked Charlie, sounding disappointed. "I thought pirates didn't get scared. What kind of pirate *are* you?"

Spit glared. "The kind who plans to die old."

"Who's Ronia?" Charlie asked.

"The captain," said Betty. "And a right scary one she is, too."

"Has *she* got a parrot?"

"No," Betty answered. "If she did, it was probably eaten by her awful cat."

"*Oh*," said Charlie, brightening a tad. "A cat!" She frowned suddenly. "Betty, where's Hoppit?"

Betty gulped. "Sorry, Charlie. He's with Fliss. I'm sure she's keeping him safe." *If she's safe herself*, she thought miserably.

She picked up the oars, trying one last time. "Make your mind up, Spit. It's a long way to those rocks and I could really use your help. Are you coming or not? I can hide you from Ronia. She won't know—"

Spit snorted. "Like you hid Fliss and Willow? No thanks. They'll see the boat coming for a start, you know."

"Just go, then," Betty snapped, close to being overwhelmed with exhaustion. "Take your chances with Rusty and the rest of the wisps!"

Spit glared at her, his nostrils flaring with angry breaths.

"Where is the pirates' ship?" Charlie asked.

"Behind those rocks," said Betty, still scowling at Spit.

"You mean *those* rocks?" Charlie said, pointing. "Where that boat is coming from?"

"Boat?" Immediately, Betty lowered her oar and stood up, gazing into the darkness. Sure enough, a shadowy shape was moving out from behind the rocks, a small lantern bobbing in front. It was, unmistakably, a boat . . . but not the pirates'.

"Is that . . . *our* boat?" Charlie asked, leaning over the side eagerly. "Betty, I think it is! It's *The Traveling Bag*!"

Betty clutched at her sister, hardly daring to hope. But the more she stared, the closer it came, and there was no mistaking it really was their very own little fishing boat. "I don't believe it," she murmured, her heart soaring. "It's coming this way. Looks like Fliss and Willow really did manage to steal the boat!"

To her surprise, Spit grabbed both oars and began to row.

"What?" he said indignantly. "If that *is* your sister, then this is your chance to get away. And the quicker you do, the quicker I can pretend I never saw any of this happen." He spat into the water. "Wisp catchers, kidnaps, disappearing dolls . . . rotten luck, all of you!"

Luck, Betty thought. Perhaps the approaching boat meant it had changed at last. But then a little doubt pricked her like a pin. *What if . . . ?*

"You didn't raise the sail," she said. "What if Ronia has sent pirates back in our boat to find out why?"

"I doubt she'd use your boat for that," Spit replied.

"Then again," he added darkly, "with Ronia, you never know."

As it drew nearer, the light at the front of the boat flashed off, then on again.

"It's seen us," said Spit, flashing the light on the little rowboat back. "It's heading this way."

He rowed wordlessly, the *shush-shush* of oars through water and the occasional chattering of Charlie's teeth the only sounds. Betty put her arm around Charlie, pulling her close. If it was Ronia, there was nowhere for them to hide now they'd been spotted.

"There's someone on deck," Spit said, craning his neck to look over his shoulder.

Betty snatched one of the oars from Spit and began to row as hard as she could. She could see the figure, too. Pixie-short hair, long, graceful limbs . . . it could only be Fliss!

"It *is* her!" Betty exclaimed in amazement. "They've done it! They escaped somehow." A vision of Ronia sailing away plundering on her ship came into Betty's mind, followed by Fliss sneaking across *The Traveling Bag* to push an unsuspecting pirate overboard. However it had happened, this was one story Betty couldn't wait to hear!

And just beyond Fliss stood a smaller, disheveled silhouette, barely visible in the dim light. *Willow.*

For a moment, Betty was so overcome with joy she wanted to hug everyone—even Spit. Betty couldn't see Fliss's face yet, but she knew she must be smiling as widely as Betty was now. She had her sisters back. And Willow still had time to try and save her father. Heck, perhaps Fliss could even charm Spit into taking Willow to the Winking Witch! All Betty knew, very firmly, was that she was taking her sisters home to Granny and Father. Everything was going to be all right.

And then . . .

And then they were closer, and a shaft of moonlight shone across Fliss's face. She wasn't smiling.

"Betty?" Charlie whispered. "What's wrong with Fliss?"

"They're not alone," Betty said, her voice trembling as she suddenly realized what she was seeing.

"What do you mean?" said Charlie, peering into the distance. "I can't see no one else, just Fliss and Willow on deck."

"Exactly," said Betty. Her dread was like icy tentacles, popping the little bubble of hope she'd felt only moments ago. "So if they're on deck, who's steering the boat?"

A white shape shifted by Fliss's leg, but this time it wasn't moonlight. This was something stealthy, something real and feline. Which meant that the person steering the boat had to be . . .

"Ronia?" Betty whispered. "What's going on here?" She turned to Spit. His face, which had been flushed with temper just minutes ago, was now draining of color. "Is Ronia releasing them? Or are they prisoners? I don't understand!"

"You think I do?" he retorted.

"She's *your* captain!" Betty said desperately.

"A captain I've lied to," Spit snapped, raking a hand through his hair. His eyes were wild and afraid. "Just shut up a minute—I need to think how I'm going to get us out of this. If that's even possible."

The Traveling Bag drew closer until the two boats were only a leap apart. By now, Fliss had rushed to the side and was leaning over, but for once it was not to be sick. Instead, her gaze was fixed on Charlie, relief etched on her face.

"Charlie! I can't believe it's really you!"

"It *is* me!" Charlie yelled back, grinning. "Betty saved me!"

"Let *me* do the talking," Spit hissed. "Be quiet until we know what's going on."

Charlie tutted. "You ain't even a real pirate," she said sulkily, but she folded her arms and kept quiet.

Spit tensed as Ronia emerged from the wheelhouse. She strode purposefully toward them and paused by the side of the boat, giving a low whistle. Bandit shot along the deck, climbed her leg, and perched on her shoulder, purring.

"Well, well," the pirate captain drawled, looking over them coolly. Her eyes flashed as keenly as the cat on her shoulder's, and Betty suddenly felt rather like a mouse that was being toyed with. Ronia's gaze rested on Betty. "Not so dead after all."

"Got her for you," Spit said, gesturing to Betty and puffing out his chest. "Gave me a right runaround she did, but I outsmarted her in the end."

Ronia gave him a hard stare that was just long enough to make him squirm. "Big, burly looters?" she said coolly. "It seems you and I both have some thinking to do, Spit."

"Th-thinking?"

"About where your loyalties lie." Her tone dropped further, becoming icy. "Luckily, we're going to have plenty of time on our hands."

"Why's that?" Spit asked, appearing decidedly nervous now.

"Because we're going on a little journey," Ronia replied. "To a place that could be very, very useful for the

Rusty Scuttlers." She looked sideways at Fliss. "If it really exists."

Betty's mouth dropped open. Surely Fliss hadn't told Ronia about the secret island? Or had Ronia discovered the mysterious map and worked it out for herself? From the way Fliss was hanging her head, Betty was pretty sure it had been her sister's doing. Either way, Ronia knew . . . and it was plain the idea of it excited her. But the thought of going on "a little journey" with Ronia was the last thing Betty wanted and—from the haunted, wretched look on the little girl's face—she knew Willow felt the same.

"All aboard," Ronia said with a thin smile. She reached out and took Charlie's hand, then hauled her onto *The Traveling Bag.*

Charlie gawped at her, awestruck. "Meddling magpies! Now *that's* what I call a pirate!"

Bandit hissed at her from Ronia's shoulder, flicking his tail. Undeterred, Charlie blew him a kiss, then rushed into Fliss's arms. Ronia's bejeweled fingers reached for Betty, but instead of taking her hand, they encircled her wrist, as tight as an iron band.

"I'm watching you," she said so quietly that her lips barely moved.

Betty tried to wrench her hand out of the pirate's

grasp, but Ronia's grip was like a manacle. She pulled Betty onto *The Traveling Bag*, then released her like she was something nasty caught up in a fishing net. Betty rubbed her sore wrist, wondering what else Ronia had discovered. Had she seen the wisp?

Rushing to Fliss's side, Betty grabbed her sister's sleeve, unsure whether to hug her or shake her. "Fliss," she croaked. "What happened? Did *you* tell her about the island? If it's real, if it *does* exist, someone like Ronia could ruin everything for Willow!"

Fliss embraced her fiercely, her breath warm against Betty's ear. "I did what I *had* to do. I made a bargain with her."

Chapter Twenty-One

The Winking Witch

"**I** CAN'T BELIEVE YOU MADE A DEAL with her," Betty whispered, her words as sour as her breath. "*And* showed her the map! She's a pirate, and you let her con you." She glowered at the wheelhouse. Ronia was inside at the wheel, but the door—and Ronia's ears, no doubt—remained open.

Next to Betty, Fliss shifted, trying not to disturb a snoring Charlie, snuggled up with Hoppit in her collar. The three of them—and Willow—had been forced to sit out on the cold deck, huddling together for warmth under Spit's watch. Though Betty was exhausted, she had managed only a few snatches of sleep over the past few hours since Ronia had set sail. On the horizon, the first stirrings of dawn light were visible.

"Well, excuse me if I've never met any pirates before," Fliss said huffily. "I thought they had a code of honor, but obviously not! Can you please stop going on about it? It's done now."

"Honor!" Betty scoffed. *"Really?"*

"It was the only thing I had of value," Fliss said in a quiet voice. "I heard Ronia saying they need places to hide themselves—and their loot. It seemed a small price to pay to escape!"

"Or perhaps you just gave her four prisoners instead of two," Betty shot back. Because they *hadn't* escaped, she thought now, uneasy. They were still firmly in Ronia's grip, on a boat that was under her control. And there was no way of knowing whether the pirate captain intended to release them or whether there was a more sinister plan in store for them.

Fliss gave an infuriated sniff. "I wouldn't have had to make a deal with her if you hadn't messed up with the dolls! Luckily, the pirates manning *The Traveling Bag* were too busy seeing what they could pocket to notice how we appeared out of thin air. And then they blamed each other for not searching the boat properly!"

"I already explained about the dolls," Betty said,

annoyed. "It was an accident." She crossed her arms. "And keep your voice down. You've blabbed enough already—we don't need her finding out about the dolls, too."

They both quieted down as Charlie shifted in Fliss's lap, grunting in her sleep. When Fliss spoke next, her voice was low and thick with emotion. "You weren't there, Betty. I was scared, and Willow started looking really strange, like she was about to collapse." Her eyes sparkled with angry tears. "I did the only thing I could think of to help us get away."

"Only we haven't gotten away," Betty muttered, though some of the anger had left her now. Until this moment, she hadn't been fully convinced that the hidden island actually existed—but something about Ronia's willingness to look for it changed things. Not to mention everything else Betty had seen since leaving Crowstone, which was certainly enough to make her believe in the impossible. As guilty as it made her feel to admit it, Betty's only concern had been to find Charlie. She'd never really imagined that they had a chance of getting Willow to the island. Now they were heading off in search of it with a conniving, murderous pirate for company, whether they wanted to or not. And Betty definitely did not. All she wanted was to go home, to Granny, Father, the musty old Poacher's Pocket—and even Oi.

They sat in miserable silence, each feeling as wretched as the other. Willow was sitting a little way away, her hair trailing over her face as she stared into her lap. She seemed to be feverish, half in a daze, and Betty was starting to worry that she was sickening. Finally, she broke her silence and nudged Fliss.

"Willow does look ill," she said. "Her skin . . . it's really pasty."

Charlie turned over in Fliss's lap, scowling. She was always terribly grumpy as soon as she woke up. "She don't look no different to me," she said with a yawn and a stretch. Hoppit nosed his way out from her collar, yawning and stretching, too.

"She *doesn't* look *any* different," Betty corrected. "I asked her if she was all right a few minutes ago, but she just kept repeating everything about her father and getting to the island, over and over."

"I'd feel pretty wretched if our father were about to be hanged," Fliss murmured. "Or perhaps seasickness is catching. Excuse me." She shuffled out from under Charlie and leaned over the side of the boat, gulping at the air. Within seconds, Spit appeared, his forehead crinkling with concern. He offered Fliss a flask of water, but she waved him away and he skulked back to the wheelhouse doorway.

Inside, Ronia stood at the wheel and was studying

Willow's map with interest through the hagstone. On the roof of the wheelhouse, Bandit was snoozing with one eye open and trained in Charlie's—or rather Hoppit's —direction.

Betty watched the pirate captain through narrowed eyes, her stomach curdling at the sight of Ronia's hands on Willow's precious magical map. To Ronia, she felt sure the map and the island were just a means to fill her pockets. For Willow, the map meant saving the life of someone she loved. Would she get that chance, or would Ronia steal that from her, too?

"You don't trust her, do you?" said Charlie. She was sitting up now, sucking one of her pigtails with her eyes on Ronia.

"Nope," Betty admitted, thinking of the things Spit had confided to her about his captain: poison . . . pillaging . . . possibly wrecking ships before stealing children away. And then, of course, there were the bones swinging from the foremast. But she wasn't about to voice any of this to Charlie. "Do you?"

Charlie shrugged. "When we got on the boat, she said she'd let us go."

"I'm not sure how much we can count on a pirate's word," Betty murmured, thinking back to the moments after they'd boarded *The Traveling Bag*.

"If the map's genuine, I'll release you," Ronia had told them, her green eyes glinting keenly as Spit had stoked the boiler. She cast her eyes through the hagstone at Willow's map. "And from the way this witch is winking at me, I'd say things are looking very promising indeed. Let's pay her a little visit."

For Charlie's sake, Betty hadn't dared to ask what would happen if the map *wasn't* genuine.

"Well, she made sure we all got fed, even Hoppit," Charlie added now, scooting over to huddle next to Willow. "That's got to count for something, right?"

"*Hmm,*" said Betty, rolling her eyes. Charlie could be persuaded of most things when it came to her tummy. Privately, Betty had other thoughts. Such as why Ronia had decided to journey to the island without any of her crew members—except Spit—with her. Could it be that she was planning to double-cross the Rusty Scuttlers and keep any loot for herself?

"Charlie's right," said Fliss, flopping back down beside her and wiping her mouth. "Surely Ronia wouldn't waste good food on us if she didn't mean to keep us alive?"

"Well, we're not much use to her dead, are we?" Betty whispered fiercely. "And I'm glad the two of you are so optimistic. I mean, Charlie's six, so she's got an excuse, but I thought you'd be smarter than that."

Fliss bristled. "Smarter than *what?*"

"Think about it! At the very least, she's keeping us alive until there's proof the island really *does* exist. And none of us will know until we see it," said Betty. "Including Ronia. Until then, she's making sure she's still got us as backup, to trade or sell or whatever she decides to do with us. And four prisoners are going to cooperate with her a lot more if they're not hungry."

"Perhaps we *shouldn't* cooperate then," Fliss said in a low voice. Her dark eyes hardened. "There are four of us and only one of her."

"What are you saying?" Betty asked. "That we try to overpower her?"

Fliss took a shaky breath. "Could we?"

Betty glanced through the wheelhouse at Ronia, her heart quickening. *Could they?* The idea was tantalizing . . . and yet . . .

And yet . . . "It wouldn't work," she said softly. "You've never been in a fight in your life, and Willow and Charlie are just children." She shook her head. "Charlie might be a scrapper, but Willow's in no state to fight off a flea. Not to mention Ronia has a cutlass as long as her leg—and she knows how to use it. There might be more of us, but numbers don't mean anything." She sighed. "And then there's him."

They both eyed Spit, who'd taken the wheel while Ronia pored over the map.

"He helped us once, but there's no guarantee he'll do it again," said Betty. She felt a strange little twist deep in her gut as she recalled Spit's story. "He's loyal—at the end of the day, the Rusty Scuttlers are all he's got. We mustn't forget that."

"You're right." Fliss sighed wearily, shaking her head. "It was a silly idea. I suppose I just wanted to think of a way to make up for getting us into all this."

"Well, maybe you could do that by getting Spit on our side," Betty muttered. "Be a bit nicer to him. He's sweet on you, you know."

Fliss shuddered. "Well, I'm not sweet on *him* or his revolting habit."

"I know," Betty said. She glanced grimly at Ronia's cutlass once more and the dagger strapped to her boot. "But if we go up against Ronia, we'll need all the help we can get."

Her gaze drifted to the glass lantern propped by the wheel. The cloth she had thrown over it had been tossed aside—no doubt in the pirates' search of the boat—but surprisingly the wisp remained inside, barely visible in the brightening daylight except for the faintest of flutterings. Judging by how close Ronia and Spit were to it, neither of them knew what it really was. Betty wondered how Ronia would react to that knowledge—and Spit, for that matter. He was certainly familiar with wisps—she'd seen that back at the shipwreck—and it hadn't made him fear them any less. As for Ronia—was there a chance that her superstitions might even lead her to abandon *The Traveling Bag?*

Betty frowned, glancing from the wisp to Willow. Was it a coincidence that, as Willow weakened, the wisp did, too? Unsettling thoughts hooked into her like claws. If it *was* Willow's mother, did this mean she was moving on? Or maybe the wisp attack on the marshes had something to do with it—neither had been quite the same since. There was certainly a marked difference to the playful, darting thing that had entered the Poacher's Pocket. It was now little more than a dying moth.

"Yo ho!" Spit cried from the bow of the boat. "Land ahoy!"

Betty and Fliss got up and joined him, rubbing warmth into their stiff limbs as they stared across the water. Through the early morning sunlight, they saw a small, craggy island with a large rock at its center. They drew nearer, glimpsing several rock pools sprouting seaweed and alive with crabs and, between them, a little sandy cove just wide enough to moor *The Traveling Bag.*

"This isn't the Winking Witch, surely?" Betty said doubtfully as they clambered off the boat and landed on the sand.

"It is," Spit said. "It's exactly where the map said. Right, Cap'n?"

"Hmm," said Ronia, surveying the island through narrowed eyes. Bandit, who had leaped onto her shoulder as they'd left the boat, now jumped down and began investigating.

"Where's the witch?" Charlie demanded. "It just looks like a load of old rocks to me."

"I think . . . *that* must be it." Fliss pointed uncertainly to the large rock in the middle. "I mean her." She took a deep breath. "Oh, to be on dry land again—*oh!*" A wave of water had surged over the sand and soaked her feet. "Darn it," she grumbled.

"Don't look like a witch to me," said Charlie, her bottom lip jutting out in disappointment.

"Perhaps there's something around the other side," said Betty, feeling her hopes slipping dangerously away. How could this pile of rocks possibly link to the figure inked on Willow's map? And if the Winking Witch didn't exist, where did that leave them? With nothing but a fairy tale to follow? She tried to sneak a look at the map, but Ronia was keeping it tight to her chest.

"That way," Ronia commanded, herding them in front of her like sheep.

With no choice except to obey, they crunched over the sand. Ahead of Fliss and Betty, Charlie and Willow walked hand in hand. Behind them, Ronia trod so soundlessly that Betty felt even more unnerved by her presence and had to stop herself from looking over her shoulder. They scrambled over shallow rock pools around to the other side of the tiny island, and already Betty could see that the hulking rock appeared to be taking on a new form now that they were viewing it from a different angle.

"Whoa," said Spit, who was a little way ahead. "Come and take a look." He reached out to help Charlie, and then Fliss, over the uneven rocks. After a slight hesitation and a nudge from Betty, Fliss placed her hand in his and allowed him to help her. Spit's cheeks flushed a deep red, and Betty couldn't help but notice that he held on to Fliss's hand a little longer than was necessary.

"There," said Spit once they were all standing in the shadow of the towering rock.

Betty gazed up and gasped, feeling a tingle of excitement and recognition. She could see it now. While the depiction of the Winking Witch had been rather elaborate on Willow's map, showing a crooked, old woman with a long, black cloak, the real thing was very different. From the other side of the cove, the rock appeared ordinary, with no special features to mark it out. But from here . . .

"The witch," Charlie breathed, shrinking back.

It was not so much a figure as a head and shoulders. The weatherworn stone snaked back and forth, creating a shape that was distinctly like the profile of a face. A hooked nose curved over a gap that had a small piece of rock hanging down like a single tooth in a mouth. Below that, another shelf of rock jutted out to look like a chin. A sprig of grass sprouting from it gave the unfortunate appearance of a hairy wart. At the top of the face, a sliver of rock overhung like a shelf, while another resting on top tapered to a point. Together they looked like a wide-brimmed witch's hat.

But it was the eye that Betty couldn't look away from. Above the nose, there was a single hole bored through the rock, which the sun streamed through.

"So now what?" said Ronia, unrolling Willow's map impatiently. "According to this, the island should be over there to the northwest." She gazed through the hagstone out to sea. Her voice was icy. "I don't see anything, and yet . . ." She glanced at the map again, clenching her jaw. "And yet she's winking at me, the old hag!"

Betty turned to Willow, aware of Ronia's thinning patience and the need to work out the link between the

Winking Witch and the invisible island. "Willow?" she asked, keeping her voice gentle. She hadn't imagined it: Willow *was* looking peaked. Her skin was waxy, and there was a sheen of sweat on her forehead and upper lip. But she seemed to have perked up a little now that they'd reached the Winking Witch. "Any ideas? Anything your father or Saul might have said before they went out on their boat that day?"

"I . . . I don't know," Willow said, swaying on her feet a little. "I feel . . . I can't remember."

"Sit her down," said Fliss. "She's worn-out, poor thing." She guided Willow and Charlie to sit by one of the rock pools and rubbed Willow's back while murmuring to her comfortingly. At the next rock pool along from them, Bandit was watching some small fish darting about in the water. His tail flicked from side to side, and every now and then, he plunged his paw into the water and yowled with frustration when he missed.

Suddenly aware that Ronia was standing right beside her, Betty's sense of unease deepened. She could see the tension in the pirate woman, her frustration building as things didn't go her way. It was a dangerous combination.

"Enough time wasting," Ronia snapped. "How do I get to the island?"

"That's what I'm trying to figure out," Betty retorted,

unable to keep her dislike of the pirate out of her voice. Fear was making her careless. If she couldn't figure it out —or worse, it had all been for nothing and there *was* no island, just a legend that had led them to a pile of rocks —then what did that mean for them? She certainly knew what it meant for Willow's father. Ronia's stare became fiercer.

"I-I mean . . . I don't know," Betty stammered. "The only clue is the map."

"It's no clearer now that we're here." Ronia stared through the hagstone in every direction. "There's nothing."

"This place must link to it somehow," said Betty. Privately, she was starting to think Ronia could be right. It was only the thought of securing their freedom—and getting answers for Willow—which forced her to keep going. "Why else would the witch on the map wink?" She went past Ronia and picked her way over the rocks, driftwood, and bits of sea glass. She set off, meaning to circle the witch. With a couple of steps, its features shifted, almost like the face was frowning. With another step, the daylight shining through the witch's eye was obscured by an overhanging rock.

"So *that's* how she winks," Betty murmured, stepping back, then forward again to observe the spooky illusion. But it still brought no answers, only despair. Could the strange island have been a hoax all along? Could the map just be some kind of clever trick? If none of it was real, then Willow's hopes were for nothing—and quite possibly, her mother's life had been lost needlessly. And what of the Widdershinses? Spit had told her what Ronia was capable of when people crossed her. Were Betty and her sisters about to experience her wrath for themselves?

She sat on the lip of the large, round rock next to the witch, trying to calm her thoughts. The top of the boulder had eroded over the years, for it dipped inward like a bowl. An array of junk had collected inside, no doubt washed up in heavy storms or blown by fierce winds.

Spit crunched over the sand toward her. "Looks like someone had a sense of humor."

Betty turned. "Huh?"

He nodded to an old broomstick that had been propped up next to the witch's chin.

"Oh," said Betty, her voice flat.

"Anything useful in the cauldron?" Spit stopped beside the boulder, picking through the bits and pieces.

"Doesn't look like it," Betty replied, barely giving the items a second glance. She wasn't in the mood to look through a load of flotsam and jetsam or make chitchat about broomsticks. She was scared now, of everything that rested on this. Even though they had Charlie, there was still no guarantee they were going to get home—Ronia was in no hurry to let them go. What was she planning for them all? On top of this, now that Betty had stopped worrying about Charlie, she was afraid for Willow. Not only did the girl look ill, but also her chance to save her father was ticking away.

Then something about what Spit had said caught, like a fishing hook. "Wait . . . *what* did you say?"

"I said anything useful—"

"In the cauldron," Betty finished, leaping off the boulder. She stood back as Spit poked about in the rocky bowl. The *cauldron!* She felt a tingle of excitement in her tummy—but just as quickly, it vanished when an eerily strange sound cut across the air from above, shocking them all.

THE CROWSTONE CHRONICLES

The Crone, the Raven, and the Labyrinth: Part III

Days stretched into weeks, and then into months after Luck vanished in search of Fortune and the labyrinth. Their father had grown thin with worry, but Hope kept him going and, in the meantime, had taken up his father's trade and was proving a worthy apprentice. Slowly, business began trickling back, and while they were far from rich, they were no longer poor.

Yet Hope could not forget his brothers. He was sure that something had happened to them, and he longed to bring them home. But as Hope was all he had left, his father would not agree to let him leave. Then one day, a year after Luck had sailed away, the boat washed up in the harbor again, empty except for two black feathers. Hope begged his father to let him search for his lost brothers, and finally, the old man relented.

Hope took the boat and the two feathers and

rowed out over the marshes in search of the crone. When she saw him coming, the crone's temper soured once again for she remembered his brothers and expected Hope to be as rude and thoughtless as they had been. So she took a breath of cloud and blew a terrible marsh mist that caused Hope to lose all sense of direction. His boat hit a rock and sank. Leaping into the water, Hope swam the rest of the way. When he finally made it, having swallowed half the marsh, he still greeted the witch politely, acknowledging that he had arrived quite uninvited.

"Why do you try?" asked the raven by the witch's side. "Why do you try?"

"Because I'm Hope," he explained. "And I must find my brothers. I'm all our father has left."

The crone nodded, passing Hope a hagstone.

"Look through, look through," the raven told him, and Hope held the stone to his eye to see the island for the first time.

The old crone silently offered him the cauldron.

"Take one, choose one," said the raven.

Hope noticed how the crone's arms shook under the weight of the cauldron. "Let me hold this while I decide," he said. "For you look tired."

The crone gladly handed over the heavy cauldron.

"I have no need for shoes," Hope said, picking through the items. "Mine are old, but dear to me because my father made them and my brothers wore them before me. The egg is beautiful, but somewhere a creature must be looking for it. The dagger and cape are worthless without my brothers to share them. As for the lucky rabbit's foot, when I find my brothers, I'll have all the luck I need. But"—he paused, checking his pockets—"a reel of yarn is always useful!"

The crone nodded, pleased with Hope's wisdom and kindness. Hope tied the yarn to his belt. He went on, "But it's only right that I should give you something in return. I don't have much, but I'd be happy to share a tune with you to brighten your day?"

Again, the witch nodded. Hope whistled a little tune he had thought up when working long hours making shoes, which kept him full of cheer and made the time pass quickly. Warmed by his generosity, the crone felt sorry for sinking Hope's vessel.

From the shoreline, she collected a large

seashell and rubbed it. Before Hope's astonished eyes, it grew to the size of a small boat. To his surprise, the two black feathers he had been carrying stretched to be as tall and strong as he was and were sturdy enough to use as oars. So it was in an enormous shell, with feathers for oars, that Hope rowed off in search of the labyrinth with a helpful breeze sent by the crone to speed up his journey. When he arrived at the island, he spied a rough path on the cliff's edge and looked for the best place to reach it.

"I knew this yarn would come in useful," Hope said to himself. He cut a length of it against the sharp edge of the shell, securing one end to a branch and the other to a barnacle on the shell boat with plenty of the string left to spare. He began to climb, sliding down one step for every two he took. He was perhaps a quarter of the way up the cliff when he wondered if the string could help ease his struggles.

"How strange," he exclaimed, for when he unraveled it, he was surprised to find a loop at the end. When he threw it, it snared a jutting root, and he found it bore his weight comfortably. He made his way up the cliff, lassoing a rock here and a branch there, and in no time at all, he had reached the top.

There he came across the old stone well with the bucket floating in its depths.

What a shame, Hope thought. *Perhaps I could collect the bucket and tie the yarn to its handle so no one ever needs to leave here thirsty again.* To his surprise, he saw an old fishing hook on the side of the well. He tied this to one end of the yarn, and the other end to the spindle, then lowered the hook into the well. At once, a voice called out from below:

"Oh, please do not catch me with your hook! For I am not really a fish but a man."

"Fortune!" Hope exclaimed, for he would know his brother's voice anywhere. "Swim into the bucket and I will pull you out."

So Fortune swam into the bucket, and Hope hooked the handle and wound the spindle. Up came the bucket and with it Fortune, now a large fish with gleaming silver scales. The two brothers laughed and cried and shared their stories of the strange, old crone and her raven. Then Fortune explained that Luck had vanished into the caves, never to be seen again.

"We will find Luck, and then a way to break this curse and turn you back into a man," Hope promised Fortune, and he unhooked the bucket with his fish brother inside and set off for the cave.

Pausing outside the cave's entrance, he noticed that he still had plenty of string fastened to his belt and it was showing no signs of running out. It was now he realized that this was no ordinary yarn, for it seemed to replenish itself at his will, as well as being extraordinarily strong.

Guessing that the caves were vast and treacherous, Hope decided to leave a trail. He tied one end of the yarn to the hagstone and left it at the cave entrance, leaving the rest to unravel as he explored. That way, if he got lost, he could safely retrace his steps at any time. He was about to step into the caves when a small voice called out to him.

"Please, take me with you."

Hope looked around for the tiny voice but saw nothing except a bog beetle clinging to the rocks.

"My brothers and sisters went into the caves, but I was left behind," it said. "My legs are small, and it would take me a lifetime to catch up."

Fortune urged Hope to leave the beetle behind.

"You already have me to carry, Brother. Why add to your burden?"

"Because we know what it is like to lose a brother," Hope replied as he lifted the bog beetle onto his shoulder and stepped into the caves. Once inside, to repay Hope's kindness, the little beetle glowed so brightly that the caves were lit up and he could see his way.

Hope trudged through the dark, damp caves. He sang to himself to stay cheerful, but the voice that echoed back was not his own.

"That's Luck's voice!" Fortune exclaimed. But no matter how much they called or where they looked, Luck could not be found. Hope realized that, just as Fortune had survived in the well as a fish, Luck had become an echo to survive in the caves. He continued to sing so that his brother's voice could follow him, and though the journey took many wrong turns, the sturdy length of yarn meant he was never truly lost.

On the third day, when the two brothers were hoarse from singing and chilled from damp, they saw a brightly lit cavern ahead. In its center was an old lantern of bog beetles and a single shoe, scuffed and stained with sea salt. Hope knew then that this was his foolish brother's. Hope returned the beetle to its siblings and together they glowed even brighter than before.

"You cannot go back through the caves," they told him. "The only way is forward, to reach the heart of the island. We will light your way out." And so, collecting the lantern and the shoe, Hope continued until the bog beetles' glow faded in the bright light of the sun, for at last, he had found his way out to the center of the island. Here, he freed the beetles, who were full of gratitude.

Thanking them, Hope turned to find that the enchanted yarn was no longer trailing through the caves. Instead, it was neatly looped on his belt, and the hagstone given to him by the crone rolled to a stop at his feet. He put it in his pocket and was about to go on with his journey when he realized that, out in the open, the echo of Luck's voice could no longer follow him.

Thinking quickly, he called his brother's name into the caves and captured the echo of Luck's voice in the empty shoe. On they journeyed, and the island became stranger. They passed trees that dripped with glittering coins and waterfalls that rained jewels, and every time they did, Fortune and Luck begged Hope to collect them. But Hope was wiser than his brothers and did not touch anything that did not belong to him.

Reaching the center of the island, Hope found a raven in a vast nest of treasure.

"You may leave with whatever you can carry," the bird told him. "But once you do, the island will vanish and you can never return."

"My hands are full," Hope replied. "I have all the riches I came for. All I ask is for my brothers to return to their rightful forms."

With a shake of its feathers, the raven granted his wish.

And this was the story of how three brothers set out to save their family from ruin, but only one returned home with Fortune, Luck, and riches beyond compare.

Chapter Twenty-Two

The Raven

THE HARSH, RASPING NOISE CAME AGAIN, making Betty's nerves crackle. Immediately, Ronia whipped out her cutlass.

Betty froze at the horrid sound. It was unearthly and chilling, but suddenly she had a very good idea of what it might be. She shielded her eyes from the sun and looked up to the shelf of rock that formed the brim of the witch's hat. Something scuffled up there, and moments later a strand of seaweed was tossed over the edge. It landed on Ronia's blade, neatly slicing into two. Then a large, black bird appeared over the rim of rock and peered down inquisitively at them.

"A raven!" Charlie exclaimed, appearing at Betty's side. "Oh. What a *beauty!*"

"Odd that it's all alone out here, though," said Betty. "They're normally seen in pairs."

"They're unlucky, either alone or in a pair," said Fliss, watching the bird warily from where she was sitting with Willow. "That's what Granny always says."

"I thought that was magpies," said Spit.

Fliss shrugged. "She says it about all of them: crows, ravens, and magpies. She even has this funny little rhyme about them."

"One for marsh mist, two for sorrow," Betty said softly, recounting the old superstition Granny often repeated. The bird tilted its head to listen, its eyes firmly on Betty. "Three, you'll journey far tomorrow." With a funny little jolt, she remembered the three crows perching on the sign outside the Poacher's Pocket on the night Willow had arrived. Marsh mist, sorrow, and a journey. All three had happened.

"Didn't Granny make up another version when she was drunk?" Fliss interjected, joining Betty now. "How did it go? Oh, yes! 'One for whiskey, two for rum, three for down the hatch in one—'"

"Shut up," Ronia said, silencing Fliss with a scathing look. "Speaking of hatches, you talk way too much—"

A rasping shriek cut her off. It was so loud that Ronia raised her cutlass in one quick movement, narrowly missing Spit's nose. And then came a voice. An ancient, creaking voice that wasn't human.

"So . . . you're looking for the island?"

"Whoa!" Spit cried, diving behind the rocky cauldron. "Did that bird just *speak*?"

"Yes," Betty answered, her mouth suddenly dry. Thoughts uncurled in her head like a hedgehog waking up after the winter. Part of her had known it, been *expecting* it, from the moment the bird had appeared.

"Get back," Spit urged, cowering behind the cauldron rock. "Talking crows . . . this isn't right! This place is cursed. It must be a sea spirit—"

"Ain't cursed!" Charlie flung him a scornful look. "And it's a raven, like I said. They *can* talk—they copy people." She gazed at the bird admiringly. "There was one that came in the yard at the Poacher's Pocket. Granny used to bang two saucepans together and swear at it till it flew off. Then one day it swore back at her—she didn't half get a shock!" Charlie snickered.

"She's right," Ronia said irritably, sheathing her weapon. "I've seen a talking raven before. It belonged to some old sea dog whose ship we stole." She made a disgusted noise and kicked a pebble. "Training it to speak about the island must be someone's idea of a joke."

"Maybe it isn't," Betty said. She had no wish to help Ronia, but at the same time she had the troubling feeling that it would be more dangerous if they didn't prove themselves useful. And the sight of Willow slumped on the rock was a reminder that, regardless of Ronia, getting to the island was crucial to the little girl and her father.

"The Winking Witch is on the map for a reason," Betty continued. "And I think . . . I think the raven is here for a reason, too." She took a step closer to the witch rock and looked up at the bird. "Yes," she told it. "We're looking for the island."

The bird stared back at her for a long moment, blinking silently. Betty squirmed, starting to feel very silly. Was her theory wrong? She'd been so sure . . .

"This is a waste of time," Ronia began, but the raven suddenly flapped up in the air, making a loud, shrill noise that sounded eerily like a person laughing.

It swooped down and landed on the edge of the stone cauldron, still cackling.

Charlie frowned. "Ravens don't normally make those kinds of noises."

"Maybe it's a crow," Spit said.

"No . . . it's a raven," Charlie insisted. "Its beak's longer, more curved. And its neck feathers are scraggy looking—"

"Scraggy?" the rasping voice sounded again. *"Scraggy?"*

"Jumping jackdaws!" said Charlie. "I didn't know they could learn to copy *that* fast."

The bird cackled again, and there was something so mocking about the noise that it cast the final shreds of doubt from Betty's mind.

"It's not copying you," she said quietly. "It's answering you."

There was a beat of silence as each of them considered what this meant.

"I'm right, aren't I?" Betty said, taking a step toward the bird. "You're no ordinary raven, are you? You've been here a long time."

The raven stared at her. "Long, long time," it croaked.

"This is nonsense." Ronia's voice sliced across the bird's, loaded with aggression. "Of *course* it's mimicking you! It hasn't answered anything—"

"Silence!" the raven snapped, turning its beady, yellow eyes on her.

Ronia's mouth opened and closed soundlessly. She couldn't have looked more shocked if someone had slapped her.

The raven hopped around the edge of the cauldron. "And you," it scolded Charlie sternly as it preened its neck feathers. "Scraggy, indeed! 'Ruffled' is a better word."

"Er, y-yes," Charlie stammered. "Sorry." She hesitated, then recovered herself. "Hang on a minute. I said you were a beauty, too, you know." Hoppit nosed his way out of her pocket, took one look at the bird, squeaked, and dived back in.

"So you did," the raven replied, less frostily now. "Now, where were we?"

"The island," Betty said. "We're searching for it." Excitement was fizzing in her tummy now, like popping candy. All those times Father had told them the legend of the three brothers, none of them had dreamed the story might be anchored in truth. If the raven could talk, then maybe it could show them the way. Perhaps Willow's father really *could* be saved.

"Of course you are," said the raven. "Just like everyone who comes here. But not everyone who comes here knows how to listen." It flapped into the air again with an ear-splitting *caaaarrrrrrrrrck!* in Ronia's face, then settled on the lip of the cauldron once more.

"I'm listening," said Betty.

"Me too," Charlie added at once.

"Good." The raven leaned into the cauldron bowl,

using its beak to dig through the contents. "Then you know what to do."

Betty peered into the jumble of items. "Take one, choose one," she murmured.

"Take one, choose one?" Fliss frowned. "Why are those words so familiar?"

"They're from the story," Betty whispered. "*The Crowstone Chronicles*, remember? The one-eyed witch, the raven, and the three brothers. We spoke about it when we set out to find Charlie, because the Winking Witch made me think of that tale!"

She hesitated. There would be clues in the story—warnings when the brothers had failed before Hope succeeded—and perhaps these things could help them now. How safe was it to reveal as much in front of Ronia? But then, Betty reasoned, if Spit had heard the story, there was every chance Ronia had, too.

"So . . . you're saying the one-eyed crone and the Winking Witch are the same thing? But . . . that's just a legend," Fliss burst out, shaking her head in disbelief. "All those stories Father told us—they're fairy tales! Made up and passed down through the generations to entertain bored children."

"Are they?" said Betty. "That's what we've been brought up believing, Fliss. And maybe some of them *were* just made up . . . but think about it! What if this one existed because it all really happened? Maybe not exactly the way it did in the story, but with some true parts and other bits that people made up."

"Or maybe it happened almost exactly as it did in the story," said Willow, speaking up for the first time since they'd set foot on the Winking Witch. She still looked unwell, her eyes bright and feverish. Perhaps it was the oddness of the witch's crag and the talking raven, but Betty suddenly acknowledged the unsettling thought that it was becoming easier and easier to forget Willow was with them at all.

"So that means there really *was* a one-eyed witch here once," said Betty. "One who knew the way to the secret island and tricked greedy travelers with her magic. And because the story never died, neither did she . . ."

"She just took a different form," Fliss said slowly, gazing at the witch rock.

"My father once told me magic goes where magic is," said Willow quietly. "It might change or hide itself to look like something else, but it'll be there forever. Even if it's only a trace. We don't always have to understand it. We just have to believe in it."

"And now we have to . . . to choose one of these things in the cauldron?" Charlie asked, peering into the stone bowl. She had been just a baby when Betty and Fliss had first become familiar with the tale and didn't know it as well as they did.

"That's right," said Betty, glancing at the raven. "Just like the three brothers did."

"Choose one," the raven agreed, bobbing its head. "Choose one."

"And then you'll show us the way to the island?" Willow asked.

The raven cackled. "The island is right there. Look, *look.*"

"We *have* looked," said Ronia, eyeing the bird, one hand resting on the blade at her waist. "There's no island in sight."

"Because," the raven croaked, "now it can only be seen through the witch's eye."

"The witch's . . . ?" Betty whipped around to face the towering rock again. "Of course! The witch's eye is a hagstone! But a much, much bigger one."

She scrambled up until she was level with the large hole that was the witch's eye. Taking a breath, she leaned out to stare through it, hoping she was at least looking in the right direction.

"Meddling magpies!" she gasped, almost losing her

footing. Grabbing onto a tuft of grass, she pulled herself up and looked again.

"What?" Charlie yelled, hopping up and down. "Is it there? *Is it?* Let me see! I'm coming up!"

Betty stared at the shimmering water before her, only realizing she had forgotten to blink when her eyes began to smart. "Yes," she whispered, believing it and not believing it all at once.

For straight ahead, with frothy waves breaking at its base, was the island.

Chapter Twenty-Three

The Witch's Cauldron

"JUMPING JACKDAWS," CHARLIE BREATHED in Betty's ear, having practically scrambled up her back to get a look through the witch's eye. "It's there. It's actually *there!*"

"And you're actually strangling me," Betty spluttered, loosening her sister's grip around her neck with one hand, while hanging on to a tuft of grass above what now looked suspiciously like an eyebrow. "Sorry," she muttered, letting go of it hastily. They dropped down to let the others, one by one, take a look at what they had seen.

"It's *real*," whispered Willow. The discovery had pulled her off the rock where she'd been sitting and brought her strength flooding back. She gazed through the enormous hagstone with a renewed determination that was as single-minded as Ronia's. "I have to get there," she said to herself. "*Have* to get there."

"I don't understand," said Fliss. "Why couldn't the island be seen through the other hagstone?"

"Like the raven said," Betty replied, longingly eyeing the stone that Ronia had claimed for herself, "we weren't looking through the witch's eye." She stared in the direction of the island, expecting to see nothing. This time, however, it was there. She turned to the raven in confusion. "Oh! I can see it now without looking through it!"

The raven cackled. "A glimpse through the witch's eye changes things."

Betty nodded, then froze.

The raven stared back at her. Or at least Betty *thought* it did. For now it was hard to tell exactly where the bird was directing its gaze. For a start, it had no eyes. Instead, there were empty eye sockets in a bleached-white skull. Gone were the black feathers, and in their place were bones. She was staring at a skeleton.

Somehow, despite everything that had happened —the warders, the shipwreck, Rusty Swindles and the pirates—the vision of the sightless bird skull that was moving and speaking was one of the most unsettling things Betty had ever seen. She recalled the swarm of wisps and realized it was the second time in a few hours that she'd seen death staring her in the face. The thought of it chilled her, like a whispered voice in an empty room. If Granny were here, she'd say it was a bad omen. A warning leading up to something bigger.

"Betty!"

Fliss's voice jolted her from her grim thoughts. Her sister was hurrying over, watching her curiously. "What's the matter? You look like you lost a cake and found a crumb."

Betty blinked, breaking the spell. When she looked again, the raven was preening its feathers. No bones or skulls in sight. "I . . ." she stammered. What *had* just happened? Clearly, no one else had seen it—they'd been too busy staring across at the island. Had she imagined the ghoulish vision? Or had looking through the witch's eye allowed her a glimpse of something that was ordinarily hidden?

"*N-nothing,*" she lied.

She followed Fliss to the cauldron, wanting to be away from the raven, even though she could feel its gaze burning into her. She chanced a look over her shoulder. Its black feathers ruffled in the breeze, but besides that, it now sat as still as a gravestone.

Fliss reached into the stone bowl and began sifting

through the items. "It's just a load of old jumble," she said, doubt clouding her expression once more. "I mean, look!" She held up a chipped cup and then a broken eggshell. "How can any of this stuff help us, Betty? In the story, the objects in the cauldron were put there to tempt the brothers, but half these things look like they were washed up in a storm."

Betty grabbed at the eggshell. "The golden egg?" she muttered, but already she could see it was not golden but a pale gray green, with speckles. It crumbled in her fingers. She tossed aside a holey sock covered in seaweed and a soaked, fraying scarf. Fliss was right: Where was the temptation? The large golden egg and the fine leather shoes that Fortune and Luck had been unable to resist?

"Unless . . ." She hesitated, sensing Ronia behind them. Watching and listening. How well did the pirate captain know the old legend? Was she waiting for the sisters to make the choice for her? "There *must* be something. Why else would the raven be here?" She glanced up at the rock. Was it her imagination, or had the witch's eye narrowed a little?

Fliss poked delicately at the contents, her lip curled. "Each item looks as useless as the next. And there are way too many things here—some of them must have washed up in rough weather."

"But one of them will help us," said Betty. "Or rather help Willow." She glanced at the girl, who was standing beside the witch rock and gazing at the island intently, as though afraid that it might suddenly vanish if she took her eyes off it. Once again, Betty felt the familiar urge to protect her. Betty had her sisters out here, but Willow had no one. If the Widdershinses had no choice in going to the island, then Betty was determined that it should be Willow who would benefit, not Ronia. And the more she thought about this, the more she felt like a fly stuck in a web. Why *had* Ronia forced them out here with her when she hadn't brought any of her crew? It couldn't be for anything good.

"What were the original objects in the story of the three brothers?" Fliss asked. "I remember the shoes and the golden egg. What were the others?"

"There were different versions," said Betty. "Don't you remember? The items were never quite the same, depending on who was telling the story. Father's version had an egg, but Granny said it was a feather. And Granny always said there was a lucky rabbit's foot, but Father said it was a horseshoe."

Fliss rummaged through the cauldron. "There's definitely neither of those in here. It doesn't make sense . . . Wait. What's this?" She plucked out something small and partially wrapped in seaweed. She cleared it off, and held it in her finger and thumb. "A wishbone. Granny says these are lucky! You don't think . . . ?"

Betty stared at it, her heart thrumming. "Yes, that's exactly what I think. It's something lucky, like a horseshoe or a rabbit's foot. What if . . . what if the items are different to the original story but linked somehow?"

"Perhaps they change depending on who finds them," said Fliss in an excited whisper.

"Exactly," said Betty. "Especially if you happen to *know* the story. We know the witch can be a trickster and that it was the humblest item that helped the brothers in the end: the ball of yarn." She stared up at the witch rock just as a breeze rippled the grassy eyebrow she'd noticed earlier, moving it into a frown. "She was never going to make it easy for us."

She turned back to the cauldron, digging through the items. More objects appeared, unearthed from the sludgy water pooling in the hollow of the rock. Betty had the strangest feeling that every time she looked, items changed, new ones emerging that hadn't been there before. Her fingertips grew numb with cold, so numb that it took her a moment to feel the sharp prick on her forefinger.

"Oh!" She snatched back her finger in shock. A bright bead of blood bloomed on its tip. "What *was* that?"

Fliss brushed aside the sock.

"Careful," said Betty, sucking her finger. "It could be glass or perhaps a needle."

"No," said Fliss, pulling something out between her finger and thumb. "Look, it's an old hatpin. Granny has one of these, but hers isn't as fancy." She wiped the gleaming silver pin on her shawl. It was sturdy and almost as long as Fliss's hand. It was the decorative end of it, however, that revealed its value. Once Fliss had cleared the muck off, a shimmering mother-of-pearl seahorse lay in her fingers.

"Beautiful," she murmured, stroking it longingly.

"Sharp," Betty whispered. Her eyes flickered to Ronia's cutlass. Perhaps it wouldn't hurt for them to have a weapon, too. One that could easily be hidden up a sleeve or pinned into a skirt, waiting for the right moment. Not quite a dagger, but close enough . . .

"And what's this?" Fliss breathed, jolting Betty from her musings. She'd sifted out something balled up. "How strange. It's not even damp . . . but look, Betty! Velvet gloves—how *beautiful*."

Betty frowned as Fliss smoothed out the expensive fabric. The gloves were a rich, deep purple edged with gold and more luxurious than anything the Widdershinses had ever owned.

Fliss's dark eyes were wide with desire. "Imagine wearing these," she murmured. "They look just my size, too . . ."

"No!" Betty blinked, knocking the gloves from Fliss's hand. They landed back in the cauldron in a shallow pool of seawater.

"Hey!" Fliss said, annoyed. "I was . . ."

"About to make the wrong choice," said Betty, staring down at the hatpin. She placed it on the gloves with trembling fingers. "Just like me. Don't you see? The gloves? They're luxurious, the perfect fit. Just like the shoes were for Fortune. And the hatpin? It's a weapon like the jeweled dagger. We nearly fell for her tricks, Fliss! We have to be more careful. We need to find the yarn, whatever it could be disguised as."

"But there's nothing like that in here," said Fliss, sounding panicked. "How does this work, anyway? We each choose an item to take with us?"

"Choose one," the raven croaked. "One, one, *one!*"

"I think it means one between us," said Betty. "In the story, each brother traveled to the hidden island alone with one object. I guess if we're a group, then we still only get to choose one—"

"Two." Ronia spoke from behind them, making them jump. She shoved Fliss out of the way, poking through the cauldron. Bandit bounded over from a nearby rock pool and leaped onto her shoulder.

Betty grabbed Fliss's elbow to steady her and her temper flared. "No, it's *one*. And we have to get this right —that's why it's important to choose wisely."

Ronia chuckled, but it was an empty sound. "I mean that we're two groups, not one." She dug deeper into the cauldron, not looking at Betty. Bandit hissed, showing off long, white fangs. "And you can choose whatever you want after *I've* had first pick. Ha!" She snatched something up. "I choose this." In her hand lay an old key covered in sludge.

"I'm sure that wasn't there before," Fliss whispered.

Ronia's eyes glinted greedily, and Betty knew at once that she was thinking of locked chests and untold riches. But was the key one of the witch's objects? Or something that had been washed up?

"Put it back," Betty said angrily, aware of precious time passing. "That's not how the island works! The wrong item will mess everything up. And whether you like it or not, we're in this together now . . ." She trailed off as Ronia gave a small cry.

The key in her hand had fluttered like a bird shaking its feathers and, as it did, years of grime and rust fell away in flakes to reveal a gleaming golden surface with a small, teardrop-shaped stone set into it.

Gold, Betty thought. And the longer she looked, the less the stone in the key looked like a teardrop—and the more it looked like . . . *an egg.*

She gasped as Ronia's fingers closed around the shimmering piece of gold like a door being closed in Betty's face. The choice had been made.

"Spit!" Ronia called. "Get the boat ready. We're getting out of here." She pocketed the key and turned away, but Betty grabbed her arm and spun her around.

Ronia shook her off, but Betty held her gaze, her eyes every bit as fierce as the pirate captain's. "You want to do this your way, fine. But we're doing it *our* way, and we won't be rushed!"

To her surprise, Ronia grinned. "You take as long as you want, my prickly little sea urchin. Spit and I will be long gone by the time you reach that island. *If* you ever reach it."

"Cap'n?" Spit said uncertainly. He cast his eyes over the girls, lingering on Fliss, then Charlie, before he met Betty's gaze.

The worry she saw there frightened her.

"You can't," Betty whispered as she finally realized

what Ronia meant. And then the whisper slipped away, and she roared. *"You can't take our boat!"*

She was suddenly aware of silence around her as everyone else stopped what they were doing to listen. Even the waves seemed to quiet down.

"If you take it, we'll be stranded!" said Fliss. "With no food, no shelter . . ."

"No food?" Charlie repeated in horror.

"I'm sure you can use that pretty face to flag down a passing fishing boat," said Ronia dismissively. "Who knows? If you're still here on our way back, we might even rescue you ourselves. I'm sure we can find a use for you." She threw back her head and laughed at Fliss's alarmed face. "Spit! What are you waiting for?"

"Spit, don't you dare!" yelled Betty.

Spit hesitated, his feet lodged in the sand. Betty could see he was wrestling with his conscience. He might not be their friend exactly—not yet—but Betty could tell he didn't want them left like this. Despite his warped loyalty to Ronia, he cared what happened to them. But would it be enough?

"Spit." Ronia's voice dripped with danger. "You've seen what happens to those who defy me."

And so have I, thought Betty, as Spit lurched toward *The Traveling Bag*, his tanned face unusually pale.

"It'll be my bones up on that mast next," he'd said.

Is it loyalty or fear that keeps him in line? Betty wondered grimly. Either way, she knew that they had lost and Ronia had won.

"Spit, *please!*" Fliss begged. "You know this is wrong."

"I'm sorry," he mumbled, not meeting her eyes. "She's my captain."

"Then do immunity!" shouted Charlie. "Chuck her overboard!"

Betty shot Ronia and Spit a furious look. "She means 'mutiny.'"

"That's what I said!" Charlie roared. "MUTINY!"

But Betty knew there would be no such thing, even as she stormed across the sand after them. Ronia leaped nimbly aboard *The Traveling Bag*, while Spit unmoored the rope and followed her. Betty lunged for the rope, snatching at it helplessly, but Ronia drew her cutlass and brandished it under Betty's nose.

"Don't even think about it," she said, "unless you want your fingers to be fish food."

"Please!" Willow cried, her voice cracking. She stumbled into the water after the boat as it began to move off. "Let me come with you!" she called. "I *must* get to the island—my father's life depends on it! Please . . . wait! WAIT!"

Charlie and Fliss joined her, wading knee deep into the water, pleading with Spit and Ronia, but the words blurred in Betty's ears along with Willow's heartbroken, hopeless sobs. And then, from the back of the boat, a faint silvery glow that could have been mistaken for light shimmering on the waves trailed over the water to flicker dimly at Willow's side.

"Her wisp," said Charlie, pointing. "It came back to her!"

Betty eyed the pale orb, so faint in the daylight it was easy to miss. It was nothing like the threatening wisps she'd seen back at Rusty's ship. This one was . . . different. Almost as delicate as Willow herself.

"Come back!" Willow croaked.

"You're wasting your breath," Betty said, clenching her fists as the boat got farther away. "They aren't coming back for us."

"Then what do we *do*?" Fliss shrieked, still flapping her arms at Spit and making a gesture at Ronia that was so rude she could only have learned it from Granny.

"Go after them," said Betty, through gritted teeth. "If we don't, Willow's father will die. We have to get her there."

"*H-how?*" Willow asked, her voice faint between sobs.

"It's too far!" Charlie added incredulously. "We can't swim all that way!"

"We aren't swimming," said Betty, turning away from the water. She had glared so hard at the boat that her eyes were smarting. "There's got to be another way across, just like in the story." *The story*. It was there to guide them, she felt it in her bones. And what else could they learn from it? What else were they missing? It came to her in a flash.

She turned to Charlie urgently. "And I'm going to find it while you choose something from the cauldron. This is important, Charlie. That's why I'm trusting you with it. You remember the story? How the least fancy object was the one that saved the brothers? That's what I need you to do. Fliss and I nearly failed—so it has to be you. Just like the story, Charlie. It was the youngest brother who made the right choice."

Charlie looked doubtful, glancing at Willow. "But, Betty, how will I know what to pick? What if I get it wrong?"

Fliss, too, appeared anxious. "There's no string in there. We looked."

"I know," said Betty, taking in her little sister's worried face and messy pigtails. Everything rested on this

—and on Charlie. "But I also know you'll choose well. You're smart. That's why I'm counting on you."

"What about you?" Charlie asked, her lip quivering. "You're not going across alone, are you? Because—"

"No, Charlie." Betty shook her head. "We're sticking together this time."

"What *will* you be doing, then?" Fliss asked.

"Searching," Betty replied, beckoning her away from the cauldron, for the urge to look over Charlie's shoulder as she chose was almost too much. "And I need your help."

"What are we looking for?"

"Anything we can use," said Betty. "In the story, Hope got across in a seashell—"

"Like *that's* going to happen," Fliss said at once.

"No, but perhaps there's some driftwood . . . We could build a raft," Betty said desperately. "There must be *something!*"

"I think there is." Somehow, without Betty noticing, Willow had joined them. She'd stopped sniffling now and was pointing across to the rock pools. Her cold fingers wrapped around Betty's, tugging her insistently across the sand with the wisp leading the way. "We saw it over here," Willow said, pushing an armful of seaweed aside to reveal a silvery sheen just above the water's surface. "Charlie noticed it earlier."

Betty grabbed another pile of seaweed and threw it out of the way. She paused, making sense of a familiar shape—the very *last* thing she would have expected to find there. She felt a tingle, a crazy sense of hope that this just might work.

It was an old bathtub, much like the one they had at the Poacher's Pocket. It was half underwater and full of debris and sand, but it was big. More important, despite having a few dents, it appeared to be in one piece.

"Fliss!" she yelled. "Help me dig this out. Willow, you help Charlie."

Fliss scrambled to her side and together they began emptying the tub, scraping out shingle and driftwood. Grunting with the effort, Betty was dimly aware that the raven was watching everything. "Hurry," she muttered, glancing in the direction of the island. *The Traveling Bag* was disappearing at an alarmingly fast rate. Soon it would vanish altogether—like Willow's father's chances of survival.

Yet even as Betty scooped out handful after handful of sand, she knew that getting to the island was just the beginning. What they found there would be something else altogether—and even if Willow got answers, she might not be ready for the truth.

Chapter Twenty-Four

Bath Time

"YOU'RE CUCKOO." Charlie stared at the bathtub sitting on the sand, shaking her head. She reached out and twisted one of the old brass taps. It spun uselessly in her fingers. "This ain't gonna work."

"It *will*," said Betty, her words carrying a determination she wasn't entirely sure of.

"But how will we all fit?" Willow asked. She looked so forlorn, so frail, that once again Betty was reminded of how young she was—and of the weight of the task on her shoulders.

"With great difficulty," Fliss muttered.

Betty ignored her. "Help me get it ready to push off."

The two girls each grabbed a side of the heavy tub, heaving it through the gravelly sand.

"Even if it floats," Fliss grunted, "how will we steer? We don't have any oars."

Betty looked up at the raven. "Any bright ideas?"

The raven didn't answer. It stuck its head under a wing and began preening. A moment later, two glossy black feathers floated to the sand in front of Betty's feet.

"You've got to be joking," she said under her breath.

"Well, that's how it was in the story, right?" said Fliss. "Feathers?"

"I know, but . . ." Betty paused, noticing something glinting in the grit by the first feather. She scooped her fingers through the sand and unearthed a large, silvery ladle, like the one Granny used for soup. "Actually, I think *this* could work," she said. She faced the raven suspiciously. "You meant for me to find that, didn't you?"

The bird made a clicking noise. "Meant to," it said.

Betty knelt by the other feather and scratched in the sand again. Her fingers met wood, curling around the handle of something. She tugged it free and found it was an old, scratched frying pan. "Looks like we've got our oars."

"You can't be serious," Fliss muttered.

Betty dropped the ladle and the frying pan into the bathtub with a clank. "Hop in," she told Charlie and Willow, as she and Fliss began to push the tub out into the water. "Oh, I almost forgot."

"What now?" Fliss grumbled, shivering and knee deep in water. "A bath with no hot water, no rose petals in it —this is *torture.*"

Betty turned to the raven. "It's only right that we should give you something in return for helping us." *Just like Hope did*, she thought.

Charlie snorted. "Helping? We dug up all this junk ourselves."

Betty shot her a warning look. "We don't really have much, but is there anything we can offer you?" *Not the dolls*, she thought silently, her fingers curling around the smooth wood in her pocket. *Please, not the dolls . . .*

The raven watched her for a long moment, thinking. "Gets cold here," it said at last. "Some of that lovely fluffy hair of yours would warm my nest."

"*Th-this hair?*" Betty grabbed a clump of frizz doubtfully. "First time anyone's called my hair lovely. All right." She searched around, scrabbling through the debris until she found a battered razor. She pried it open and began hacking at a handful of hair. It came away in a shower of rust. The raven swooped down and snatched it up in its beak, before returning to the top of the witch rock.

"Come on," Betty said, returning to the bathtub. "Let's go."

They pushed the tub farther out, buoyed by the water.

"That," said Fliss, "was silly. Don't you remember what Granny always told us about cleaning the hair out of our combs properly? If a crow steals your hair and puts it in its nest, it's supposed to lead to an untimely death!"

"It wasn't stolen," Betty reasoned, trying to reassure herself as much as Fliss. "I *gave* it away." She tapped the side of the bath. "Now in you go. Chop-chop."

"I just think it'd be nice for once if we could get back home from an adventure without one of us losing our hair," Fliss said. "Chop-chop indeed."

"We're not home yet," Betty answered, feeling a pang of longing at the thought of the Poacher's Pocket. But as much as she wished she could return there, she knew it would be with a bitter taste if she hadn't done all she could to help Willow. There was no turning back now.

Charlie clutched her pigtails tightly. Grumbling, Fliss clambered in, earning shrieks of protest from Charlie.

"Watch where your foot's going!" Charlie demanded. "And why do I always get stuck at the end with the taps?"

"Because you're the littlest," said Fliss, curling her knees under her. "Now budge up so Betty can get in, and make sure the plug doesn't come out or we'll sink!"

"It'll sink anyway," Charlie protested.

The bath bobbed like a cork, dipping lower as Betty squeezed in to more yowls of indignation. But it didn't sink. When she had squashed between Fliss and Willow as best she could, she handed the frying pan to Fliss and swung the ladle into the water. "Row," she said.

"This is ridiculous," Fliss puffed, thrashing around with the pan. "It'll be sunset by the time we get there at this rate! Charlie, poppet, I don't think turning the taps is doing anything."

"It is," Charlie said indignantly. "I'm steering!"

"At least we'll get there," Betty answered. Because slowly but surely, it *was* working. She could no longer see the sandy bottom of the seabed; it had slipped away to a deepening blue. She paused from her rowing to look up. The island shimmered distantly, like a road on a hot day. "Even though it's still a long way off."

A sudden wind rose up, lifting the hair off the back of her neck and capping the far-off waves with white froth.

"Does it seem . . . breezy to you?" Fliss asked, a note of concern in her voice.

"A little," Betty admitted, searching the sky for storm

clouds. She saw Willow's hands tighten on the edge of the bathtub. Water slopped over the sides as it rocked, and Betty gulped. She turned back to the Winking Witch, uttering a silent prayer. Could they have done something wrong? she wondered. Had they angered the witch by taking a second item after Ronia had helped herself to the key? *Please, please, don't let us sink . . .*

But while clouds swept across the sky and the wind built, there was no sign of a storm.

"What's happening?" Fliss yelled. "How are we speeding up like this?"

Above the rock, Betty could make out the outline of a large, black bird staring in their direction and beating its wings in the wind. And then she almost dropped the ladle as the rock beneath the raven shifted and rearranged into a cavernous yawn.

"Hold on!" Betty yelled, aware of what was about to happen.

A huge gust of air whooshed out of the witch's mouth, sending water spraying up and the bathtub spiraling through the water at speed. The four girls shrieked, holding on for dear life until the tub eventually slowed to a gentle spin.

Charlie was the first to recover. "Jumping jackdaws!" she whooped. "Can we do that again?"

"No," Fliss moaned, clutching her tummy queasily. "Oh, someone make it stop."

Betty stared back at the Winking Witch, now tiny in the distance. She could no longer see the raven, but just for a moment, she thought she saw rocks shifting back into position, like a rocky mouth closing up. The wind died down as quickly as it had arisen, lowering to a breeze that faded to something that sounded a lot like a gentle sigh.

She only managed to turn away from the Winking Witch when she realized goose bumps were dotting her arms. The bathtub had fallen into shadow. Betty looked up and felt her breath catch.

The island was right in front of them.

Chapter Twenty-Five

A Wooden Reel

THEY FOUND *THE TRAVELING BAG* moored around the other side of the island. As quietly as they could, Betty and Fliss brought the bathtub alongside the boat, using the frying pan and the ladle. There was no sign of Ronia or Spit.

"I'm really getting the hang of this now," said Fliss, looking slightly less green.

"You're not completely useless with a frying pan after all," Betty agreed.

"Hey!" Fliss scooped water into the pan and flicked it at her, but Betty ducked easily. The mood changed as they looked up at the island.

"I can see the bottom," said Charlie, peering into the

water. "Well, rocks, anyway. What should we do with the bathtub?"

"We'll sink it here where it's shallow," said Betty. "It looks like Ronia's moored the boat at the safest point to get onto the island. If we walk across it, we'll avoid going into the water or over the rocks."

One by one, they scrambled onto *The Traveling Bag*, with Charlie and Willow going first, followed by Fliss. Betty pulled the plug out of the bathtub, then jumped out as it began filling with water. It sank with a gurgle, landing on the rocks on the seabed with a dull *clunk*.

"It's there if we need it again," said Betty, fervently hoping they wouldn't.

"We did it," said Willow, gazing up at the island in awe. "We're actually here." She stared up at the vast cliff. In its shadow, she appeared younger and smaller than ever. Here the wisp glowed a little brighter, bathing her pale face in silver. Silently, Charlie went to stand beside her, pigtails askew. Something tugged in Betty's chest at the sight of the two girls dwarfed by the island.

They should be playing and carefree, she thought. Instead they were caught up in an adventure bigger and more dangerous than anything they could have expected.

Before now, the island had always been a story. A cautionary tale that had not actually been real. Now it was, and the Winking Witch had only been the start. What else lay in store for them? Here, on their boat, Betty knew she and her sisters still had a choice. A chance to return home. How much more were they willing to risk for a stranger?

You got her this far, said a little voice in her head. *You can't save everyone, but you can save yourselves.*

"You want to go home, don't you?" Willow asked, her voice quiet. She smiled, a sad, little smile that left her eyes dull. "I understand."

For a moment, Betty almost caved in. She thought of her family, and the Poacher's Pocket, and even Oi curled up on his favorite barstool. She wanted, desperately, to go home. But as she pictured herself warm in bed while rowdy voices filtered up through the floorboards, she knew that in every quiet moment, her mind would return to this one. Wondering what might have been. Who *she* might have been.

"That's not who we are," Betty answered softly. "You can't do this alone. But it's more than that. I don't want to look back and know we chose to be selfish over what was right. I don't want to carry on thinking a little less of ourselves." She glanced at her sisters. "Do you?"

Fliss was silent for a long moment. Finally, she and Charlie shook their heads.

Betty surveyed the island. At a glance, it was like any other, but there was something about the *feel* of it. Look a little too long, and the edges seemed to blur, as though its magic was bubbling up from within. Halfway up, between rocks and greenery, a sketchy trail was visible. "That must be the path leading to the caves," she said.

Betty's eyes swept the deck of *The Traveling Bag*. "We should check to see if there's anything here that could be useful. But I'm guessing that, if there was, Ronia's already taken it." She spotted the old potato sack lying discarded by the wheelhouse door and picked it up.

"It's empty," Fliss confirmed. "Ronia gave all the tobacco tins to the pirates when she took the boat the first time."

Betty let the sack drop. For the first time since they'd left the Winking Witch, she dared to ask something. "Charlie," she said tensely. "What was the object you chose from the witch's cauldron?"

"Oh." Charlie produced a wooden reel from her pocket. It was the kind of thing found in sewing boxes, but it was twice the size of her hand and empty. "I found this."

Betty gaped at it, her heart sinking. "That . . . that's what you brought?"

Charlie's face fell. "You said choose something simple. Did I . . . did I do it wrong?"

Betty swallowed, forcing herself to shake her head. "No. I just . . . keep it. It may come in useful." She shot Fliss a worried look, which was returned. If they were to navigate the island, all their hopes were stacked on this one object. Right now, Betty didn't like their chances.

"Perhaps it got blown in there," said Fliss. "There was so much flotsam and jetsam on that place, it was hard to know what was meant to be there and what wasn't."

"I don't think a witch would have anything in her cauldron that wasn't meant to be there," Charlie said stiffly, clearly hurt. "But maybe someone else should have picked." She went to put the reel back in her pocket, but it caught on a fold of fabric and dropped to the deck.

"Charlie, don't be upset," Fliss began.

Charlie ignored her and went to grab the reel. Curiously, it rolled away from her and out of reach. She darted after it, missing it again.

They all froze as the reel continued rolling at an impossible angle that defied the swaying motion of the boat.

"Jumping jackdaws," Charlie muttered, her eyes widening.

"How . . . how is it rolling that way?" Fliss breathed.

The reel stopped next to the potato sack, settling on a stray thread that had come loose. Before their astonished eyes, the sack unraveled . . . and the reel continued to roll at speed, until the sack was completely gone and the wooden reel was still and fat with twine.

Betty picked it up, feeling something flutter in her chest. *Hope.* "Looks like we have our yarn, after all."

The first signs of Ronia and Spit were on the path leading up to the caves.

"Look." Betty pointed, breathless, to a scuffed area of dirt and a handful of weeds that had been half wrenched from the soil. "One of them must have slipped and grabbed on to that to keep their balance."

"Hopefully Ronia," Fliss said viciously.

"But not her cat," Charlie added, a crease of worry appearing between her eyebrows.

Fliss looked over her shoulder and grimaced. "It's a long way down." She tightened her grip on Charlie's hand and urged her onward. "Don't look."

"Just keep heading for the top," said Betty. She thought back to the story. Would they find something there, an answer to the mystery of what had happened to the friend of Willow's father? Even if they didn't, it would surely be safer there than on this precarious path.

They continued to climb, picking their way along, saving their breath for the climb rather than conversation. Only when the ground leveled and stretched away to a grassy area before a crumbling cave did Betty allow herself to pause, resting her aching legs. Her mind was fraught with worry. What she had said was true: they had to help Willow. But at the same time, she was afraid. If the stories of the witch and her magical objects were true, then this vast island really was a trap. How likely was it that they would find the evidence they needed when they didn't know what they were searching for? And then of course, there was Ronia . . .

Betty forced the doubts away. The map—and the Winking Witch—had gotten them this far, and Charlie had chosen correctly from the cauldron. She needed to continue to trust in the magic of the island—and herself.

One thing she couldn't reassure herself of, however, was Willow. If the girl had seemed sickly earlier, she appeared almost deathly pale now. She looked fragile, like a bleached twig about to snap off in the wind.

"Willow?" Betty said gently. "Are you sure you can go

on? You look so unwell. You've been losing strength ever since we had to fight off those wisps."

Willow blinked slowly, as if trying to clear her thoughts. "My head feels . . . fuzzy," she admitted. "My thoughts are jumbled. But we're so . . . so close now. I need to know the truth. If my father can be saved, I have to go on." She looked at Betty, her eyes feverish. "I can't give up now."

"I found something!" Charlie shouted from behind an area of scrubby bushes near the cave entrance. "Over here!"

"What is it?" Betty called, hurrying to her with Fliss on her heels. "Careful—don't touch anything!" The thought of the island's traps leaped to the forefront of her mind.

"Look," said Charlie, pointing. "An old well."

A circular wall of gray stones stood around a deep hole in the ground. Above it, a wooden spindle was bare of rope. There was no sign of a bucket.

"It says something," said Fliss, tracing her fingers over letters that had been scratched into the stones around the rim. "Some of them have been worn away over time. I can't make them all out. 'he well of ost . . . tune . . .'?" She squinted, her lips moving soundlessly. "'The well of most . . . tunes?' That doesn't make sense."

"The Well of Lost Fortune!" said Betty, the answer arriving in a flash. "The eldest brother in the story was called Fortune, and he fell into the well and turned into a—"

"Help!" a voice cried faintly, interrupting her. "Is someone there?"

"Was that . . . ?" Charlie began. "Someone's calling from down there!" She peered into the depths of the well. "Hello?"

"Charlie, don't!" Fliss grabbed at her. "It could be dangerous!"

The voice sounded again weakly from below. "Someone, please help!"

"Wait," said Betty, recognition sparking. "I'm sure that's . . . I know that voice!" She leaned over the side of the well, cupping her hands to her mouth. "Spit! Is that you?"

"Yes!" Spit's voiced echoed back up at them. "Get me out. I'm stuck down here! And there's a creepy fish that won't leave me alone!"

"*Fish?*" Betty whispered, recalling the three brothers' tale. "The story! Spit, are *you* a fish?"

There was a pause, then Spit's voice sounded, faint but incredulous. "*What?* No!"

"Never mind!" she yelled, feeling rather silly. "Is the bucket in there?"

"Yeah," Spit shouted up. "It snapped off!"

"We're getting you out," Betty called, but the memory of the brothers' tale made her wonder if the fish, too, had any significance. "Get the fish in the bucket and bring it with you."

There was a bewildered pause before Spit answered. "Whatever. Just get me out!"

"Charlie, quickly," said Betty. "The string!"

"Uh-uh." Charlie shook her head, arms crossed defiantly. "Nope."

Fliss gaped at Betty. "Surely you're not helping *him?* He left us on that rock, or have you forgotten that?"

"Yeah," said Charlie. "He nicked our boat!"

"Ronia stole the boat," said Betty. She was angry at Spit—there was no question about that. Yet at the same time, she'd seen another side of him back at *The Sorcerer's Compass*. He could have turned his back on them—but he hadn't. He'd helped, even though he was afraid of Ronia. She swallowed, trying to imagine living in fear of the only family she'd ever had. "I know Spit went along with it, but he didn't *want* to!"

"Then that's even worse," said Charlie.

"It is," said Betty. "He was wrong. But before that, he helped us. We can't just leave him. He'll die."

Sulkily, Charlie passed her the reel.

"Tie this to the bucket!" Betty shouted, throwing the string into the well. She felt the end of it moving as Spit complied. Under her fingers, the string felt flimsy, like it was about to break any second. It would take some very strong magic, she thought despairingly, to haul a person up.

"This could still be a trap," said Fliss, looking over her shoulder as though she expected Ronia to come charging at them at any moment.

"I know," said Betty. "But there's no way either of them expected us to turn up here."

"It's ready!" Spit yelled.

Betty felt a weight at the end of the string. She pulled, and slowly a battered wooden bucket came into view. Inside, a large, silvery-green fish with strange little tufty fins stared up at them with unnervingly human eyes.

"Spit's right," said Fliss. "That's one creepy fish!"

"It speaks, too!" yelled Spit. "Keeps telling me it's a sole. Don't look nothing like a sole! Don't look like any fish I've ever seen!"

"Sole?" Betty frowned glancing at Willow. "Wait . . . Saul? SAUL! Jumping jackdaws! Could it really be—"

A small cry escaped Willow's lips as she leaned over the bucket, gripping its edges tightly with her fingers. "Saul?" she whispered, her voice trembling.

The fish flipped in the water, breaking the surface. "Saul," it said, bubbling through the water. "*Saul.*"

Willow gasped. "Saul! My father—you have to tell me what happened that night."

"Saul," the fish repeated, staring back, unblinking.

Willow's face fell. "He can't tell me."

"Maybe it's not really him," said Fliss gently. "For all we know, it could be one of the island's tricks."

"Talking ravens," Spit muttered in the well. "Now talking fish!" He spat loudly.

"Swim clockwise if it's really you," Willow urged.

Immediately, the fish changed direction, swimming to the right.

"It's him!" Willow insisted. "I knew it. It has his eyes! He's *alive.*"

"And still a fish," Betty said grimly. "If we take him back, it doesn't prove a thing, especially if he can't tell us anything."

"Then we have to go on," said Willow.

"If it's really him," said Betty, "then yes, we do. And we've gotten this far. There's no turning back." She thought of the three brothers and how Fortune and Luck had only been restored to their true forms after Hope had navigated the island. Just as the brothers had, they were being drawn deeper into its clutches with no real answers. What if Fliss was right—what if it wasn't Saul? Either way, they had no choice but to go on. "But first we've got to get Spit out."

"You can't get him out with *that*," said Fliss, plucking the string. "It'll snap."

"Perhaps if we twist it double, or even triple it . . ."

Betty never got to finish the sentence for before her eyes the reel of string rolled out of her grasp and began weaving itself deftly into a thick, strong rope.

"Meddling magpies," said Betty as the rope coiled neatly at her feet. "It's definitely strong enough now!" She picked it up. "Spit, watch out! I'm throwing you a rope. Grab on!"

She launched the rope into the well.

"Got it," came the faint reply.

"I'm going to need help pulling him up," she said. "It's a long way down." Together, Betty, Fliss, and Charlie hauled on the rope. "Keep going," Betty panted.

"I see him," Charlie exclaimed. She dropped the rope and leaped onto the edge of the well for a better look. "He's nearly at the top!"

A moment later, Spit's golden head emerged and he flung an arm over the side of the well. Then he pulled himself out and rolled onto the ground, chest heaving. Behind him the rope began unraveling as quickly as it had made itself, looping back around the wooden reel at Betty's feet.

Spit eyed it warily. "More magic?" he said eventually. "Follows you everywhere, doesn't it? Just like bad luck."

Betty ignored him. "Where's Ronia?" she asked. "How did you end up in the well?"

"Did she push you in?" Charlie asked, barely concealing a smirk. Betty elbowed her.

Spit shook his head, his expression darkening. "She may as well have." He hauled himself to his feet and spat on the ground. "That pesky cat of hers pounced on a bird at the edge of the well. Missed it but fell straight in. Ronia ordered me to climb down and get the cat in the bucket so she could wind it back up. She got Bandit out, but of course it wasn't strong enough to pull me up. Snapped right off." He shrugged, rubbing his nose angrily. "She said she'd come back for me."

"Maybe she was planning to," said Betty. Privately, she doubted this, but Spit looked so crushed, so broken, that it was all she could think of to say. In any case, he remained unconvinced.

"You didn't see her face," he said, a haunted look in his eyes. "Once she got that key, it was like . . . like that was all that mattered. The closer we got to the island—"

"On *our* boat," Fliss interjected coldly.

He nodded, shamefaced. "The closer we got, the less she seemed to care about getting back to the Rusty Scuttlers and the more she talked about what riches there might be. All I wanted was to help her and to prove myself. But I'd started to wonder if . . ." He hesitated, still struggling with some deep-rooted loyalty. "If she wanted me with her at all." He gulped, his voice cracking. "If you hadn't come along . . . I . . ." He broke off, frowning. "How *did* you get here, anyway?"

Betty exchanged glances with her sisters. "You wouldn't believe us if we told you," she said. "But one thing's for certain: we're leaving on our boat, and neither you nor Ronia is going to stop us."

Spit nodded, hanging his head. "Got it. I hate to break it to you though, but I reckon Ronia's going to get to it first. Same goes for the treasure."

"We're not here for treasure, so Ronia can keep it," said Betty. "We're here for her." She turned to where she had left Willow and felt a stab of panic. Willow wasn't there. "Where is she? Willow?" she called, searching frantically.

"Here." Willow's voice sounded softly from the cave entrance. She continued to stare into the gloom as, one by one, they joined her. The wisp hovered at her side, barely visible in the daylight. "The brothers went through the caves, didn't they? That must mean we have to follow their path."

Betty tied the end of the string to the low branch of a tree just outside the cave.

Spit raised an eyebrow. "That so we can find our way back?"

Betty nodded. "In case we take any wrong turns. It's all we've got now that Ronia has the map."

"She doesn't." Spit reached into his shirt, removing a roll of paper. He handed it to her.

Betty gasped, seizing it. She unrolled it, flicking water off the waxed surface. "How did you get this?"

"Ronia dropped it in when she was leaning over the well," Spit replied. Anger flashed across his face. "Even that wasn't enough for her to get me out. She said we didn't need it anymore, that it had gotten us here and she could do the rest."

"Wait," said Charlie, pointing at the map. "It's changed again. Look! That wasn't on it before."

"*There*," Betty breathed, her finger tracing the lagoon as she spotted what Charlie meant. For, sure enough, a large wooden chest had appeared at the center of it and, as she watched, she could see the inked surface of the water softly rippling. A thrill of anticipation stole over her, the magic of the map making her fingertips tingle.

It had led them here. Now they had to trust in it if they were to find their way home. "The lagoon is at the heart of the island. That's where we need to get to."

"Looks like Willow was right about going through the caves," Spit murmured, nodding at the map. "Look."

Sure enough there was something else on the map which hadn't been there before: a tiny lantern in the mouth of the inked cave. Flickering, as if it were inviting them in.

"Let's go," said Betty.

Fliss nodded at the bucket by Willow's feet with an expectant look at Spit. "Grab that."

Spit raised an eyebrow.

"If it wasn't for us, you'd still be stuck down there," said Fliss. "The least you can do is carry the fish."

"You planning on eating this?" he grumbled.

"No," said Willow, horrified. "My father's life depends on that fish—it needs to survive, so stop slopping the water everywhere!"

Spit looked at her quizzically. "Your father's life . . . this fish?"

"If this is Saul, then it proves my father didn't kill him," said Willow. "He's innocent."

Betty watched the fish, once again unnerved by how human its eyes appeared. She could swear there was sadness in them — and regret. Had Saul been seduced by the idea of the island's riches and double-crossed Willow's father for them, allowing his friend to take the blame for his murder? If that were true, Saul had paid a high price for his greed. But not as high a price as Willow and her family.

"Everyone ready?" Betty asked, nodding to the caves.

"I am," said Charlie, slipping one hand into Betty's and the other into Willow's.

Together, they stepped into the murky cavern, pausing as their eyes adjusted to the gloom.

"How will we find our way through?" asked Spit. "We've no torches, no lanterns . . ."

The wisp trailed ahead, bobbing in a narrow part of the black tunnel. Its glow lit the craggy walls, casting an eerie, pale light on everything.

"Whoa!" Spit staggered back, noticing the wisp for the first time. "Where the heck did *that* come from?" He crossed himself, eyes wide with fear and confusion. "Did it follow us from the wreck?"

"It's been with us all along," said Betty quietly. "You just couldn't see it. It's not like the others — it's with Willow. And it means us no harm." As she spoke, she watched Willow. There was a look of worry in her eyes, like a haze had momentarily lifted.

"I . . . I thought it was Saul," she said, staring at the glowing orb. "But now I know it can't be." Her expression became drawn, haunted as she made the connection —the possibility Betty had considered but left unspoken. "When I got split up from Mother, I never saw what happened to her . . . What if—?"

"We can't know what happened," Betty told her gently. "Or who it is. All we can do is keep going, for your father's sake. He needs you, Willow."

Willow stared at the wisp, her eyes growing steely once more. "Father needs me," she repeated, stepping farther into the caves. "He *needs* me."

"Great," Spit muttered unhappily. "*Perfect.* Haven't you ever heard that you're not supposed to follow will-o'-the-wisps?"

Don't follow the will-o'-the-wisps—that's what everyone always said, thought Betty. Yet here they were, about to risk everything. Their own lives for that of a stranger's.

"We're not following it," said Betty. "It's just lighting the way." She set down the wooden reel, hoping that, once again, it would help them. "We're following this."

For an awful moment, she thought it wouldn't work. The reel stayed still. Then it quivered, like a creature scenting the air, and began to roll into the darkness.

Chapter Twenty-Six

The Caves of Lost Luck

"I DON'T LIKE THIS," SAID CHARLIE, moving closer to Betty as darkness pressed in on them, swallowing them up. "I don't like it one bit."

"I know," Betty answered, her eyes following the glow of the wisp ahead. Already the temperature in the caves had dropped, and there was a shift in the air. A sensation of things closing in. "Neither do I. But as long as we have this yarn, we won't get lost." She repeated it in her head, trying to convince herself of it as much as she was trying to convince her little sister. *We won't get lost . . . we won't get lost . . .*

But they all knew that Luck, the second brother, *had* gotten lost. It was easy to see why. The tunnels twisted and turned, branching this way and that. Every word and every movement came back to haunt them as an echo, and Betty could not get the story out of her mind. How Luck had shouted and shouted for help, until all that was left of him was his voice.

The temperature dipped further, chilling Betty's bones as she eventually took the lead. She was already starting to lose track of time. Repeatedly, Betty had to pause as she followed the string in the dim light, causing Fliss and Spit, who were right behind her with Charlie, to bump into her. Willow moved silently close to Betty, her eyes fixed on the wisp. The farther they got into the caves, the harder it became to ignore the evidence. Discarded objects littered the damp corners or lurked out of sight, waiting to trip them up. Betty cussed as she stumbled on a worn-out shoe, and her skin crawled as she crunched over broken eggshells. A squeal stuck in her throat as she accidentally kicked a wishbone. All signs of the people —and their wrong choices—who had gone before.

"I can feel fresh air up ahead," she said, sensing a cool breeze on her cheeks. But then the tunnel narrowed, forcing them to stoop, and the air turned stale once more.

"You sure this is right?" Spit asked. He was breathing heavily, clearly not enjoying himself at all, and his blond hair was damp with sweat despite the chill. He lugged the bucket at his side, spilling so much water that Betty was fearful that the fish wouldn't have enough left.

"I'm not sure of anything," she said. "Except that we need to keep moving." The words were sour in her mouth, and her cheeks and neck itched with sudden heat. The enormity of what they were doing closed in on her, like a tomb, as the tunnel narrowed. Could they really place their trust in an old legend and a reel of yarn? With time running out and no other options, they didn't have much choice.

"What happens when the string runs out?" Spit demanded. "For all we know, these caves could go on for miles."

"They probably do," said Betty. "But we've already come quite some way, and the reel still looks as full as ever." She eyed it with a tingle of fear. "It's like . . . like it's as long as you need it to be." She edged a little farther, sharp pebbles digging through her worn boots. "Looks as if it's opening up again here, thank goodness."

The cavern was so dark that the wisp's glow barely seemed to light it at all. Afraid of losing sight of it, Betty bent down to pick up the string trailing behind the reel and held it carefully, allowing it to slide through her fingers. She knew she wasn't imagining it now: the wisp *was* dimming. Hanging on by a thread, like Willow. All of a sudden, the cavern widened and forked off in two directions: one narrow tunnel and one higher and wider. Both were as dark as each other. Betty paused, the rest of the group catching up to gather around her. She was glad that, for once, she was not in the lead.

She moved closer to the higher tunnel for a better look. As she did, something clattered under Betty's foot. She lifted her boot and bent down, recognizing the object immediately. It was a golden key, set with an egg-shaped stone.

"Ronia," she whispered, her eyes darting to the two dark caves ahead. There was silence, no sign of the pirate captain.

Spit stared at the key. "She wouldn't have left this. Something must have happened to her." A strange look crossed his face: a mixture of relief and regret. Would he return to the pirates without Ronia, Betty wondered, or take the opportunity to be free of them? Because, as he'd already said, if he wasn't a Rusty Scuttler, then who was he?

"Her and everyone else who came through here," said Betty, her thoughts moving to the shoe, the eggshells, and the wishbone. The only traces of people who had taken on the island—and lost. Could Ronia, so fierce and invincible, really be one of them? If so, what hope had they, a group of mere children, a wisp, and a fish? "Who knows what else we'll find farther on?"

Spit shook his head "That's it. I'm not going another step through these tunnels."

"Thought you were a pirate?" Charlie demanded. "You ain't a real one, are you?"

Spit gulped. "Maybe I'm not," he admitted. His eyes were wild, glassy with fear at the thought of his fearsome captain being defeated. "But I'm not staying here another minute." He dumped the bucket on the ground and turned toward the dark tunnel they'd come through.

"Spit, wait!" Betty protested. "Stay with us! You'll get lost—the only light is the wisp!"

Her voice echoed back at them, shrill and loud like a slap. And then another voice came out of the darkness, and another and another: whispered voices that echoed all around them. The words were low and fast, like dry leaves skittering in the wind. Betty's scalp prickled.

"Take us with you . . ."

"So dark in here . . ."

"We'll follow you . . . follow you . . ."

Spit turned back in the tunnel, his face almost as drained as Willow's.

"What *is* that?" he gasped, the string slipping from his fingers. "Where's it coming from?"

"All around us." Betty thrust the bucket at Fliss. "Move, quickly!"

Scuffling in the darkness, Betty grappled with the string, following it hand over hand as the reel rolled into the wider of the two tunnels. There was only blackness stretching ahead and a dim glow from the wisp. It was not enough to light the way, and time and again, Betty bit her lip as she tripped on jutting rocks or crunched over more discarded objects. How much longer could Willow last in here? And how long would the fish survive in the bucket? If they stumbled or dropped it, there was no hope of reaching water in time.

Behind her, she heard panicked breathing. All of them were too terrified for words now and had only one thought between them: escape. Echoing voices surrounded them from every direction until it felt as though they were inside Betty's head. With each one, the tunnels seemed to shrink. Some were pleading, others malevolent.

"This way . . . follow us . . ."

"Lead you to untold riches . . ."

"Stay away! Mine, mine . . ."

Terror drowned Betty's thoughts, making her clumsy. Twice she dropped the string as she tripped and was forced to put out her hands to save herself. Grit flew up and peppered her eyes, making them stream. Behind her,

Charlie let out a whimper—or perhaps it was Fliss. Betty's hand closed around the string and she almost wept in relief, vowing not to let go again. If she got lost, they all did.

"How much longer, Betty?" Charlie clutched at her with hot hands. "It feels like it's getting harder to breathe!"

"Not long now," Betty babbled, with no way of knowing if it were true. Surely they were nearly out? She couldn't work out how long they'd been in the tunnels. It felt like hours, but there was no way of telling. All sense of time had vanished, leaving only fear and the urge to survive. "It has to be soon, it has to be!"

"*Has to be . . . has to be . . .*" the echoing voices chanted back, mocking and relentless.

Beneath her, the cave dipped without warning. Betty's ankle jarred, her foot suddenly ice-cold. "Water," she gasped. "I think it's a rock pool . . ." She took another step, feeling the coldness rise. "It's getting deeper. I'm going to try and wade through it."

"Betty, be careful," Fliss begged, sloshing well water at her back. The icy shock of it made Betty turn and catch sight of the bucket containing the fish.

"Saul," it burbled. "Saul!"

"Yes, we know!" Fliss snapped. "If it wasn't for you, we wouldn't be in this mess!"

The fish blew a stream of indignant bubbles, its eyes full of misery.

A third step took the water to Betty's knees. The fourth, deeper still. She strained her ears, trying to listen over the whispers. From somewhere nearby, she thought she heard a faint trickling. Was there water above them? Below? She took another step, shivering as the icy wetness rose to her hips. "It's getting higher," she told the others. Above her, the ceiling of the tunnel sloped lower, forcing her deeper, before rapidly declining to meet the water. *It's underwater*, she realized, the thought striking her with trepidation. But how far did it go?

"How do you know this is *really* the way out?" asked Spit. "And that the string isn't just another one of the witch's tricks?"

"It can't be," said Betty, but as she said it, doubt began to creep up on her like fingers along her spine. Could they really trust anything from the witch's cauldron? Betty had been so certain of the legend and everything she knew of it, but now it wasn't just a spooky story. It was her life and her sisters' lives. Spit's life and Willow's life. But in the dim light, with echoing voices in her ears, she couldn't be sure of what was real anymore.

Betty took another step. She had no time to gasp as the ground below seemingly vanished. Water stung her eyes and gushed into her mouth. She scrabbled around, desperate for the breath she never got to take. She fought to keep hold of the string, looping it around her wrist. Breaking the surface, she heaved in a lungful of air and swam back to the others, scraping her knee on the shelf of rock.

"Betty!" Fliss shrieked. "What happened?"

Hands grabbed her, pulling at her soaking clothes. She coughed, her teeth chattering. "I'm all right . . . but it gets deeper. I don't know whether we can get through —or how long it goes on for."

"But this is the way," Charlie protested. "Isn't it? Did we go wrong?"

"No . . . this is the way the string's taking us," said Betty. She tried to keep her voice from rising as an awful thought occurred to her. "Perhaps this *was* the way out long ago. Things change over time. Maybe it flooded. Maybe it . . ."

An eerie, echoing laugh surrounded them. This time there was no mistaking its menace. "*Maybe it flooded . . .*"

"SHUT UP!" yelled Fliss. "Just leave us alone!"

"There must be another path." Willow's voice was weak, the light from her wisp dimming even further. "Pull the string back in. Perhaps it'll lead us somewhere else."

Betty tugged the string, but already she knew that the

reel was ahead in the underwater tunnel, and it was hold-ing firm. Resisting. "It's like it . . . *wants* us to follow."

"We can't risk it," Fliss croaked. "These sorts of under-water caves . . . there's no telling how far they stretch. We could all drown!"

Betty squinted above their heads, searching in vain for some rocky shelf that they might cling to, but there was nothing. "I can't see any other way," she said desperately. "We have to go through the water." She swallowed down a sob. "I'll . . . I'll go on ahead, swim a little way. For all we know, it could just be a dip."

"No," Fliss growled. "No way!"

"We can't go back," said Betty. "We don't have a choice. Someone needs to go. If I get through, I'll tug the string three times and you can follow. If it goes on too far, I'll come back. I promise."

"Don't make promises you might not be able to keep," Fliss said hotly. Betty could just see the outline of her face, but the little light there was showed that her eyes were sparkling with tears.

Betty gritted her teeth. "I *promise*," she repeated, readying herself to go into the water again.

"Betty?" Charlie said anxiously. "What about Hoppit? He can't swim that far!"

"Oh, Charlie," Betty said, feeling a rush of love for

her little sister. "You and that pesky rat. He'll make it." She sighed, ruffling Charlie's hair. "Because he'll be with you."

Charlie took the rat out from her collar and kissed him on the nose. "You can do it, Hoppit," she whispered. "And so can you, Betty."

"Right then," said Betty, steeling herself. "Before I lose my nerve."

She slid into the water, moving to where the roof sloped quickly to meet the water. Taking a breath, she plunged beneath the surface and swept her arm from side to side, feeling her way. Rocks scraped her back, and slimy weeds tangled in her hair. A boot, still with its laces tied, drifted past her nose. She kicked further, jarring her ankle. Her lungs began to burn. How had she held her breath so long at the shipwreck? It was too much effort now, and she was so very tired. Dark spots flickered at the edge of her vision, threatening to overwhelm her. She clung to the thought of her sisters, and Granny, and home. But she had to breathe, cold water rushing in . . .

The rocks at her back gave way, sloping up, and she emerged, wheezing, into a pocket of damp air. She lifted a hand in the pitch darkness, feeling cold, wet rock an arm's length above her. Tentatively she swam a little farther, hoping the tunnel roof might remain high enough for her to continue with her head above water—but only a short way along, her outstretched fingertips brushed sloping rock once more.

Aware of the others waiting behind her, she tugged the string three times, feeling one in return, and time stood still. Water rushed and churned. *Come on*, she willed. *Come on!*

It was Charlie who popped up first, immediately followed by Willow and the wisp. After the blackout, the wisp's glow, though faint, was welcome. "It stinks in here," Charlie gasped, her pigtails plastered to her head. On her shoulder, a soggy Hoppit squeaked as if in agreement.

"Charlie!" Betty gasped, hugging her joyfully. "You did it!"

To Betty's immense relief, Fliss emerged next, followed by Spit. To Betty's shock, she saw he was bleeding.

"It's nothing," he muttered, rubbing his forehead. "Just a scratch on the rocks."

Betty nodded, gulping at the air gratefully. Stinking or not, it was keeping them alive a little longer.

Spit was bobbing an arm's length away, the bucket containing the fish beside him. "There's another opening here," he said, motioning underwater. His chest heaved, and he blinked watery blood out of his eye. "Just need to . . . to get my breath. I'll go first."

"Spit," Betty croaked. "No! You've hit your head."

"I'm going," he repeated. "You three have each other. If one of you gets hurt . . . I have no one. No one to miss me, anyway." He gave a wry laugh, passing the bucket to Fliss. "I don't even have a proper name."

His words tugged at Betty's heart. "Be careful," she said, reluctant. "Three tugs, remember?"

He nodded, then breathed deep and vanished in the murky water.

"The echoes have stopped," Fliss whispered in the silence that followed, holding Charlie tightly. The bucket bobbed next to her. "I don't know if that's better or worse."

Worse, Betty thought. For though she didn't say it, it made the place seem even deader than it was already.

"Is he still there?" Charlie asked, shivering.

Betty pulled the string gently, feeling the same resistance as before. "He's there."

"He should be through by now," said Fliss. "It's been too long!"

"Give him a chance," said Betty, trying to convince herself. "He'll do it." An image of Spit, open-eyed but unmoving, floated in her mind. How long could he last under there? She held in something that might have been a sob. Words sounded in her head: *I have no one. No one to miss me . . .*

"That doesn't mean it's all right," she whispered. What Spit had risked for them mattered. *He* mattered.

The string pulled in Betty's hand, tight around her fingers. *One, two, three.*

"He's there!" Betty yelled. "He's made it—he's *some-where*. Come on!"

Charlie and Fliss each took a gulp of air and vanished. Betty squeezed Willow's hand, so cold that her own hand was almost numbed. She looked into the girl's face and was gripped by doubt and fear.

"Willow," Betty began, alarmed. "You're looking paler than ever!"

"I can make it," said Willow, edging closer, her face ashen. "Just don't let go of me." With an iron grip, Betty pulled her under the water. It was worse here, colder, the water heavy with silt. Her knuckles scraped rock. Slime caught under her nails. Not meaning to, she opened her eyes and wished she hadn't. All around Willow the water glowed eerily, lit faintly by the wisp. Her terrified eyes locked on to Betty. Bubbles escaped her lips.

Betty kicked, closing her eyes. Seaweed tangled in her hair, trying to pull her back. To keep her in the darkness.

"*Noooooooo!*" Betty yelled, losing precious air.

Blinding light waited up ahead, so close. Water shot up her nose and into her throat, choking her. Then water turned to air as she came up to dazzling brightness, coughing and retching. Muffled voices reached her, becoming clearer as her ears emptied of water. She staggered from the water, a spluttering Willow following her. Finally, Betty released her hand as three figures came into view, ankle deep in a cave of shallow water. Beyond them, warm sunlight streamed through trees into the cave.

"Fliss, Charlie!" A cry forced its way out of her and she ran to them, pulling them both into her arms with a rush of love and relief.

"We made it!" Charlie laughed, thrusting a wet-nosed Hoppit in Betty's face. He snuffled happily, shaking water from his whiskers. "All of us!"

"Saul!" the fish repeated from the bucket, now topped up almost to the brim.

"Yes, you too," Betty added with an unexpected pang of sympathy for him. One by one, they waded out of the water into the open air, still blinking after the darkness of the tunnels. The warm sun was like a balm on Betty's skin and, from its warmth and position, she could tell that hours had passed during their passage through the caves. They were now on a rocky path that ran alongside a high cliff edge to the right and curved down into the distance. To their left, a vast area of forest began at the path's edge and dropped away steeply. Far below, past the thick vegetation, was a small circle of brightest turquoise. *The lagoon.*

Betty's heart galloped at the sight of it, but just as quickly she felt a flash of worry. She knew distances could be deceiving, and already it looked a long way to the lagoon. The quickest route would be off the path and through the trees—but the thought of this made the hairs on the back of her neck stand up. In all the fairy tales she knew, leaving the path was always a mistake.

Something knocked at her feet. She looked down to find the wooden reel there, and before her eyes, it began raveling up the string. She watched as the yarn twisted around, trailing back through the mouth of the caves, and finally stopped. She collected the reel, fat with string once more, and some of her doubts melted away. Whatever lay ahead, the magical object had done its job by leading them safely through the caves. "Strange," she murmured. "It's bone dry. Not a drop of water on it."

"Nothing about this place makes sense." Spit shook water off himself like a dog, then winced, pressing a hand to his head.

"Let me," said Fliss. She lifted her sleeve, gently touching it to his skin.

Spit's mouth dropped open. He blushed a deep red and gazed into her eyes.

"Thank you," Fliss said. "For what you did. If it wasn't for you, risking your life like that, we might not have made it through." She rested her fingers lightly on his cheek.

"Yes," said a cold voice. "You've been *very* useful, Spit. Perhaps you're worth more than I realized after all."

Betty spun around, dread rising like a tide.

Ronia stood in the mouth of the cave.

Chapter Twenty-Seven

Bewitched

"OH," SAID THE PIRATE CAPTAIN in a mocking voice. "I'm sorry—am I interrupting something?" She stared at Fliss and Spit with a look that would wilt a flower.

Fliss dropped her hand, her fingers curling into a fist.

"You're *alive*," said Spit hoarsely. "We thought . . ."

Ronia stepped toward them, dripping like a sea witch. There was a gash in one of her sleeves, dark with blood, and her hand trembled slightly. In her other hand, she held her cutlass, and it was as steady as ever. Next to her, Bandit slunk out of the caves, sneezing. He gave Ronia a baleful look and began licking his wet fur viciously.

"You thought I was dead," Ronia said. "Or whatever

it is that happens to people once they lose themselves in those caves." She smirked, advancing on them like a vulture. "Sorry to disappoint you, but I don't plan on leaving this island empty-handed."

"But the key," Spit stammered. "We found it—"

"*This* key?" Ronia produced it from her pocket. The stone glowed golden in the blazing sunlight. "I heard you blundering through the tunnels and managed to hide just before you saw me. By that time, I admit I almost welcomed the company." Her eyes slid over Betty. "How *did* you get here, by the way?"

"Never you mind," Betty growled. She thought back to the forked tunnels earlier. If they had checked the narrower one and found Ronia, would it have made a difference? Or would she simply have marched them through with her blade at their backs? "You followed us."

"I wasn't doing too badly." Ronia shrugged. "But you made it so easy." She grinned triumphantly. "You even found the key I'd mistakenly dropped—I thought I'd lost it! And when you'd gone, I picked it up and I trailed you. Or should I say your lovely bit of string. All that noise you were making! What with that and the echoes . . . you never heard a thing." She turned to Spit. "I always thought you were a lily-livered waste of space, but you were braver than I suspected. Perhaps I'll promote you after this."

"After this?" Spit repeated faintly. He took a step toward Ronia.

Betty watched in disbelief. Surely after all that had happened, Spit wouldn't double-cross them now?

"There won't be an *after this*," Spit continued, his voice shaking, but with anger, not fear, Betty realized. "I'm through with the Rusty Scuttlers—and you."

Ronia stared at him thunderously. "You dare to desert your captain?"

"I looked up to you," said Spit. "All this time, I tried to prove myself. And you left me in that well. You're not my captain anymore."

"Mutiny!" Charlie cheered.

"I was coming back for you—"

"Liar!" Spit said. "All you care about is whatever's at the heart of this island, and you want it for yourself."

"I thought pirates stuck together," Charlie put in. "But you left him!" Hoppit squeaked as if to back her up.

Ronia curled her lip. "Silence!" she said. "If you're good, I might even let you keep your rat a little longer before I feed it to my cat."

Charlie glared, eyes alive with defiance. "Funny," she growled, "I was planning on feeding *you* to my rat."

Hoppit hiccupped unconvincingly.

"What are you waiting for?" Spit said angrily to Ronia.

"You got through the caves. You're free to go ahead and loot whatever treasure there is. We're not stopping you! And after this, we never have to see each other again."

Ronia sighed, inspecting her blade. "That's not how it works. You see this island is tricky. It caught me off-guard. But one way or another, I'll make it down to the heart of it, to that lagoon. So it's handy having someone to go first in a place like this. A bit like having a cat with nine lives. There's always room for a few . . . mistakes." She smiled thinly. "And you girls are certainly proving useful, with your magical map and string."

Fliss gasped. "You're saying you want us as . . . as spare lives for you in case things go wrong?"

"Glad we understand each other." Ronia flicked her cutlass dangerously close to Spit's nose. "You first. Go."

Spit stayed where he was, his hands in tight fists. Betty glanced sideways at him, heart racing. They had Spit on their side now, and there were more of them and only one Ronia.

"We're not going anywhere with you," she said. And then her daring thoughts crumpled like paper. Soundless as a breath, Ronia seized Charlie and held her cutlass to her throat.

"I don't think I made myself clear," Ronia said softly. "Don't test me." She nodded in the direction of the steps.

"I said *move!*" She pointed at Fliss, then the bucket. "You, carry the dinner."

"*Saul!*" the fish protested in alarm, but Betty didn't react. She was too afraid to make any move with the blade at Charlie's neck. And if Ronia knew the fish was valuable to them, there was no telling what she might do.

Spit shot Betty a helpless glance. *Disappear!* he mouthed, as he moved past her. Betty followed, heart hammering as her fingers went to her pocket. If she could use the dolls to make them all vanish, perhaps they could escape. But Ronia was too sharp—and she already had Charlie in her clutches. If Betty made her vanish now, Ronia would still feel her—could still *hurt* her.

"Now walk," Ronia said, gripping Charlie's collar. Charlie's eyes filled with tears, but she pursed her lips, seemingly determined not to cry.

Betty bit back her rising anger. They had no choice but to obey—for now.

The sun shone down on them as they left the caves behind and set off along the path. Brightly feathered birds called from above and flower heads nodded at the foot of the trees. Fruit none of them recognized hung heavy from the branches beside the path. Instead of the rocky cliffs they had climbed up to enter the caves, rough steps were hewn into the stone leading down. Betty gazed at the rocks sloping up and around, curving gently inward as far as the eye could see. It gave the disconcerting feeling of being inside a giant cauldron.

Though she kept taking worried glances back at Ronia and Charlie, Betty couldn't help her attention being drawn to the trees beside them.

Swaying branches brushed them like curious fingers. The farther they went along the path, the higher the trees and bushes around them got, blocking the view of the lagoon, but Betty saw that the ground beyond the trees sloped even more steeply than she'd first realized. If any of them fell, their chances of survival were slim. It was no surprise Ronia had chosen to stick to the safer path down to the lagoon, Betty thought, however desperately the pirate craved the island's riches. She recalled what Spit had told her: She's clever and cunning and, most danger-ous of all, she's *patient.*

And relentless. They marched along in silence as the sun crawled through the sky, gradually losing its heat as time slipped away. The march became a trudge. Betty's feet blistered, and even Fliss was breaking a sweat. The only suggestion that Ronia was tiring had been her sheath-ing her cutlass with a cool warning to Charlie: "Don't pull any tricks."

"Fliss?" Charlie called hesitantly after quite some time.

"Hoppit's tummy's rumbling. And so is mine. Could we pick some fruit?" She paused to stare at a strange, bell-shaped fruit in wonder. "Looks tasty."

Betty shook her head, remembering stories of enchanted feasts and trapped humans. "Don't eat *anything*, Charlie. This whole island is bewitched. It could be dangerous."

Ronia sneered. "Your sister's right. Eating here could be risky. So if the time comes, you can have first bite."

"Can't even tell what it is on these branches." Spit looked up uncertainly at another tree. "Is that fruit?" Gold gleamed from above.

"An *egg*?" Charlie peered into the leaves. "A *golden* egg. What kind of bird—?"

"Look," said Betty, mystified. "There's a stalk attached, and leaves. It's *growing*."

"Oh," Charlie breathed, eyeing a tiny egg barely the size of an acorn.

"Don't touch *anything*," Betty said, unsettled. "All this stuff . . . it's not right."

"But look how dinky that egg is," Charlie said mournfully.

"Don't touch," Fliss whispered, but even as she said it, the longing in her voice was evident. Betty gazed up, not really wanting to but unable to help seeking out those tantalizing flashes of gold. Would it really be so bad to take just *one?* Before she knew it, she found herself reaching up into the branches. A mouthwatering smell wafted down like powdered sugar.

But it was Ronia who got there first. Out came her cutlass to slash down one of the golden eggs, which was almost as large as a pumpkin. She stepped aside neatly as it fell, smashing next to her feet. Betty held her breath, half expecting to see an oozing yolk. Instead, a plume of black feathers puffed into the air before landing on the path.

Unsettled, they forged along the winding path. Between Betty and Fliss, Willow staggered along, dragging her feet. Trailing her, and unnoticed by Ronia, was the wisp — so insubstantial now it looked like a shimmer of moonlight. It seemed that the farther along they went, the lower the nearby branches hung, dangling temptation in their faces. Before she knew what she was doing, Betty realized her hand was reaching for one of the strange, bell-shaped fruits Charlie had been hankering after earlier.

She plucked one, but the instant the stalk snapped, the flesh withered and rotted in her hand.

Betty began to withdraw her arm, but as it brushed against the leaves, she noticed a peculiar sensation, as if the leaves weren't really leaves at all. Instead, they felt like feathers. The shock of it made her freeze, her hand suspended between the branches. Without warning, something rushed at her, a scrabble of bird-like claws, a sharp jab like a beak snapping, pecking her skin.

Betty reeled away, foot tangling in a tree root, and lost her balance. She threw her arms out to steady herself, but her ankle twisted and, with a sickening lurch, she felt herself fall away from the path and down into the trees. Her head bumped against a trunk, sending a painful flare of stars before her eyes, but she continued to plummet endlessly. Roots and vines scratched over her, jolting and jostling as she spun like a wheel.

I'm off the path, she realized somewhere through the pain and lights flickering before her eyes. *I'm falling, and there's nothing to stop me.*

Voices yelled for her. From somewhere above, she heard sobbing, and Fliss shouting her name, the last thing Betty was aware of before everything faded to black.

Betty opened her eyes and winced. Why was it so dark? How much time had passed since she'd fallen? Panic snatched at her, making her bruised head throb. She prodded it cautiously, feeling an egg-size bump. There didn't seem to be any blood. *How far did I fall?* she wondered, opening her mouth to call out, but her voice emerged as a dry croak that sent another shooting pain through her head.

Her fingers caught in something at the same time as she realized she was swaying from side to side.

The odd sensation sharpened her mind, pulled her more fully out of her daze. Her hands felt something rough and thin in a cocoon around her.

The string. It had saved her, netting her like a fish and hanging her from the branches above. Groaning, Betty stepped out of it carefully, lowering herself to the ground. She swayed, trying to get her balance on the sloping ground. Reaching out, she steadied herself against a rough tree trunk, but the longer her fingers remained there, the less it felt like bark and the more it felt like something scaly, like the leg of a giant bird. She recoiled hurriedly. Through the darkness, she felt blindly for the string, giving it a cautious tug. It held firm, anchored somewhere in the branches above—but there was no way to find the reel, she realized with mounting dread.

A breeze lifted, ruffling through something that sounded like feathers. Betty held her breath, unable to work out which way to go. She was lost.

She was alone.

Chapter Twenty-Eight

Treasure

F EAR TOOK OVER BETTY'S SENSES, rendering her unable to move. How was it so unnaturally dark when the sun had still been on the path only moments before? She looked up, seeing swaying branch movements. And yet . . . they didn't seem quite like branches. Instead, she had the sensation that she was under feathers, like a large, black wing was smothering her, disorientating her.

A sob lodged in her throat. How could she ever find her way back without the magical reel? Could it have snared somewhere near the path, leaving the trail of yarn for her to follow? She gripped the string tightly, uselessly. Even if she could follow it, doing so blind would be treacherous. She pictured jutting rocks, looping vines. Unseen raven claws and beaks . . . And even if she retraced her steps to where she had fallen from, what use would that be? She had no idea how much time had passed. She'd be way behind—her best chance now was to try to continue through the trees, on to the lagoon where she could intercept the others. Yet the thought of moving farther into the trees in any direction terrified her.

"Betty Widdershins," she told herself shakily. "Get on with it. It's no safer going back to the path than it is to try and find your way forward to the heart of the island." She bunched her hands into fists, trying to squeeze strength into them. This was for Willow, she reminded herself, remembering the haunted look in the girl's eyes as she'd told Betty about her father. And she had to get back to her sisters—they weren't safe with Ronia and her blade that had already been at Charlie's throat.

She took a step, screwing up her courage. Something flickered in the darkness, and her breath caught. *The wisp?* No, this was a brighter, warmer kind of light. Betty took another step, and another light came into view. More flickered on before her, dozens of tiny lights like fairy lamps, gliding over the ground, leading the way.

"Beetles," she whispered, the story leaping into her mind. "The beetles lit the way for Hope out of the dark caves. If I follow them . . . ?" She hesitated. Was this a trick of the island? A test? Perhaps. "Hope," she whispered. "That's what I have to hold on to."

She took a breath and followed. The beetles marched on, swarming in a line that dotted the darkness like pinpricks of light. The ground descended sharply. Gritting her teeth, Betty went after them, legs and throat burning, crunching over undergrowth like eggshells. With every step, her feet rustled through twigs like she was treading through a giant bird's nest. She strained to listen, trying to track her sisters' cries, their panicked voices. There was nothing, only her padding footsteps and the chirruping of the beetles, but she could see a little now, the beetles' glow illuminating branches and roots.

Her head throbbed with every movement. How long had she blacked out for? Seconds? Minutes? Though she recalled her sisters calling for her, she now doubted whether it had happened at all. She imagined them sobbing, pleading, wanting to search . . . and Ronia forcing them on without remorse, driven by her own greed to secure whatever riches lay at the island's heart, no matter what the cost.

Her throat ached with the urge to cry, but she held it in. Crying wouldn't help. All it would do was give her away to whatever might lurk unseen nearby. If she was going to catch up to them, she had to be as fearless and stealthy as Ronia.

She continued to stagger on, following the tiny lights. All hopes pinned on them leading her to safety. It was several minutes before she noticed the unnerving chill. A coldness sweeping over her that wasn't from any breeze. She stared ahead at the beetles and then behind, desperate for any sign of her sisters or the glow of the wisp.

And that was when she saw the figure—no more than a shadow, unmistakably female, with long, ragged clothes and hair to match. Something feathered on her shoulder, claws and hooked beak. *A raven.*

Betty's gut twisted with terror, as if an invisible hand were wringing her out.

It's a trick of the light, she thought. *Shadows always look like something, the way clouds do when you stare at them for long enough.* She took a step, looking over her shoulder, waiting for it to stretch. Expecting to laugh with relief as it became a cluster of branches.

The shadow remained unchanged. Exactly the same distance away, though Betty hadn't seen it move. A sickening feeling gathered in the center of her chest, and she felt feverish, shivering and sweating all at once. How hard had she hit her head? She moved farther away. The shadow moved with her.

A sob lodged in Betty's throat. She stumbled, scraping her elbow on a nearby tree trunk. The shadow figure followed, spilling over the ground like ink. Not walking or moving in any way, yet *somehow* following.

Betty began to run, breathing ragged. The distraction had slowed her, allowing the glowing beetles to slip a little farther ahead. Every glance over her shoulder told her the figure was still there, neither falling back nor coming closer. Always the same, as constant as her own shadow. Perhaps there was a way she could hide? She tugged the nesting dolls out of her pocket, standing still in the dark. Carefully she undid them, nudging the third doll out of alignment so that only she, not her sisters or Willow, would be affected—and left the second doll with her hair inside lined up. She twisted the outer doll to render herself invisible and continued after the fading beetles. Quickly, she saw it made no difference. Somehow she knew the shadow could see her—or perhaps sense her.

She sped up, forgetting to be quiet now and not bothering to readjust the dolls. Not caring about noise, just wanting the shadow to be gone and the beetles to lead her somewhere, *anywhere* out of the never-ending dark. *Keep hope*, she thought, chanting it in her head, but with every step, it slipped further away from her. What if her sisters fell afoul of Ronia's determination to find riches? What if they were already gone? *What if . . . ?*

She felt dampness on her cheeks and realized she was crying. The little lights of the beetles dimmed, like mist over a starlit sky. She looked back, then wished she hadn't. The witch's shadow blurred, somehow even more terrifying in its ambiguity. *She's waiting for me to give up*, Betty thought, faint with fear as things twisted in the darkness at her feet. Roots snaring her ankles, clinging to her legs. *She knows it's only a matter of time . . .*

Time. The word lit up in her mind like a match. Time was running out for Willow and her father, and for her sisters in Ronia's grip. They couldn't be parted like this! She *had* to make it back to them. She dashed the tears from her cheeks, desperately searching the undergrowth for the fading glow of the beetles. There! One tiny spark remained, trailing into the darkness.

Betty plunged after it, summoning all that was left of her courage. She had to keep going, couldn't lose it, this last little speck of light that was her only hope . . .

And then, when she no longer knew whether her knees or her heart might give way first, a sound broke the silence: the trickle of running water.

Betty forced herself onward, stopping abruptly as her foot left the crackling undergrowth and sank into sugar-soft sand. The instant her boot set down, it was as though a veil had been lifted, light flooding over her, its brightness almost blinding. She glanced back into the trees, curiously no longer coated in darkness. On the fringes of the wood, the tiny beetles glittered like light on glass. How long would she have been wandering in the darkness without them? How long *had* she been wandering? The sky was still light but fading to pink, the sun having vanished beyond the steep cliffs encircling the island. A thin slice of moon and faint stars were already visible.

"Thank you," Betty whispered to the beetles. One by one, they flickered out, vanishing.

And yet the shadow remained, no closer but no farther away, silent within the trees. Waiting and watching for her next move.

Braver now that there was light, Betty took a few more steps onto the pale sand. It swept from side to side in a curve, smooth as fresh snow, with only a few rocks and boulders dotted here and there as it tapered away to a shore. Water lay ahead of her, crystal clear and turquoise. She had reached the lagoon. *The heart of the island.* Without the shadow at her back, she might have enjoyed the beauty of it, but as her eyes swept across it, her gnawing uneasiness grew.

The water's surface was flat and glassy, a mirror of the sky. And yet that made no sense, for at the back of it, a waterfall was churning, its spray a pale blur at the furthermost edge of the lagoon.

A movement drew her attention. Betty passed a boulder and stared along the crescent of sand. Farther up in the distance, a group of figures stood along the shoreline, surrounding something on the ground half in the water. Fear clutched at her. Was it a person lying there? It was too far to tell or make out any expressions. She headed closer, counting them. She made out Charlie's tangled hair and Fliss next to her. Spit was beside them, and there was Ronia, sword drawn. Willow stood a little way back, appearing to be swaying on her feet. Miraculously, the bucket containing Saul was next to her.

Betty crept closer, weak with relief. They were all there; they still had a chance. She just had to get them past Ronia and—and . . . ?

She scanned the lagoon, thinking of the three brothers' story. They'd had to reach the heart of the island in order to get Fortune and Luck returned to their true forms before they could leave. And for Betty, it must end here, too—but how were they to return home and restore Saul to his human self?

Betty glanced over her shoulder warily. The witch shadow lingered in the darkness, but Betty felt stronger now, revived by the sight of her sisters, for however much danger they were in, there was still . . . *hope*. The word chimed in her head. Was it her imagination, or had the shadow faded a little? She took another step toward her sisters. Unmistakably, the witch drew farther back.

She's losing her hold on me, Betty realized. *In the dark, when I was afraid, she almost caught me. And now she can't*. She edged closer to her sisters, heart soaring at the sound of their voices—just fragments at first but becoming clearer with every step. When she looked back next, the shadow had vanished—but a movement caught her attention.

The wooden reel, fat with twine, emerged from the fringe of the trees and rolled to rest against her foot, as though someone had accidently nudged it. Betty picked it up and pushed it safely into her pocket before continuing.

She moved closer still, glad of the cloak of invisibility the dolls provided. Soon Betty was near enough to hear every word. Charlie was sniffling, not interested in whatever the thing on the sand was. She stared back up the beach toward the path leading up the cliffs, tugging Fliss's hand.

"We have to find her, Fliss! Betty's out there somewhere—"

Fliss wrapped her arm around Charlie's shoulders, making shushing sounds, but her own face was tear-streaked and fraught.

Betty crept nearer, almost close enough to touch. A mixture of love for her sisters curdled with loathing for Ronia. And then Charlie gripped Fliss's hand hard, pointing. Betty froze—she *was* invisible . . . wasn't she?

Betty looked down, understanding at the same moment as Fliss. Her footprints were visible in the sand! Quickly, she dropped to her knees, using her finger to scrape a word: *Shh!*

A gap-toothed grin broke out on Charlie's face, but Fliss pressed a finger to her lips, shaking her head slightly. Charlie stopped grinning immediately and pretended to give a little sob.

"Stop that child from sniveling. Or I will," Ronia snapped. "And get the lid open."

Lid? Hastily, Betty brushed away the writing in the sand and peered past Ronia.

A huge wooden chest was half submerged in the sand. It lay at an angle, its curved lid tilting down, crusted with seaweed. Even though the lower half was buried, Betty could see that it was easily big enough to fit a person inside. A terrible sense of foreboding prickled at her, and it seemed she wasn't alone.

"I don't think we should open it," said Spit, his voice low, urgent. "Anything could be inside. It might be a trap. We know what happens when people touch things they shouldn't—Rusty Swindles showed us that." His eyes were haunted.

"Yes," Ronia said, swinging her cutlass. "That's why *you're* opening it."

Reluctantly, Spit heaved at the lid with Ronia, Fliss, and Charlie looking on. Only Willow stood back, caught by some strange shaft of the fading light that illuminated her, almost painting her in blue. Betty frowned, further unsettled, although she couldn't explain why . . . but as the chest creaked open, her gaze was pulled away from the little girl.

A collective gasp went through them. Betty clapped her hand over her mouth, afraid of giving herself away, but Ronia was too busy staring into the chest.

It was full of maps, more maps than Betty had ever seen. Glimpses of ink—black, gold, and silver— peeked out from rolls of fine parchment. Their curling edges were like beckoning fingers and, almost in a trance, Betty felt herself taking a step toward the chest. What kinds of maps were to be found on an unmapped island? The mystery of them sang to her, luring her like a siren's song.

"*Oh,*" Charlie whispered, breaking Betty's thoughts. "Look at the toffee on those apples! And those fruit drops —I've never seen so many colors!" She squeaked and pointed in delight. "And those sugared mice are bigger than Hoppit!"

Betty shook her head faintly. *Toffee apples? Sugared mice?*

Ronia elbowed Charlie out of the way, leaning over the chest. Amber light played over her features, lighting them up in a way that didn't make sense. In a way that might have been light reflecting off gold. "This isn't a game, you stupid child! It's riches. And they're *mine.*"

"Riches?" Spit said faintly. "Is that what you see?"

"Mice!" Charlie insisted, her eyes still huge. "Great big ones with licorice whiskers and tails!"

Betty blinked in bewilderment, seeing only maps.

"That's not what I see," Fliss murmured.

"Nor me." Spit's expression was haunted. "I see . . . a *family.*"

"No, it's a staircase," Fliss continued, a faraway look in her eyes. "The one leading up from the cellar into the

Poacher's Pocket." She grabbed Charlie's hand. "If we took it, it'd lead us home, I know it!"

"Ain't no staircase!" Charlie protested, licking her lips. "That's sweets, that is!"

"Stop with your nonsense," Ronia hissed. "It's clear what's happening here."

"Untold riches," breathed Spit, pausing, his eyes wide. "It was all true! Only everyone's ideas of riches are different. It's showing each of us what we want."

"Well, only one of us will be leaving with them," Ronia said viciously. She thrust a hand into the casket, and in that moment, the maps Betty saw vanished. Golden coins and bright jewels tinkled through Ronia's fingers. She laughed delightedly, unearthing a firestone the size of a lump of coal before plunging her arm in even deeper.

"What?" Charlie whispered, eyeing the glinting coins in confusion.

A strange expression crossed Spit's face, and Betty followed his gaze to Ronia, the captain he had so admired. She cackled like a magpie, her face contorting into something almost unrecognizable. As if the treasure itself had possessed her in every way.

"It's huge, *vast*," she crooned, admiring the casket like it was the crib of a longed-for child. "Bigger and better than any chest we've ever found."

"Yeah," said Spit softly. "And you want everything inside it for yourself, don't you? To heck with the Rusty Scuttlers."

Smirking, Ronia dug her arm deeper into the tumbling coins. But then the smirk faltered, replaced by confusion. She withdrew her arm and swung a foot into the chest, pushing down through the treasure. "I—it must end somewhere . . . It's—"

The coins gave way beneath her, as if a trapdoor had fallen open. Ronia screamed as she was sucked into the coins that were disappearing into the chest's hidden depths like quicksand. As her fighting arm flung out to save herself, her cutlass dropped silently into the sand.

Fliss swooped on it, but already Betty could see that Ronia was shoulder deep and in trouble. Gold spilled over gold, and gemstones crushed against each other, grinding like pepper in a mill.

"It's swallowing her!" Charlie yelled, wide-eyed in horror and fascination.

Instinctively, Spit grabbed Ronia's arm, his face pinched with shock.

"Spit, no!" Fliss shouted. "It'll take you, too!"

"I can't let her die!" he cried. Coins flew up, hitting him in the face. One of them landed on the sand, rolling to a standstill to reveal it was nothing more than Willow's hagstone. Another layer of coins gave way and Spit was jerked farther into the chest.

"No!" Betty yelled, breaking her cover. She leaped forward, grabbing his waist and holding on. "Fliss, Charlie, help me! Don't let him go."

Coins slid all around them, golden light shining in their eyes, blinding them. "Pull!" Betty roared.

Ronia's eyes were bulging, one arm locked on to Spit's, the other gripping the edge of the chest.

A growl rumbled from within the coins.

"Ronia," Spit gasped. "Take my other hand."

With an effort, Ronia released the side of the chest and began reaching for Spit. A firestone rolled away from her, flashing red on her skin . . .

"Don't!" Spit yelled. Unable to resist, Ronia lunged for the stone, her fist closing around it. Her eyes registered jubilation . . . then shock as she plummeted back, slipping from Spit's fingers. Gold light played across her terrified face.

The lid crashed down, sealing Ronia inside the chest.

Chapter Twenty-Nine

Hagstone

"GET BACK!" BETTY CRIED, feeling the sand beneath them sliding inward toward the lagoon. The water began to glow and stir, sucking hungrily at the chest. They scrambled back up the shore, watching in disbelief as the chest was dragged through the sand like a spoon through sugar. Then everything—water, sand, and chest—lurched to the left as the lagoon began to swirl. They could only stare in shock as the chest rushed inward, drawn closer and closer to the center of a giant whirlpool.

"That was our way home!" Fliss cried, blinking tears away. "I saw it!"

"No," Betty answered. She twisted the dolls in her

pocket, rendering herself visible. "It was temptation. A trap, like Spit said. Nothing more."

Fliss hugged Charlie close. "Then how do we get out of here? How do we get *back*? The map pointed to the lagoon—but why?"

"What if we can't get back at all?" Charlie added tearfully. "I want Granny!"

"Wait," Fliss said suddenly. "Where's Willow?"

Betty turned, shaking herself. She had almost forgotten the strange girl who was the reason they were on this island in the first place, and the realization unnerved her. Yet as she clapped eyes on Willow, that feeling only grew.

Next to the pale little girl, the wisp flickered faintly, but it was clear at a glance that it was losing its light. Vanishing. As if it were being leached away somewhere . . .

"What's wrong with it?" Fliss asked. "It's like . . . like it's dying."

Willow swayed on her feet unsteadily. But now, in the near darkness, Betty could see why she looked so strange. At first, she had thought it was the moonlight making Willow appear so white and unearthly, but now that she looked properly, she saw it was nothing of the sort. A strange, pale light was glowing out of Willow, blurring her edges and rising off her almost like steam . . .

. . . or marsh mist.

"Willow?" Betty managed in a choked voice.

"What's the matter with her?" Spit asked, backing away. "Why's she glowing like that? She looks . . . she looks like a *wisp!*"

Willow lifted her hands, staring at them in puzzlement. "I don't understand," she said. Her voice sounded muffled, far away. "What's happening to me?" She looked around with pleading, confused eyes. "I needed to do something, but it's getting harder to think . . ."

"We were helping you," Charlie said gently. "Remember? You escaped from Torment. You were running away, trying to reach this island. You came to us in the night . . ."

You came to us . . .

Something sparked in Betty's mind. A memory of words uttered by Willow herself.

Wisps hold on because of unfinished business. Sometimes it's a feeling: anger or sadness. Sometimes they're vengeful; sometimes they want justice . . .

"Justice," Betty whispered with a glimmer of understanding. "That's what you said. Holding on to clear your father's name. Now it makes sense." Thoughts tumbled over and over in her head, piecing together.

"And Charlie found you," said Betty, remembering. "I didn't see you at first. I only saw Charlie, but then . . . there you were."

"Betty, what are you saying?" Fliss hissed. "This still doesn't answer why she's . . . *glowing* like that!"

"I think it does." Goose bumps raised on Betty's arms and neck. "Because Charlie saw her, so could we. Otherwise we might not have seen her at all. And then we invited her in. We made her . . . *real*."

"Please, stop," Willow whispered, her hands trembling. "I don't . . . I don't . . ."

Another memory pushed its way into Betty's head. Voices, rippling around the Poacher's Pocket when the news of the escape had broken out.

Two runaways . . . one washed up, half-drowned, not expected to survive the night . . .

But something of Willow *had* survived . . . or had clung on to what little life she could.

"Something happened when you escaped from Torment, didn't it, Willow?" Betty asked gently. "The boat got into trouble. You went into the water. All this time, I thought the wisp was your mother, that she hadn't survived. But it was *you*."

Willow frowned, her forehead creasing. "I . . . yes. We hit a rock, I think. The boat tipped, and I fell into the water. Away from Mother. It was so, *so* cold, and I couldn't breathe, but I . . ."

Images flashed in front of Betty's eyes: of Willow,

surrounded by marsh mist in the backyard. Dripping water that had never properly dried out. Breath that hadn't misted the air. Pale as the fog itself.

Pale as death.

". . . I don't remember getting out," Willow finished, frowning. "I just remember thinking about the map and knowing I needed to get here. And running, and running . . . and hiding."

"What are you saying?" Spit whispered.

"Don't you see?" Betty asked. "Willow hasn't just been followed by a wisp. She *is* the wisp!" A sense of loss threatened to overwhelm her, and she blinked back tears. Poor, lost Willow. Dimming through the night, a soul fallen to the marshes. Trying to make someone listen. Trying to make someone *follow.* "When someone's lost on the marshes . . . or at sea . . . that's what becomes of them. Heck, we even missed the biggest clue of all." She chuckled, but it was mirthless and empty. "Your name. It's not really Willow, is it?"

A silent sob shook Willow's shoulders. She seemed to be almost hovering now, flickering like the tiny light beside her which, before their eyes, merged into her to become one. "I don't know!"

"Willow-the-wisp," Fliss said, her eyes flooding with

realization. "And she led us here. We . . . we *followed* her and that's the worst thing we could have done!"

"We didn't follow her," said Charlie. "We followed the map. We helped her." She took a tentative step toward Willow, the pale glow from the girl playing over her face. "I'm *still* helping her."

"There's still a chance," said Betty, summoning her courage. "Whatever she is . . . she's holding on. If we can get off this island, maybe we can save her. And we have to hurry—now the wisp has . . . has *joined* her, she's running out of time!"

"How *do* we get off, though?" Spit asked, his gaze locked on Willow. "We found the lagoon, but I sure as heck don't want to end up like Ronia!"

"The brothers made it back," Betty whispered to herself, thinking of the story. "There *has* to be a way." She took out the map once more. Nothing had changed; no words had appeared. Only the cave mouth, the well, and the lagoon at the island's center were visible. The chest, however, was gone.

"Let's see that," said Charlie.

"I've looked." Exhaustion crept into Betty's voice, but she passed the map to Charlie. "There's nothing different."

"Not different," said Charlie. "But the *same*." She

lifted an object to the waxed paper—Willow's hagstone spat from the treasure chest. Charlie laid it on the map next to the island. "They're the same shape!"

Betty stared at the inked drawing and the barnacled stone. They were, undeniably, identical.

Fliss clutched at her arm urgently. "She's right!"

"It's a hagstone," Betty said slowly, her eyes drawn to the swirling water. "The lagoon at the center . . . it must go all the way through. The island itself is a *hagstone!*" She lowered the map. "And if you can only find it by *looking* through a hagstone, maybe you can only leave it by . . . by . . ."

"Going through the middle," Fliss finished.

"You want us to go through that?" Spit repeated. He threw out his arm, gesturing to the wildly swirling water. "Look what happened to Ronia!"

Betty shook her head, understanding sparking within her. "Ronia came here for riches that weren't rightfully hers," she said. "It made her cruel and selfish, and she was punished for it. But Willow brought us here to clear her father's name. She came for someone else. That's how the island works. The greedy are punished and the selfless are rewarded."

"Then that must mean us, too." Charlie tugged at Betty's sleeve earnestly. "We came for Willow, didn't we?"

She glanced worriedly at the chest. "I never actually *ate* any of the sweets, even though I really wanted to. And I promise I would've shared."

"I know you would have," Betty said, hugging her. "And you're right. I think this *is* the way home, for all of us. We have to trust it."

"Betty?" Fliss said, her voice trembling. She jerked her head back at Willow. "What about her?"

Willow was still glowing, brighter now, her eyes glassy and unseeing. A wave of panic took hold of Betty. Willow had to hold on, had to get back. They knew the truth—that her father was innocent. But until they returned, no one else would—and Willow would stay a wisp. Roaming the marshes, unable to rest. But even if they succeeded—what then? Could Willow still survive somehow? Or was she already lost?

"How will we stay together?" Fliss exclaimed. "It's a whirlpool; it'll tear us apart!"

"With this." Betty pulled the string out of her pocket and unraveled it. "Loop it around your hands, and don't let go." She grabbed Willow—almost afraid her hands would pass straight through her—before bundling her toward the water. She glanced fearfully at Charlie, squeezing her other hand, then Fliss. All holding on to one another. All holding on to hope.

"And the fish?" Fliss gasped, suddenly remembering the bucket.

"Give it here," said Spit, pale-faced, taking the bucket from Fliss. "I'll try and keep it above water for as long as I can."

"Now us," said Betty. She took Willow's hand. That cold, glowing, pale, little hand that had sent shivers through her ever since they'd met and she only now understood why.

"Hold on, just a little longer," Betty told her, squeezing her hand. Whatever happened, they owed it to Willow—and themselves—to see this through to the end. "It's nearly over. Everyone ready? Let's go!"

She waded into the churning water, screwing up her courage, breath held. Instantly, her feet were swept from under her and she was pulled sideways with such ferocity that it knocked the breath from her lungs. The string pulled tightly around her wrist as she was sucked to the left.

"Betty!" Charlie shrieked, hurtling past her with Fliss and Spit close behind. They whipped in dizzying, ever-decreasing circles that dragged them toward the center of the maelstrom. The water roared, a black void opening up in the center, twisting and plunging, faster and faster until all Betty could see and hear were blurs. A leg, a

glowing hand, a tufty fin. A waxed, yellowing map . . .
a blur of yowling, white fur and Willow's eyes, closing as
they were sucked down and down and down . . . water in
her ears, over her head, and the surface far, far above . . .

. . . then up, rushing through light and bubbles, and a
roaring noise that gave way to something like a cackle and
a raven's screech echoing in Betty's head.

She burst to the surface, the terrible sound still ringing in her ears. Spluttering noises surrounded her, water
thrashing and splashing, hungry breaths being drawn in
and misting the air.

"Fliss? Charlie?" she choked, tasting salt. The sky
above was inky now, the moon hidden by cloud. "Spit?"
She glanced around frantically, lifting the hand that had
been holding Willow's and finding only an empty wooden
reel.

"Over here!"

Grateful sobs shook Betty's body as she swam to her
sisters.

"We're out," Fliss gurgled. "It's gone. The island has
vanished!"

For the first time, Betty saw it was true. They were
floating in a vast expanse of water with no island in sight.
Only their slightly battered, old, green fishing boat was
bobbing a little way away, tethered to nothing.

"So has Willow," she whispered, tightening her grip on the reel. "I had her . . . and now she's gone." She whipped around, searching the water and teetering between hope and anguish.

"And who's that?" Spit asked, pointing to a figure floating motionless in the water nearby. He struck out, swimming quickly, and arrived by the person's side, turning him over. The man groaned, clutching his head. A tuft of hair poked out from above each ear in a vaguely familiar way.

"Feels good to breathe . . . air again," he murmured. "And to speak words instead of bubbles."

"The fish," said Charlie. "It's Saul! We did it." Her face crumpled, tears spilling down her already wet cheeks. "We did it for Willow."

Betty continued to search the waters desperately, but there was no sign of Willow. What did it mean that she was gone? Where was she now? *What* was she now? A pale, little wisp haunting the marshes? Or had the Widdershinses' help been enough? The thought that they might have failed to save her was too much to bear, but Betty hadn't the heart to speak her thoughts aloud and dash her sisters' hopes.

"Come on." Betty's voice was clipped in her effort to

contain her feelings. She shivered, nodding toward *The Traveling Bag.* "Before that gets away from us for good."

One by one, they scrambled aboard, pushing and pulling until everyone had finally collapsed on the deck. Stars peeked through the clouds. On top of the wheelhouse, a thin shape licked water droplets from its fur, then paused to stare into the water with a mournful yowl.

"Bandit!" Charlie exclaimed, undeterred as the cat hissed back at her. "I *knew* we'd end up keeping you."

"Charlie," Betty said, passing her a blanket from the wheelhouse. "Don't even *think* about it."

"What?" Charlie stuck out her tongue, grinning mischievously. "I've got a plan." She tickled Hoppit's chin, whispering, "Don't worry. You're still number one."

"There's only one plan we need right now," Betty answered, stepping over to the wheel. "Getting home." But as she took the wheel in her hands, she stiffened. For there, in front of the window, was a familiar map.

"How did that get there?" Fliss asked, pausing from rubbing her hair dry. "I thought it was lost in the whirlpool."

"It was in the lagoon with us," Betty said, frowning. "It doesn't make sense that it's here now. But then . . . perhaps magic and sense don't go together."

"Or perhaps the map can't be destroyed," Fliss said, yet despite her quietness, her voice was heavy with a responsibility that Betty also felt. It was upon them to ensure the map wasn't passed on. To prevent others going in search of the mysterious island.

Carefully, Betty rolled the map up and replaced it with a larger one, one that showed the way home. "Here, take the wheel a moment," she said to Fliss, pushing her way out of the wheelhouse. "There's something I need to do."

She made her way to the back of the boat. The water stretched behind it, as black as a raven's wing and fathomless. Guarding the island and its secrets.

Betty lifted her hand, letting the wooden reel slip from her fingers.

It slid beneath the waves, vanishing as completely as the island itself.

Chapter Thirty

Spitting Feathers

CROWSTONE HARBOR WAS TEEMING with warders by the time *The Traveling Bag* arrived back.

"There's Father!" Charlie squeaked, pointing through the dark uniforms. "And Granny! Ooh, she looks awful cross with them all."

"Spitting feathers," Fliss agreed. "Oh, look—she's seen us!"

"Just remember our story," Betty murmured, her pulse racing as the crowd swarmed toward the boat, lanterns in their hands and questions on their lips. "We discovered Charlie at *The Sorcerer's Compass*, no sign of her kidnappers. On the way back, we got lost and went off course, ending up at the Winking Witch, where we found Saul."

"Reckon anyone will believe that?" Spit asked.

"Well, it's the only story they're getting," said Betty. "And they'll sure as peck never believe what *really* happened." She barely believed it herself. "And, Saul," she said. "You have to tell the truth. I mean, not all of it . . . not the fishy part. But the rest—or most of it. And you have to hurry. Willow's father is due to be executed tomorrow—you can stop that."

But what of Willow? She glanced at the sky dotted with bright stars. Betty gulped, on the brink of tears. Had they been in time to save her? Or were they too late?

They had sailed through the night, and during those dark hours, when nothing seemed quite real, Saul's story had emerged. How he had been the one to discover the strange, old map on a drifting boat and convinced Willow's father to join him in the search for the mysterious island. And shamefully, how, at the discovery that the island existed—and the thought of what it held—he had been overcome by desire and determination to keep any riches for himself.

"We fought," he'd whispered, hanging his head. "Conroy insisted we split whatever we found or he'd return home. But I didn't want to lose the boat. There was a struggle—he caught me in the face and drew blood." His face crumpled. "And I . . . I hit him with an oar. I thought

I'd killed him, so I panicked. The island was in sight by then, close enough to swim to. So I . . . I left him in the boat to drift. I cheated my friend, and I deserved all I got. But you *have* to believe me—I didn't mean for him to take the blame for my disappearance."

"Perhaps not," Betty had replied more kindly than Saul deserved. She had seen what the island did to people, witnessed the madness in Ronia's eyes and her own brief temptations. "But his life is at stake. It's up to you to save him now."

As the sisters, Spit, and Saul stumbled onto the dock, Granny came stomping through the crowd, sweeping the three of them into a hug that was strongly scented with tobacco and whiskey. "Charlie! You *found* her," she wept between a slurred stream of questions. "You got her back! But *how*—?"

"Granny," Betty said in a rush, her voice almost lost in the depths of her grandmother's ferocious hug. "The girl, the runaway . . . did they find her? Is she . . . is she alive?"

Granny hiccupped, eyes clouding with fresh tears. Betty felt a wave of dread engulf her, steeling herself for what Granny was about to say.

"Poor mite," she muttered, making the sign of the crow. "Horrible business, all of it. No one expected her to survive—half-drowned she was! Barely alive, from what people have said, but then just a few hours ago, she pulled through, against all the odds. Her poor mother was frantic."

"She's *alive?*" Betty burst out, a lump coming to her throat. Joy bubbled up inside her, and somehow within Granny's hug, she and Fliss found each other's arms and squeezed so hard that it was sure to leave fingerprints for a week. They *hadn't* just saved Willow's father—they'd saved her, too. *Willow was alive!*

"We *did* it!" Fliss whispered, sharing a jubilant look with Betty. Her eyes were bright with tears.

"Jumping jackdaws, we really did!" cheered Charlie.

Granny's mouth puckered. "They still haven't explained how Charlie ended up involved in all this." Her eyes flashed dangerously. "But what we *do* know is that her kidnappers were that pair of warders who vanished a couple of months ago. Let everyone believe they were dead, so they did! The *real* warders were out searching for Charlie, but it was Fingerty who led them to a secret cave over near the cliffs by Skinny Woods. They found a hideout and a copy of a blueprint for that old ship of Rusty Swindles's." She snapped her fingers. "I *knew* I'd heard them right when they threw me in that lockup— but what I don't understand is why they'd drag a child out there." Her eyes were mutinous. "If they ever find those two, I hope they lock them up and throw away the key."

Betty and Charlie locked eyes, a look passing between them.

"They won't be coming back, Granny," Charlie whispered.

Bunny glowered. "Well, we still want answers, don't we, Barney?"

Betty twisted around in Granny's fierce grip, glimpsing her father's bloodshot eyes.

"Yes," he said. "But first I'd like to hug my daughters."

Granny gave them one last, enormous, rib-crunching squeeze before reluctantly letting go. The girls went from her plump, smoky embrace to Father's solid, strong arms, where he held them so tightly that Betty wondered if he'd ever let go—and was quite happy for him not to. After the adventures and terrors of the past few days—runaways, wisps, pirates, and everything else—she couldn't be happier to be home. *Safe.*

"Charlie, *why* is there a white cat on the boat?" said Granny, still sniffling. Her voice was muffled through Barney's hug. "I *hope* you're not thinking—"

"Oh, no, Granny." Charlie grinned, wriggling free of Father's arms. "I don't want to upset Oi. This is Bandit.

He's going to be the harbor cat now. I've got it all planned out."

"And who might *this* be?" said Father, quirking a bushy eyebrow at Spit. "Felicity?"

"Long story," Fliss muttered, sharing a look with Betty as she squeezed Father tighter. Spit grinned awkwardly, then pressed his lips together in an obvious attempt to avoid living up to his name.

These were only the start of many questions, endless and awkward, that none of them knew how to answer. So they stuck to their story: one of crooked warders, shipwrecks, and people found adrift. A cobbled version of half-truths, like so many tales before, with no mention of will-o'-the-wisps, witches, hagstones, bathtubs for boats, unmapped islands . . . or the old coin Betty found in her pocket sometime later . . .

. . . which had once belonged to a pirate.

Epilogue

THREE WEEKS LATER, A COPY of the *Crowstone Herald* landed on the Poacher's Pocket doormat.

WRONGLY CONVICTED MAN FREED AFTER "VICTIM" FOUND ALIVE

A Crowstone prisoner narrowly escaped the death sentence after being proven innocent of murder. Conroy Gill was jailed for almost a year after his fishing partner, Saul Heron, vanished, but this week Heron was discovered ALIVE.

In events that have shocked the Sorrow Isles, Gill's daughter—too young to be named—almost drowned after escaping Torment with her mother three nights before Heron reappeared. It has since emerged that the family was condemned to live on Torment until Gill revealed the whereabouts of Heron's body, prompting demands from locals for a change in the law.

"It's disgusting," said Seamus Fingerty, a former Crowstone warder. "They should never have jailed the man or punished his family without proof!"

In a further twist, two corrupt warders kidnapped ANOTHER child, mistaking her for Gill's daughter. Both men are now missing, although the child in question was found unharmed.

Gill, now reunited with his family, has left Crowstone. Both families are expecting considerable compensation.

When asked about his whereabouts, Heron claimed he had been stranded on an unknown island. His account bears a striking resemblance to a local legend*—*(continued on page 7)*

*From *Winking Witches to Sorsha Spellthorn: A History of Crowstone's Sorcerers*—page 9.

"Did you see this?" Fliss slapped the paper on the bar of the Poacher's Pocket, her eyes bright with excitement. "It's us! On the *front page*, if you don't mind!"

"Where?" Charlie demanded, pigtails bobbing as she tried to decipher the words. "Where does it say 'Widdershins'? I can't see!"

"Well, it doesn't," Fliss admitted. "Granny insisted they keep our names out of the paper, but everyone knows it was us."

"Hardly surprising when you and Father have blabbed about it to anyone who'll listen," Betty remarked, sealing up another box of their belongings.

"Lucky for us we did," said Fliss, though she had the grace to look slightly embarrassed. "We might've waited forever to sell this place if something exciting hadn't happened. Now where's that box I was about to start packing?"

"I think Oi's sitting in it," said Charlie. "Good luck getting *him* out." She scurried upstairs, and moments later, the slam of the larder carried down from the kitchen. "Has someone packed the jam?"

"Nope!" Betty yelled back. "You've just scarfed it all!"

Then, "Has anyone seen Hoppit?"

"How can anyone *see* him," Fliss exclaimed, "when you keep making him invisible?"

There was a silence before Charlie replied, "Found him!"

Betty stared out of the window across Nestynook Green. Loud bangs came from outside where, with Spit's help, Father was changing the FOR SALE sign to one that said SOLD. At least Spit was meant to be helping, but Betty had caught him three times already gazing through the window at Fliss.

"Reckon he'll stick around?" Fliss asked.

"He will for as long as he can gawp at you," said Betty, watching Spit with a rush of fondness. "Who knows? Maybe our strange family could be the one he needed all along."

Next to Hubbards' sweetshop, Betty spied an impatient-looking Granny with her basket, surrounded by curious neighbors who were pestering her for gossip.

"I can't help thinking Charlie knew all along, you know," Fliss went on as she dusted a shelf above the bar. "About Willow and what . . . what she was."

"How could she when *Willow* didn't even know?" Betty replied, feeling a chill. "Charlie says she didn't." The floorboards above creaked as Charlie scampered about upstairs. "Reckons she just knew Willow needed help, but . . . perhaps in some way she *was* aware." She shook her head. "Nothing scares Charlie, that's for sure."

"Do you think Willow's all right?" Fliss asked.

Betty smiled faintly, though it wasn't without a pang of sadness at the knowledge that they were unlikely to see Willow again. They hadn't, she thought regretfully, even had the chance to say a proper goodbye—but there was, at least, comfort in knowing she was now with her family. "She is now." Betty glanced over the newspaper article again, her eyes lingering on the word *compensation*. "Fliss?" she said softly. "The money that we got. You don't think . . . ?"

The question hung in the air like a feather. They both knew what Betty meant.

"Five hundred golden Crows is more money than we've ever had," Fliss said, lowering her voice. (This part, she and Father *had* kept quiet about.) "And probably ever *will* have. Granny says it's hush money, but it seems . . . well, a lot." She hesitated. "I know that without what happened, we'd never have received it, but it seems strange that it came to us after . . . after the island."

"Untold riches," Betty whispered. Had it been the island's doing? The most money she had ever had was a couple of silver Ravens. She could probably count on one hand the number of times she had even *seen* a golden Crow. Now the Widdershinses not only had the chance to leave Crowstone for good, but they could do so with money in their pockets.

"I know Crowstone's gloomy and all," Fliss said quietly, "but I'm going to miss this place. Even if it *is* shabby, it's home." Her eyes glistened suddenly, and she looked away.

Betty stared around at the swept fireplaces, gleaming brass, and drafty windows. She nodded. "I've always moaned about it here, but I'll miss it, too," she conceded. "Only here's the thing: it's not where you are, but who you're with that matters. As long as I'm with you, and Charlie, and Granny, and Father, I *am* home. We all are. But there'll always be a little piece of us that belongs at the Poacher's Pocket."

And of course what Betty meant was the memories they had made there, which could not be swept away with a broom or glossed over with a lick of paint. The beer glass of flowers they left the new owners eventually wilted and were thrown out, and the note Granny wrote to go with the enormous bunch of keys was pushed to the back of a drawer. But, like memories, other things of the Widdershinses remained, out of sight and undiscovered.

Such as a strange, old map, hidden under a cobwebbed floorboard with a tarnished coin. It might once have been part of an old childhood game.

Or something else entirely.

TRAVEL TO ANOTHER WORLD WITH THESE MUST-READ FANTASY BOOKS